T0287078

Acclaim for

BREATH OF BONES

"*Breath of Bones* grabs early, *very* early, and does not let go. A captivating weave of legend and reality, this story will draw you in and make you say, 'I need the next book in the series *now*.'"

—JAMES L. RUBART, Christy Hall of Fame author

"A riveting piece of history welded with science fiction. Readers intrigued by steampunk, dieselpunk, or World War II will devour this well-researched, wonderfully crafted tale and come back for more."

—JAMIE FOLEY, award-winning author of *Sentinel* and *Emberhawk*

"*Breath of Bones* is a tale of forgotten legend, tragic hope, and faithful courage. Goyer and Goyer leave no stone unturned in their masterful research and transport the reader across time with a fantastic blend of fiction and history."

—NADINE BRANDES, award-winning author of *Romanov* and *Fawkes*

"Tricia and Nathan Goyer deliver the best of their respective worlds in *Breath of Bones*. Fans of historical fantasy, steampunk, dieselpunk— and WWII fiction-lovers looking for something delightfully different— this is a can't-miss first installment of what's sure to be a stellar series."

—LINDSAY A. FRANKLIN, Carol Award–winning author of *The Story Peddler*

"History, legend, and imaginative tech come alive in *Breath of Bones*. Josef and Kateřina's story will send you exploring architectural secrets, fighting for impossible choices, and cheering every victory."

—KATHERINE BRIGGS, author of *The Eternity Gate*

"Breath of Bones is a fascinating WWII story that takes place in an alternate reality with a guardian for the Jews arriving in the form of a golem. Yet it also portrays the same courage and sacrifice that existed in our own history, of people who chose to save others in the face of evil. I was moved, I cried, and I was encouraged. This is a story for all readers. Highly recommend!"

—MORGAN L. BUSSE, award-winning author of the Ravenwood Saga, Skyworld, and *Winter's Maiden*

"With intense and imaginative storytelling and brilliant detail, *Breath of Bones* uses alternate history to bring us a vital reminder of a very real evil we must never forget."

—JAMES R. HANNIBAL, award-winning author of *Lion Warrior*

BREATH
OF BONES

Books by Tricia Goyer

The Liberator Series
From Dust and Ashes
Night Song
Dawn of a Thousand Nights
Arms of Deliverance

The London Chronicles
A Secret Courage
A Daring Escape

Chronicles of the Spanish Civil War
A Valley of Betrayal
A Shadow of Treason
A Whisper of Freedom

The Gabi Mueller Series
The Swiss Courier
Chasing Mona Lisa

Songbird under a German Moon

Twice-Rescued Child

By the Light of the Silvery Moon

View more of Tricia's books at triciagoyer.com.

BREATH
OF BONES

TRICIA GOYER & NATHAN GOYER

To my husband, John,
who always chooses movies with strange creatures
and otherworldliness, expanding my imagination.
To Nathan,
who jumped on board when I paused my sweeping to ask, "What
do you think about a novel like this?"
To Steve Laube,
who was the first to read my work and say,
"This is going to get published," and who turned to me at my first
Realm Makers Conference and said,
"Come to the dark side," inviting me to write in new,
creative ways to share God's true light.
—Tricia

To my brother Cory,
who always listens to my crazy ideas
and tells me if they're good or not.
To Tricia, my mother,
who has fostered my writing skills ever since I was a child.
To my dad, John,
who helped come up with some of the
fantastical elements you're about to read.
—Nathan

For the glory of God we all had to die,
For the mercy of God we only could cry.
On the eve of the feast, they began their foul deed,
When they grabbed every Jew they found in the street,
And forcibly tried to make him give up,
The creed of his fathers, his trust in our God . . .
May the offering please God be it lamb or sheep
Or the innocent children over whose suffering we weep . . .
O God, put an end to such murderous deed:
It follows us everywhere. The thought makes us bleed.
It made us a target of cruel contempt
In the Land of Bohemia and wherever we went . . .

—RABBI AVIGDOR KARA, 1389
QUOTED IN HANA VOLAVKOVA

Judah Loew dodged sword strikes, unsteadily wielding his longsword while pressing a fistful of his tunic into his side, attempting to stop the flow of blood. Behind him, cries of enemy soldiers rose, as did the crunch of bones and blows against armor. On each side, bodies flew this way and that.

Then, as if moving in slow motion, the soldier standing before Judah lifted his gaze. His eyes widened in horror as an ominous shadow fell upon them.

Judah saw his chance and lunged, slicing open the man's neck. Bright red droplets splattered across the ground. Crumpling, the Roman soldier's sword fell, glistening with the fading sunlight and Judah's blood.

He whispered a quiet prayer for the man, hoping for God's mercy. Then Judah gasped and sank to a knee, gripping his side as heat spread through his abdomen.

Warm, sticky liquid spread over his fingers. Judah's stomach clenched at its sweet, metallic scent. His blood mixed with that of his enemies as it dripped onto the clay and grass of the riverbank. Would the madness ever stop?

Judah had never wanted this slaughter, yet he would do whatever it took to protect his people. *Will we ever be safe? Will the wolves always seek Jewish blood?*

Using his sword as a brace, Judah attempted to rise. His knees wobbled. He pulled in one breath, then another, as if trying to suck air through clay at the river's edge. His second attempt brought him to shaky feet, and his gaze danced over the surface of the Vltava River. *Maybe my fight will end tonight.* For the first time, this thought brought no sadness.

The looming shadow grew closer, darkening the water. Judah turned slowly, and his breath caught. *And maybe yours, too, my friend.*

The massive figure stood before him, bearing a man's shape. Its opposing presence appeared as tall as the trees at the river's edge and as wide as the castle wall beyond. It was not flesh that composed its body but deep-red clay, which still bore the marks where Judah had pressed and shaped its surface. A roughly formed face turned to Judah, and two glowing red spheres peered down.

Golem approached with halting steps, and the riverbank trembled under Judah's feet. Dozens of arrows, spears, and even a sword pierced its body.

He's only clay. He feels no pain, Judah reminded himself.

Judah stepped forward and gasped as the figure raised a closed fist, ready to crush Judah into dust. *Will this be my end? The creator destroyed by the creation?*

Holding a halting gesture toward Golem, a whisper escaped his lips. "Calm, now. *Hněv je špatný rádce.*" *Yes, anger is a bad advisor.*

Golem took a jerky step forward, hesitated, and slowly lowered its fist.

"Good." A raspy breath escaped, and then Judah coughed. "You did well."

Movement caught his eye. Beyond Golem, another soldier writhed on the ground, his final breaths labored. More lifeless bodies dotted the river's edge. Golem had fought them all. Golem had meant only to stop the threat. Stop them, he did. Death was only a living thing's concept. Golem was not alive. Not touched with the breath of their Creator. But still. Golem did *too* well.

Judah motioned Golem forward. "Come, follow me now."

Six steps, then Judah's feet sunk into the red clay. He stumbled and fell to his knees. Judah gritted his teeth as pain surged through his battered body. He again pulled himself up with great effort. Step by labored step, he led Golem away from the battlefield.

Soon, cobblestone replaced the clay and grass from the river's edge. Single-story homes and buildings lined the roads. The quiet streets mocked him. Despite his efforts, no one exited the doorways to cheer on this victory. Occasionally, a nervous face peered through a cracked window, but each face pulled back once Golem appeared. *It's not only the enemies who fear.*

Lagging steps took them to the synagogue. The oldest Jewish temple in Prague, the Gothic Old-New Synagogue, stood silently on Maiselova Street. Its black, jagged-shaped roof jutted into the sky like the tip of a spear. Golem hunched down as he approached and shuffled through the entrance.

As Golem entered, the wooden beams that framed the doors knocked arrows from its shoulders, sending them clattering to the ground. Together, they shuffled to the back nave and peered up the stairs to the attic.

Red streaked the walls, evidence of the pogroms of 1389, where three thousand Jews sought refuge within the synagogue but met their deaths instead.

In the two hundred years since, there had been seasons of peace. Then, thirteen years ago, the priest Thaddeus claimed that the Jews of Prague used the blood of Christian children in their rituals. Ordinary men and soldiers made it unsafe for Jews to leave their homes. That's when the words came to Judah in a dream: "*Ata Bra Golem Dewuk Hachomer W'tigzar Zedim Chewel Torfe Jisrael.*" *You shall create a golem from clay, that the malicious anti-Semitic mob be destroyed.*

Judah created Golem with the help of his son-in-law, Isaac, and his disciple, Jacob. Now, with their enemies destroyed, Golem had fulfilled its purpose. Judah's chest heaved with labored breaths as he lifted one foot and then the other, dragging his body up the first step and the next. Golem filled the stairwell and moved with the same slow gait. With great effort, master and creature made their way to the attic.

Approaching an open tarp, Golem lowered himself to a sitting position. His eyes now level with Judah's.

"It is the Sabbath, dear one." Vision blurring, Judah neared Golem and reached out toward its face. Golem's mouth opened, revealing a parchment covered in words. Judah removed the parchment, and Golem slumped. Its eyes faded, and its body stilled. Again, a lump of clay, lifeless.

"Yes, rest now. Rest." Judah coughed again and then limped to the wall by the stairs. His body weighed heavily, and the world grew darker with each labored breath. Judah leaned against the wall, slid down its cold surface, and closed his eyes. "I will rest now, too."

THURSDAY, 14 MAY 1942

PRAGUE, PROTECTORATE OF BOHEMIA AND MORAVIA

God who does not abandon the people of Israel . . . . let them again find mercy before the monarchs of the land. —Vitalis

Josef Loew pressed himself against the shadow of the ancient gate that once marked the entrance to Josefov in the Jewish district. Nestling in the stone archway, he felt the cold, mossy surface against his back. A column of *Wehrmacht Sturmtruppen*, in their meticulously tailored uniforms, marched down the narrow street. The gas lamps' flickering lights caught the polished edges of their attire, causing them to shimmer menacingly.

The rhythmic clomping of their heavy leather boots, reinforced with metal toe caps, echoed through the alleyways, harmonizing with the frantic beat of Josef's heart. Their uniforms, a mix of deep charcoal and forest green, were immaculate, with golden epaulets and badges that shone under the ambient light. These were no ordinary troops. Their status was evident in their dress's finery and march's discipline.

Gleaming in steel and brass, their weapons were not mere tools of war but works of art. Rifles with ornately engraved barrels, pistols with wooden handles adorned in intricate patterns, and backpacks fitted with curious devices that emitted gentle puffs of smoke and the soft hum of machinery. Small gadgets with rotating gears and flickering lights attached to their belts showcased the blend of military might and the pinnacle of craftsmanship. The sight was both awe-inspiring and deeply foreboding.

Josef's fists balled at his sides. *This madness has to stop.* For months, he'd dedicated his life to moving Jewish men, women, and children around the city to keep them one step ahead of the transports that rounded them up and shipped whole families off to the camps. But they couldn't keep running forever. There was a time to hide and a time to fight. If only his inventions could puncture the Germans' confidence and remind his people they didn't have to be led away like lambs to the slaughter. Like David, Gideon, and Joshua in their ancient Scripture, perhaps it was time for the warriors to rise among · them for the salvation of their people.

Josef pressed himself closer to the ground. Trailing the platoon of soldiers, a spider tank advanced with deliberate grace on its curved, elongated legs. Its brass-and-steel body reflected the muted light, revealing intricate gears and steam vents that hissed intermittently. Having been field-tested in Spain during their Civil War, the rumors of these eight-legged monstrosities capable of scaling walls and descending into trenches were chillingly accurate.

Each leg, expertly engineered, had joints decorated with ornate patterns, giving it a fusion of intimidation and elegance. The central body of the tank bore multiple viewing slits, with a rotating upper turret equipped with steam-powered cannons. The spider tank was manned by a team: a commander who dictated the strategy, a gunner who aimed the weapons, a loader responsible for ammunition, a driver who navigated the mechanical arachnid, and a radio operator ensuring seamless communication.

For all its engineering marvels and tactical advantages, the tank had one unmistakable flaw. The loud *click, click, click* of its legs echoed ominously as it traversed the medieval cobblestone streets, announcing its presence to anyone within earshot. Those in the resistance knew to listen for this sound as a harbinger of the approaching menace.

"*Pavouci*," Josef mumbled under his breath. *Spiders* were out today. It meant only one thing: more families would be swept into their web. For eight months, men, women, and children had been hauled away "to the east." While many hoped the families were simply relocated, the evil glints in the soldiers' eyes told Josef a different story.

Above the medieval streets of the Jewish district, an airship navigated, floating over the gabled roofs and tightly packed buildings inhabited for over a thousand years. Under the dirigible, dressed in dark-blue uniforms with quilted layers for warmth, rode the *Zeppelintruppen*. Perched in the rigid basket, with rifles poised, they appeared like hunters aiming at skittering rabbits. Additional air scouts peered into the streets and alleyways with steel binoculars pressed to their faces.

The Wehrmacht column marched out of view, and Josef hurried to his place of refuge—soon to be the center of deliverance for his people. He was a Loew, after all. Like his father and grandfather, it was his turn to make his mark.

With quickened steps, Josef hurried toward his grandfather's clock shop and the warehouse once used as a storehouse by Jewish merchants of the Prague markets. His advance turned into a jog as he moved past the Old Jewish cemetery with its rows of rock headstones, tilted and blackened with age. How many of his people had already died in this war, shuttled away to walled camps by the *Einsatzgruppen*, the killing units, with no tombstones to record their names or mark their final resting places?

The weight of his call rested on Josef's shoulders. For centuries, his family had accepted the vocation established by his great-grandfather to protect the Jewish people. And today, Josef could be one step closer to doing that—if he could only get his newest weapon to work. An ache pinched in the pit of his stomach as he thought of the last words his father had spoken to him before joining the others being marched to the train station. *You are a Loew. Remember that . . .*

There wasn't a day he didn't remember. Not a day he didn't strive to prove himself worthy.

Pulling a heavy key from his pocket, Josef fumbled with the lock on the door. He blew out a breath. *I will make myself worthy. I will prove it by my deeds, Father. I will live up to that name.*

Someone touched Josef's shoulder, and he jumped. Gripping the key harder, Josef turned with a swing.

"Josef, it is I!" a woman's cry split the air.

He quickly dropped the key into his pocket and placed a finger over the woman's mouth. "Quiet, do you wish for the soldiers to come? Do you wish for us both to be killed?"

The woman's dark eyes, red-rimmed and puffy, widened. A single brown curl slipped from her cap. Freckles dotted her nose. Josef blinked as recognition came to him. "Hermina?"

She nodded, and he quickly apologized and removed his finger from her face. The woman whimpered, her body shivering while she gripped his sleeve as she inched forward.

He'd known Hermina Roth since he was a child. At least a decade older than his nineteen years, she had worked as a seamstress at the dress shop his mother favored. Yet this waif standing before him was a withered replica of the round, jovial young woman she'd been before the German occupation.

Josef's gaze darted to the dirigible overhead from which the Zeppelintruppen aimed their rifles, their focus fixed on something beyond him. He slowly released a breath. Moving his key to the lock, Josef opened the door. Hermina relaxed her grip on his sleeve and followed him inside.

The now-slender woman with sunken cheekbones crumbled into his arms as soon as the door shut. He awkwardly patted her back until she drew a shaky breath and righted herself. Her pale, blotchy face caused his stomach to tie into knots.

"We are next on the list." She pulled a photograph from her pocket and held it out. "We will be required to report to the train station in three days. My uncle sent me a warning. My husband has already been taken away. I am strong. But the children . . ."

Josef took the photo and peered at the image of two small girls in smart frocks, hair curled in ringlets, sitting on matching white wicker chairs. Their toddler brother stood beside them, solemnly staring off to the right as if he alone knew the danger to come. A flare of anger rose, and Josef ground his teeth.

The hunters and the rabbits. Soldiers seeking children.

Yet how much more could he do? He worked tirelessly on weapons. On shuttling Jews. What more could he give? Must he start hiding families, too?

I know what my father would do. And what Judah Loew had done before us—risked all for our people. Josef ran his thumb along the photo's edge and offered it back. Pain tightened the back of his throat.

He swallowed it away. "I will do my best. I will see what locations are available. Yet even if we find someplace to hide your family for a while, it's nearly impossible to get anyone out of the city, children especially."

The woman pulled her coat tight around her and lowered her gaze. Her shoulders visibly shivered. He touched her arm and sucked in another deep breath. *You are a Loew. Remember that.* Josef forced a smile. "It is *nearly* impossible, but I will do my best to find a place. And then we will see about getting you out of Prague to safety."

Hermina's face lifted, and tear-filled eyes met his. "Thank you. Thank you. God bless you."

Josef straightened his stance. "I will get word to you within a day."

Hermina nodded, accepting his word as a promise. Then she slipped out, and Josef secured the door. He closed his eyes and, for a moment, wished he didn't carry the weight of these responsibilities on his shoulders. So many lives at stake, so many more futures to be cut short. He wiped his forehead and then rubbed his eyes. Although weariness caused his head to ache and his senses to dull, he needed to continue.

For as long as Josef Loew could remember, stories of his ancestor Judah Loew ben Bezalel had been told. Or, more accurately, of the creature the esteemed rabbi had created. Magical, mysterious. What some would claim a monster. But Josef believed there were times when a beast was needed to fight madmen. If only he could believe in the legend. A creature like that could help his people, the Jews, against this new Nazi horror.

Some families passed down romantic legends—with stories of love and adventure. But not Josef's family. Josef's family had been called to protect the weak in the ancient city of Prague, known for Bohemian rulers and artists.

I will do what I can, legend or not. I might die, but I'll protect those who cannot defend themselves, as the Loews have always done.

Josef's feet shuffled across the aged, wooden floor of the clock shop and down three steps toward Grandfather's workbench, which separated the front of the shop from a brick wall at the back. Before the occupation, when the shop was a busy place of commerce, the hum of customers' voices filled the space. Now only dozens of clocks ticked in unison—their chimes ringing out on the hour and half hour. These days, Grandfather only left one clock unwound, an iron-and-copper mechanical clock dating from the sixteenth century.

Next to that elaborate mechanical clock, a dull silver wall clock with a cracked face hung on a hook on the back wall as if waiting to be repaired. Pausing before the wall clock, Josef glanced over his shoulder to ensure the dark curtains blocked the front windows completely. Satisfied no one from the street could see in, he opened the glass in front of the clock face. Then Josef wound the clock until it read 10:17.

A small *click* sounded, and to his left, a tall grandfather clock gently swung open, revealing a hidden doorway. It remained ajar long enough for Josef to slip inside. Then it closed again. The Pavouci might be crawling the streets of the Jewish district with the racket of their feet on cobblestone, but Josef refused to struggle without hope like a fly within their web.

GAS WARFARE?

Industrial circles in New York claim the tip that accused the Germans of making ready-to-use poison gas came from the glass producers in Czechoslovakia and Belgium. The Nazis, it is reported, are forcing glass companies to manufacture cylinders designed as gas containers. Recently, production of these cylinders has been stepped up.

Winston Churchill has substantiated the alarm registered by observers in the glass, manufacturing, and chemical fields. It is agreed that if Hitler, in desperation, employs the outlawed weapon, it will be a confession that his other resources are exhausted.

Our scientists say that while the Nazis have been among the pioneers in the chemical field for many years, there is no evidence they have anything new or startling—anything in gas warfare that is unknown to the United States or Britain. We are familiar with the substances most likely to be used, the effects to be anticipated, and the technique of protection.

Moreover, if retaliation is forced, we have the production and distributing advantage. If the fiendish Hitler orders a gas war, he and his people must accept the consequences.

Before tonight, Kateřina Dubová had never attended a formal party. Her father thought her too young for such things. Yet now, a distinguished officer—one of the Nazi elite—pulled her undeniably close and led her across the dance floor. If she were to prove to her father she could write a story to make the newspaper's front page, she had to pay attention She had to learn the secrets of their enemy, all while making the Nazis believe she could be trusted.

Who wouldn't trust someone who'd landed the job because of who her father was, not due to her skill? Her date believed so. She felt it in the way his warm touch spread across her back as if he'd already claimed his prize: her belief in him, his party, and the conquering of their enemies. Nothing could be further from the truth.

Sturmbannführer Langer smelled of cigarettes and a heavy cologne that reminded her of sage and an earthy aroma similar to the dark clay that lined the banks of the Vltava River near her home. It was the first time Kateřina had danced with a man who wasn't a cousin or childhood friend. The first time she was given a real story to write. Even though she was twenty and had already finished her journalism degree, her father still saw her as a child. Well, at least he had before tonight.

An SS officer dancing with a reporter, an unlikely pair. Yet they were one of a half dozen couples on the makeshift dance floor. A string quartet played nearby. So close that if Kateřina tried, she could reach out and touch the cello.

When her father had first asked her to write a story for his newspaper, *Zemědělské Listy*, about new products coming out of the glass factory in Sázava, Kateřina had been disappointed. What story could one find in a small village southeast of Prague? That was until Father told her to dress formally and be prepared by five o'clock, when a car would arrive. A car and driver? A formal Nazi affair?

Even more intriguing, the banquet was set up in the glass-cutting room of the factory where the finest Bohemian crystal in all of Czechoslovakia had once been crafted. The simple workroom had been staged with the familiar decorations of swastikas, eagles, and other symbols of Nazi power. Yet, unlike extravagant Nazi events with carefully arranged seating plans that emphasized the hierarchy and importance of the attendees, only eight round tables had been set up tonight with an open seating plan.

Why this factory? Kateřina had wondered on the drive down. *And why invite me?*

When she arrived, her questions found their answers. This factory was no longer used to manufacture fine crystal pieces. Since Adolf Hitler came to power, the Nazi regime had transformed many industries to support the war effort. This was the Reich's newest accomplishment.

With a turn and a step, Kateřina's escort spun her. She had a full view of a table ladened with glass cylinders approximately 30 centimeters in diameter and 60 centimeters in height. The glass glimmered in the flickering candlelight.

Kateřina's stomach clenched. The words clicked through her mind as if she were already sitting in front of her voice box, watching black-typed words appear on crisp white paper as she spoke them into existence.

Furnaces that once produced delicate crystal stemware now manufacture glass cylinders for Nazi chemical warfare.

Another spin and the officer's breath on her cheek reminded Kateřina not to get lost in her thoughts. His grip tightened, and she glanced away from the clear canisters to his piercing blue eyes. Probably the most beautiful eyes she'd ever seen, yet like the canisters, they hid death inside.

"Such a beautiful young woman. Yet why is such a rose among the thorns?" Sturmbannführer Langer's words purred over the music. His uniform was starched straight, and his medals glinted in the candlelight. Unlike her father, who acted as if the occupation of the Germans was simply another bit of news to report, Kateřina wished she could speak out against the changes, especially the imposition of Nazi ideology and suppression of Czech culture and language. Czechs were forced to learn German, and their language was banned in official settings. With a Czech father and German mother, Kateřina had thankfully grown up knowing both languages. But that still didn't prevent her from wishing for how things used to be. *Mother would have stood against it. She would have said something—German-born or not.*

Kateřina straightened her spine as she replied to the officer in German. "I may be a rose, but I am not weak. I have heard that a flower is a soldier standing in attention to the sun."

He shot her a glance of delight. "Ah, I see. So you are here to honor *der Führer und Reichskanzler?*" The man's German accent thickened as his leader's name rolled from his lips.

"My duty is to *report* on this new regime." Kateřina pressed her lips into a thin line. She wanted to say more, but not now. Not to him. Her throat tightened with emotion. Reporting was precisely what she'd tried to do for the last six months, only to find herself covering food shortages and long queues. She was made out as a fool in the eyes of the other reporters, even more so since she was the editor's daughter. Her chin trembled at the humiliation of it.

The man slowed his steps. "Fräulein, what is it?"

Kateřina forced the edge of her lips up and wiped at a tear on the corner of her eye that threatened to break through. *Not here. Not in front of him.*

Yet when she noticed sympathy in the man's gaze, she changed her mind. Perhaps she didn't need to appear strong. Her weakness might be what got her what she wanted most—a front-page story. A story to get her father's attention.

A story to make Father *see* her for once in her life.

As the music rose, she allowed her body to shift slightly closer to her dance partner. Kateřina eyed the glass canisters again, more boldly this time. "There is little need for new crystal vases; am I correct?"

The officer's brows lifted. Then laughter rumbled from Sturmbannführer Langer's chest, catching Kateřina off guard and causing her to miss a step. Yet her feet found their way before her dance partner noticed her fumble.

"*Ja,* you are correct. There is no need to purchase new crystal vases or other valuable items. We've already stripped everything of worth from Josefov."

Kateřina's brow furrowed. *Josefov, the Jewish district?*

He glanced at the canisters and offered a lopsided grin. "And soon we'll claim everything they have, even their very breath."

The breath of Jews?

An ache pressed on her chest as if the air in her lungs had become concrete. It took every ounce of focus to keep in step with the music. To keep inhaling and exhaling. To smile.

She jutted out her chin and swayed with her steps, like she'd seen in the picture movies. Yes, she could play the part of a character in one of the talking films. She could act like the doe-eyed reporter the officer believed her to be. Maybe who Father thought her to be, too.

Black-typed words filled her mind again. *While industrial leaders believe the Nazis have plans for gas warfare on the front lines, the German high command may have a different enemy they wish to destroy.*

The music stopped, and Kateřina pulled back from his embrace, swallowing down any hint of emotion. "Thank you for the dance, Sturmbannführer Langer."

"Please, call me Hilbert."

"*Danke,* Hilbert."

Pulling from him, Kateřina turned and eyed the room. As she

scanned the cluster of dining tables, she noticed only a few open seats. At every table sat members of the Nazi elite.

When Kateřina arrived, she was one of the few women in attendance. As she stood before the group, the men's hungry gazes caused her knees to soften. Hilbert touched her elbow and directed her toward the factory machines. Kateřina was thankful for his closeness. Better to become an ally of one wolf than face the pack.

"I am certain the glass workers are thankful to have jobs again." Kateřina kept her tone light. This was the story she'd been sent to write.

Since the occupation of the Germans, the Nazi regime took control of the media. Many newspapers and other media outlets had been shut down or forced to comply with Nazi censorship and propaganda. *Zemědělské Listy*—the newspaper her father worked for—was carefully observed by Nazi censors. She knew the type of stale story her father expected her to turn in.

Still, the journalist in her wanted to know the *whole* story. And maybe she could mold her words to spotlight this new German industry while encoding a warning to Czech citizens that poison gas was being used in other ways. *Yet surely not against innocent women and children.* War was one thing, but heartless genocide?

Kateřina tucked her arm into Hilbert's and allowed him to guide her toward the tables where glass cutters had shaped valuable art pieces for nearly a hundred years. "So, can you tell me more about this new production?" she asked as simply as if she were inquiring about the weather.

"As you know, the glass industry has a long and rich history in Czechoslovakia." Hilbert puffed out his chest, taking on the role of a tour guide. "For decades, Bohemian glass has been exported worldwide. We have no desire to destroy this great land of artisans and skilled laborers. The workers have work—work that still requires skill. Perhaps you can relay this in your story?"

Kateřina nodded, understanding. The Nazis wanted better press from her father's paper. And Father had sent *her.* Did he believe she'd get caught up in the glory and the splendor and not realize the truth?

Fine, at least Father thought of her. At least he, for once, gave her a shot at the front page.

"Ja, of course," she answered in a thick German accent—one she knew from visiting her mother's family in Berlin. "The Czech people need to know they still have a place. That not every industry has been stripped from our—*their*—grasp."

As Kateřina paused, Hilbert's arm came around her waist and pulled her close. "And why did the newspaper wait so long to send you? A hidden asset. I can already see you'll be a great gift to our cause."

Kateřina beamed. "Maybe that will change? Maybe soon I'll be allowed to interview der Führer himself?" She winked.

Sturmbannführer Langer burst out in a fit of laughter that caused him to bend at the waist. "My, you are ambitious, aren't you?" He kissed the top of her head before he straightened. "Maybe in time that will be possible. And while I cannot offer up our great leader, perhaps the *Obergruppenführer* will do?"

Kateřina's lips parted in surprise. "Reinhard Heydrich?" The name escaped in a whisper.

Hilbert's eyes sparkled, knowing he offered a front-page story on a silver platter.

"Will you honestly arrange for me to interview Reinhard Heydrich?"

His fingers reached up and tucked a strand of her blond hair behind her ear. "Ja. Would that please you?"

"Very much." Kateřina tightened her grip on his arm. Reinhard Heydrich, *Stellvertretender Reichsprotektor* of Bohemia and Moravia, was said to be the darkest figure of the Nazi regime. From the wolf's lair to the den of the devil himself. *Father isn't going to believe it.* Maybe when the invitation arrived, her father would finally meet her eyes and tell her she'd done well.

A shaft of light shot down from a high window inside the sheltered workshop, and Josef paused to wipe his brow. Setting down his welding tool, he adjusted the blackout curtain to block the natural light. With the curtain secure, he pushed the switch to turn on the bright electric bulb hanging from the center of the room.

This could be the weapon that gave his people a fighting chance against the Nazis. They didn't have the manpower to conquer their enemies, but if they could damage their firepower and sting their pride, perhaps Jewish lives could be saved.

As dim yellow light filtered in, a fluttering in Josef's stomach told him today could be the day he finished his newest creation. Over the last year, he'd spent most of his time moving Jews from Josefov to other parts of the city and the countryside. Yet his people could only scatter like seeds on the wind for so long. Soon, they'd have to root themselves and fight.

The workshop was twice as large as the clock shop storefront. Aromas of gas fumes, acetone, and lubricating oil mixed with the mustiness of faded paper journals and dusty wooden boxes, some dating back to Judah Loew ben Bezalel himself.

Josef's newest weapon sat on the wooden workbench in the center of the room. A two-foot crafted metal shaft with interlocking parts glimmered under the hanging lights. Fitted to the end of the shaft was an octagonal mallet larger than his two fists put together.

Forged from steel, the average observer would guess the object to be a blacksmith's hammer. Josef knew its true power. Or at least the power it could possess once he perfected the fuel ratio. He whistled, picturing a torch of fire shooting from one end of the mallet toward the enemy.

Wielding a weapon like this would allow resistance fighters to superheat the metal armor of the Sturmtruppen to blister their enemies, cook them within their metal suits, and take them out of the fight. Because of the required proximity for the blast, it wasn't the weapon patriots needed to win their war. Still, capable of providing two dozen flaming shots with its limited fuel, it was something to fight with.

Picking up the mallet, Josef grinned at the heaviness. Eyeing the metal pieces he'd crafted before dawn, he chose the bracket he needed to control the fuel flow. The sounds of metal components clinking against each other sounded as Josef fitted the small pieces onto the metal shaft. The precision of the mechanisms would make the difference between success and failure.

Hours slipped by. The growling of Josef's stomach told him he'd missed dinner. Not that he had much to eat these days.

His fingers, stained a blackish brown from the lubricant, trembled as he slid the last pieces in place.

With the new mechanisms in place, he fitted a collection of small canisters into the iron head of a hammer. With *this* design, a small amount of fuel should ignite when expelled, providing the expected blast.

Josef swept his brown hair away from his forehead, his forearm grazing the patch of his eyebrow that had been singed a few days earlier.

The hidden door creaked from behind. He whipped around toward the room's entrance. An aged man stood there. His gray beard touched the first button on his shirt. A small black cap covered his head, and his dark coat hung from his frame. The only spot of color was the yellow star pinned to his jacket.

Instinctively, Josef moved his arms over the canisters. "Grandfather, you're still awake?"

Samuel Loew answered with a raised bushy eyebrow. He hobbled to Josef's side, eyeing the canisters.

"Fire again?" Grandfather scoffed. "There are many other methods, my boy. Most are not so destructive."

Josef folded his forehead into a scowl, winced, and rubbed the back of his neck, turning away from his grandfather's probing gaze. "I think I have it this time. See, the flames will come out *here* in a focused stream." He pointed to the revolving cylinder on the flat part of the mallet opposite the canisters. "And now, I have the flames focused, so there is less spread."

Josef lifted the hammer with effort and raised it above his head. "I used solid metal pieces to minimize the seams and make the overall structure sturdy."

"And what is the purpose of a flaming hammer?" Grandfather tilted his chin downward and eyed Josef over the top of his glasses. "You forget what our people need. Not more destruction. Every weapon you turn against others will cause two more to be turned against you."

And what if we have a thousand weapons turned against us already? Josef dared not say such things aloud while under the steely gaze of his grandfather. "I understand."

"Good." Grandfather nodded and stepped back from the worktable. "Now, bring it and come along."

"What? Where are we going?"

Grandfather turned back and offered a smirk before waving for Josef to follow. Confused, Josef picked up the hefty device and followed him through the hidden passageway and into the clock shop. Despite his six decades, Grandfather moved at a pace that would be a light jog for most. Walking out the clock shop's side door, Grandfather entered the high-walled garden. Outside, cloud cover filtered the moonlight and cast the courtyard in shades of gray.

After latching the door behind him, Josef quickly paced to catch up. As Josef was about to question his grandfather again, he opened the warehouse door and ushered Josef inside. With a twinkle in his eyes,

Grandfather closed the door and locked it tight. Then he hurried to the far corner of the expansive room.

"Both the best and worst part about being an inventor," Grandfather spoke as he moved boxes and pushed aside scrap wood, "is that your inventions will be used in ways you never expected."

Josef eyed his weapon and twirled it about. "It shoots fire. How else could that be used?"

"You would be surprised. The airplane was invented in 1903. A few decades later, it is used to rain explosives from the sky." Grandfather simulated a bomb dropping and then exploding.

Josef lowered the mallet to his side and nodded. "Be careful what you make, yes? It could be used for bad purposes. I get it."

"Not at all. The opposite. If an honest invention can be used for such terror, then any weapon can be made into something new." Grandfather walked to Josef's side and gestured for him to raise the weapon and shoot its flame. "Ah, on the lowest setting, if you would."

Josef swallowed a lump in his throat. *Now? Here?*

Taking a deep breath and sending up a quick prayer for success, Josef raised the shaft in front of him, aiming toward the empty, expansive area of the warehouse. He twisted the shaft's handle, switching the number of open compartments to one, limiting fuel and flame.

Failed attempts flashed through Josef's mind, including the fire that nearly engulfed his head during his last try. He stretched his arm a little farther, closed one eye, and scrunched his face.

"Here it goes," he whispered to both Grandfather and himself. Finally, he twisted the handle with one quick motion. Flames erupted from the head of the mallet. Josef had expected a steady flame. Instead, a raging river of fire shot out, blasting as hot as a furnace.

He attempted to steady his stance as the unguarded flame grew in intensity. Then, with another burst of fire, the mallet lurched and twisted toward him. Flames flashed toward his body. It took every ounce of his power to redirect the orange-and-yellow stream away.

Another sudden jerk almost wrenched the weapon from his grasp, but his grandfather was quicker. The older man's strong fingers wrapped around the shaft, helping to hold it steady.

"It's too strong!" Josef called over the roar of the torch. Heat bore down on his hands, and his arms trembled under the exertion.

"Extinguish it!" Grandfather shouted.

Josef twisted the handle in the other direction, and the flames flickered to a stop. The force of the mallet switched off, and only the object's weight pulled against Josef's fatigued arms.

Sucking a deep breath, he gingerly set the weapon on the tiled floor. His arms flopped like empty sacks at his sides. He ached from the exertion. He flexed his fingers and then rubbed them together.

"The gasses burn and expand too quickly," Samuel explained as he examined the shaft on the ground. "As a result, all the force from the flames shot directly back toward you."

"It's a design flaw, then." Josef shook his head. *Not again. I have to start from scratch.*

"I would not say that. It is an interesting concept I have never thought of." Samuel rose to his feet and patted Josef's shoulder. "Good work, Grandson. It gives me something to consider."

"Consider? For what?"

Grandfather rose and moved toward the door once more. "For something I'm thinking about. A project I am working on myself."

MONDAY, 25 MAY 1942

ŽIŽKOV, PROTECTORATE OF BOHEMIA AND MORAVIA

The glass factory in Sázava has a new breath of life as a record number of glass cylinders are being produced. Cylinders for a wide range of applications are being manufactured at additional factories nationwide to meet the booming demand. This is good news for the workers who used to be employed by the Czech glass and crystal production industry. Because Bohemia was once the seat of royalty, such production has existed throughout Europe for hundreds of years. Bohemia was at the forefront of glass production and design for much of the Middle Ages. Kamenický Šenov in northern Bohemia, which remains the center of Czech glass production today, is the site of the oldest known glassworks, founded in 1250. —Kateřina Dubová

Kateřina drew a slow, steady breath through a clenched jaw as a hundred rotating metal teeth, powered by a complex system of steam pistons and gears, tore her story apart. The paper shredder, boasting a gleaming brass maw and an intricate mesh of exposed cogs and adorned with ornate dials and pressure valves, stood as tall as her father's mahogany desk. Its insatiable appetite was notorious. In her six months of working for her father, Kateřina had witnessed numerous news pieces being devoured, but witnessing her work being destroyed was a first. Then again, she'd never penned a story of such significance until today.

Bits of white drifted into the trash bin like snowflakes, but not her resolve. *If Father doesn't respect me, I will find a way for him to respect my words.*

The shredder's grinding stopped. Other than the noise of the newsroom beyond her father's door, the steady ticking of the wall clock was the only sound in his office. The iron-and-copper mechanical clock was said to be from when Rudolf II was Holy Roman Emperor, King of Bohemia, and member of the House of Habsburg. Rudolf ruled from *Prazský Hra*—the castle Kateřina could see out the window beyond her father's desk. *How things have changed.*

Rudolf would roll over in his grave if he saw what was happening in his beloved Prague. Called the Father of the Scientific Revolution, Rudolf was a mystic who spared no expense to expand the arts. He dabbled in astronomy and alchemy and even had a court poet.

Now, most Czech intellectuals, scientists, and artists had been swept away to camps for fear of their influence over the common people. And those allowed to stay? Their work was censored. However, the Nazis did not need to send a private censor to the offices of *Zemědělské Listy*. Her father did a fine job controlling every word printed in his newspaper.

Seeing her efforts scattered like sawdust in the metal bin beneath the shredder, she glanced away. Heat crawled up her neck, yet she fixed her face as if carved by stone. *I will not give my father the pleasure of tears.*

Then again, the man standing before her with salt-and-pepper hair, a wrinkled brow, and tight, thin lips did not resemble the father she once knew. Even his pressed suit seemed too large on his frame.

The clock ticked on, and Kateřina struggled for words. Her father, too, refused to speak. Where was the laughing man who used to take her to feed the swans, tossing breadcrumbs from the Charles Bridge under the shadows of the saints? Or the tender man who would embrace her when she skinned her knee? As a child, her father would blow on her scrapes to make them better and then take her for ice cream in Old Town Square. That man had been lost to her years ago. Like the statues of the saints that lined the Charles Bridge, he was a stiff shell of the man he used to be.

Pavel Dub, Editor in Chief, the sign on his door read. *Dub*, meaning mighty oak. And that was how she used to see her father, even though all she'd ever known was his broken body from his fight in the Great War.

Kateřina glanced at the empty sleeve of his suit coat pinned at his left elbow. All her life, she'd known her father's missing arm had resulted from his wartime exploits. Still, Kateřina hadn't given much thought to the fighting he'd faced or the trauma he'd endured until the German annexation of the Sudetenland four years prior. As the German tanks had rolled into their homeland, the father she'd known had disappeared like fog over the Vltava River under a bright, shining sun. After months had passed and he had still not returned to her, she'd attempted to reach him the only way she knew how—through words.

After years of study and hard work, she'd earned a spot as one of her father's reporters. Or had she? Kateřina pressed two fingers to the bridge of her nose, fighting the mounting pain in the center of her forehead. Would anything she wrote be good enough? Would she ever see approval in her father's gaze?

"I don't understand the problem." Kateřina kept her tone steady. "Why did you shred it? I could have fixed—"

"There was nothing to fix." Her father pulled his arm behind him. He straightened his shoulders and turned to peer out at the sea of red tile roofs spreading through the castle district. "You can't fix accusations."

"Accusations?" Kateřina turned and shut the office door behind her, muting the rhythmic click of typewriter keys and the monotone voices of secretaries and reporters, including Evka, her only friend among the staff. Evka wore an elaborate headset fitted with tubes and wires winding down to a brass dictation machine. She spoke steadily into its funnel-like mouthpiece. Despite this shield from the outer commotion, her father remained unmoved, his back to her. In the *Zemědělské Listy* newsroom, the clock counted the hours until the paper was due. Unlike years prior, no one was in a rush. Even though the keys of their voice-activated typewriters and dictation machines clicked endlessly, no phones rang. No reporters called with last-minute stories. No messengers rushed in with breaking news. Instead, the printed stories were stale—as if there was no war or occupation and there were no trains hauling away intellectuals, politicians, or Jews.

Heat once again flushed Kateřina's body. She had not mentioned the Germans or their plans for the new gas cylinders. Then it hit her. "You never intended to use the story, did you?" She spoke to his back and grasped her hands to control their shaking. "So why did you send me? What could you have gained from Sturmbannführer Langer pulling me close as we danced or from him kissing me?" She didn't tell him the officer only kissed the top of her head. She'd let her father think the worst.

Her father's fingers flinched. A movement so slight she would have missed if she'd blinked.

An eerie stillness came over the room, and finally, her father turned. His narrowed gaze fixed on hers. "If you want to be one of my reporters, you must not cast such accusations upon our occupiers." His voice trembled. "Do you wish to be arrested? Locked away?"

"Locked away? What are you talking about? I didn't mention the Germans at all."

Her father's eyes locked on hers. "So maybe the Germans will not take offense by phrases such as *was once the seat of royalty*? Or how you revealed that their cylinders will be used for applications beyond military warfare." He paused.

Instead of meeting her father's gaze, Kateřina focused on the vein in his neck pulsating with his heartbeat. He cleared his throat. "Not to mention your embedded secret message."

Kateřina's lips parted, and she lifted her eyes to his. "Embedded secret message?"

Her father narrowed his gaze. "The glass factory has a *new breath of life*? Cylinders are being made in *record numbers* to meet a *booming* demand. These cylinders are being produced for *various* uses?" He snarled. "Any intelligent person will understand. Germans are sending poison gas to the camps. The lack of food and poor hygiene aren't the only things killing the imprisoned Jews—even women and children." He pointed to the bin of shredded paper. "Do you know what they'd do to you if word got out?"

Kateřina took a step back. She shook her head as a sudden heaviness moved into her core, making breathing hard. "Are you saying that's *true*?"

The color rushed from her father's face. He touched his temples as if trying to compose himself. "Kateřina, I thought—" Her father's eyes searched her face pleadingly. "From your words, I thought you'd figured it out." He mumbled under his breath as if scolding himself.

Women and children, too? Kateřina's brow furrowed. Is that the reason she'd seen death in Hilbert's eyes?

She attempted to process what her father said. "From what I was told, I guessed the gas was being used against *s-some* Jews," she stammered. "But surely the Germans would not be using gas to rob innocent women and children of their breath." Her words emerged labored, even as the ticking clock on the wall quickened to a double stroke. She blinked, unsure if her eyes and ears were playing tricks on her.

Kateřina would have thought the double stroke was her imagination until her father moved toward it. He opened the glass front and took out a key. Yet instead of placing the key in the keyhole on the clock face, he moved the key to a second keyhole in the iron frame and turned it. Then, returning the key and closing the glass door, her father turned back to her as if nothing unusual had occurred. Emotion flickered on her father's face. Worry? Or maybe fear.

Alarm sent moisture to her palms. "You've been hiding the truth from me, haven't you?"

Her father lifted his chin. "What do you mean?"

"You thought I knew about the gas killing women and children, didn't you?"

He released a breath, almost as if in relief, then stared at the tiled floor before her feet as if picturing his unintended confession there and attempting to find a way to retrieve his words.

Finally, her father lifted his head and spread his fingers across his chest. "I did not say such a thing."

"You stated that any intelligent Czech would understand that lack of food and hygiene weren't the only things killing the Jews—the women and children." Kateřina's gaze flickered away. He wasn't going to answer her, and she knew it.

Kateřina took in the shredded paper. "I worked hard on that, and now it's a thousand pieces."

"If I printed that, you would soon be in a thousand pieces." Her father lifted a shaky finger and pointed straight to her chest. "Did you forget who has control of this country?" He released a low growl. "I have one job here. It's *not* to report the news. It's to keep my reporters alive." He balled his hand into a fist, released it, and pointed to the shredder. "I've saved your life three times this week already. How bent are you at ending up in one of those camps?"

"What do you mean you've saved my life three times this week?"

He brushed back his thin hair. "Twice withholding the stories that I knew you wanted. And now, shredding the one that could have harmed you a third time."

Kateřina's thoughts raced back to a conversation she'd had with Evka, who, with her dark hair and piercing eyes, always seemed to know exactly what Kateřina was going through and was eager to hear what was going on in her life. Over a cup of steaming tea, nestled between gears and pneumatic tubes in the reporters' break room, Evka had listened intently as Kateřina poured out her frustrations about her father.

Remember, he has lost a wife, just as you've lost a mother, Evka had told her, her voice soft yet firm. *Also, consider the treacherous path he treads daily. He's sharing news to aid the Czech people while trying not to incite the wrath of the Nazis.*

Kateřina's mouth dropped open at his words. *He's protecting me.* The weight of Evka's words now bore down on her. She resisted the urge to rush forward and embrace her father. He was right. She would become a prime target if the Germans misconstrued anything she said. And if their anger reached a boiling point, the entire newspaper could be shut down.

"But now that we're aware," she said, her voice trembling with passion, "what can we do about it? How can we speak for those who have no voice? For the women—the children—forced to leave their homes and—"

"Nothing," he said. "There is nothing we can do but wait."

"What do you mean wait?"

"*Kdo jinému jámu kopá, sám do ní padá.*" He spoke the proverb slowly, emphasizing each syllable.

He who digs a hole for someone will fall in it himself.

Her father returned to his chair behind the desk. The chair automatically adjusted to his form as he sat. Then, with one smooth motion, it slid his body forward. He placed his fist on the desk, and Kateřina noted its trembling.

"Every night, I toss and turn, hating myself for allowing you to have this job, wishing you'd go back to writing folk legends and novels." He glanced up from under his bushy eyebrows. She saw a glimmer of humor in his gaze for the first time. Warmth flooded her chest, and her wrinkled brow released. Kateřina pressed her lips together, and they lifted softly. Her story may lie in shreds, but the invisible thread that tied her heart to her father's mended with his one tender look.

"I suppose you're speaking of my novel about the alchemists and magicians during the reign of Emperor Rudolf II?"

He sighed and rubbed his brow. "*Magic Castle* was the title, if I remember correctly."

"Yes, and if only a king ruled from Hradčany Hill now."

"If only I could believe that devotees of the stars and cultivators of the spagyric arts were no longer in play in Prague . . ." As if controlled by his mind, his chair turned. It slid toward the window to give her father a view of the city.

Kateřina almost laughed, thinking of her childish tales, but the haunted expression on her father's face urged her to hold it in.

"Alchemy was a thing of the past, wasn't it?" Her words lifted in a tentative question. "To create precious metals out of basic materials. Or bring to life that which has no breath—it's impossible. Science has taken us in a different direction." She strode to the window, standing next to him.

"Many believed Paracelsus was a fool when he thought that chemicals could poison or heal the body," her father answered. "But today, we consider him the father of toxicology and a pioneer in the medical revolution. Paracelsus's religious beliefs heavily influenced his approach to science. He believed science and religion were inseparable and scientific discoveries were direct messages from God. Thus, he believed it was humanity's divine duty to uncover and understand His messages."

Kateřina settled herself on the windowsill, blocking part of her father's view. Finally, after minutes passed, he took his eyes off the city and met her gaze.

"Father, you're no longer talking about the poison gas, are you?"

"No, I wrote something myself under your name. It's already been submitted. It's benign. It'll keep you safe."

Ten minutes ago, that statement would have made her angry, but something in her father's gaze told her that story was the least of his concerns. And it should be the least of her concerns, too.

"So what is it then? What's going on?" She kept her voice low, hoping not to break his odd trance. From the dark circles under his eyes and the curious words coming from his mouth, it was clear sleepless nights were catching up with him.

"Sometimes the truest story isn't what we see happening, but the unseen directing the players." He swallowed loudly and stroked his chin. "There *is* a story to pursue on Hradčany Hill. It might come to you soon enough." Her father thumped his open palm over his heart. "But I want you to see with your heart, Kateřina, not just your mind."

"A story on Hradčany Hill? The Germans control Prague Castle now. How—"

The ringing of the telephone interrupted Kateřina's words. It rang once, then twice, but her father continued to stare out the window.

"Do you want me to answer it?"

He gave the slightest nod, wincing.

Kateřina hurried to the desk. She lifted the receiver and placed it to her ear. "Hello?"

"Kateřina? This is Sturmbannführer Langer—*Hilbert*—calling from Prague Castle."

Prague Castle on Hradčany Hill. Goosebumps rose on her arms. She watched her father, who stared out the window, focusing on the castle beyond. *How did he know?*

"We reviewed your story of last night's events. You did a fine job. Thank you for offering such high praise for our efforts."

"You read my story, and you approve?" she said aloud for her father's benefit.

Father already submitted my story even before I arrived today. Kateřina didn't know whether to be angry or thankful.

"We not only approve of you, we commend you. The Obergruppenführer Reinhard Heydrich wishes for you to interview him." The German-accented voice was as soft and clear as if he spoke directly into her ear.

"He wants me to interview him? The Obergruppenführer?" Her heart leaped to her throat. The thrill at the prospect of meeting Reinhard Heydrich disappeared as quickly as a gust of wind, replaced by a strange sense of unease.

Father had said there was a story to pursue on Hradčany Hill. But what? *What is he getting me into?*

"Yes, is that a problem?"

"No, it's not a problem at all. And Sturmbannführer Langer, I mean, *Hilbert,*" she cooed, "what will this be about?"

"You will interview the Obergruppenführer concerning his *Nacht und Nebel,* Night and Fog Decree, and his role as Protectorate of Bohemia and Moravia. Can you come in two days at noon?"

Kateřina glanced at her watch. "Yes, I will be there."

"Very well. An escort will await you at the front gate upon your arrival." The words were curt and efficient, and then the man hung up without a goodbye.

She stood with the phone in her hand, uncertain how her father knew that call was to come—and that she'd be the one to answer it. Or did he? Had it been a coincidence? A tingle ran down the back of her neck.

Her father rose from reporter to editor in chief at a young age because he knew what to focus on, where to send his reporters, and what stories needed to be front and center. Twenty years into the job, his luck hadn't seemed to run out . . . unless it was more than luck.

As Kateřina gathered her wits to face the second most powerful man in the Nazi regime, she would take her father's advice. She had to see with her heart and not only with her eyes. The question was, what would she see?

Josef carried a small stack of boards through the secret doorway into their hidden workroom. He moved to the back wall and set them on the floor. He stretched his aching back and shoulders, then pulled a handkerchief from his pants pocket and wiped his eyes. They burned, and he blinked rapidly. Then he pressed the handkerchief against them, refusing to sit. If he sat, he'd be asleep in minutes. He'd made a promise to Hermina two days before, and he had to see it through. He would not let her and her children be swept away like all the others. Building a secret room to hide them wasn't the answer, but at least it would buy him more time.

"Almost done," he muttered, eyeing the back wall.

As expected, her husband had already been rounded up, and Sturmtruppen could be at her door any day now, returning for the rest of them.

As promised, he'd reached out to his contacts. He'd received the same reply from all of them. There was no place to hide families, especially children. A frightened child could cry out. He'd heard too many stories of families being arrested after Jewish children were discovered among them. Still, Josef had no choice.

What would my father do? he'd asked himself. His father would hide Hermina and her children in whatever space he could find. Thankfully, as had become the standard practice, his grandfather Samuel had left for a few days. Josef did not know where he went, but

Grandfather was working on something. Josef noted it by the calluses on his hands. Smelled it in the chemicals of Grandfather's clothes. Then there was something else: clumps of clay from Grandfather's boots at the doorway. If Josef were to guess, it was clay from the banks of the Vltava River. But why would he be at the river?

To protect and to shield, a plan took its birth, with whispered prayers and clay of earth.

Josef considered the words he had written as a schoolboy. Before the age of eight, stories shared around their home about a clay protector crafted by their great ancestor had been as true to him as the cobblestone under his feet. It was only after the taunting of other children that he'd discovered the creature was a myth. If only such a protector were true.

Returning his handkerchief to his pocket, Josef studied his work. Since the room was deeper than wide, the false wall hid the secret room perfectly. After taking down shelving, he'd almost had enough to make a wall that ran from floor to ceiling, but not quite. And that's when Josef decided to find whatever boards he had inside the house.

Seeing his task almost finished, Josef worked with these last boards to assemble a secret door that would slide in and out of place. He waited to secure the last of the panels with nails when the spider tank's clacking and the roar of motorbikes on patrol met his ears.

At least they're good for something.

He'd just finished the last nail when the other secret door, between the clock shop and the hidden workspace, slid open with a soft grind.

Josef spun, dropping his hammer and barely missing his toe. Only once he recognized his grandfather's face did he release his breath.

Grandfather paused inside the room. "Expecting someone else?"

Josef retrieved his hammer. "I don't know. Maybe. We can't hope our secret workroom will remain hidden forever."

Grandfather perched his fists on his hips and eyed the new back wall. Josef's heart fell at how his grandfather's clothes now hung on him. "At least I know what happened to the pantry."

"It's not like we had anything in it anyway. Or the cellar, for that matter." Josef shrugged. "I'm not sure how we'll continue to stretch the last of our food supplies."

"God promises only enough for the day, does He not?" Grandfather didn't wait for Josef to reply. Instead, he hurried forward and studied Josef's work. "Yes, this is good. Once you move the metal shelving back against this wall, it will not appear any different from the other walls."

"That is the point." Josef motioned toward their secret door hidden behind the grandfather clock. "If anyone discovers this room—"

"They will not find Hermina and the children." His grandfather finished his sentence. "Once this is finished, you will hide them well."

Josef's eyes widened. "How did you know?"

"Nothing happens in Josefov without the knowledge of others." Grandfather ran a hand down his cheek. "I was told of Hermina's visit, not once but twice. Did you promise her protection?"

"I promised her I'd figure something out. And I have."

"Yes, and then we must consider how we will feed this family."

Josef tilted his chin and locked his gaze on his grandfather's eyes. "Will not God provide for them too? Enough for each day?"

Grandfather nodded once. His eyes wandered to the wall, but from the odd gaze, Josef knew his mind was lost in another place. "A chamber crafted, hidden from sight," he finally mumbled. "A space of hope, where fear should subside."

"What is that?" Josef searched his mind, trying to remember if it was something he'd heard before, but nothing came to memory.

"Oh, I was thinking how our occupiers do not know the lengths we'll go to win, do they?"

"We are not winning, Grandfather. Not when I hear the clicks of the spider tank's feet on cobblestone, moving up and down the streets of Josefov day and night."

"You are wrong. Each life we protect from those monsters is a win. All around this city and into the countryside, we have sanctuaries, havens, and secret spaces." Grandfather jutted out his chin. "For every moment of solace, grace, and hope we produce for another—at the risk of our own lives—we win again. The room is small but a place of trust," he finished, more to himself than Josef.

"If only we could truly fight." Josef thought of his weapon. He hadn't touched it in days.

"You want to fight, do you?" Grandfather puffed up his chest and crossed his arms. "Well, good. This is the very reason I came for you."

Josef brushed back his disheveled hair, and with his grandfather's words, new energy surged through him.

"A meeting has been called tonight. My presence will be required, and it would be best if you also came."

"A meeting?" Josef asked.

"When we have nowhere to turn, we've turned to each other." Grandfather tilted his head as if recounting each person in attendance. "We've often been gathering as of late."

"Often? Why haven't I been invited?"

"The subjects we discuss are quite difficult. There is much we don't know, and . . . well, you're being invited now."

Josef nodded, too weary to press the question. He was twenty now and still treated like a child. His father respected his input and ideas. *But Father is not around.*

June 1939. News had arrived that *Schutzstaffel* Adolf Eichmann had come to Prague, ordering Jews to register, sell their property, and surrender their investments. When they heard the news, Father— Adam Loew—Josef, and Grandfather had returned from visiting Mother's grave. Mother had died of cancer a year before, and their only consolation was that she didn't have to witness the Germans selling or carting away all their beautiful possessions.

When the first Jews were transported to the Terezín ghetto five months later, Father was the first to volunteer, saying, *How can we send our friends and neighbors without a Loew to protect them?* It wasn't a question. A question expects an answer. They all knew it was their family's duty. If not his father, then Grandfather or Josef would have to go.

Since then, a few notes from his father had arrived, sent on official Terezín postcards. The censored postcards had to be written in block letters and couldn't exceed thirty words. And when the most recent postcard came, Josef doubted he'd ever hear from his father again.

MONTHS OF MISSING. I AM HEALTHY STILL.
I WILL GO TO THE EAST. DO YOUR BEST TO
CARE, AS I KNOW YOU WILL. KEEP HEART
SOFT. WITH LOVE UNENDING.   FATHER.

Emotion tightened Josef's throat. He reset the metal shelf against the new false wall, filling it with dusty boxes, bins, and tools. Then, without another word, Grandfather led the way out of the workshop and into the street.

Josef forced thoughts of his father out of his mind. He couldn't think of his father behind barbed wire walls if he wanted to stay focused and alert. He couldn't let his mind wander. If it did, he'd soon be the one writing postcards to those left behind. Or worse, sent away "to the east."

Rádek Ježek pulled his coat tight and strode toward the Charles Bridge. In a world of gears and steam, where machines tended to draw one's attention, the ancient bridge held an enchantment Rádek could not deny. For centuries this city had been a place for artists to gift the world with beauty and alchemists to turn worthless elements into something valuable. But today was the day for neither. He'd use his art and his skill to claim a private victory and, in doing so, secure the triumph of a very public war.

As Rádek neared the Gothic Old Town Bridge Tower, he eyed one of the guardians of the gate that flanked the bridge. Carved numbers decorated its arched surface: 135797531, a sequence of ascending and descending odd numbers. According to the royal astronomers, construction of the bridge commenced at the suitable, lucky time of 5:31 on 9 July 1357. When complete, the bridge measured 9.5 meters wide and 13 meters high and sat on 15 pillars.

Three stories tall, this stone tower had stood the test of time for centuries, spanning the waters of the Vltava. Each stone set with precision, as a coded message for anyone wise enough to see it as more than a relic of time.

Standing tall from the tower, the statues of Charles IV, St. Vitus, and King Wenceslas IV stood on the first floor. Beside the guarding Bohemian Lion, the Czech patrons St. Sigismund and St. Adalbert perched transfixed on the higher ground.

As Rádek passed under the tower and onto the bridge, a German jeep rolled by, fitted with armor plating, large wheels, and a gun mounted on the back—a contrast between the two worlds. The old world, in which people believed religious figures could help them. The new world, in which prayers went unanswered.

In this time of German occupation, destruction and chaos ruled the city. Long gone was the peace the statues of the saints lining the bridge suggested. Not that Rádek had any sense of peace. It disappeared years ago when the one Rádek loved most had been lost to him.

Long and sleek, an oblong tank followed the jeep and reflected the stone statues on its mirrored surface. Shades of the city in spring transformed the tank's polished plating to blues of the sky, grays of the stone, reds of the tiled roofs, and greens of the trees at the river's edge.

Unlike the spider tanks that crawled, the Czechs called these rolling tanks *syčící* švábi. Hissing cockroaches. They rumbled past with serpentine pistons pounding and gears whirring. With cannons primed above the rolling treads, smoke and steam poured out from behind the tank.

Rádek counted as he walked, numbers spinning in his mind. Sixteen arches, two tall towers, thirty statues. The bridge was finished in 1402—even numbers representing completion.

He marked off the stone statues as he passed them. A half smile curled on his lips. Writers saw the Charles Bridge as a story unfolding, connecting the past and present. To artists, this bridge was an inspiration, a canvas for creativity.

The Wehrmacht saw the bridge as a thoroughfare, connecting the castle district to Old Town and Josefov—a route from power to plunder. The soldiers ignored the river that flowed gently below, the water and waves in play. They ignored the clay at the river's edge, not understanding that it was perhaps the most potent element in the city.

As a scientist, Rádek saw the bridge as an alchemist's experiment. The numbers, the link between two worlds, the frozen heroes, and the clay below that pulsed with life.

Rádek's partner, too, believed that ancient tales could be retold. That cold, lifeless form could animate. That legends and myths of the past could birth new heroes. In a way, Rádek pitied this fool who had no idea that in seeking life, death would come. Many deaths. Yes, it was all part of Rádek's plan.

Pausing beside the statue of St. Assisi, Rádek pulled out a cigarette and lit it. As time passed, Rádek saw darkness engulf the castle, remembering when it once glimmered as if adorned with a thousand jewels. Fearful of drawing the attention of bombers in the air, not a light had shone since the Nazi occupation. This was a fact and a symbol, as most things in Prague were.

Soon, the statues along the bridge stood as dark forms, waiting silently as another hissing cockroach rolled by. The crew of this tank was a daring bunch. Smartly uniformed soldiers rode on the back of the silver beast. They crouched down with goggles perched on their heads as if they had a second set of eyes pointed at the airships zigzagging across the sky. Even though they had no spotlight, the near-full moon provided enough light for a night watch.

The crew's laughter told Rádek they were off to Josefov, most likely to gather more timid Jews to refill their camps.

Footsteps approached, yet Rádek didn't turn.

"Where there is hatred, let me sow love," the sultry female voice beside Rádek mumbled.

Rádek attempted to hide his smirk as he picked up where the woman left off. "Where there is injury, pardon; where there is doubt, faith; where there is despair, hope; where there is darkness, light; where there is sadness, joy." His last word trailed off, leaving a sour taste in his mouth. When was the last time he'd experienced joy? Years. Yes, it had been years.

He stood in silence. The moment he'd been waiting for had come. A glint of metal drew his attention to his hand. His glove had slipped, exposing the mechanical limb beneath. He pulled the glove back up. Showing his scars here would make him weak.

"If these saints could talk, they would say much." She sighed.

"Silent witnesses. Oh, what they've seen. And oh, what they have yet to see."

"This is not the first conflict along the banks of the Vltava, and it will not be the last." Rádek's eyes moved to the river's edge downstream from the bridge. So much had changed since then, yet more had remained the same. He pictured the battle of long ago when a roughly formed creature slayed an enemy and saved a generation of Jews.

"The requested items will be delivered tonight at your desired location."

"And your name?" he asked.

The woman turned, studying his face as if it were a painting mounted on a wall. Then, lifting her eyebrows, she fixed her dark eyes on his. "I'd be a fool to give you my name. You can call me Persephone."

"Persephone. Destroyer, yes?"

She tilted her head, amused, and smirked. "Have you read much of the Greek legends?"

"I know enough. Persephone was a daughter of Zeus, and she was taken to the underworld."

"And allowed to return to the earth for six months of the year," she added.

"Bringing death with her. It seems fitting." He leaned forward and rested his arms on the bridge's stone side wall as if he had all the time in the world.

"Says the man who has made a deal with the devil himself." A chuckle slipped from her lips. "And your name?"

"You can call me Kelley."

"Ah, after the famous alchemist Edward Kelley, who was known for his ability to speak to the angels. It is also said that he was the one man who turned lead into gold." She winked. "And who is also said to have struck a deal with the devil."

Rádek shrugged. "Flasks, powders, and coils can go only so far. Sometimes a higher power is needed."

She twirled a strand of dark hair around her finger. "Many searched for gold . . ."

He could tell by how her words trailed off that she didn't understand what would soon be delivered. She was simply a messenger. Even if she knew the material, she'd never guess the power soon to be displayed. Not entirely, anyway. "I've created something greater than gold."

"Can it be duplicated?" Persephone placed her hand on his. It was soft and warm. His insides heated as if he'd swallowed a magic elixir. Did she think him a fool? Did this woman believe romance was the tonic that could distract him from his goal? He kept still, letting her believe her touch intoxicated him.

Instead of answering, Rádek turned his attention to the stone saints. "Do you know a lot about the statues on this bridge?"

"I wouldn't be a good Czech if I didn't."

"That one over there." Rádek pulled away and pointed. "Johánek z Pomuka, yes?"

"Of course. John of Nepomuk was tortured to death after he refused to give away the confessional secret of the queen. And allegedly, his tongue stayed preserved hundreds of years after his death—thanks to his honesty." Her dark hair ruffled in the breeze. "Many people believe it brings luck if you touch the statue."

"I do not need luck when I have the truth. Just like Johánek."

She smirked. "So these Jews believe you? That you have an answer? Their answer? They are not always trusting of outsiders. Many Czech people like yourself are joining our cause."

"Our" cause. He nodded placatingly. "One man believes me, and this man is all I need. He trusts that I am his friend."

"And the others?"

"The other Jews trust and believe him. He comes from an important family—a family of protectors."

"Ah, you must speak of the descendants of Rabbi Loew. Golem is a popular legend." She chuckled. "Of course, a Jew's legend of choice would be about when they were on the brink of extinction. They should have learned by now that they are not welcome in this world."

"Nothing but an old legend." Rádek nodded. "And I agree, some people need to be exterminated, down to the last man. Our partnership will make that dream a reality." Rádek extended his hand to her, palm up. While he'd enjoyed their cat-and-mouse game with words, he needed to go. He was expected soon.

In one swift movement, Persephone placed a key in his palm. He fisted it and tucked it into his pocket. "Everything I requested? The whole list has been provided?"

"Yes, of course." She took a step back and straightened her spine. "And how soon should we expect the . . . presentation?"

Rádek's stomach churned like the spinning treads of a cockroach tank. "Soon. Don't worry. All will be seen soon enough."

Josef followed one step behind his grandfather as they crept down the narrow alley of Josefov. Their feet moved swiftly but quietly, despite Josef's heartbeat pounding in his ears. Fear gripped his throat, making it hard to breathe. What had Grandfather been up to? What was worth the city's men congregating at the threat of their very lives?

He did not doubt that the strolling night patrols also roamed the streets. Unlike the spiders or the motorcycles, they made no noise—gave no evidence of their presence. The Night Crawlers wore dark clothing and moved in pairs, striding from shadow to shadow. Perhaps luck would be on the side of the Jews tonight, and the few pubs open near the Vltava would be of more interest than the streets of the Jewish district.

Even though Prague had been under blackout conditions since the arrival of the Germans—and light from every window hidden behind dark cloths—the moon waxed bright and bold overhead. Like a traitor's spotlight, it emphasized their movement upon their path and splayed across the cobblestone in muted shades of gray.

A distant shout rang. Josef and Grandfather halted in their tracks. Josef braced himself for a pair of Night Crawlers to rush out and grab them. He pressed tighter against the stone wall, sending up a prayer and seeking refuge in the shadows of the night. After a minute, Grandfather motioned Josef to continue.

When they arrived at a crossroad, Josef scanned the streets ahead.

He sucked in a deep breath. How had their existence come to this? One step forward out of the shadows was a life-and-death risk, and crossing a simple roadway a dangerous feat.

Grandfather shifted to move, but Josef grabbed his arm. The faint sound of Nazi boots echoed off the cobblestone. They huddled lower and pressed against the wall, hoping to blend with the shadows.

Josef's breaths turned shallow as a Night Crawler staggered through the crossroad not five feet away. The German reeked of beer. Josef gripped his chest over his pounding heart, thankful the Germans enjoyed the popular Czech drink. More than anything, the beer hindered the hunters from catching their prey—like a secret elixir dulling their sharp, piercing eyes.

The lone German Night Crawler shuffled forward, and even before he was entirely out of sight, Josef and his grandfather darted across the street, defying the evil in their path.

One block past the crossroads, his grandfather approached a broken metal gate and shifted it to the right. Josef followed him inside.

They padded through the courtyard that used to belong to one of the local bankers, Petr Herrmann. Petr had been among the first Jews to be transported to Terezín with Josef's father. After his arrest, not an hour passed before the Nazis arrived to strip the banker's home of everything valuable, leaving the large house as an empty shell.

With his long coat swirling around him, Grandfather led the way around the house to a separate structure. Its exterior hinted at a summer kitchen, with ornate copper pipes curling around its brick walls, intermittently releasing soft puffs of steam. Josef trailed behind the rhythmic hum of gears and the faint click of hidden machines accompanying their steps.

Upon reaching the entrance, Grandfather rapped two quick knocks on the door, its wood aged and reinforced with metal bands, then added a third distinct tap. The door creaked open, revealing hydraulic mechanisms and cogwheels that operated the lock. They slipped inside.

The atmosphere inside was dense with age. The scent of musty air, tinged with the oily aroma of machinery, hung heavy in the summer kitchen. This was compounded by the thick stone walls, laced with intricate metalwork, and curtains—a blend of velvet and chain mail—drawn tight over the windows, filtering the outside light into a soft, dim glow. Gleaming brass chandeliers with flickering gas flames hung overhead, illuminating the figures below.

A dozen men, some wearing leather vests adorned with various tools and gauges, others with goggles pushed up onto their foreheads, were gathered in animated discussion. Faces Josef hadn't seen in months, if not years. Recognizing them, Josef's heartbeat steadied, and a warm sigh escaped his lips. Here, surrounded by the comforting hum of gears and the companionship of old allies, he felt recognized and cherished—reconnected to a community he had dearly missed.

The room is small, but a place of trust. His grandfather's words from earlier replayed in his mind.

The gathering of twenty men sat in a circle with their knees nearly touching so they wouldn't have to raise their voices as they spoke. Candles flickered from high shelves, reflecting on discarded pots and bins. Shadows danced. Specks of dust drifted in the light. Their downward spiral reminded Josef of falling stars. He rubbed his weary eyes in an attempt to hide tears. He didn't know if the lack of sleep over the past few days made him want to cry or that others were missing from these ranks—others he doubted he'd ever see again, including his father.

Three empty chairs waited. Josef sat next to Grandfather and took a closer count of the faces in the room. Each of these men had been friendly enough before the German occupation, but he felt an unexplained closeness with them at this moment.

Teachers and engineers. Clerks and carpenters. They'd become a brotherhood of loss. Each of them had become shells of their former selves as they hid away and fought for survival—their own and of those who remained in their community. Whether they liked it or not, they were in this together.

Josef paused on Hugo. The baker's thick beard could not hide his worried grimace as he stared at Grandfather. As if sensing his gaze,

Grandfather fixed his eyes on the baker. Hugo opened his mouth and then closed it again. Then, shaking his head slightly, he glanced away.

Maybe he has a question but doesn't want to know the answer.

"Just when we think things won't worsen, Jews can no longer use public transportation. Yet the Germans still demand work," one of the local shopkeepers said, breaking the silence.

"I can't feed my family." An older man's head dropped low. "It's like the Turnip Winter, the Bolshevik Revolution . . ."

"This is not like 1918. This war is in *our* homes. On *our* streets." Hugo thoughtfully stroked his black beard.

"As if hunger is our worst problem," another man spoke. Josef recognized him as one of Hermina's uncles, Moshe. "Our men, women, and children live behind the barbed wires of Terezín." He refused to meet Josef's gaze.

Moshe knows Father is there. Josef entwined his fingers on his lap. He wasn't sure if he wanted to learn more about Terezín. His mind already pictured harsh conditions. He'd dreamed about the horrors. What if the circumstances were even worse than his nightmares?

Moshe's chin trembled. "I've heard Jews are being murdered in Charkow and Ukraine. What if the same is happening at Terezín? I have cousins there. My niece and her children are going—we have been warned they will be on the next transport."

Josef straightened in his seat. He wished he could tell Moshe there was already a plan—and a secret room—to help Hermina and the children. Instead, he absently brushed at the sawdust clinging to his pant legs, evidence of the room he'd finished for them today. The rules had been the same for the dozens of families he'd helped hide— the fewer people who knew the location of hidden Jews, the better.

"I've heard of sterilizations of those with mixed blood," Ivo, one of the cemetery's caretakers, said in a hushed tone. "It's not only the Jews now who are in danger . . ."

Josef shifted in his seat. *Things have gotten a lot worse.* The tragic news was easier to take when one heard it piece by piece over the months. To listen to it simultaneously was overwhelming. Fresh energy moved through Josef's limbs. Even though his mind ached with weariness, a new resolve flowed through his veins. He had to keep working on weapons—only then would they have any chance to fight.

"My brother took his own life last night," an elderly man stated simply. "He heard he would be on the next transport, too. He said he'd lived all his days in Prague and wanted to die here." The man's voice caught. Then he faced Grandfather before moving his gaze around the crowd. "Where can we find hope? Is it even possible? Will they not be satisfied until we are dead? Or maybe . . . living in fear is worse than death itself."

Men nodded, their faces etched with pain and fear. There was something else—a longing for what had passed. A thirst for what would never be again.

Many gazes were drawn toward Grandfather, as Josef expected they would be. Even though these men spoke, they all waited to hear what Samuel Loew had to say. Grandfather remained motionless, his sightless eyes revealing he was lost in his thoughts—as if the men in this room did not exist. He would speak when the time was right and the words were found.

Josef's eyes moved to Nikolai, who sat at his left. Josef had seen him at events and shared a few conversations here and there. They had been friendly but never close. Nikolai had a number of years on Josef, which always kept a barrier between them..

Nikolai set his square jaw, glanced to the side, and his dark eyes locked with Josef's. He gave a curt yet polite nod.

Josef returned. Did Nikolai expect something? *Are they all waiting for me to speak? I am a Loew, but I have no answers.*

He wanted answers more than anything. He wanted to know he could rise to the occasion and be the protector everyone wished he could be.

Goosebumps rose on Josef's arms, and his mind spun like a whirlwind. It was enough to think about helping Hermina and her children. And to keep working on his weapons. He couldn't comprehend how he—one man—could do more than that. *But I am a Loew . . .*

Grandfather sat straighter, arms crossed and eyebrows pinched in thought. Finally, he cleared his throat. "I wish we could meet here and share friendly conversation, food, and our faith as we have cherished in the past." He looked upon them sorrowfully as if the good times he spoke of were only a finger's length out of reach. He blinked the sadness away and then refocused. "There are no mincing words. We face an enemy who does not only want our riches, land, or servitude. They want our very breath. Their only victory is our death. For our bodies to return to the dust from which God formed us."

"It is not that bad, is it?" Ivo asked. "They boycott our stores, keep us in this side of the city, and send our families to cities like Terezín. Cruel and unnecessary. But are they trying to kill us? No. They are not."

Josef tried not to smirk. Was it the man who cared for the graves of the dead who had the most hope?

"My friend, to talk of Terezín—and other German prisons—is why we're here." Grandfather leaned forward and placed a gentle pat on Ivo's shoulder. "Terezín is not what the Germans told us. It is not simply a walled-off ghetto where families can live together in relative safety. They don't even have enough food or water to survive. It's a prison, of which there are many. But this prison is not large enough for all their evil plans. Other places are being built to put an end to our people as quickly as possible."

"This is true." Nikolai leaned forward as if telling a secret. "A man came in last night. One who had escaped the walls of Terezín itself. He helped the Germans at the ovens—yes, ovens. This man says they are building camps designed to kill. Not one or even a dozen. Camps to hold thousands of us. Extinguish thousands more."

"I don't believe it."

"It's true." A side door opened, and a man stepped into the room. The man was tall and thin. Josef believed him to be a stranger until he met the man's eyes. He sucked in a breath. *Petr?* Petr had been a neighbor, a friend. Now he appeared as a ghost—a frail representation of who he'd been before. Clothes draped his body like rags. With his chiseled cheeks and chin, Petr resembled a talking skull.

"Every word is true," Petr stated simply. "I got away. I offered to transport the dead." Petr's Adam's apple rose and fell with silent sobs. "I survived by lying among them, in the piles." He closed his eyes, and his body trembled. "They didn't think to search for me there. And finally, I rose and escaped under the cover of night."

Josef turned to his grandfather as if still not comprehending what was being said. Piles of bodies? And camps that could hold thousands. Tears rimmed Grandfather's eyes. *It is true.*

"Thousands?" Josef repeated the word before he had time to think. "If this is true, then they are from hell itself. We can't let them do this!"

Horror and bile rose within his throat, though only the latter could be swallowed down. What had the Jews, God's chosen people, ever done to Germany to extract such *hate*?

"We won't let them get away with this, my son," Grandfather assured him. "This is why I have gathered everyone. We have tried to survive, but it will not be possible within this city for much longer. It's time for all of you to leave Prague. Leave and hide." He gestured widely before them as if presenting a banquet.

Josef's heart clenched. *Loews do not run. They fight.*

"We must move fast. We must think of leaving in days, not weeks," he continued.

The words pierced Josef like an arrow to the chest. A tight pressure pinched his knees. He glanced down to see that his whitening grip caused it. Though he fought them, words built up behind gritted teeth. Words he had before been able to tame.

"You want to *run*, Grandfather? Run and hope that most of us are not caught?" Josef all but spat the words. It was like Grandfather to do this. He didn't have a drop of fight in his veins. He had the following of the people but never once forged a weapon for them. Even worse, he constantly told Josef *not* to.

"We have to do something. We have to fight. We need to fight." Josef jumped to his feet. "Surely there are those who believe the same as me."

No one moved.

"I do not believe what I am hearing, Samuel." Hugo jutted out his chin toward Grandfather. "You are a Loew. There has to be a way. You *need* to have an answer."

Grandfather stood, too. Not quite as tall as Josef, but far more imposing. "Do you think I'm God?" He moved to the window and peered at it as if he could see through the black curtain to the synagogue across the street.

The synagogue where a Loew laid down his life for his people.

"I understand how some have had to leave, but this is our home, Grandfather." Josef's voice trembled. "That is our synagogue. Should we leave it all behind? These streets connect a community. The walls remember our laughter and our songs. And it's from this we must escape?"

"Escape, yes, and survive." Grandfather spoke calmly, though Josef could feel the anger hidden within. "Raising arms and ambushing the Germans will only hasten their plans. Instead of camps, they will send us bombs and bullets. Any allies we have will reject us, and our blood will fill the streets. For what? A house? A shop? People are important, not buildings."

Josef stared at his grandfather's back for a long moment. None of the other men showed readiness to fight for their home. *Why?* It was the best way to deal with this threat. The only way.

His knees softened, and he sank onto his chair once more. He'd stop his words for now, but he would not stop his work. He found solace in the weapons he had made. His flaming hammer, though that was still in progress, and a throwable device even more effective than a soldier's grenade, though since he had made it with Grandfather, it was not as destructive as he would have liked.

The meeting continued, but their words buzzed in Josef's ears. The community elders talked about smuggling people to other countries and finding families to hide them. They spoke of getting more messages out to the neutral countries in hopes of spurring their action against Germany. Despite not liking any of these ideas, Josef kept his mouth closed.

Eventually, he stood and moved to the door. Listening to this was useless—especially when he had work to do. After peeking outside to ensure no patrols, he stepped into the cool evening air.

A strong arm gripped his shoulder as he crossed the threshold. He turned, expecting to see his grandfather, but instead, it was Nikolai.

Leaning close, Nikolai whispered in Josef's ear, "You are not the only one who wants to fight. Samuel is a good man, but we need action."

The urgency in Nikolai's voice sent Josef's heart racing. Before he could reply, Nikolai steered him into a shadowed alcove, distant from prying ears. "Come by my courtyard at six o'clock tomorrow morning. You'll see what unity and resistance can achieve."

In the dim light, Josef leaned in and focused on the man's dark gaze. "Are you sure, Nikolai? The risks are . . ."

Nikolai's eyes, intense and unwavering, met Josef's. "The price of silence is too steep. We must act before we're forever silenced."

Thoughts swirled in Josef's mind, memories flooding back. His grandfather's lap, the warm embrace, the tales of Rabbi Judah Loew ben Bezalel—the Maharal of Prague. The stories weren't just of wisdom and leadership. They were tales of a golem, a protector born of clay. For young Josef, these stories weren't mere bedtime tales. They were a legacy, a bridge to a time when his people stood defiant.

But innocence is fleeting. A memory of older boys laughing at the "childish tales" stung even now. The golem? A mere fable. And with that revelation, a sliver of Josef's trust in the world had chipped away.

Now, facing Nikolai, doubt battled determination within him. How could his grandfather, a descendant of the revered Rabbi Judah Loew, stand by while their people suffered? Josef might be ill-equipped, but he'd worked on a plan to protect Hermina and her children. He may not possess the wisdom to craft a protector from dust like the legends of old, but he would not remain passive. Unlike the legends, he was taking action, however small.

Nikolai's grip tightened on Josef's shoulder. "It's not about matching the deeds of legends, Josef. It's about writing our own."

Torn between the legends of his youth and the realities before him,

Josef nodded. "Tomorrow, at six," he whispered, steeling himself for the dawn of a new chapter—one he would take part in writing.

CHAPTER 8

TUESDAY, 26 MAY 1942

PRAGUE, PROTECTORATE OF BOHEMIA AND MORAVIA

"Effective and lasting intimidation can only be achieved whether by capital punishment or by means which leave the relatives and the population in the dark about the fate of the culprit. Deportation to Germany serves this purpose."
FIELD MARSHAL WILHELM KEITEL
Nacht und Nebel Decree, 12 December 1941

Kateřina had settled in her father's home office five hours ago to prepare for her interview with Reinhard Heydrich. Then, there was a knock at the door. A uniformed officer had presented her with a personal invitation from Sturmbannführer Langer, inviting her to the concert that Heydrich himself would attend. Yes, she would go, she'd told them. What better way to prepare for her interview than to see the Obergruppenführer in his element with his guard down? More than that, she'd gain the trust of Sturmbannführer Langer. Prove to Hilbert that she could be a valuable asset to his cause. His pride wouldn't allow him to think of her as anything else.

A car had arrived and picked her up, and now she stood at the grand, tall entrance of the palace itself. Although she had walked through these gardens numerous times, she'd never been inside.

Kateřina's high heels clicked on the polished marble floors of the Wallenstein Palace foyer as she walked to Sturmbannführer Langer's side. She'd passed this baroque palace in the Malá Strana district of Prague hundreds of times. The palace was one of the city's masterpieces, with multiple wings and courtyards. Yet she never thought she'd be here under these conditions.

Entering the central wing's main hall, Kateřina's heels echoed on the mosaic floor, an amalgamation of brass, bronze, and tarnished silver tiles. Above her, frescoes depicting scenes from Greek mythology were interwoven with intricate tubes and steam outlets, all half-hidden by Nazi banners boasting cogwheel insignias.

The chuff of distant steam engines and the whir of clockwork mechanisms faintly reverberated throughout the hall. She glanced around and saw that the palace was a fusion of ancient grandeur and industrial innovation. Intricate carvings of mythological creatures now donned aviator goggles and bronze armor, while ornate moldings of gods were rendered as inventors, their hands brandishing tools rather than lightning bolts.

Pipelines crisscrossed the richly decorated ceilings, while walls became canvases for ornate tapestries and steam-driven contraptions. Overhead, the massive chandeliers boasted shimmering crystals and a network of exposed gears and cogs, rotating and interlocking in mesmerizing patterns. These mechanical wonders had become the standard of high fashion and decor the past two decades as the world embraced a new age: one where steam ruled, even amidst the tumult of war.

The men in the room sported sharply pressed uniforms adorned with brass buttons and gear-shaped insignias. Their epaulets shimmered with an array of metallic colors as tubes and dials jutted out from their belts, each connected to ornate pocket watches. At their sides, women draped in silk and leather wore corsets accentuated with copper buckles and intricate lacework. Ribbons and hairpins resembling miniature steam pistons held up their elaborate hairstyles.

Kateřina smiled, her lips curling confidently over her custom-crafted, gear-encrusted choker, giving the illusion that she belonged among this elite crowd. Hilbert's shoes clicked rhythmically as he led her down a hall where white-and-gold stucco worked seamlessly with twisting bronze pipelines. The ceiling boasted a fresco that seemed to move—airships navigating a sky full of gods and mechanical creatures—thanks to the clever incorporation of clockwork mechanisms.

As they passed, paintings showcased the traditional masterpieces and scenes where steam-driven contraptions soared above landscapes. Sculptures melded the classical with the mechanical, portraying ancient and innovative figures with marble and bronze cog limbs. Her mouth dropped slightly, not just at the art but at the audacity. With news of bombing raids over Germany coming in daily, the Nazis seemed to believe that, surrounded by a world of steam and wonder, their art—like them—was untouchable.

Two and a half years ago, when the first dirigibles had entered the Czech skies, she couldn't imagine anything in her future beyond chaos and fear. When the spider tanks had crept into town, she'd pictured war-torn streets and fighting in the alleyways. If not for the airships that floated over the palace and the air scouts peering down, she would have believed it was like any ordinary day in Prague before the war.

Laughter and snippets of conversation continued to vibrate around her head like the rotors on an airship. Kateřina smoothed her burgundy velvet dress, thankful her father hadn't been strong enough to empty her mother's closet after her passing. Mother's dresses fit her well enough.

Brass buttons adorned the fitted bodice with a high lace neckline and long sleeves. The skirt swooped behind her, full and flowing, layered with ruffles. It was her mother's style, not hers. Yet Kateřina blended in with the other women in attendance, even down to the black broach she'd pinned onto the lace at her neck.

Around her, the atmosphere buzzed with anticipation. The murmurs of the other concertgoers pricked her ears. It was hard not to eavesdrop on their whispered conversations, especially when she walked among the Nazi elite.

"Is this your first time inside Wallenstein Palace?" Hilbert offered an arm.

She slipped her fingers around the crook of his arm and squeezed. His uniform jacket felt rough under her touch, and Kateřina imagined his heart the same. Something seemed off with Hilbert's white-toothed grin, which gleamed like polished marble in the glow of a gas lamp.

Kateřina tucked a blonde strand of hair behind her ear. "Inside, yes, but not in the gardens. I remember the first time I snuck into the gardens alone. My father was meeting a friend for coffee here in Malá Strana, and I told him I would walk around. I must have been eleven or twelve. There was a wall with an unmarked door. I watched as a few people walked in." She pointed her thumb over her shoulder, back toward where they'd come. "As I saw, the entrance is well protected today."

"What isn't well protected in this city?" Hilbert commented, his shoulders straightening even more.

Notes of the orchestra rose, and Kateřina tipped up her chin to listen. A genuine smile lifted her cheeks. "The warming up always feels like a call to hurry, as if the notes say, 'Listen, listen, we're about to get started.'"

Hilbert chuckled. "Yes, well, tonight is a special night."

"What do you mean?"

"They will be playing Heydrich's father's compositions."

Kateřina paused and blinked twice. "His father . . . is a composer?"

Hilbert stirred beside her. "Was a composer, yes. He died a few years back." He motioned her forward and led her into a mirrored room. Royal-blue plush seats lined in straight, neat rows. They settled in seats in the fourth row. Kateřina attempted to act as if this was an ordinary day, yet in her mind, she was clicking through the names of the men who sat around them.

SS-Gruppenführer Karl Hermann Frank, *Generalleutnant* Rudolf Toussant, *Generalarbeitsführer* Alexander Commichau, and *SS-Brigadeführer* Karl von Treuenfeld. And sitting in the third row, front and center, Obergruppenführer Reinhard Heydrich himself. A beautiful wife sat at each of the men's sides.

Before long, the conductor walked onto the stage, wearing a tailored black suit with a high-collared shirt and waistcoat with brass buttons and gears. A pocket-watch chain hung on his waistcoat, and a top hat sat upon his graying hair. He wore an embellished glove on his left hand. A simple white glove on his right gripped his baton.

"The concert will be given by the string quartet of Arthur Bonhardt, accompanied by pianist Kurt Sanke," the conductor announced. "The Bonhardt players are from Halle, where Obergruppenführer Heydrich was born. A music academy has prospered there, and because of that, we have music to enjoy tonight."

The musicians lifted their polished instruments, and notes rose like delicate butterflies. Music wrapped around her like a warm and soothing embrace. Kateřina's breath caught as Hilbert leaned close. Her heartbeat quickened at the spicy aroma of his cologne, his nearness.

Hilbert pressed nearer until their shoulders touched. "Piano Concerto in C-minor." He explained. Then he breathed deeply through his nose like the music was a sweet fragrance. "One of Richard Bruno Heydrich's greatest works."

She noted how the stringed quartet swayed as they played as if in a dance with their instruments. The pianist's fingers skipped across the keys lightly and flawlessly, notes rising soft and lilting. She pressed her back into the blue velvet seat, leaning slightly on the armrest. Her fingers swept back and forth ever so slightly, following their pattern.

Then a scowl grew on the pianist's face, and his fingers tapped harder on the keys like the heavy thud of boots hitting the pavement. A chill coursed through Kateřina like cold steam escaping a pressure valve as the staccato of notes rose sharply, assaulting the room with the precision and force of a clockwork mechanism in overdrive.

As if attempting to escape the battle cry, Kateřina's eyes darted to the back of the stage where a steam-powered organ stood—a silent sentinel from bygone days. Her mind recalled listening to Alice Herz-Sommer play such an instrument. As a young teen, she'd enjoyed attending concerts highlighting the Jewish musicians. Kateřina remembered those sweet days gone by and evenings out with her mother, attending the concerts and walking home with the twinkling of a thousand lights of Prague Castle bearing down on them. She wiped at a tear.

Nothing was the same. Nothing would ever be the same again. Everything changed with the pounding of those boots. And even though she wasn't Jewish or considered a political enemy of the Germans, the echoing of boots haunted her. They plagued her father, too.

She pressed her lips together. *He's trying to stay one step ahead of them.* While she wanted her name and her words splashed on the front page, Father knew allowing that would be the same as waving a red flag to draw the bull's attention, which for those in Prague was Heydrich himself.

Kateřina pressed a hand over her heart and shrank back as if she could feel his intense disapproval resting on her. How foolish she'd been to think she could use her stories to reveal what the Nazis were truly up to, as if Hitler's henchman wouldn't see it for what it was and punish her for it.

Then, as quickly as the pounding of the keys had started, they eased again. Kateřina's shoulders softened. Her frame sank into the chair, and it wasn't until the music washed away her worries that she realized how fast her body had reacted to the rhythms that pranced and pulsed through the room.

Following the same gentle and forceful pattern as at the beginning of the composition, the music rose like a swell of waves crashing against the shore. Standing erect with his back straight, the conductor waved like a magician casting a spell.

Hilbert shifted beside her, his cough jolting Kateřina from her reverie. She chastised herself for being so engrossed in the music that she might miss vital details for the news story she hoped to convince her father to allow her to write. Many in the audience had turned their attention away from the performance, their gazes now focused on Heydrich. The Obergruppenführer, usually so formidable, seemed almost diminished, hunched in his seat as if transported to another time by the music. It was difficult for Kateřina to reconcile this seemingly vulnerable figure with the man known for orchestrating such brutality—the one responsible for sending countless Jews to their tragic fate.

Heydrich lowered his head even farther, and Kateřina held her breath. Time stood still as he wiped away a tear. The concert drew to a close. Applause erupted, and a wave went out in every direction as men and women rose to their feet.

Music triumphs even in a time of war. Kateřina pressed her lips into a thin line. Was it true? Was this truly a triumph? Unexpected anger smoldered like an unwholesome fire in the pit of her stomach, and the emotions she'd been pushing away caused her skin to grow clammy and her heart to pound.

She stood, clapped, and then smoothed the skirt of her dress. Smiling broadly, she pulled her lower lip between her teeth and bit down, tasting blood. Then she released it.

What about Jews or political opponents whose only music now is the death wails for those taken first . . . knowing they will soon follow?

And here the Obergruppenführer sat in a plush seat—in a room that had pulsated with his father's music—with nods of approval from all. As if realizing the music had stopped, he leaped to his feet and clapped with the exuberance of a peasant boy viewing a circus act for the first time.

As the Obergruppenführer turned and acknowledged the audience, Kateřina could only think about the tens of thousands, if not hundreds of thousands, who sat in camps. Not to mention other enemies who disappeared without a trace.

Even though every college professor had instructed Kateřina and the other students that a reporter should state the news impartially, that seemed impossible. Truth couldn't triumph in times like these. Well, as long as one wanted to stay alive, it couldn't.

She thought of her father's downturned scowl, followed by the glisten of concern in his gaze. He did more than keep neutral as he ran the newspaper. He smoothed his words—all their words—so the Germans' deeds seemed understandable, acceptable even.

What would Mother think of that?

While her father filled the pages with black text, her mother read between the lines. Where her father tried to protect himself and others by cowering before those who were more powerful, her mother had always done the right thing—or at least had tried.

As the musicians exited the stage, voices rose around her. The excitement on their faces was broad and bright, yet Kateřina thought only of escaping into her thoughts.

She walked by Hilbert's side as he spoke with the other officers exiting the theater room. She was starting to hope they were finally headed toward the exit door when a foreboding presence appeared ahead. Obergruppenführer Reinhard Heydrich himself paused not ten feet from her.

He stood a few inches taller than Hilbert, an imposing figure, over six feet tall. Heydrich's sharp features and piercing blue eyes took her breath away. It wasn't that he was handsome. He was intense—from an impeccable, perfectly tailored uniform to neatly styled hair. As if drawn to her, the Obergruppenführer walked in her direction.

Heydrich's reputation preceded him. She had read about his cruelty. She'd overheard the stories that didn't make it into the newspaper. He was mostly known for his brutal treatment of the Jews. Yet, meeting the monster face-to-face, Kateřina spoke the only words that came to her.

"Your father's compositions were both lovely and powerful, Herr Obergruppenführer. You must be very proud."

Focusing teary eyes on her, Obergruppenführer Heydrich's lips parted slightly. They opened even more, as if preparing to speak, and then pressed tight again. Only after his pregnant wife patted his arm, urging him to respond, did he try again.

"Ja, of course. Very proud." Then Heydrich's gaze narrowed on hers. "And while tonight was a celebration of my father's efforts, Miss Dubová, tomorrow will be a celebration of mine. I eagerly await our talk."

Kateřina gasped and reached for Hilbert's arm, gripping it tight. *Reinhard Heydrich knows me? Knows my name?* A clash of pride and fear rose in her chest.

"Yes," she managed to whisper. "I'm eager for that, too."

As the crowds pressed in to personally speak with Obergruppenführer Heydrich, Hilbert steered Kateřina toward a set of stairs with the gentleness of a father leading his fearful child away from a snarling pit bull. Even though Heydrich neither snarled nor snapped, he'd imposed the same fear.

This will never do, she urged herself. *I have to push that fear aside. I need to see the true story behind the façade, the true man behind the high position.* Only then would her words matter and not simply be another piece of propaganda on the newsstands in whatever province the Nazis had claimed under their control.

They walked to the second level, and she released the breath she'd been holding. She'd worry about sitting face-to-face with Heydrich tomorrow, but first, she had to get through tonight.

Kateřina tipped up her chin, mouth parting as she saw a large table on the second level spread with an elaborate array of food. Sliced beef, cheese, fresh white-bread rolls with butter, chocolate. Her mouth watered. These things, and so much more, were rationed or unavailable to the general population.

"Our fears can seem as insignificant as ants when faced with the delicious aroma of freshly baked bread, can they not?"

Kateřina knew Hilbert spoke of the interaction with Heydrich moments before. "Was it that obvious?"

"Who wouldn't be afraid of interviewing one of the most powerful men in the world? At least getting that first interaction out of the way can help with tomorrow's nerves."

She nodded and put on a show of faux approval. "Yes, of course." If only nerves were her singular fear. How would she ever talk to the man who had formalized the destruction of so many people and act impartial?

I will consider the deeds of the wolves when I'm not walking among them, she urged herself, pushing all thoughts of tomorrow from her mind.

Hilbert guided Kateřina to a small table on the balcony. A brass candelabra sat atop it, with multiple twisted arms reaching skyward. Each arm held candles whose flames danced in the cool evening breeze. Although blackout drapes covered the palace windows, the candlelight on the balcony was subtle enough to provide a festive mood, yet it could soon be extinguished if needed.

With the warm glow of the moon, the aroma of flowers on the breeze, and the handsome man at her side, Kateřina could almost imagine there was no war. She could forget there were news stories to write. Forget a father was sitting at home waiting to reprimand her. Forget this father was a newspaper chief who would listen to the night's events, sifting through her stories in search of headlines like a gold miner sifting through dirt in search of precious nuggets.

Soon a half dozen other junior officers joined them. The men laughed and talked to each other while the women did the same. A white-jacketed waiter served each guest a small plate of appetizers. Kateřina shifted in her seat, forcing herself to eat slowly, despite wanting to consume one morsel after another without taking a breath.

Hilbert sat with a straight spine in the chair next to her. The other uniformed men watched Sturmbannführer Langer with the same awed reverence as Sturmbannführer Langer watched the Obergruppenführer.

Hilbert—a mere man—appeared almost godlike in the light of their approving glances. His words fell like gospel to the lower-ranking officers as he reflected on the music. When he smiled, his blue eyes grew larger, and in the flickering candlelight, she had to admit he took her breath away. There was no denying his power, beauty, and eloquence. And still, he'd chosen her to be at his side.

Kateřina's chest warmed. Without warning, her attraction to him rose like bubbles to the surface of the champagne glasses sitting before them.

Sensing her gaze on him, Hilbert turned and met her regard. He lifted his eyebrows as if appreciating a fine painting or sculpture. Her heart caught at the appreciation and respect in his gaze.

Heat rose to her cheeks, and she hoped the redness rising wouldn't be obvious to others. Then again, maybe the brightness in her eyes at Hilbert's nearness revealed even more than the light from the candles on the table and the round moon overhead that glowed dully like tarnished brass. Then as quickly as the moment came, it passed as Hilbert spoke of the movement of troops in recent weeks.

Watching the other women from the corner of her eye, Kateřina took bites from her plate at the same slow, steady pace. As the men talked about world events, she attempted to keep her reporter's mind alert for anything she could later weave into a story. Yet it was hard to ignore the ripples of pleasure that moved through her taste buds at the first nibble of fine chocolate in years.

"How is work in Terezín?" Hilbert asked the man sitting on his right.

Kateřina bit into a biscuit. The flaky, buttery crumbs melted in her mouth, and it took all her control not to close her eyes and savor the moment.

"Terezín? Overrun with vermin," the man joked.

Hilbert grinned. "So, you have a rat problem?"

"Ja, that too." The man threw back his head and laughed. "No worries. Now that we've caught them, the extermination is the easy part. Harder is keeping them tightly locked behind the gates."

"Not easy to do when the pests manage to escape. Days ago, one of the rats fooled some guards by lying among the log pile of bodies on the death cart. He escaped when the guards rolled the cart out of the gates, taking it to the ovens." He smirked. "Imagine being desperate enough to cover yourself with decaying bodies."

The crumbs in Kateřina's mouth grew bitter. She dropped her biscuit back onto her plate and took a sip of her drink, forcing the crumbles down.

"If word gets out—"

"*If* word gets out?" Hilbert's sharp voice snapped but swiftly turned humorous. "It *will* get out, especially with a mouth as large as yours. Did you not know a Czech reporter sits among us? No doubt she's already writing the story in her mind as we speak."

Every set of eyes turned in her direction. Kateřina again attempted to swallow down the biscuit. Clearing her throat, she hid her disgust behind what she hoped was a playful smile.

"I have every word recorded." She tapped the side of her temple. "I have the deadline for tomorrow's story already met." She pretended to write with an invisible notebook and pencil. "Can I have your name, sir, if Jewish freedom fighters or Czech rebels wish to confirm your words?"

Laughter from the group rose louder than before, and Kateřina's heart pounded. *What am I doing here?*

"Yes, well, we're about to have more vermin to corral," one officer said between sips of wine after the laughter died. "Another roundup is happening in a few days, and no doubt another after that until every dark corner of Josefov is swept clean."

"Spring cleaning, ja. This is good." Hilbert covered Katrina's hand with his own. What started as a soft squeeze grew more intense. She sucked in a breath, and it took everything within her not to wince.

Even though a smile crinkled the corners of Hilbert's blue eyes, Kateřina knew this was a warning, and she had a strange sensation that she could as easily be seen as *vermin*. The only difference was, while the Jews were hidden, she'd walked proudly into the mousetrap, and she could almost picture Hilbert licking his lips in his pursuit.

Her shoulders tightened as an eddy of fear swirled around her stomach.

"Now it's time to resurrect Bohemia. More Jews will have to leave Josefov, and we have a plan for that," Hilbert spat.

A chill rushed over her, and Kateřina pushed her plate away. As their conversation switched to the newer steam trains that could carry their transports around their protectorates even quicker, Kateřina turned her attention to the shaped garden hedges. She leaned forward, thankful for the moon's light that hinted at their display. Although she'd walked along these pathways, the view from overhead revealed something new: triangle shapes with straight hedges intersecting the lower half of the triangle.

Kateřina scratched her eyebrow. She'd seen those symbols before, but where? In a way, the intricate patterns on the hedges resembled the symbols used by alchemists to unlock the secrets of the universe.

"You like the garden, yes?" Hilbert's breath was so near Kateřina's ear she jumped. Yet instead of longing, disgust pulsed on every nerve. She balled her hands into fists, pressing her fingernails into her palms. How could her body betray her in such a way? She swallowed the lump of regret forming in her throat.

Thankfully Hilbert stood, putting space between them and giving her a moment to release an angry breath.

Kateřina rose and allowed herself to be led to the balcony's edge, overlooking the garden. "Yes, I do like the garden." She pointed, hoping he didn't notice her slight trembling. "I especially enjoy those symbols. Of course, they can only be seen from this height. I wonder what they mean."

Hilbert lifted a brow and offered a half smile. "It resembles the alchemy symbols."

Kateřina released a sigh. "That's what I thought. Yes, that makes sense. It has been said that the elixir of life was found here. Emperor Rudolf II attracted many alchemists to his court."

"Alchemy has some value, but I'm more interested in the Golem of Prague."

Her head pulled back, and she gave a side glance.

"Are you surprised?"

"Truthfully, I wouldn't think Jewish folklore would interest you."

"Mystical rituals, incantations . . ." Hilbert shrugged. "Our great Führer would not have risen to such heights without these things."

She submerged another jolt of surprise. "So Hitler is a patron of such arts and sciences?"

"More like a master."

Instead of focusing on Hilbert's gaze, Kateřina looked toward the garden bathed in a ghostly, moonlit radiance and the city's darkness beyond. With no lights to be seen, the Vltava River, with the city rising on each shore, appeared like a deep, dark valley, nestled between two ominous mountains.

"And you think the descendants of the Maharal of Prague are still out there? Do you wish to hear the legend from their lips?" she teased. "Or maybe you want to search the synagogue's attic where the golem still waits as a lump of clay, marking time before he is resurrected?"

"No. I care little about tales of the past or a lifeless lump of clay." He smirked. "I wish to learn from those who hold the keys behind the power."

Kateřina turned away from the garden to study Hilbert's face. There was a haunting tone to his words as if this mattered more than anything he'd spoken of this evening. "And you are certain Rabbi Loew's family is still there?"

"Yes, we know the names of every Jew—those still in Prague and those who are gone." One eyebrow lifted. "The Jews keep track of every name. Their obsession with knowing and honoring their ancestors has been very useful to us."

"Then, if you know of these descendants, why haven't you arrested them?"

"My father was a butcher. He always told me patience is like giving a heifer the time it needs to produce the best quality meat. While some believe in Jewish folklore, I know a trusted man can lead many to destruction." Then, as if worried he'd said too much, Hilbert waved the words away.

He reached over and placed a gentle hand on her arm. "The driver is waiting. I must not keep you with my musings. You have a big day tomorrow." He led her to the banquet hall with his hand pressed to the small of her back.

They moved through the room of well-dressed women and

uniformed men eating from small plates and speaking in clustered groups to the upstairs hall and the staircase to the first level. They reached the stairs, and her footsteps halted. She grasped the railing, an uneasiness filling the pit of her gut.

Concerns about tomorrow's interview rushed in again. A gaslight that resembled a flaming handlight brightened only half of Hilbert's face, making him appear phantomlike.

Kateřina tightened her hold on the stair railing, her face turning a shade paler. "What did you say Obergruppenführer Heydrich wanted to discuss with me?"

"*Nacht und Nebel*," Hilbert whispered, leaning closer. "The Night and Fog decree. It's an edict for those who dare to defy the Reich across occupied territories. Disappearances without any explanation."

Hilbert moved down one step, positioning himself so that their eyes met. "Out of all the reporters in Prague, Obergruppenführer Heydrich wishes to confide in you about its implications. Are you not curious?"

Kateřina swallowed hard, trying to steady her voice. "But why me? Surely, there are others he would trust with this information."

"Yes, but for his own reasons, he's chosen you." Hilbert watched her closely.

She took a deep breath, attempting to calm the storm of anxiety raging within her. "Why would he reveal such a chilling edict to me?"

Hilbert tilted his head, observing her with a keen eye. "Perhaps the better question is, why wouldn't you want to be in the know?"

Kateřina paused, her gaze distant as she grappled with her whirlwind of thoughts and emotions. She drew a deep breath, searching for the right words. "While my father believes knowledge is power," she began hesitantly, "my mother always said that too much knowledge is like a mirage, leading you toward an illusion of safety."

"Wise mother." Hilbert stepped closer, and his lips neared hers. For a moment, Kateřina thought he would pull her into a kiss, but then his whispers met her ear. "But we need you. Imagine that." His voice was husky. "The Obergruppenführer needs you. I need you."

She didn't know what to do or say, and she inwardly cursed the warm sensations in her body at his closeness.

Hilbert pulled back ever so slightly, ignoring the conversations that filtered from the open doorway at the top of the stairs and acting as if they were the only two souls in his building.

"We need to control what is said about *Nacht und Nebel,* the sweeping away of our powerful enemies so they are never heard from again. The rest of the world frowns on this, even during war."

Kateřina swallowed deeply as she tried to keep her fear down like a ball held underwater—straining to keep it from surfacing. "What do you mean?"

"We could not be doing what we are now if it weren't for the newspapers. If we control what is in the newspapers, we shape their opinions."

She nodded. *And if you control me, you govern my father . . . and his newspaper.* "And this is why Heydrich wants to speak to me?"

He ran a finger down her cheek. Her eyelids fluttered closed for the briefest second. Then she opened them, maintaining her composure.

"After what you wrote about the glass factory, ja. We see the potential in you."

We?

"We appreciate your explanation—that gas is humane and less lethal than conventional weapons." Hilbert stroked a finger down her neck, smiling. "What you came up with was better than what we could have devised."

Kateřina nodded and then pulled back slightly from his touch. She repeated her father's printed words—words with her byline. "It is not meant to kill but rather to incapacitate the enemy by causing temporary blindness, coughing, and nausea." She shrugged. "It does sound better than painful and sudden death, doesn't it?"

He leaned forward by inches, finally resting his lips on her ear lobe. "You are very useful to us, my darling. *Kleine Blume,* little flower, standing so strong. Very, very useful."

Josef took the long way back. While Grandfather followed the shadows toward their home, Josef chose a route past the clock at Židovská radnice, the Jewish Town Hall. He took comfort in the Hebrew numerals and the hands that moved counterclockwise around the dial.

Time is more precious than money, his mother had told him as her illness progressed. If only, like those clock hands, he could turn back time and seek her advice. Mother would have convinced Father to stay in Josefov instead of going to Terezín. She'd also be able to persuade Grandfather to fight. But since she wasn't here, it was all on Josef's shoulders. If he couldn't urge his grandfather to pick up arms, he'd have to find a way to be the Loew this generation needed.

Folding himself against the white stone wall, Josef stood in the shadow of the Old-New Synagogue on Maiselova and Červená. The night air took on a chill. A heaviness pressed on his heart as he thought of the familiar nightmare that had plagued him from childhood. An image of a gigantic clay figure, made of mud and grime, rising from the soil imbued with life.

He tilted his face skyward toward the attic where Rabbi Loew had laid his golem to rest. Although the creature had haunted Josef's nights for two decades, these days he wished for nothing more than to believe such a creature was real and could protect them.

The Germans had entered their city 1,168 days ago. From that day, the Jews in Josefov had scurried into every basement and rushed into every attic to hide, but it hadn't stopped the predators from collecting their prey. Instead of devouring them, the Nazis had shipped them off, hiding evil deeds behind stone walls and barbed wire. Men, women, and children were rounded up like sheep.

Giving one last glance at the white-faced clock, Josef crept back home. By the time he staggered into the living room, Grandfather had already gone to bed. Two slices of brown bread without butter sat by a shriveled apple on the small kitchen table. Tears sprang to Josef's eyes. Where had his grandfather come up with bread and fruit? He always found a way when he wanted to.

Weary, Josef moved to the living room. He sank into the worn sofa, too tired to walk up the stairs to his third-story bedroom. Closing his eyes, the image of Judah Loew appeared—a man who dared to create something from nothing.

Josef often found himself yearning for the legends of old, particularly the golem story. There were days when he could almost sense its mighty clay presence, looming protectively in the shadows. But no matter how much he wished, the protector of yore remained a figure of myths.

"Judah and his people found hope when Golem, their silent sentinel, came to life," Josef mused. "They had a guardian crafted from the very earth, and with its strength, victory had been assured all those years ago."

He often wondered how different things might be in the present if the golem were more than a story. What if his grandfather, with his vast knowledge, could breathe life into such a being once more? Would they, too, experience the security and hope Judah's people had felt?

A heavy sigh escaped Josef's lips. The weight of his yearnings and fears pressed on his chest, making it hard to breathe.

Glancing around the dimly lit room, Josef's gaze settled on an oil-painted portrait of his celebrated ancestor, Rabbi Loew. The wise old face seemed to gaze back with knowledge of generations. Josef whispered to the painted figure, his voice heavy with emotion, "What would you do, Rabbi Loew, if you were standing in my shoes today?"

The light of a lone candle flickered. Even though weariness racked his body, his mind turned like a waterwheel, repeatedly spinning yet going nowhere.

Judah Loew's presence still filled this room as if he'd lived there 35 years ago, not 350. *If only Judah could have an answer for me now.* Bringing a clay creature to life was impossible. But Josef's desperation made him think otherwise.

Dust and cobwebs clung to the books lining the shelf, proving most hadn't been touched in months. One volume bore a brighter shade of red. Josef gasped. Unhindered by a layer of dust, it blazed like a beacon on the shelf, and Josef wasn't sure how he didn't notice it sooner.

He hurried to the shelf and pulled out Judah Loew's greatest treasure—his holy book. Josef rubbed his eyes and sat in the chair closest to the candle. A piece of cloth rested between two pages as he opened the book. Josef had learned Hebrew in school, but it still took a few minutes for him to focus on the marked words.

"But you are our father, Lord," he whispered the translated Hebrew. "We are like clay." Emotion caught in his throat. "And you are like the potter. You created us . . ." Words from the great prophet Isaiah.

Tears sprang to his eyes, and he slammed the book shut. What nonsense. Josef knew what he was—a weakling. He didn't have the wisdom of his ancestors or the ability to raise a creature to save his people like Rabbi Loew.

Something shuffled at Josef's side. He jumped to his feet, sure a German soldier had followed him home, ready to arrest him for being out past curfew. Instead . . .

"Grandfather."

Grandfather moved to sit in the next chair over, wearing a thin nightshirt. He pointed to the book that Josef still held. "Do you remember the Hebrew word for *ark*?" His voice was soft and calm as if they sat side by side in Torah school.

"*Teivah*, Grandfather."

"And what did God command Noah to do?"

Josef's eyelids ached as if full of grit. He didn't know what this had to do with anything, but he was too tired to fight the questions. "God commanded Noah to enter the ark."

"The holy Scriptures are the same, are they not? They are a door, and we must enter them. It's there we will find the refuge we need." Grandfather cleared his throat. "Judah Loew ben Bezalel wasn't just a rabbi of Prague. He was *the* Rabbi of Prague. Yet when our ancestor was summoned to the castle to speak with Emperor Rudolph II, the king of the Holy Roman Empire did not discuss the Jews in Bohemia. He wanted to talk about alchemy and magic." Grandfather shook his head. "The king sought answers but missed out on the truth."

Josef didn't argue.

Grandfather bit his lip, implying he had more to say. "There is something I have wanted to tell you, but I am worried the truth will do more harm than good."

"What is it?"

Grandfather closed his eyes and drew several deep breaths. Then he wiped the corners of his eyes as if tears had formed. "I did not tell you about the meetings because I worried you would focus on the wrong things. No, more than that, I *am* worried because you want to fight against the Germans—to kill them. Yet if you strike them, their wrath will come full force, turning against you. Unstoppable force. Evil . . ." He huffed in disbelief. "That's not the path we should be heading down."

Josef froze. Had his grandfather been told of his upcoming meeting with Nikolai? Or had he heard a rumor and was trying to confirm its truth? "I can't talk about this right now. I need to go." Without a glance back, Josef rose and hurried to his room. Turned out he did have the strength to make it upstairs after all.

Kateřina walked to the front door of her house with slow steps as her mind attempted to process all the night had held. Reinhard Heydrich knew her—knew her name. Hilbert had plans for her. No, *they* had plans for her.

Perhaps her father thought he'd protected her by writing that piece about the glass factory. He'd done the opposite. In his effort to protect her, Father had led her to the jaws of the wolves.

She entered the front door and noticed a light in the study. She moved down the hall in that direction, searching for the words to tell him all she'd learned.

Father glanced up. He sat at his desk, still wearing his buttoned-up shirt and tie. He regarded her with an air of business, seeing her as the reporter, not his daughter.

"I saw you leave earlier, heading to Wallenstein Palace. What did you notice?" He spoke with clipped words, as if telling her he wanted his questions answered without questions in return.

"It was a concert. There was a string quartet and a pianist. Blue velvet seats. Obergruppenführer Heydrich sat front and center. The musicians played his father's compositions. Heydrich was very moved." Kateřina's emotionless words applied armor around her heart piece by piece, creating a fortress impenetrable to whatever questions he asked.

"Did you know that palace is being used by the German military and as the headquarters for the Gestapo? Prisoners are being held within those walls. I wouldn't be surprised if there was an interrogation center near where you listened to the lovely music." His nose curled up in a snarl, and he tapped his fingers on the desktop. "I wouldn't want to guess how many Czechs have been tortured and killed. Maybe one, even as you enjoyed your evening."

His accusations stung like a thousand bees, leaving Kateřina's heart throbbing. Hadn't Father started this? Hadn't he been the one who told her about the party at the glass factory?

"Why are you telling me this? Are you trying to make me feel guilty?" Her fingers twitched, and she crossed her arms tightly.

"Just think, maybe tonight a person breathed his last while he listened to a Heydrich composition drifting down." Father's tone was flat, but still, emotion carried on every word.

"And could I have stopped such a death?" She scoffed and gritted her teeth. "How could I have known anything other than the concert was happening within those walls?"

"Then why did you go?" His features softened, and at that moment, Kateřina wondered if they were having two different conversations about two separate topics.

"I dressed up and mingled with the Nazis because Hilbert asked me to go. I assume I am supposed to write a story about the event—a sympathetic story about a son who finds pride in his father's work. To make a killer appear human."

She turned her back to him. "Of course, nothing I write will be good enough, and whatever words I put onto paper will no doubt be put through the teeth tomorrow morning. Why bother with me at all?" She jutted out her chin. "Or maybe tonight is just another way to feel like a failure in your eyes."

Kateřina paused, waiting for his response. All she heard was the tapping of his fingers.

Finally, he cleared his throat. "You're wearing your mother's dress," he stated simply.

"Yes, I am. I had nothing appropriate of my own, and it's not as if I had time to go to a dress shop to have something made . . . if the fabric could even be found to make one."

He said nothing after that, and she wanted to turn, to stomp her foot, and to tell him that she was tired of whatever game he was playing. "Oh, I get it. I understand your plan now. Let's tell Kateřina to dress up and mingle with the Nazis so I can shame her for doing that very thing when she returns."

She swept back around in time to see the color drained from his face. Guilt ricocheted off her heart like pebbles, pinging with pain. Just because he could be heartless to her, she didn't need to do so with him. What would Mother say about that?

Tears welled up in her eyes like an unexpected rainstorm, catching her off guard. Kateřina hurried from his office and raced up the stairs into the bathroom at the top.

Sucking in a big breath, she turned on the water and tilted her face over the sink. Then she scooped handfuls of water, splashing it over her face and neck. She undid the buttons on her neck and stepped out of her dress, standing there in only a slip.

At first, she believed that she was only hiding her tears, but as Kateřina moved to the tub and started to draw a bath, the truth hit her like a headline. Tonight she'd mingled with the most powerful and wealthy in her country, yet her skin felt grimy, as if she'd been sitting in a slop pit with swine.

The bathtub had filled when she heard a knock. Kateřina slid on her robe and opened the door. Her father stood pensively waiting. Gone was the emotionless newspaperman who'd been speaking to her moments before.

"I'm sorry I got you into this." He released a heavy sigh. "We needed to know if the rumors about the glass canisters being made were true." He paused as if trying to decide how much to reveal.

Kateřina focused on the water drips from the tub faucet, plinking in a slow, steady rhythm as she waited for his words.

"The Germans have created false news reports about the nature of the gas and their intentions to use it." He combed his fingers through his hair, causing it to stand on end.

He continued, "You had no idea of this information, but I wanted you to know how I knew what to write. I used your voice and name to hold up a mirror, reflecting the Germans' goals. They believe the world will believe these things, but anyone with wisdom will see the lies and be alerted of the increasing gas production. I am sorry I didn't tell you sooner."

She moved back to the tub and twisted the handle harder, stopping the water flow. "We?" Kateřina did not turn. "You said, 'we needed to know if the rumors are true.' Who is we?" She did not meet his gaze lest he turn and walk away.

"That is all I can tell you." His words flowed slowly like a symphony of sadness. "I've already said too much." Without another word, he turned and exited the room.

Kateřina dried her face and looked at the bath, needing even more to sink into the hot water in hopes of washing away the grime that seemed to crawl on her skin. She had told her father nothing, yet she had told him enough. Tomorrow, there would be another piece in the paper concerning the concert, and she wouldn't have to write one word. There would be reflections she wouldn't have thought of. There would be facts she didn't know. And it would be precisely what the Nazis would want—music to their ears. She was a source for her father, but not the only one. Now that he'd pulled her in, how much longer would she have to continue to play this game?

Precisely seven hours after leaving the community meeting, Josef approached Nikolai's courtyard. A teen boy waited expectantly. With quickened steps, they walked a few blocks to the business district, slipping down a narrow passageway to a large warehouse. Finally, he'd be with men who believed in action and not just words. He was ready to take a stand—to fight—like Judah Loew had done.

Josef entered the warehouse and took stock of his surroundings. Half a dozen men milled about, examining weaponry and supplies. His heart dropped, and his faith wavered. He didn't expect a standing army of Czechs prepared to invade Germany. Still, he had imagined more than the collection of ill-prepared men. He recognized some from last night's Jewish community meeting. Others he did not know. Two men stood with straight backs like soldiers and appeared the most prepared.

One man glanced up and met Josef's eyes defiantly. Then he turned to Nikolai. "Why are you bringing in someone new now? This could blow the whole mission."

Nikolai didn't acknowledge the man's words. He fixed his eyes on Josef. "There he is, Josef Loew." Nikolai approached with a slight grin. Whether intentional or not, Josef noticed a more significant inflection on his last name. It confirmed his suspicion that Nikolai didn't care about him. He would likely be much happier if Grandfather were here, but having a member of the Loew family added a level of validity to their movement, at least within the Jewish community.

Josef approached. He crossed his arms, a headache pricking his temples. He regarded Nikolai and looked around. "Don't take this as rude, but is this all?"

"All?"

"Of the resistance." Josef motioned around the room. "What can you accomplish with so few men?"

"You would be surprised." Nikolai set his jaw and narrowed his gaze. Then he leaned in close. "A massive operation is happening within hours, young Loew, a blow to the Nazis that will shake them to the core."

"How could we pull off something so large without an army?"

"Not everything requires a large fighting force." He dropped his voice to a whisper. "This group is small for a reason. It must stay quiet, hushed until the day of reckoning comes to pass."

"What type of operation is it, then?"

Pressing his lips into a thin line, Nikolai stared off into the distance as his nostrils flared. "The type which will surely put a large target on our backs, no matter whether we succeed or fail. Every Germany will be out for our deaths."

Josef considered the words. Nikolai was hiding something. Was he spouting nonsense because he had no specific goal to offer? Or was he being cryptic so as not to leak details to someone who wasn't wholly committed—even a Loew?

"I believe I understand," Josef started. "Merely knowing of your plot will endanger me, right? I need to either join or walk away." He raised an eyebrow.

Nikolai nodded, then motioned to the two unfamiliar men. Both peered at him from the corners of their eyes as they whispered between themselves. "It is not just for your safety but others as well. I am serious when I mean it will put a target on our backs."

Straightening, Nikolai grasped Josef's shoulders. "You can choose to leave now. Walk out that door and slip back into your normal life— as normal as it is these days." His grip tightened. "But even then, know you will not be out of danger. Today . . ." He gritted his teeth. "Today can change everything, but I feel things will get worse before they get better. Much worse."

Josef thought of his grandfather. Something had brought Grandfather to tears last night—something he'd wanted to tell Josef. No doubt it was the same familiar warning: hold back. Josef scratched his head as another word came to memory. *If an honest invention can be used for such terror, then any weapon can be made into something new.*

What did Grandfather mean by that?

He wouldn't want Josef to get mixed up in a plot like this, that was for sure. It didn't make sense. Being a pacifist was one thing. But what did you call someone who refused to fight against pure evil? A coward? Even though Grandfather no longer had the youthful energy to pick up a weapon and attack, surely he could do more than cower when so many they knew—even his son—were being shipped away.

Since Grandfather would not help solve their dilemma, Josef would find others who could.

"I'm in." He eyed two men preparing by adding a metal canister into a satchel. "Whatever this is, I want to be part of it."

A small smile tugged on Nikolai's cheeks—a smile that grew as he walked toward the two men who were obviously in charge. Soon, the warehouse hummed with whispered words. Plans were being made and secrets shared.

No one gave Josef any mind, so he folded his arms and stood against the wall. Fear pulsated through him. By the end of the day would anyone from the Jewish district, including Grandfather, understand that men were planning to fight? Even die? Did ordinary people understand this was the price of freedom? Then again, what was the alternative?

Just when he was confident he would not be accepted, the two leaders slipped on long coats, shot glances at each other, and then, with mirrored nods, turned to Josef. For three heartbeats, he stared disbelievingly as they approached.

One man pulled a black metal object from his coat pocket and extended it to Josef. He hesitated briefly before accepting their offering. From the determined fix of the men's gazes, Josef knew they had only one thing on their minds: death.

TEREZÍN PRISON OF HORRORS

Terezín, the former military fortress once built to protect the people of Bohemia from occupation, has become a prison for Jewish families. The German dictator, Adolf Hitler, has built a city for the Jews, but it is a place of horrors. One of the prisoners escaped by hiding among bodies on a death cart taken outside the gates of Terezín to the ovens to be burned. Men, women, and children live in appalling conditions. Families are separated within the high walls, and other members sent away to camps farther east, to unknown fates. Sickness and malnutrition impact every person, and those imprisoned waste away within ragged clothes. Scholars and philosophers, artists and musicians are being lost. With very little food, children are dying daily. "Whenever you see a transport leaving our stations, know the fate these Jews are being sent to," one escaped prisoner urges. "We must do something. We must all do something now." —*name withheld.*

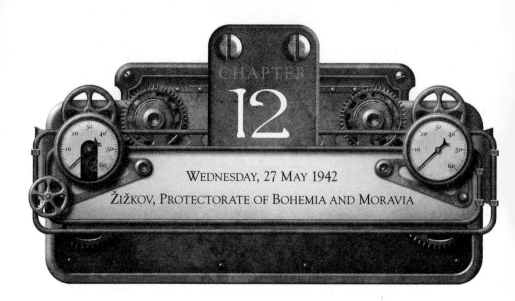

Kateřina's heels clicked against the floor as she briskly entered the newsroom, the rhythmic tapping of typewriters echoing her determined pace. Holding her chin high, she met the eyes of several reporters who looked her way. Their gazes a mixture of pity and disdain.

Evka called her earlier that morning, her voice tinged with sympathy, to inform her that word had spread within the office. "They're saying your father wrote that article about the glass factory."

Kateřina felt a sting at the back of her eyes but refused to let it show. Everyone assumed she was employed only because of her father's influential position at the newspaper, not because of her merit. Let them think she was there due to nepotism, she resolved. Let them underestimate her. She would prove them wrong, and her words would soon be the ones to make a difference.

She paused near her father's door without a story. She hadn't written one. What was the use? This morning, she'd been determined to read whatever her father had written before it was published. Then again, last night's story mattered little. She'd let him print what he wanted, keeping her attention focused on today's interview.

Reversing, she eyed her desk. No, she wouldn't be able to sit either. She'd be interviewing Obergruppenführer Heydrich today, and her nerves were twisted like a tangled ball of yarn. Instead, she strode to the window.

Three stories below, a Nazi jeep rumbled by on the cobblestone streets. Soldiers with red armbands, marked with white circles and black swastikas, marched past in two columns. Overhead, an airship bearing the same markings floated between the office buildings—the ever-present eye of the Germans.

She vividly recalled the day, three years prior, when Hitler's troops had first rumbled into Prague. Immense snowflakes, as large as gears, gracefully descended from a steel-gray sky. Soldiers, wearing helmets adorned with intricate metalwork and gas mask visors, marched in grim formation.

Behind them trailed an array of fantastical machines that showcased Germany's audacious blend of steam and steel. Monstrous tanks, fitted with myriad rotating gears, belching steam, and articulated legs, looked like mechanical spiders from a nightmarish dream. Skyships hovered overhead, their propellers whirring and casting dark, fleeting shadows upon the cobbled streets below.

Flying machines with ornate, winged designs sputtered skyward, their engines leaving trails of smoke and steam. Articulated armored suits clanked alongside traditional troops, making the ground tremble with their every step.

It wasn't solely the overwhelming might of the German war machine that had made her heart skip like a misaligned gear. Beyond the cold steel and steam of their machinations, there was an unmistakable ruthlessness in the eyes of the soldiers. Their expressions were as unyielding and mechanical as the machinery they operated. It was as if their humanity had been stripped away, replaced by gears and cogs, turning them into living extensions of the very machines they controlled. In Germany's ambition, they had seamlessly merged Victorian innovation with modern warfare techniques—tools they believed would grant them an unyielding grip over any nation they desired.

The city had been blanketed with snow on the day of their arrival, and a hushed silence had permeated every corner. The shouts of the soldiers had assaulted the air, and snow in the streets soon gathered at the edges in dirty clumps, evidence of the enemies arriving in every district of Prague.

The brilliant blue sky had dared to peek out from behind gray clouds that day, giving Kateřina a glimmer of hope that somewhere a sun still shone, no matter the darkness the Germans cast. The Nazis could not blot out all light. Or at least that's what she had thought before last night. Would anything be able to stop them? Anyone?

She drummed her fingers on the windowsill, remembering the punctuated music of last night. At first, Kateřina had attempted to find some good in the German's presence. It was why her father was promoted.

Father had taken the place of the former editor in chief, a Jewish man named Goldberg who had fled for his life. While her father didn't celebrate the Nazis' presence, he hadn't disapproved either. *War sells papers,* he'd said in his first weeks at his job. *We may not be able to change history, but we can profit from it.*

Even those words never sat well with her.

Behind her, the other reporters talked in low tones. She'd have a hundred knives in her back if their jealous sneers could shoot daggers. She was getting the attention they desired. But they didn't believe she deserved the role. This was why she needed to prove herself even more. Maybe she *could* capture the right story today—one that would please her father *and* earn her a spot on the front page. Yes, that could happen. She could make it happen.

With new determination, Kateřina marched into her father's office without knocking, ignoring the glances of others. Beams of sunlight glinted off the gold-plated lamp Mr. Goldberg had left behind, and her father glanced up with curiosity as she entered.

"I will write my own story. I want you to hold my spot."

Father returned to the text before him, proofing with a sharp pencil.

Kateřina took another step forward. "Did you hear me? I know you're trying to help me, but I know what I'm doing. I know what Obergruppenführer Heydrich expects of me."

Still, her father did not lift his head.

"Are you going to answer me?"

"Are you going to shut the door?" he said without emotion.

She turned and did as he requested. Then she sat in the chair opposite him, peering across the desk.

Finally, he sighed at her. "If you want me to argue, I will not." He rubbed his brow. Then he placed his palm against his heart. "I remember the last war vividly. I was part of the Czechoslovak Legion, fighting for the Allies on the Eastern Front. Our orders were to move through Siberia to Vladivostok to secure a seaport for the Allies."

Kateřina frowned. She'd heard this before. Had he forgotten? Then Father's eyes widened, full of emotion, and she realized he was speaking to her as a daughter now—not as a reporter. Kateřina pressed her lips tight and allowed him to continue.

"As we advanced through Siberia, we established control over large parts of the region. However, we began to clash with the Bolsheviks as we moved further east and became increasingly involved in the Russian Civil War.

"In July 1918, we heard rumors that the Romanov family, including Tsar Nicholas II, was being held captive in Yekaterinburg. We knew we had to do something to try and rescue them.

"Our leaders dispatched a small unit of soldiers, led by Captain Jaroslav Řezáč, to undertake the dangerous mission of freeing the tsar and his family. We knew it was a mission that could end badly, but we had to try.

"On the night of 16 July, I was one of the men with Řezáč who attacked the Bolshevik-held city of Yekaterinburg." He closed his eyes and paused.

Pained emotion carried with his words as he continued, "It was one of the most intense and brutal battles I have ever experienced. We knew the mission was dangerous, but we were determined to try and rescue Tsar Nicholas II and his family. When we entered the city, we were met with fierce resistance from the Bolsheviks. They were heavily armed and had fortified positions throughout the city.

"The fighting lasted all night long. We engaged in close-quarters combat, fighting from building to building and street to street. We could hear the sounds of gunfire and explosions all around us, and the smoke from burning buildings and wreckage made it challenging to see and breathe.

"Despite the odds stacked against us, we fought with everything we had. Captain Řezáč led us fearlessly, and his tactical skills helped us gain ground against the Bolsheviks. But as the night wore on, we realized the mission would be more difficult than we had ever anticipated."

Kateřina leaned forward in her seat. Yes, she'd known her father had fought in the war, but for the first time, she pictured him there as a scared young man. And as he spoke, he sounded like a terrified young man still.

Her emotions twisted like a kaleidoscope, shifting and changing, but always a mix of pride, sadness, and fear. She needed to listen, truly listen. In a few hours, she'd be sitting before the Obergruppenführer Heydrich. There had to be a purpose for her father's story; the only way to discover it would be to listen well.

"The next day, we learned that the Bolsheviks had brutally executed the Romanov family. It was a devastating blow to us and our hopes of rescuing the tsar and his family. Our efforts had been in vain, and we mourned the loss of innocent lives."

As her father spoke, she saw the pain in his eyes. This was a challenging story for him to tell. But as he recounted the bravery and sacrifice of his fellow soldiers, she couldn't help but feel proud of him and all the men who fought alongside him.

Does Father feel the same now? Is there the same pride in this secret fight of his? He had a stake in this somehow, but it was one she knew little about. And today wasn't the day to demand answers.

"The fate of the Romanovs remained a mystery for many years. We all had hope, of course. We didn't want the rumors of their deaths to be true."

Father sighed, and Kateřina wiped the tears that pooled at the corners of her eyes. Her father's stories—his service—were like an old pair of boots that no longer fit but ones he kept as a reminder of where he had been.

Or ones that warn me about the path I'm about to walk? Yes, that could be the case, too.

"I will never forget that night in Yekaterinburg and the bravery of Captain Řezáč and my fellow soldiers in trying to rescue the tsar and his family." His words drifted off. He would not hold a spot for her on the front page, and now she understood why.

Instead of feeling awkward, the silence between them seemed like a gift. Instead of an argument, there was understanding.

"Perhaps we shall both wait and see what today holds," she stated simply. "No use arguing about tomorrow, is there?"

His eyes met hers, and he offered a placating hand. "Yes, we will see what tomorrow holds, won't we? Until then, we will fight with all we can."

She knew their talk was over when he returned his attention to the proof spread across his desk. No more words were needed, so Kateřina stood and exited his office.

The newsroom seemed quieter than usual. Those who worked alongside her cast side glances, no doubt waiting for her to say or do something in hopes they could determine what had happened behind the closed door. Kateřina knew her every movement would be judged as long as she was in this room. She decided not to give them the opportunity.

She glanced around, offering only a smile and no explanation. She then read her watch. She still had an hour before her interview but could no longer stay in the newsroom.

Grabbing her camera and satchel, Kateřina left the noise of the clattering of typewriter keys behind her. After walking down two flights of stairs, she emerged on the busy street.

The sounds of traffic mixed with voices on the road. A bell tolled from a distance, and a church bell clamored. A man in a disheveled suit strode past, face red. As he passed her, he paused from his quick walk to catch his breath, wheezing like a sick horse.

Just up the street, three soldiers had gathered around two dark-haired women, their rifles slung over their shoulders and pointed into the sky like new saplings. The soldiers eyed the women's papers with skeptical frowns. Their voices rose as they thumbed through the pages, causing the winded man to launch into his hurried pace again.

If she could ignore the groups of soldiers or the rumbling of tanks crawling past, it would seem like nothing had changed in Prague. But one could not overlook the Germans.

Rhythmic thuds of metal pounding on cobblestone drew her attention to a German spider tank. Its eight legs moved in pairs, alternating steps. A terrible sight that made her long for the days when tanks simply rolled by.

As a show of force, it turned its tank cannon toward a group of young Jewish men, which caused them to scramble and flee. One of the soldiers operating the tank opened the hatch on top, mocking the terrified civilians as they ran.

She paused and patted her satchel, wishing to ask Obergruppenführer Heydrich the questions she wanted:

If you want to win the war, wouldn't it be better to send your troops to the front lines instead of rounding up and assaulting ordinary citizens?

Why did you choose Prague to be your headquarters above all places?

And finally, what have you been told about me, Obergruppenführer Heydrich? What do you think I have to offer?

Of course, those were not questions she'd be allowed to ask. Instead, she'd listen closely—both to hear and to understand—for the second time today. As Kateřina moved to the trolley, she knew one thing for sure. Even when one tried to fight the present, one must first consider the past. The past is what made her father who he was today. History made Obergruppenführer Heydrich who he was today, too. Until those rising against Heydrich understood the demons of the past, they wouldn't be able to rise against his demonic acts in the present.

Kateřina joined others on the sidewalk as she made her way to the tram stop. Around her, commuters hurried past each other like leaves blown by gusts of wind. Ahead, an older woman walked hunched, shuffling among the men in suits and the mothers with shopping bags and prams. Kateřina would get to the castle grounds early and take a position in the waiting room of Heydrich's office. No one would pay her any mind as she waited, watched, and listened, which would benefit her.

What juicy bits could she discover when everyone trusted she was there to interview Heydrich? A puppet to mold the Obergruppenführer's words into a story befitting the retelling of their German fairy tale: *Protectors of the great land of their ancestors, Bohemia and Moravia, rising to claim their rightful kingdom.* Yes, she, too, would make them think she believed that.

Absorbed in her plans, Kateřina momentarily lost herself in the potential narrative she could weave. She imagined the tale she'd tell, a story that would make them believe she was on their side. But as she plotted, the reality around her began to change.

The atmosphere shifted. It felt like the impending onset of a storm. The sensation of ground vibrations, like a spider tank lumbering past, caused her to pause her steps. Yet nothing was in sight.

She wasn't the only one who felt it. The older woman nearby appeared equally perplexed. The woman's bright yellow scarf stood out, tightly wrapped around her graying hair and knotted neatly beneath her chin. Their eyes met in mutual bewilderment.

The woman inhaled a deep breath through her nose, and her forehead creased in question. "This air . . . it smells of the factory where my husband once worked, right by the Vltava River." She paused, her nose wrinkling. "I can almost smell the water and clay, the tang of metal, and the slick of oil."

Kateřina wanted to dismiss it as mere ramblings of age, but she couldn't deny it. She perceived the same scents. As passengers gathered at the corner for the upcoming tram, Kateřina found herself inexplicably drawn to the elderly woman, captivated by their shared experience. But as seconds ticked by, the surroundings began to feel more surreal. It wasn't just about the peculiar scent anymore.

A shiver ran down Kateřina's spine. The air before her seemed to shift and shimmer. She paused her steps and pulled her satchel closer to her body. The atmosphere was as heavy as a leaden sky before a storm. There was only one problem—not a cloud dotted the blue expanse above her.

She took a deep breath. Yet even as she did, it was as if she was breathing through a feather pillow. The air itself seemed thick with tension and weight, with a hint of ozone and the electric particles that built up before a storm blown in by the gods.

In the distance, near the Vltava, the sky grew dark and gloomy. She brushed her arm, and an unexpected humidity bore down, an unexplainable sense of impending moisture, making breathing even more difficult.

On the street, a black sedan drove past more slowly than usual, and instead of watching the road ahead, the driver stared out his side window. She quickly took another step before realizing the older woman in front of her hadn't moved.

Even though Kateřina stopped mid-step, her satchel swung and hit the woman's back hard enough to make the older woman stumble. The woman's body slumped forward as if in slow motion. Kateřina reached out and grasped the woman around the waist, but not before her shopping bag hit the ground, spilling its contents in every direction.

Apples rolled out of the bag, bouncing down the street. Eggs hit the sidewalk, spilling their yolks. A milk jar crashed onto the ground, creating a white puddle. A pot of pickles shattered, too, emitting a sour smell into the air.

The line of men and women who waited for the tram turned toward the commotion. Kateřina's satchel fell to the ground as both hands reached out to help the woman steady herself. "I am so sorry. Please forgive me. I wasn't watching where I was going."

Instead of answering Kateřina, the old woman reached out to the empty space beside her as if expecting something there.

Even though she was in no rush, an odd sensation moved from the base of Kateřina's neck down her limbs. A gut feeling urged her to leave the area and do so quickly.

Should I run to catch the tram? She had plenty of time before her meeting, but something told her to head straight to Hradčany Castle. But first, she needed to assist this woman.

"Let me help you pick up your things." Kateřina kneeled on the sidewalk, forgetting about the milk and pickle juice. Both liquids seeped into her skirt. Somehow it didn't matter, even though she knew she'd meet Reinhard Heydrich in an hour. *Or will I?*

Kateřina picked up the bag, marveling that it was not torn, and promptly put two apples inside. Those were the only two items worth salvaging from the groceries.

Standing, Kateřina grabbed her own satchel and slung it onto her shoulder. Then she reached inside for her wallet. She opened it, pulled out a roll of bills without pausing to count them, and pressed the money into the woman's hand.

The woman's fingers pinched around the money.

"Again, please forgive me." Kateřina tightened her grip on her satchel. "I am certain that is enough money to cover what you lost and more, but I need to go."

She darted toward the trolley stop and lined up behind the others.

Standing before Kateřina, two young mothers held their children's hands. Businessmen waited with briefcases.

At the end of the line, Kateřina shuffled her feet slightly from side to side, suddenly eager to get on the tram that would take her closer to Hradčany Castle. She had to get this right. She couldn't mess up this story. And she hoped that Obergruppenführer Heydrich would understand why she smelled of spilled milk and pickle juice.

The grinding of the tram rose above the noise of the automobiles traveling by as it climbed the slope from the Troja bridge. It neared, and something else caught her attention—a Mercedes driving by with its SS flag flowing high. Her back straightened slightly. Obergruppenführer Reinhard Heydrich rode in the backseat of an open-air car, sitting in his uniform like Napoleon riding into a conquered city.

Although others had told her the Obergruppenführer followed this route, traveling from his flat to Hradčany every morning, it was the first time she'd seen him riding in his open-air car. The buzz of an electric current caused the hairs to rise on her arms.

Strange I'd see him on his ride to the castle today. Then again, of all days, it had to be today. *Or maybe it isn't strange.*

A slight sound barely registered her attention. Her left ear caught a subtle ticking sound like a pocket watch but *different* somehow. As she turned to see what it was, a rush of wind moved past her. Goosebumps rose on her arms, and she clutched her camera tightly to not drop it.

A tall woman with red hair glanced over her shoulder at Kateřina and smiled. "Windy today."

Kateřina lifted her face again. The breeze was as erratic as a flickering flame, changing direction with each gust as the tram approached. She blinked twice. "Yes, the wind has picked up. Maybe it's coming in with the storm."

"Storm?" The woman's brow wrinkled, and she offered a weak smile. Then the redhead laughed. "I was certain there were no clouds when I left my apartment."

Kateřina nodded, looking up at the now cloudless sky. "That's what's odd. The weather's been acting strangely today. But maybe it's just the winds of change," she offered with the softest chuckle.

The woman with the red hair tilted her head, a glint of mischief in her eyes. "Winds of change, you say? Interesting choice of words. Well, take care and hold on tight to your camera."

Then with quickened steps the woman left the line and hurried away, disappearing into the crowd.

Josef walked down the bustling streets of Žižkov, on the outskirts of Prague. He hurried toward the bend in the road at Holešovičkách, navigating through the usual foot traffic and patrolling German soldiers. Today, he'd join the fight—not against the ordinary soldiers on the street, but against one of the untouchables, the greatly esteemed Obergruppenführer.

Leaving the Josefov district an hour ago, he had moved through the narrow alleys that wound through the city like a labyrinth, finally catching a tram a stone's throw from the bend. Each member took different transportation modes to get to their meetup. Then, if any got caught, it wouldn't impinge on the whole mission.

Josef glanced over his shoulder to ensure he wasn't being followed. He had a job and couldn't afford to get caught by the Germans. The resistance claimed they had been planning this mission for months, and they couldn't let it fail. He couldn't be the weak link. Nikolai trusted him, and so did the other men. The resistance needed to strike a blow against the occupying forces and show the people of Prague they were not powerless. If his grandfather didn't take him seriously, these men did.

He moved quickly through the city, avoiding main roads and sticking to the shadows. Now that he'd emerged on one of the main streets leading through Žižkov, he felt exposed, like a tightrope walker without a safety net.

Every part of the city seemed different somehow. Old buildings loomed like vigilant giants. The roadway was as dangerous as a minefield, with the constant threat of hidden dangers lurking beneath the surface. Tension was thick in the air, as if the streets of Prague themselves were tightly coiled springs.

A small group of Nazi soldiers marched in the distance, the cobblestones echoing with the sound of their boots. Their rifles glinted in the sunlight like beacons of danger. German supporters walked with heads lifted high and chins thrust out. Czech patriots and Jews with yellow stars walked with eyes cast down. If Josef wasn't mistaken, many trembled as the Germans strolled past.

Josef lifted his face and dared to eye one of the German soldiers patrolling the thoroughfare. His coat displayed no star, so they didn't give him a second glance. Still, Josef's stomach trembled, and he silently prayed no soldier would stop him and demand his papers. He walked steadily, keenly aware of the firearm hidden in his coat pocket.

Just this morning, the resistance had added Josef as a third man in the plot in case the other two failed. He tried not to appear suspicious to onlookers. Thankfully, no one noticed as he planted his feet at his lookout spot—the corner of the building near the tram stop.

Minutes ticked by, and Josef bought himself a paper. Nikolai had told him Heydrich left Panenské Břežany every morning at nine o'clock. Josef glanced at his watch. Just in time.

Today even the sounds of traffic and chatter made his skin crawl. Many times in his youth, he'd imagined what it would be like to fight for something he believed in, as many boys did. But as he stood here living the moment, he could barely keep the contents of his stomach down.

He waited. Ten minutes crawled by. Twenty. An hour. The plan was simple. Josef Valčík, from Silver A group, was positioned up the hill. He would signal with a mirror when Heydrich's car was sighted. Adolf Opálka from the Out Distance team would cross the road in front of Heydrich's car, slowing it down further as it entered the bend. Gabčík had been the one who agreed with Nikolai that an extra lookout would be handy. And that's where Josef fit in.

And, of course, you chose the right man, Gabčík had said with a slap on Josef's back. *Jan needs yet another Josef to keep him safe.*

With the sun warming his shoulders as he leaned against the side of the building, Josef could not see Jan Kubiš or his 9mm submachine gun. The Sten's magazine held 32 rounds and had a detachable stock. It was relatively small and easy to break down and conceal, making it suited for today's operation.

Although he was recently added to the team, Josef's role was to step in if both Kubiš and Gabčík failed.

Josef turned up from his paper and met eyes with Gabčík across the street. The two locked gazes but didn't make any sort of acknowledgment toward each other. They each simply turned, acting as if the other was unimportant.

It will soon be time. Josef clicked through the plan of events. Gabčík's bicycle would be ready across the road, pointed down the hill to Libeň in preparation for his escape. Kubiš's bicycle was no doubt situated against the railings by the bend, even though Josef could not see it from this location.

Opálka sat on the stairs by the newspaper office, dressed as a construction worker taking a morning coffee break.

Humor tickled Joseph's lips. *Those in the news office will undoubtedly have something to report about soon.*

By now, Gabčík would have assembled his Sten, hiding it under a raincoat he'd grabbed for that specific purpose. The plan was to load one magazine into the Sten and hide the other in a briefcase on the handlebars. Minutes passed, and there was still no sign of Heydrich. Minutes turned into an hour.

Josef's nerves stretched like a rubber band, taut and ready to snap with the passing minutes. Why had Heydrich not arrived by now? *Has something gone wrong?*

Trams came and went, and Josef told himself to stay strong until Gabčík or Kubiš called off the mission—for today, at least.

He scanned the area again for anyone who might suspect him. No one spared him a glance, but his eyes wandered to a beautiful woman standing nearby on the sidewalk.

His breath caught. Had he seen her before? No. He would remember if he had.

Golden hair cascaded in waves, each strand shimmering like spun silk. Her eyes were light—maybe blue or green. Her features were delicate, with high cheekbones and a pert nose that gave her an air of elegance and refinement. Full, pink lips turned down in a pout. With a satchel over her shoulder, she held a camera and helped an older woman who'd stumbled.

Once the old woman's things had been gathered, the blonde reached into her purse and handed the woman some money. Yet, instead of smiling, the old woman frowned.

This beauty is either an angel or a saint—and neither is appreciated.

The beautiful woman straightened and then hurried toward the tram. Two businessmen regarded each other as she stepped in line behind them.

The blonde glanced at her watch and scanned the street both ways. She seemed to be waiting for something.

Could she be part of this plan? No, Nikolai hadn't mentioned it.

Maybe she's meeting someone. Josef shook his head slightly. Unfortunately, if all went as planned, their appointment was about to be interrupted.

Strangely, the tension knotting his neck relaxed. *Beautiful* was a simple way to describe her. Still, she had a visage of focus and ambition that told him she was more than mere beauty.

Josef scanned the road for any sign of Heydrich's vehicle. He sighed, still not seeing it. Then, out of curiosity, he peered back at the blonde. Her gaze was now fixed on a redheaded woman who'd joined her in line. The redhead turned and eyed him next.

At that exact moment, a German soldier approached. Josef stiffened as the Nazi stopped before him. "I have been watching you."

Josef's fingers tightened around the pistol grip in his pocket.

The soldier's eyes moved from Josef to the blonde and back again, shaking his head. "*Dummkopf.*" The guard laughed. "You think you *vell* get that woman? Maybe set your sights lower." Then he continued walking down the hill.

Josef released his breath, still feeling the lingering effects of the soldier's presence. His heart pounded like a drumbeat, and his body shook. He couldn't afford to let his guard down, not when the stakes were so high.

Focus, you fool. He returned to his task. Thankfully, nothing had happened yet, though now he was sure Heydrich's vehicle could cross into view at any moment. Josef readied himself by repositioning his hand inside his coat pocket near the grip of his pistol.

Dampness caused his hair to cling to his forehead, no doubt from nerves. Or was it? Seemingly within a minute, the air grew as thick and humid as a steam room, causing sweat to bead on his forehead and making it hard to catch his breath. The air snapped with electricity, like the crackle of a live wire, making the hair on the back of Josef's neck stand on end.

Then, with no fanfare or warning, a light flashed from up the hill. The sun was hitting Valčík's mirror! Heydrich, the Butcher of Prague—as the resistance fighters called him—was on his way. Josef checked his watch like a seasoned general timing his troop movements, marking the moment before a critical battle: 10:32.

Reinhard Heydrich's vehicle came into view as it drove casually up the road. As if welcoming the approaching leader, the breeze picked up. As strong as a giant's breath, it blew with great force, shaking trees and windows as the tram rumbled nearer.

Something else caught Josef's attention—an apple rolled from the sidewalk into the street as if kicked by an invisible force.

Then the No. 3 tram turned on the apex of the bend just as Heydrich's Mercedes approached. As if planned with perfect timing, the SS driver veered the Mercedes right, taking the vehicle closer to where Gabčík and Kubiš were positioned. The Mercedes slowed as Opálka walked in front of the car. The SS driver braked hard to keep from hitting Opálka, as planned.

Josef readied himself and kept an eye out for any nearby German soldiers. For the moment, there were none in sight. That could change at any time. Unable to hold back any longer, Josef hurried up the sidewalk to see around the tram. Within the blink of an eye, Gabčík dropped his raincoat and pointed the Sten at Heydrich's car.

Gabčík's hands shook as he aimed at the Obergruppenführer. His finger tensed on the trigger, but nothing happened.

Seconds passed. Josef's heart pounded. "Shoot! Shoot!" he wanted to scream.

The silence was deafening, each passing moment an eternity.

The car glided past Gabčík, who stood rooted to the spot. His mouth opened, and his eyes widened as he stared at his malfunctioning weapon.

"*Anhalten!* Stop!" Heydrich's voice cut through the air like a sharp knife.

Josef wasn't sure if Heydrich spoke to Gabčík or his SS driver, but the vehicle stopped abruptly. Gabčík's face contorted. He tried his weapon again. Stuck.

Then, as if in slow motion, Heydrich stood from the back of the vehicle and drew a pistol from the car's door pocket.

A bolt of fear and adrenaline shot through Josef, and his fingers tightened on the grip of his pistol.

Heydrich aimed at Gabčík. Seconds flipped like frames, as if Josef viewed a movie outside himself, detached from the moment. At the same time, he was acutely aware of every detail, every movement, every sound.

Gabčík desperately tried to unjam his weapon again. His eyebrows pinched together, and he erratically pointed and pulled the trigger repeatedly, but to no avail.

"Drop your weapon!" Heydrich commanded. "Now." Heydrich fired.

Josef surged forward. His hand shook like a leaf trembling in the wind. He closed his eyes and steadied his breathing, trying to push the fear aside. He opened his eyes again as his fingers tightened around the gun's grip.

He was no longer playing with weapons—with his inventions. Josef set his jaw. This was for his country, for the countless lives that had been lost. *For Father.*

Stop! Josef, stop! A voice called, but Josef needed to find out if he heard it with his ears or soul. Two businessmen rushed to Josef's side. His hand remained inside his coat, and he stepped back.

Then movement. Kubiš stepped from the shadows. Kubiš's action was swift and silent. He pulled something from a briefcase and hitched back his arm. Something small and dark flew through the air and landed near the rear wheel of Heydrich's Mercedes—a grenade.

An explosion rose like a cannon blast. A thick cloud of smoke and debris mushroomed upward. Heydrich's vehicle lifted and shook. The blast wave shattered the windows of Tram No. 3 and rattled the windows of the building behind Josef.

A stunned silence fell over the crowd, followed by the cries of women and children. The explosion had severely damaged Heydrich's open-topped Mercedes, sending plumes of smoke and twisted metal into the air. Heydrich, visibly injured but alive, was attempting to regain his footing amidst the chaos.

Josef's heart sank as Heydrich emerged from the vehicle like a demon rising from the flames of hell. He bent over slightly, with his left hand on his back, then pointed his handgun at Gabčík.

No!

Josef put his fingers to his mouth and whistled loudly. Still, Gabčík didn't budge. "Run! Run!" Josef shouted.

Heydrich fired.

Gabčík hesitated, shocked perhaps that the bullet missed him. Then he dropped his Sten and took cover behind a telegraph pole. He drew his pistol.

The apparent pain in Heydrich's back caused him to stagger. Heydrich fired but missed, and then he crumpled. His knees hit the ground hard.

"Run! Run!" Josef called to Gabčík, but his voice was lost in the crowd's cries.

Heydrich rose, winced, reached toward his back, and stumbled. Seeing his opportunity, Gabčík turned and ran. Passengers barred the route to his cycle from the tram, so Gabčík ran up the hill, the road Heydrich's vehicle had carried him down.

A wave of relief rose in Josef, followed by a sense of dread. This wasn't over yet. They could still be caught. Josef's gut twisted, and a new resolve shot a bolt of energy into his limbs. He had to finish this.

Kubiš stumbled toward Josef, his face smeared with blood from the shrapnel wound caused by his own grenade.

Rapidly processing the scene, Josef released his hold on his pistol to support Kubiš, whose hands were clamped to his bleeding head. "Go, now! I'll handle them," Josef urged.

Kubiš nodded weakly in gratitude, discarding his briefcase over the railing. Struggling against the incline, he mounted his bicycle and pedaled uphill, but the panicked civilians from the tram stop and adjacent buildings flooded the street, creating a human barrier.

To clear his way, Kubiš fired his pistol skyward, causing the terrified crowd to scatter further. This, however, drew the attention of Heydrich's driver, who, despite the shock and smoke, staggered out of the damaged vehicle. Spotting Kubiš trying to flee, the driver aimed his weapon, only for the magazine to clumsily fall onto the cobblestones. He stared, bewildered by the malfunction.

Heydrich, though weakened, displayed the domineering nature he was known for. Pointing at Gabčík, trying to flee up the hill, he rasped, "Get him!"

Without hesitation, the driver turned in pursuit, leaving the wounded Obergruppenführer amidst the chaos.

Joseph's eyes darted between Heydrich and the driver. The decision was agonizing: eliminate the high-ranking Nazi official or ensure Gabčík's escape? But as more German soldiers arrived, converging on the smoky scene from both directions, Josef's priorities crystallized.

He shouted to the incoming soldiers, pointing to the SS driver. "That man's an imposter! He's responsible!" Using their momentary confusion to his advantage, Josef moved assertively toward Heydrich, fingers tightening around his pistol.

Josef's pulse drummed in his ears, each beat accentuating the adrenaline coursing through his veins amidst the tumultuous scene. The surrounding area looked like a war zone. The tram had derailed slightly from its tracks, the sounds of its alarm bell ringing incessantly. The sheen of broken glass and debris from the grenade's force glinted, contrasting against Prague's historical architecture and cobblestone streets. The staccato gunfire resonated, reminiscent of a storm's fury, mingling with the anguished cries of stunned civilians and shouts of panic.

Soldiers' shouts filled the air, followed by gunfire. Looking over his shoulder, Josef spotted the SS driver, his uniform stained dark with blood, sprawled at an unnatural angle amidst the wreckage. Each gasping breath he took seemed more laborious than the last, signaling the man's impending demise.

Drawing nearer to the epicenter of the chaos, Josef's gaze settled on Heydrich. The Obergruppenführer had staggered toward a small crowd, perhaps in a futile attempt to find refuge or help. Haggard faces surrounded him, their expressions a mix of horror and morbid curiosity. Heydrich's once-imposing form was now hunched, his uniform torn, and his face contorted in evident pain, the sweat causing his hair to cling to his forehead. The sharp, metallic scent of spilled blood competed with the acrid fumes of the smoldering Mercedes.

Suddenly, the shocking sight of a motorcycle arcing through the air diverted Josef's attention. It crashed onto the cobblestones, the echoing clang of its frame a gruesome harmony to its tires' wailing protest. The electric atmosphere grew more pronounced, a static charge palpable, making Josef's hair stand on end. It was as if the very air crackled with tension, humming with an intensity that was deafening yet silent, overwhelming yet intangible. The sensation was unsettling, like the world had shifted slightly off its axis, and Josef struggled to catch a breath.

Josef's senses were on high alert, trying to grasp the absurdity of what he'd witnessed. How could a motorcycle simply fly? Was it the result of another hidden explosive, or was it one of the Germans' rumored secret weapons? The pungent smell of gunpowder lingered in the air, punctuated by the distant wail of sirens—an anthem of a city on edge.

Directing his attention back to Heydrich, Josef's heart clenched. The Obergruppenführer lay sprawled, each labored breath sounding wetter, more ragged than the last. The stench of his blood was overpowering, further tainted by the bitter tang of the vehicle's fluids that pooled around him. Heydrich's once-commanding presence was reduced to a grim spectacle of vulnerability.

Suddenly, like a specter, the blonde woman appeared in Josef's peripheral vision. Her rapid steps on the cobblestone streets barely registered as she closed the distance. "You have done what was needed. Leave this place," she urged in a hushed tone, her striking blue eyes radiating an intensity he found impossible to ignore. "The SS will be swarming here soon. You mustn't be found."

Her urgency pierced through Josef, turning caution into full-blown alarm. With a swift nod, he shot toward the Vltava River, the scent of its familiar dampness pulling him closer. Behind him, sporadic gunfire sang its treacherous song, but he was already drowning it out. The ancient cobblestones beneath his feet were a sprinting blur. Josefov lay ahead, an oasis in this barrage of chaos. He had to believe it would be his refuge in the storm.

Kateřina opened her mouth to respond to the redheaded woman, but an explosion cracked the air, nearly knocking her off her feet. She gripped the sidewalk railing as glass sprayed from the tram's windows in a thousand pieces. On the street, the Mercedes shook, and a thick cloud engulfed the scene. Heydrich's car had been hit.

They are after the Obergruppenführer.

All noise faded except for the ringing in her ears. A stunned silence fell over the crowd. Kateřina lifted her trembling camera and snapped photos. With each shot, descriptions of what she witnessed scrolled through her mind as transcribed words on the page.

Shock struck the line of people waiting to board the tram as they witnessed Reinhard Heydrich's vehicle being bombed in the street.

As the noise of the explosion died away and the dust drifted downward, Kateřina spotted a man across the street with a gun. Heydrich emerged from the car, facing the man, pistol drawn. He staggered forward and shot at the rebel who ducked behind a pole.

Instead of retreating, the Obergruppenführer stumbled in the direction of the assassin, unwilling to crumble without a fight.

Bullets flew.

Kateřina ducked behind a nearby vehicle for cover, but the camera burned in her palms. She *had* to get pictures of this event. She peeked out from safety, camera poised and ready. She snapped one photo and then two.

A loud crash came. Kateřina yelped as something massive tumbled through the air. She covered her head in horrified anticipation. The tree beside her shook and cracked. She peered up to see a twisted motorcycle lodged within its branches. Tentatively, she lifted the camera to capture that too.

"Stop! Stop!" Obergruppenführer Heydrich lurched toward the gunman with awkward steps. "Stop them!"

There are two of them.

One man jumped on a bicycle. The other raced away on foot. A third man approached a group of soldiers who'd arrived at the scene. It was the dashing, dark-haired man who'd been staring at her. More security forces raced down the hill. The black Mercedes sat broken and useless with one door ripped off and fragments scattered on the roadway. SS jackets waved from the trolley wires like flags. Heidrich slumped against the bonnet of his wrecked car. Yes, this was real.

She gaped in awe as the dark-haired man's jaw set and he sprinted up to the cluster of approaching soldiers. Her lips parted slightly, and she wanted to tell him to stop. To turn and run.

Instead, he paused before one of the soldiers and pointed to the SS driver.

"He's an imposter. He did this!" His clear voice reached her ears even over people's voices and cries.

Then, without waiting for a response, the man strode toward Heydrich.

I have to stop him. Kateřina moved toward him as if being drawn by a magnet. It made no sense, but she knew she could not let this man shoot Heydrich. The Obergruppenführer was as good as dead, but the man would be arrested. An image of him hanging on a gallows flashed before her mind—as if she'd been there and had witnessed his hanging herself. Kateřina quickened her steps, running faster toward the man. *No. Wait!*

The sharp aroma of hot metal and explosives wafted on the breeze. As Kateřina reached the man, he paused. Electric energy in the air grew like a tidal wave, building to a crescendo.

"You have done your work here. You must go," she whispered.

Dark brown eyes fixed on hers as if he clung to her words like a lifeline. "Leave before the soldiers discover you've tricked them. Hurry now."

With the slightest of nods, the man turned and walked down the street. Emotion swelled within her. Had she stopped him from assassinating Heydrich? Yes, she was sure of it.

The man walked away from the danger like a fearless warrior, leaving the panicked crowd behind. Pulling her camera from her satchel, Kateřina returned her attention to the scene and snapped photos.

Her heart pounded as the chaos continued to unfold around her. Glass crunched underfoot, and the confused cries of passengers mingled with the heavy footfalls of German soldiers pounding on the cobblestones.

Just as she tried to make sense of the situation, the ground shook again, even closer this time. She turned to see, but there was nothing there.

"What was that?" she whispered to herself.

One of the soldiers noticed her and shouted in her direction, causing her to instinctively wave her press credentials and move closer to the vehicle. As she drew near, someone moaned. A man lay crumpled by the side of the road. He was shot multiple times, and she realized from his uniform that he was the SS driver.

The injured man motioned Kateřina closer and held out a slip of paper. He opened his mouth. She drew nearer, leaning down and taking the paper from him.

"It's not what it seems . . ." his words gurgled out.

Her mind raced with questions. She tried to open the slip of paper. The man shook his head. "Hide it. Go, go . . ."

"What do you mean?" she asked urgently. "What's not what it seems?" The driver's eyes fluttered close. His breathing became labored.

"Please, can you tell me anything more?" she asked.

His shallow breaths became fewer and further between, like the dying embers of a fire.

The air around her grew still as if creation waited for the man to breathe his last. Kateřina stood and tucked the note into the front pocket of her satchel.

As she absorbed her surroundings, her mind thought through tomorrow's headlines. *Obergruppenführer Heydrich Struck Down by Brave Patriots.* She could never say that, of course, but it was the headline emblazoned around her heart.

She turned and hurried to the newsroom. No matter what her father said, what happened today would be her story.

The ringing of phones and the clacking of typewriter keys met Kateřina as she rushed into the newsroom. Trembling fingers touched her face and hair, feeling the ash and remnants of glass. The scent of burnt clothing and the sharp tang of explosives clung to her, a testament to her proximity to the blast. Reporters prided themselves any time they found a reliable witness to any great event. Kateřina didn't need to find one. She was one.

The horror of witnessing the assassination attempt on Reinhard Heydrich still roiled her mind. And now her father could no longer dismiss her capabilities as a journalist. Every person in Prague—and indeed from around the world—would hunger for an eyewitness account of the explosion near the tram, the chilling aftermath, and the attempt on the life of one of the highest-ranking Nazi officials. She'd be the one to satiate that hunger.

"Kateřina!" a voice cut through the chaos. Matěj, a fellow reporter who had never missed an opportunity to belittle her. However, his tone now bore no mockery, just genuine concern. "By the gods, were you near the explosion? Are you alright?"

She met his gaze, steeling herself. "Close enough to give the world a firsthand account."

The room was a hive of flurry. Journalists tapped away at typewriters, their fingers dancing over keys inked with the morning's trauma. Others shouted into phones, seeking confirmation, validation, or any scrap of detail they could churn into a story. And yet more huddled in groups, whispers of speculation, trying to piece together the narrative of the attempt on Heydrich's life and the chaos that had turned Prague's streets into a theater of smoke and fire.

She took a deep breath, attempting to calm her nerves. The snapshots of events danced in her mind like scattered beads, each needing to be carefully strung together to create a meaningful whole.

The smell of fresh coffee mixed with the pungent aroma of ink. The printers in the back rooms, usually churning out pages of the evening edition, sat silent.

As Kateřina walked to her desk, she imagined the words bursting from her father's lips when he first heard about the attack of Heydrich, "Stop the presses!"

She caught snippets of conversation as she made her way to her desk.

"Has anyone been able to confirm the victim's identity yet?"

"I'm heading back to the scene. I want to talk to some of those in local shops and learn what they saw."

"We need to be careful about jumping to conclusions before we have all the facts . . ."

Amidst the chaos, a few reporters packed their bags, no doubt heading to the hospital to await information about Heydrich's condition. One adjusted his camera. Another checked her output slip from the voice recorder, and a third frantically scribbled in a notebook. Energy and excitement pulsated through the room as Kateřina settled into a chair near the voice box. A sense of purpose washed over her.

When Father first purchased the office machine, she'd been skeptical. Yet, as she'd watched it record voices and type for reporters, she now saw it as a marvel of form and function.

It was a large, imposing contraption, standing over six feet tall and made of gleaming brass and copper. Intricate gears, levers, and dials adorned its surface, whirring and clicking as it worked.

A large hornlike device at the front of the machine served as the microphone. When a reporter spoke into it, the engine translated their voice into a series of complex mechanical movements, which would be recorded onto a long spool of metallic tape.

At the same time, a series of minor keys typed out the reporter's words onto a roll of paper fed through the machine. The keys were intricately crafted, with each one resembling a miniature typewriter.

A large steam engine powered the machine, chugging away in the background as it worked. It was a noisy, clanking contraption but also effective. Over the last three months, Kateřina learned to quickly and accurately record interviews without relying on shorthand or memory.

Despite its size and complexity, the machine was relatively easy to use, with clear instructions engraved onto its surface. However, it did require a certain amount of skill and finesse to operate correctly, as even the slightest mistake could throw off the entire recording process.

Kateřina focused on the words racing through her mind, attempting to slow them. Then, when her thoughts were clear, she leaned close to the voice box, speaking slowly and precisely. "As Heydrich slumped on the pavement, an off-duty nurse assisted him. She waved down a vehicle that attempted to pass, 'Quick! There has been an attack. You must take the *Herr Protektor* to the Bulovka hospital.' End direct quote."

She paused and bit her lower lip, still not understanding how some called him that: *Protektor.*

"When the nurse noticed the first car was packed with sweets, she approached a second. A small Tatra van, belonging to the Holan Company, rushed away with a delivery other than the typical polishes and waxes."

Kateřina leaned back, and even though she had more to tell, her mind kept darting back to the handsome man she'd seen. Unlike the two assassins who'd fled—attempting to escape capture—the dark-haired man had stayed. There was an innocence about him, too. He didn't move like a trained soldier.

Why was I so drawn to him? Why did I urge him to leave? Kateřina rubbed her brow. Nothing made sense.

"Obergruppenführer Heydrich's caravan was attacked!" the

reporter who sat closest to the door shouted into the telephone. "I will head to the hospital now to wait for the news."

A second reporter picked up one of the ringing phones and pressed it to his ear. His free hand blocked the opposite ear, allowing him to hear better. "They carried his body away? What state was it in? Is he dead? Surely, he's not dead."

Kateřina took her output slip and rose. As she strode to her desk nearest the window, no one gave her any mind. Her desk was neat except for the coffee cup she'd left that morning. Under the cup was a slip of paper. She immediately recognized her father's handwriting in neat square letters.

MY OFFICE AS SOON AS YOU RETURN

The adrenaline still pumping through her veins made every sensation sharper, every sound more pronounced. The hum of the fluorescent bulbs overhead seemed louder, the smell of the newsroom ink more pungent. She felt an electric charge skitter across her skin when she sensed someone behind her.

"Oh, I wouldn't want a note like that on my desk," a woman's voice spoke.

Kateřina jumped, turning sharply to find her coworker Evka grinning, reading over her shoulder.

She's smiling?

Evka, with an age advantage of five years, had been a cornerstone of the newspaper long before Kateřina's father had taken the helm as editor in chief. She was known for her reliability but often settled into mundane, routine stories unless prodded to explore more dynamic narratives. Today, despite the chaos, her appearance was impeccable: her dark brown hair was intricately curled and pinned. Her tan skirt and coat bore no sign of the day's mayhem, looking either brand-new or meticulously maintained. This perfection, juxtaposed with the morning's terror, made Kateřina's senses jolt.

She looks like she's just stepped out of a ballroom, not a war-torn city, Kateřina thought, a pang of envy and suspicion intertwining.

Evka's unnerving smirk—the one she habitually wore, even during their lighthearted evening outings to the tavern—lingered as she waited for Kateřina's response.

"Why the smile, Evka?"

Evka's eyes darted, briefly focusing on the note left by Kateřina's father before the bombing. "Just glad to see you made it," Evka responded, but her attention seemed split, the note weighing on her mind.

Kateřina's heart raced. The events of the day, the near-death experience, the disbelief that someone she trusted could be so eerily composed. Every fiber of her being was on high alert.

Why does she care about that note? Why isn't she as shaken as the rest of us?

Evka's mouth opened slightly, as if she were unsure what to say next. Then, a strange dance played out on Evka's face. Her features shifted and twisted as if she were cycling through a myriad of masks. A hint of sorrow here, a touch of empathy there, her eyebrows knitting and relaxing in quick succession. It was as though she was internally experimenting, trying to settle on the perfect countenance of genuine concern. Kateřina watched, fascinated and a tad unsettled, as Evka's practiced façade finally settled on an expression that was a blend of all those she had tested.

Evka leaned closer. Compassion overflowed from her gaze. "Honestly, are you alright? I can't imagine how you feel after being there today. I'm sure the experience was like a nightmare coming to life. Witnessing the attack must have left you feeling so unsettled."

"Yes, well . . ." Tears sprang to Kateřina's eyes, and she brushed them away. She couldn't cry, not now. She had to stay strong. *I can crumple after I deal with Father.*

Evka brushed a strand of dark hair from her cheek and shrugged. "And then to have to talk to your father. He's all business, you know," Evka said as if reading Kateřina's mind. She reached forward and touched her arm. "I am not sure I should say anything, but I have heard he is already writing a column about the events." She sighed. "I suppose it's working to his advantage . . . " She pressed her lips together, halting her words. "Never mind. I should not bother you anymore. We both have work to do."

A chill slithered down Kateřina's spine as she realized Evka hadn't mentioned her father's acknowledgment of her byline. The weight of the day's horrors, combined with the looming shadow of her father's approval, pressed on Kateřina, making it hard to breathe. The tender, raw edges of hope and fear tangled within her heart. Even if masterfully penned, would her firsthand account ever see the light of day? Or would her father write and publish his own piece under her name? She felt the sharp sting of that reality more acutely now, especially after facing death and chaos head-on.

Struggling to maintain composure, her voice threatened to waver. "He's been particularly harsh on me lately," Kateřina admitted, the trepidation evident in her eyes. Trying to mask the vulnerability seeping through, she added a light shrug. "I don't know why." The sentiment hung heavily in the air.

Kateřina's brows furrowed at the mention of her father's peculiar behavior.

"He's especially heated today," Evka remarked, her heels clicking rhythmically on the tiled floor as she approached the break room. Her silhouette briefly blurred behind the frosted glass door before becoming clearer again. Evka continued, not bothering to lower her voice, indifferent to the potential prying ears in the newsroom, "Been holed up in his office all afternoon. Only came out a few times—once to leave that note on your desk. Hasn't so much as peeked out in the last fifteen minutes, even after the explosion." A brief pause allowed the hissing of the steam-powered coffee machine to fill the air. "I heard his voice rise a bit on the phone, so maybe you'd best let him cool down before your visit."

Suddenly, Evka's head popped back into view from the doorway, her dark eyes meeting Kateřina's, a steaming cup in her hand. "Cup of coffee, dear?"

Kateřina nodded and motioned for Evka to keep her voice down but to no avail. As soon as she had begun to nod, the woman dropped out of view to fulfill her offer of the heated beverage. Only when

Kateřina sat on her desk did Evka reappear, offering a steaming cup of dark liquid.

"Oh, uh, cream, and . . ." There was no need for Kateřina to finish her request. The coffee appeared already to have some in it. After a careful sip, Kateřina realized it had the exact amount to her liking. She looked quizzically at Evka, who winked in response.

Even with all the rationing, Evka always ensured some cream and sugar at the office for her coworkers to enjoy. "If I can't even notice how my coworkers take their coffee, I wouldn't be a good reporter." She tapped her temple right next to her eye. "Have always to keep an eye out, you know?"

Kateřina nodded. On the other hand, she had no idea who drank coffee in her office. Small matters like that often slipped by her. Instead, she'd focused on the big stories above all else. But could she miss something larger by ignoring small details?

"Evka," Kateřina chose her words carefully, "why do you think my father is unhappy today?"

Evka's signature grin rose, lifting her cheeks. She leaned into what seemed like it would be a whisper, only for the words to come out at the same volume as everything else. "He's been on the phone all day, but it really ramped up when news of the attack came in. He opened the door and peered out. Sweat beaded on his brow. I'm not sure what that was about."

It was a very Evka description, but Kateřina could picture it. Her father wasn't often known as a nervous man.

"I see." Katrina smiled to match the woman's energy and tried to push her worry away. "I'll let him cool off a bit, as you suggested. Thank you for the coffee."

As Evka departed, Kateřina pushed the coffee cup and her father's note to the side. Since another colleague was using the voice recorder, she sat, pulled out a sheet of paper, and fed it into the typewriter on her desk. Kateřina's mind still reeled from the conversation with Evka, and the memories of the attack on Heydrich haunted her.

She'd write the story first, her way. The way she saw it. Then she'd talk to her father. She had no time to spare if they wanted to get her story on the front page before the morning, and why wouldn't they? Unlike the hearsay and scattered reports over the phone, she'd been an eyewitness.

The typewriter was an old, clunky machine, but Kateřina loved it all the same. Each keystroke produced a satisfying *clack* as the letter was imprinted onto the page.

Typing had always been a relaxing activity for Kateřina, something that helped her focus and calm her nerves. As she began, the rhythmic sound of the typebars tapping against the paper brought a sense of order to her scattered thoughts.

The images of what happened replayed at the forefront of her mind. Her fingers moved across the keys, conveying the scene in perfect detail. The hum of activity around her in the newsroom faded as Kateřina focused on the page before her. She was lost in her thoughts, typing furiously to keep up with the words that spilled out.

They took on their own life, shaping and reshaping themselves as she typed. It was a story unfolding before her very eyes, each sentence leading her further down the path of her memories.

Her only pause was the time it took to reset her typewriter and ready the following line. It was as if she were in a trance. The memories were clear as she relived them, minus the fear. This was her element, the telling of the story. She neared the end of her retelling when she was struck with hesitation for the first time.

The motorcycle had found itself in the tree above her at the scene of the attack. Despite being present, she didn't know what had flung the heavy machinery so high. It was an important detail, but how would she explain it? Would she gloss over the fact or perhaps leave a vague mention? If she neglected to mention it, another outlet might say it and throw her account into question. However, if she tried to come up with a way to explain it and was proven wrong, that would put her entire reputation at stake. *Not that I have much of a reputation these days.*

Typically, she'd skip past each bullet scar or the dislodged cobblestones beneath her feet. But that particular event was so peculiar. She had photographed the stuck motorcycle, which would make an excellent front-page image. She needed to include it, so vagueness might be her best option.

By the time she finished typing, Kateřina felt a sense of calm and clarity she hadn't felt since the attack on Heydrich. The words on the page were a tangible record of her thoughts and feelings—a way of making sense of the chaos inside her. She leaned back in her chair and read over the pages she had typed. It was nearly a perfect narrative if she'd ever written one. It had to be enough.

Collecting it from the typewriter, she admired her handiwork. She'd conveyed the scene perfectly but kept the word count low enough that they would have no problem printing it.

This is it. Kateřina's lips curled upward in excitement. *My story. This will finally get me the respect I deserve.*

Now, for the tricky part. Kateřina glanced down at her father's note. She didn't want his sour mood to dampen her chance at true success. She needed to choose every word as if the stern editor were also critiquing her speaking. No matter what conspiracies her father had been led to believe, she knew a story this big would have to be included—every detail.

Kateřina rose, stood upright, chest slightly puffed out, and strode toward her father's office door. The glass windows surrounding the office were still shuttered. The only evidence of her father's presence was the glow of his desk lamp inside. She forced herself to be brave and knocked on the door twice, waiting for an answer.

"Who is it?" Her father's voice was low, weary.

"Kateřina Dubová," she responded confidently.

The silence that followed built like a wall, blocking her even more from her father. *And he's the one who asked me to come into his office in the first place.*

She waited a few more long moments, considering whether to return later. Finally, her father's voice called out. "Enter."

She blew out a breath and relaxed her posture. Then she stepped into the dimly lit office chamber.

He sat, tightening his tie and adjusting his collar. His hair had appeared styled earlier in the day but was now disheveled. She wasn't sure what to make of the sight. Father was always strict about the dress policy for the office. She had never seen him unkempt while at work. Even at home, he often stayed sharply dressed until he changed into night clothes.

I'll ask him about that later. For now, the story.

"Mister Dub," she started, choosing professionalism over their familial ties. "I—"

"You're off the story. Head home, and I'll have a new assignment for you on Monday." His words doused her like a bucket of ice water. He hardly regarded her as he turned his attention to some papers on his desk.

"Excuse me? I—" A rush of panic surged through Kateřina, making her voice waver. Taking a deep breath to center herself, she thrust her story forward with determination, placing it squarely in front of him.

"Here's my account of the incident regarding the attack on Reinhard Heydrich. I was there, and I saw it all. Every other outlet will have the story only through interviews and secondhand accounts. I have the whole truth right here." The force with which she placed the story in front of him was like a hammer striking an anvil. Her palm hitting the wood echoed through the room.

Father's brow furrowed. He took her words like a disrespectful slap to the face. He met her eyes with sudden fierceness.

Neither backed down for a long while as they glared silently, until he finally shifted his gaze to the story below. His mouth opened as he read her account. He shot her a glance that she could almost interpret as impressed. He read the story twice, and she felt her panic fade and excitement grow. Then, there was a sudden, inexplicable shift in her father's demeanor. He reached over and grabbed a red pen.

Horror struck Kateřina as he began crossing out line after line of her story. He was gutting it, removing details she knew to be accurate, like the death of Heydrich's driver. She held onto a tiny bit of hope until he crossed out her account of the motorcycle. Without that, her photo would be useless. Her story as she dreamed it was lost.

Her patience snapped. "How can you dismiss this? Every word is the truth!"

"I'm saving you from being humiliated. Reinhard Heydrich's driver did not die on the side of the road. Oberscharführer Johannes 'Hans' Klein, Heydrich's driver, followed the second assassin into a butcher shop, where he was killed. I talked to the butcher shop owner myself. And what is this nonsense about the motorcycle? You couldn't even clearly say how it ended up in the tree. Were your eyes closed?"

"But I saw the man. I talked to him. The driver died on the road." She thought of the slip of paper still in her satchel. She tugged at the sides of her dress tightly. "And I was watching the entire time. I took a photograph of the motorcycle up in the tree."

Father's gaze narrowed. His nostrils flared. "Are you calling me a liar—or worse, a bad journalist? There's a reason I'm the head of this paper. I've been doing this since before you—"

Kateřina held up her palm, halting his words. "And you say you talked to someone at the scene, but I was there."

"And *you*." He snarled his nose. "You're still trembling. You're filthy. You're shaken up. No wonder you assumed—"

"I didn't assume anything," she said between clenched teeth. "I know what I saw." Her anger warred with her need for control as she struggled to contain her emotions. She'd never let her feelings get in the way of her writing. Then again, she'd never had her father treat her like this. She'd take the aloof father she'd known for years over this.

Snatching back her story, Kateřina turned. He believed her to be an unreliable witness. She had no grace for anyone who doubted her account. Not for her father. Not today, not tomorrow, or anytime soon. No unbiased journalist would place more value on a secondhand account than the words of an eyewitness. Her gut tightened, and bile rose in the back of her throat. From her first day on staff, Kateřina understood she'd have to climb from the depths, no different from any other newcomer.

She hadn't expected that, unlike the others, her stories would always be pushed to the side or, worse, covered with so much red ink that it was impossible to read what words remained under the bloodshed.

I'll never be taken seriously.
I was there. I know what I saw.
The man died. He handed me that slip of paper.

Without glancing at her father, she strode from his office. The paper was proof. She returned to her desk and sat, remembering the man's eyes. They'd widened in pain and fear, yet there was something else there, too—an urgency. As if whatever he was holding was more critical than the spilling of his blood on the pavement—more than life itself.

"Go home, and return on Monday only if you listen to me!" her father shouted after her.

She reached into her satchel and felt the paper there.

Monday it is. I'll have a story not even you can ignore.

Rádek scanned the crowd in Old Town Square, noting no excited faces or rush of troops. Yet it was only a matter of time. Sitting in the outdoor café, he sipped coffee and read the astronomical clock. Less than an hour ago, he'd received an urgent phone call.

They attempted to kill Heydrich, Persephone had stated simply. *You were on his calendar today, but now that is impossible.*

You were on his calendar today. A simple statement for such a massive undertaking. They'd agreed to meet up in Old Town Square. *Better to act as if one has nothing to hide, especially during times like these.*

He had to meet with her. Rádek had to know if she could still provide him with the last weapons needed to finish his great work. He refused to come this far simply to be pushed aside. Heydrich would have never set him aside. No, the Obergruppenführer believed this great invention would turn the tide of war.

Yet even as he waited for Persephone's arrival, Rádek couldn't help but marvel at the beauty of the clock tower. It was a masterpiece of medieval engineering and design, a testament to the creativity and ingenuity of the artisans of the time. Maybe his work of art would be appreciated as such someday. Or it would have been. The clock's face was adorned with several numerical displays—hours of the day, days of the month, phases of the moon, and the golden number, which was used in calculating the date of Easter.

Ornate carvings and sculptures adorned the tower, including figures of various saints, significant historical figures, and intricate decorative elements, such as rosettes and coats of arms.

As the hands of the clock ticked off the minutes, Rádek wondered if Heydrich's very life was slipping away with each tick. Either way, time was of the essence. He had to find out what had happened to Heydrich and whether he was still alive. But he also knew he had to be careful, as the authorities were undoubtedly on high alert. If anyone other than Persephone knew about his meeting with Heydrich, they would note his every move. Today's events could ruin everything, and Rádek cursed himself for putting such faith in the Obergruppenführer.

Heydrich was one of his most important contacts. If Heydrich had been attacked, it could mean only one thing. Rádek's whole plan could be over. If those who had attacked Heydrich had even a whisper of Rádek's masterpiece, all would be lost. Rádek's neck muscles coiled with tension at the very thought.

Persephone walked into the café with quickened steps, her dark hair blowing around her face with the breeze that had picked up. She smiled broadly, showing perfect, straight teeth, but it failed to mask the fear in her eyes.

She sat, ordered coffee, and complained that there were no pastries—even though there hadn't been pastries for sale in most cafés in Prague for months.

Only after the waiter moved out of earshot did she narrow her gaze and lean close. "If you hadn't heard, Heydrich is in the hospital with serious injuries. It won't be soon if he recovers and makes it out." She twirled a dark strand of hair around her finger. "If I were you, I'd stay inside as much as possible. The Gestapo is rounding up anyone they think could have been associated with those who attacked Heydrich. Of course, they're also using it as an excuse to kill anyone else they've had their sights on."

"It's a wonderful excuse, then," Rádek stated bluntly. "They couldn't have planned it better. The reprisals might even be for their—*our*—benefit."

Persephone continued as if the cogwheels of her mind were

operating at full steam, oblivious to his words. "They've already executed six persons of one family, including two women, with cold, steam-driven efficiency. They've sealed the frontiers with brass walls and clockwork sentinels. It's as if this whole country has been transformed into a vast concentration camp."

As they spoke, armored vehicles with brass plating and whirling gears drove into the large central square, spewing steam puffs and emitting their engines' low hums. Behind them, spider tanks with intricate ironwork and rotating chimney stacks followed in groups of two, their multiple legs clicking and whirring like an army of mechanized insects.

Rádek squirmed in his seat. *Before the day is done, how many will be rounded up and interrogated?*

"It should make all of us fear, shouldn't it?" Persephone's eyes blinked rapidly. "If they got to Heydrich, then no one is beyond their reach, are they?" She dipped her head forward. "Of course, that is where you step in." Persephone's voice rose above the murmurs of the other café guests—louder than he expected.

"That is where I *would have* stepped in." He picked up his cup and put it to his lips. "Now, I am not certain it's possible." He glanced at her over the rim of his glasses, remaining silent, for they both understood that the next move was hers.

Persephone gently tapped the spoon on the tabletop as if considering her next course of action. "My orders were direct from Obergruppenführer Heydrich—to provide you with the weapons needed."

He didn't answer right away. He didn't want to appear desperate. "Yes, you are correct. Are you saying that's a problem now?"

"I work for one man, who can no longer give me orders." She wrapped a strand of dark hair around her finger. Then she paused and smiled. "But if Heydrich trusted you, who am I to question that?"

He leaned forward, resting his elbows on the table. "I'd be a fool to believe you answered to Heydrich alone. My guess is you've already made contact with Zelewski. And if you have, I have no doubt you've already told him about me."

Persephone blinked slowly and then glanced around. "How do you know?" She leaned closer and lowered her voice to no more than a whisper. "No one is supposed to know he's even coming to Prague."

"Everyone knows SS General Erich von dem Bach-Zelewski is even harsher than Heydrich ever was. Who else would they send to kill ten thousand politically unreliable Czechs? And that is their plan, correct?"

"Himmler shot down Hitler's idea. This is a critical industrial zone. The military depends on it. Indiscriminate killing—"

"Could reduce productivity." Rádek finished the woman's sentence. "Not that it will stop the soldiers on the streets."

Persephone sighed. "It's unfortunate."

Rádek nodded, his mind racing. He had to act quickly and carefully if he wanted to save his plan and his own life. "Thanks for the warning, Persephone," he said, his voice low. "I need to find Heydrich and get out of here as soon as possible."

Persephone's face grew as distressed as a lost child.

"I heard they've tightened security all around the city. It's going to be almost impossible to get anywhere without being noticed. But I will go ahead with the plan. I will leave the, uh, items where it was previously agreed."

Rádek gritted his teeth. She was right about not transporting the weapons to his warehouse, but he couldn't give up now. He had come too far and sacrificed too much to let it all go to waste.

"I'll find a way," he said firmly. "I have to."

Persephone nodded. Her eyes filled with a mixture of admiration and concern. "Be careful, Kelley. I don't want to lose you, too."

With that, she rose and walked away, disappearing into the crowd and leaving Rádek alone with his thoughts. He had to move fast. *They* had to finish their masterpiece in record time.

He took one last drink of his coffee and glanced around the square again, trying to stay calm and collected. He couldn't afford to panic or draw attention to himself. He needed to blend in with the crowd and escape before the Gestapo arrived.

A group of soldiers marched toward the square. His heart raced.

Even though they had no reason to target him, Rádek could not be too careful. He had to keep his wits about him, stay focused, and trust his resourcefulness and skill.

He paid for his coffee, then stood, adjusting his coat and hat. He walked briskly toward the outskirts of the square, scanning the faces of the people he passed for any signs of suspicion or recognition.

Rádek set off toward the meeting place, his heart pounding. The fate of his plan and maybe his own life hung in the balance. As he disappeared into the crowded streets of Old Town, he steeled himself for the challenges ahead, determined to do whatever it took to win his war. Determined to see it through to the end, no matter the cost.

Josef stepped into an alleyway. He moved cautiously, like a soldier entering enemy territory. Everything was familiar, but nothing was the same. He needed to get back to the rebels' warehouse to check on the others, yet he also had to ensure he wasn't being followed. Even worse than not making it was leading the Germans there.

He had stood on that street corner and watched rebels attempt to kill Heydrich with a Sten gun. More than that, he'd slipped away unnoticed, even while the others had been chased down.

Yet they still needed to succeed. And when Josef had his opportunity to finish off Heydrich, he'd run away.

The blonde's beautiful face filled his mind. Did he know her from somewhere? He didn't think so. Yet why had she been so bold to approach him and tell him to run before he was discovered? *And why did I listen?*

He'd meandered deliberately through the city, vigilant of any tails. Now, he was just a few blocks from Josefov, navigating the industrial district by the Vltava River. Josef darted from one shadow to the next, feeling like he'd entered a dream steeped in fog and ambiguity. Despite his best efforts to tread lightly, every step he took reverberated through the alley, sounding like a drumbeat in a vast chamber.

While this part of town no doubt used to be a lush, grassy spot by the river, it was now a dark and foreboding place. Towering brick buildings with soot-stained walls flanked the narrow passageway, rusted metal pipes snaking up their sides. The cobbled street glimmered with spilled oil and dirty puddles, and the air was thick with the bitter scent of coal, smoke, and gunpowder.

The sound of machinery echoed through the alley, from the clanging of metal gears to the hiss of steam escaping from valves. Flickering gas lamps dimly lit the alleyway, casting long shadows that stretched toward unwary passersby.

During the daytime, this alleyway was usually a hub of activity. Men and women in goggles and leather aprons scurried about, working on machines that clanked and whirred. Yet this afternoon, all was silent. News of Nazi reprisals had spread around the city. Now and then, the occasional burst of gunfire or the rumble of an explosion sounded in the distance, a reminder that the Germans would leave no stone unturned when hunting the attempted assassins.

The alleyway squeezed in like a trap, with hidden corners and dark alcoves, ready to fold in on Josef at any moment.

A dozen heavy German boots thundered by as a squadron passed, heading to Old Town Square, where they'd gathered suspects. The Nazis had a purpose: vengeance. Rebels had dared to fight against them, and they would not have it.

All this for a failed assassination attempt?

Though the assassination faltered, the Germans perceived the attempt as a direct challenge to their authority. They sought to instill fear, to deter the rebels from reigniting their cause. But the rebels' resilience unsettled the Germans and ratted their confidence.

Fear gnawing at your edges? Better hold on. We're just getting started.

Josef turned a corner and halted. The sudden appearance of the spider tank was like a nightmare coming to life, jarring Josef out of his thoughts.

The tank, a hulking behemoth of cold metal and menace, moved with surprising speed, its legs cracking against the cobblestones. A sizable squad of Sturmtruppen marched briskly behind, their boots pounding in synchronized cadence, revealing the German determination to hunt him down. Attempting to slip past them would be not only foolish but potentially fatal. Josef's heart raced as he doubled back, his mind desperately scanning for another pathway to the rebels' warehouse.

Yet, after weaving through a labyrinth of narrow streets, he was met again by the oppressive force of the Germans, strategically positioned to block the moves of those attempting to enter or exit the Jewish area of Josefov. Panic gripped him, and his breathing grew ragged. Everywhere he turned, the path was barred, and he was cornered. The city he once knew now felt like an insurmountable maze with no way out.

What now?

The alleyway he found himself in was narrow and cramped, with little room to move and even less room to hide. The spider tanks and squads of soldiers patrolling the streets made it clear that the Germans were taking no chances. As Josef leaned against the nearby wall, the old, rough stone pressed unpleasantly against his back.

The roads were similarly narrow, designed for horses and carriages rather than the massive war machines that now prowled the streets. If Josef were cornered or deemed suspicious in any way, the Germans would not hesitate to round him up with the others in Old Town Square or ship him off to one of their camps. He needed to think carefully before making any moves.

Waiting for the roads to clear later into the night was the best action. He needed to find somewhere safe to lie low until then. But where could he go that the Germans wouldn't think to search?

As he stood thinking, the sounds of war echoed through the streets. Gunfire and explosions sounded in the distance, a constant reminder of the danger surrounding him. The air was thick with the smell of smoke and burning, a grim reminder of the destruction wrought upon his city.

He couldn't let fear paralyze him. He needed to keep moving, keep thinking, and keep fighting. Josef pressed himself closer against the wall, trying to become one with its shadows. He could hear the distant footfalls of soldiers and the mechanical hum of their machines. Taking a deep breath to steel his nerves, he darted into the alleyway.

Every corner held the potential for danger, and his mind raced with scenarios of ambushes and traps.

The cobbled streets he had known like the back of his hand now seemed to twist and shift. As he approached one street, the intense beam of a German searchlight, designed to penetrate even daytime shadows, splashed over the cobblestones. Its brilliance was such that it unveiled every hidden nook and cranny. Forced by the revealing light, Josef had to double back and find an alternative route. Another alley led him to a group of Sturmtruppen, talking animatedly. Josef held his breath and slipped into a concealed doorway, waiting for them to move on.

His steps were now more erratic, less the steady metronome, and more the frantic rhythm of survival. But then, after what felt like hours of evasion, he finally glimpsed the familiar façade of the shop.

In this world dominated by German occupation, the shop stood as an island of familiarity. Its windows were undamaged, its door unmarked. A beacon of hope in a sea of chaos. He retrieved his key with trembling hands, letting himself in. Before he locked the door behind him, he took one last glance outside, ensuring he had yet to be followed. The relief of safety was almost overwhelming.

The clock shop was relatively quiet, aside from the dozens of clocks ticking and the slight mechanical whirring of their inner workings. The peace, however, was soon disturbed by muffled talking from the hidden room—*aggressive* talking. Fear struck Josef as he pictured a German soldier searching the place. He stepped closer to the secret door.

"We can't be hasty!" That was Grandfather's voice. "If we show our hand too soon, it could come at the cost of lives. You know that!"

Show our hand? The words gave Josef pause. This wasn't a discussion with a German soldier. His first instinct was to enter the secret room and make his presence known, but growing curiosity kept him at bay.

"I have what we need. The time is now. It is foolish to wait."

Josef didn't recognize the second voice. He stepped to the side in case Grandfather exited the hidden room.

"You're not listening to me. I need you to listen." In the dimness, Grandfather's voice took on a deeper, sterner tone, starkly different from the warm and jovial cadence Josef had always associated with him.

Blackout curtains shrouded the room in heavy darkness, allowing only the feeble candlelight to break through. Tension weighed heavily, almost tangible, in the air. As the candle flame danced, it cast ghostly, undulating shadows on the walls, deepening Josef's sense of unease and making it even harder to decipher the gravity of their whispered conversation.

Grandfather said something about "the purpose of the construction." What sort of construction could be so important that it would be worth risking everything to keep it out of German control? The answer was a puzzle with missing pieces, leaving him unable to solve it. Josef held his breath, afraid to draw attention to himself.

"I assure you, the construction is ready," the other voice said.

Josef paused, finally recognizing Rádek Ježek's voice. Rádek and Grandfather had a history that dated back to their childhoods. Sometimes they would reminisce, and he would hear stories of Rádek and Grandfather running around Prague and getting into trouble. Rádek never cared about Grandfather's faith and didn't once join in a Jewish community event. He only cared for Grandfather, even cracking a few heads when other Czech boys would tease him about his religion. Though times changed around them, their friendship remained an unwavering constant. And now, hearing Rádek's voice, that emblem of unity and shared history, Josef felt a comforting sense of normality amidst the chaos. With a sigh of relief, he stepped toward the room.

"You see the city out there," Rádek said. "It will all be lost if they find it before we activate it. We must keep it out of German hands at all costs!"

Josef froze just before entering. Candlelight flickered as if a gentle wind had blown past. Josef blinked. What sort of construction could they be referring to? He stepped back and listened again.

"I understand that." Grandfather's voice lowered but became even sterner, a manner of speaking Josef had become more accustomed to hearing as of late. "But you sound like you are forgetting its purpose when you say *at any cost*, my friend. It is being built to save lives, not being made at the cost of them. The construct will not be dangerous once enabled. Until then, leave the core in the seat at the synagogue."

The synagogue, is it? I'll need to see what the core *is.*

The conversation ended. Josef crept back and made a loud show of entering the shop for the first time. He called for Grandfather, who emerged from the back appearing somewhat confused yet relieved to see him.

"Josef! Come in, come in." His grandfather welcomed him warmly. "It is good to see you well, with everything happening."

"It's chaos out there. The streets are swarming with soldiers." Josef jerked his head toward the window. "I caught whispers about a German official being ambushed. They're scouring the area, desperate to find those behind the attack before they strike again."

Grandfather frowned and approached the window, peeking out as a pair of soldiers marched by. "You heard wrong then, my boy. There is nothing left to finish."

Josef gasped, excitement welling up in his chest. "They got him?"

"By *him*, you mean Reinhard Heydrich, one of the highest-ranking German officials? I have heard he's badly wounded and in the hospital." Grandfather scowled at the floor. "He could very well die, and I will not mourn his death."

"I'll toast to it." Josef grinned. As he spoke, the moment of the assassination attempt played out in his mind in slow motion—the grenade's trajectory, the glint of metal, the surprised expressions. He could feel the weight of the event pressing on him, causing the vein in his neck to pulse more noticeably. Shaking his head slightly to clear those thoughts, he hoped his grandfather hadn't caught his pulse quickening. "I had heard that the attackers missed their shots. What happened?"

Rádek suddenly appeared from the back as well. His face was devoid of emotion. An unusual sight, as the man was often the depiction of the word *passionate*. "From what I heard, four bullets were removed from him during surgery."

Four?

That couldn't be right. Reinhard had stood up and shot at the attempted assassins as they retreated. A man hit four times wouldn't have been able to do that. More than that, the Sten hadn't fired. "Four bullets? Are you sure?"

Rádek shrugged. "It's hard to say. The Germans aren't giving anyone hospital reports, although many reporters are swarming, hoping for news. That won't stop the rumors, but it's too soon to tell what will happen to him."

Grandfather placed a reassuring hand on Josef's shoulder, the warmth feeling like the comforting weight of a well-oiled cog in a vast machinery. "For the moment, lad, we must confront the grim truths of our time. Such audacity against the Germans carries a heavy toll. They'll comb the city like a clockwork hound on the scent, seeking retribution until they extract their pound of steam and steel. Did you come here to take refuge in the hidden chamber? To remain concealed from their prying eyes?"

Josef nodded. "Too many soldiers right now. I'm hoping for a clear path later on."

"That's a good idea, Josef." Rádek's face was sour. "The Germans are arresting indiscriminately. Even if you had nothing to do with the attack, it doesn't matter. And you do not want to know what they do to those they arrest."

"Of course, everyone knows the rumors," Josef said, but Rádek didn't drop his earnest gaze. He seemed to be talking from experience. As far as Josef knew, the man had no family and never had one. Not to mention that Rádek wasn't even Jewish. What would he possibly know of something like this?

Regardless, Josef had already known better than to try and draw the attention of the Germans, especially in the Josefov district. Josef and his grandfather waited until midafternoon before departing. The soldiers had already made their way through the area, so Josef headed toward the rebel warehouse again. But as he approached the city's edge, he stopped himself. A nagging feeling pawed at his mind. One he couldn't seem to ignore. The synagogue. What were his grandfather and Rádek doing there? And what implications did it have against the Germans?

As much as he wanted to check in on the rebels and ensure their safety, he needed to know. Grandfather was a secretive man, but something seemed different this time. Josef felt the weight of uncertainty pressing on his chest, like gears grinding in a clockwork heart running out of steam. Every step toward the synagogue felt like a step into the unknown. What would he find? What secrets lay within those ancient walls?

Reinhard Heydrich, Heinrich Himmler's chief deputy as head of the Nazi Gestapo and Reich protector for Bohemia-Moravia, was in grave condition tonight, according to the Vichy radio, after being wounded in an assassination plot in Prague, former capital of Czechoslovakia.

A bomb, either planted in his automobile or thrown as it passed at high speed along the road to Berlin inside Greater Prague, exploded, wrecking the car, and seriously injuring the Nazi secret police chieftain, notorious throughout occupied Europe as "the hangman."

EXECUTIONS REPORTED

A manhunt for the assassins, led by Himmler himself, who rushed to Prague from Berlin, began immediately. Unconfirmed reports via the Budapest radio announced that several executions already have taken place. The threat of swift reprisals hangs heavy over the country.

(The Associated Press reported from London that Heydrich was shot, and his assassin escaped.) The Berlin radio made the following announcement:

Sturmtruppen's upper group leader, Heydrich, was injured, but there is no danger for his life. A million-crown reward (nominally $235,000) has been offered for the apprehension of the assassins. Martial law was proclaimed in Prague.

Kateřina walked with slow, steady steps through a sea of uniformed soldiers. They filled the streets of Prague like a disturbed nest of ants. She'd briefly glanced at the paper earlier and discovered it was a symbol with no words of explanation. Immediately, Kateřina knew she would need help determining its meaning. Her fingers closed tightly around the piece of paper as she studied it. The image of the Jewish Star of David was evident, but the rectangle surrounding it reminded her of some type of box or maybe a throne. She needed to uncover its meaning to prove herself to her father.

It's not what it seems, the driver had said. She instinctively felt the clues would lead her to Old Town to find answers. She had to understand who had decided that the facts of the driver's death needed to be altered and why.

The arachnid-like legs of the spider tanks clacked against the cobblestones. Heavily armored with machine guns and cannons, their turrets swept back and forth, scanning for any sign of resistance. Designed for urban warfare, their presence clearly indicated the Germans' intention to stamp out anyone deemed a threat.

Overhead, airships hovered like dark, ominous clouds. Engines hummed as they circled above the city. Their massive hulls bristled with guns, and their crews peered down through binoculars, prepared to strike against anyone resisting arrest.

The airships were a constant reminder of the Germans' dominance.

They would rain down destruction from above. Their mere presence was enough to strike fear into the hearts of the people below.

Kateřina walked through the streets, thinking of the men waking the sleeping giant. Where were they? Safe? The military presence proved they were still unaccounted for. Unless the Germans also used this as an excuse to wipe out more of their enemies. The glint of pride and dominance she saw in Hilbert's gaze told her this was likely the case.

The spider tanks and airships were a tangible reminder of the danger she and her fellow Czechs faced. Yet at the same time, she also felt a flicker of hope. The fact the rebels dared to strike at Heydrich—one of the highest-ranking officers in the Nazi regime—proved Czechs could fight back. And even in the face of overwhelming odds, they would continue to resist.

The soldiers' presence pressed on her heart like a weight. She strode with her head down to blend in with the crowd.

Last she'd heard, Obergruppenführer Heydrich was in critical condition. Kateřina thought of the dark-haired man. She guessed he was her age, barely twenty. She hadn't seen him before, but he seemed familiar—someone she knew from her past and, strangely, someone she expected to know in her future.

Who are you? Where did you go? He wasn't a soldier, but he was with the rebels. What was worth fighting for? Possibly dying for?

She thought of the conversation after the concert. The officers had teased about rounding up more Jews. Even now, preparations were in the works to send them away. The man's dark features pervaded her mind again, and her lower lip quivered.

It was clear what he was fighting for—his people.

Walking through Malá Strana after the assassination attempt was a surreal experience. Everything was the same, but in light of what happened, everything was different, too. No debris or rubble were in sight, but the city seemed broken. The sun hung high, but it was almost as if the smoke and burnt metal followed her like a dark cloud over her soul.

And as Kateřina saw men and women being hauled out of buildings and herded into the streets, her mind advanced to months from now. Would this attempt be the start of more fighting? Had the Czechs had enough?

Even as she eyed the unmarked buildings on either side of the street, she pictured them pockmarked with shrapnel and windows shattered into a million pieces. As she walked, distant sirens wailed, broken glass occasionally clattered underfoot, and an icy sensation crept along her back. The rebels might have stirred a sleeping giant, but perhaps they had also shot a boost of courage into the conquered people.

More than that, there was a sense of defiance in the air. With the bravery of a small group of men, they had shown they would not be forced into complete submission. Her fellow Czechs had been through so much, yet they continued to fight for their freedom and independence.

Her steps paused near the Charles Bridge. A line of soldiers stretched across it, stopping all who passed. Reaching into her pocket, Kateřina's fingers touched her press badge. Then she paused, pulled out a handkerchief, and wiped away some of the dust and dirt left over from the chaos.

She pressed her thumb and finger against her eyes, causing them to water. Blinking back tears, she stepped into the queue, pausing behind other men and women. With silent efficiency, the soldiers checked papers and waved them through. As she neared the front of the line, shouting erupted beside her, and an older man was pulled to the side.

"I have done nothing! I have done nothing!" the man shouted as officers dragged him to a waiting vehicle.

As the scene unfolded, a chill coursed through her like cold steam escaping a pressure valve. A soft cry escaped, and she jumped. Before her stood a Wehrmacht soldier, his uniform impeccable, blond, and tall—every inch the archetype she'd seen in German propaganda posters.

"Fräulein?" The man's voice was softer than she expected.

Kateřina blinked back real tears. "Any news of the Stellvertretender

Reichsprotektor?" she croaked out as she displayed her paperwork showing that she was a German and Czech citizen..

The soldier barely glanced at her paperwork. "We know only that he is alive." He smirked, which soon curled into a snarl. "And the dogs who dared to attack our great leader better hope that does not change, unless they wish for even more blood on their streets."

Kateřina's knees softened at his words, and the soldier wrapped an arm around her shoulders. "Oh, please forgive me. I do not wish to cause such distress. It may not be a good day to be out."

"I'm on an errand. I have something I must do for my father." This, she knew, was not a lie.

"Yes, of course." The soldier motioned her forward. "But after your visit, plan to remain home for the upcoming days. One never knows what will happen to the rebels among us, and I'd hate for you to be caught up in such matters."

"Thank you. I will do that. I appreciate your concern." She dabbed her eyes again, though her jaw tightened. Danger snapped like static electricity in the air. How many others in the city shared this soldier's sentiments? Was she safe? She kept her eyes downcast, hoping not to draw attention to herself.

As she walked from the checkpoint, Kateřina couldn't help but think of the Stellvertretender Reichsprotektor's fate. She had heard rumors that he was in critical condition, but the soldier's words suggested he was still alive. She couldn't imagine what kind of retribution the Germans would exact upon those responsible for the assassination attempt.

She tried to shake off her fear as she approached the Klementinum library near Old Town Square and the Astronomical Clock. She had always found solace in books and hoped that the serene atmosphere of the library would calm her nerves. Still, today's purpose was a different matter. She needed answers. What did the symbol mean, and why was it so important?

Kateřina's press pass gave her immediate entrance. She stepped through the ornate doors of the Klementinum library and was immediately enveloped by awe. The grand hall stretched on for miles, with towering shelves of books on either side. She craned her neck to take in the stunning frescoes that adorned the ceiling, marveling at their intricate detail and vibrant colors.

Still, the soldier's words haunted her. What kind of future lay ahead for her and her fellow Czechs? Would they ever be free from the tyranny of the Nazi regime? Or was their fate already sealed, with more bloodshed and violence to come?

She went deeper into the library, reverent of the countless volumes of rare and valuable books containing knowledge and insights passed down through generations.

Despite the grandeur of the space, there was a palpable sense of tranquility within these walls—the opposite of what was happening outside in the streets. Visitors moved about with hushed footsteps, their voices lowered to a whisper in respect for the sanctity of the space. The scent of old paper and leather added to the atmosphere of quiet contemplation.

"Can I help you?" A gentle voice startled her.

She turned to see a thin woman her height in a pressed white shirt and long skirt. Her daily uniform?

"I'm looking for a book of Jewish symbols."

"Symbols?"

"I'm looking for one in particular, which includes the Star of David."

"The hexagram. It's often used to identify Jewish communities, as an architectural element, yes? I have books that will interest you. And your name?"

"Kateřina."

"And I am Dita." The woman frowned slightly and motioned to a table. "Wait here. I have a few books in mind."

Within thirty minutes, a small stack of books sat at Kateřina's elbow. Only the occasional shifting or the rare cough permeated the otherwise silent library as she pored through the reference books. She hadn't found an answer, but she'd at least narrowed her search to the history of Prague. She found the same image in numerous historical sketches, but none of the books explained the symbol or its meaning.

A dead end.

She closed the last book with a huff, feeling defeated. Was she cut out for this type of work? It was a far cry from the investigative journalism she had dreamed of as a student. Kateřina couldn't shake the feeling she was wasting her time. She couldn't ask a deviously loaded question to coax out data from a book or catch a tome in a compromising situation to reveal a hidden truth.

And she couldn't ask for help. At least, not without her father hearing about it. How could she discover the symbol's meaning if she couldn't find it in a book?

Kateřina sat up straighter. Books, of course, were written by people. If she couldn't find the answer by searching through a history book, she could find someone who *knew* the history and extract information from them.

She found Dita sorting books. The older librarian peered curiously above the frames of her glasses as Kateřina approached. "Did you find information about that symbol?"

"Unfortunately, no. I looked in the books you recommended about old Prague architecture but didn't find anything." Kateřina hid her frustration by keeping a straight face. "I was hoping to find someone who might know more about Jewish symbols. Do you know where I could find someone like that?"

The librarian put down the book she held. A sparkle lit her eyes and splayed out her wrinkles. "Well, Dr. Emil Urban is a history professor at Charles University. The university closed a few years ago because of the . . . occupation," Dita said barely above a whisper. "He comes here often, but I haven't seen him today."

"Do you know where else he might frequent?" Kateřina tried to keep her voice calm. She wasn't expected anywhere until Monday but needed this story to be perfect by then. Every minute counted.

"Even better, I know his address." Dita pulled out a small notebook and wrote it down. "I wouldn't normally give it out, but I know Emil. He's a very kind man who would be interested in a mystery like your symbol. He won't mind a visit from a pretty young woman like yourself, either."

"In that case, you should visit him too. Thank you again." Kateřina winked then accepted the address. Thankfully she recognized the street name. It wasn't too far.

It was midafternoon now. German soldiers, out in force, paid her little mind. When she got noticed, it was only a stray whistle or catcall from a soldier trying to find companionship during their nights of occupation. A jeep packed with soldiers came rolling down the narrow road. Though they slowed down, Kateřina had to step into the old Uzlaté koruny building long enough for it to pass.

Finding the flat, she saw movement inside the door, and she gently knocked. "Professor Emil? I was hoping to speak with you for a little while?"

"One moment, please!" An older gentleman called from inside. Then she was left relatively quiet, disturbed only by shuffling or thumping from beyond the door. After a minute or so, the door opened, and a tall man in his late sixties greeted her. He had white hair, and a neat mustache, curved downward at the edges. He wore a simple suit that seemed hastily put on and held a pipe that was half-smoked. "I apologize for the wait, miss. I was not expecting any visitors. Are you perhaps an aspiring student of the university?"

"Oh, no, nothing like that." Kateřina pulled her press badge from her satchel. "I'm a reporter, actually. My name is Kateřina Dubová. I'm following a story of great importance, and I hope you can help me."

Distrust crossed Emil's face. Gesturing for her to enter, he moved aside. As she stepped in, the door closed ominously behind them. "I don't know how you expect me to help you. I'm a historian and don't involve myself in current affairs. Not when I know what I say can be used against me."

"Your name doesn't need to be included at all. Rather, I have it on good authority from a friendly librarian named Dita that you would be interested in the subject." Kateřina tilted her head toward Emil endearingly. "She seems quite knowledgeable of your comings, goings, and interests."

Emil's neck and ears turned red, and all signs of distrust faded. He cleared his throat and waved her to come in. "Well, a small chat should be fine."

She was welcomed to a cozy flat. A lone armchair sat close to the rear window, and nearly every wall had a tightly packed bookshelf. One such book, an incredibly lengthy read, sat open on the table next to where Emil presumably had been sitting before her arrival. He directed her to the armchair, the only sitting spot in the room, and approached a small nearby kitchen area.

"Would you like some tea?" he asked.

"Please, and thank you." Sitting in the armchair, she carefully lifted the book on the table to read the cover without accidentally closing it. *Rudolf II und seine Zeit. Rudolf II and His Time.*

"I know, I know. Not casual afternoon reading for most." Emil filled his kettle with water. "It's a fascinating era, though. Perhaps one often overlooked. I find that the least famous stories can have the most meaning."

"How so?" she asked with genuine curiosity.

"Well, people generally don't like confronting uncomfortable truths. They like to hear about their heroes and how they overcame adversity." He grinned and held up a cup before her. "But I don't suppose you came all this way to merely chat about history, did you, Kateřina?" He asked as he poured her a cup of tea, which she sipped politely.

"Pleasant as this is, I am afraid not." She reached into her coat pocket and pulled out the paper with the symbol drawn on it. She examined it once more herself and then passed it over.

Emil scrutinized it. "Ah, what's this now?"

"I have no idea," she admitted. "Dita mentioned it resembled a symbol she had seen in Prague before, especially on older architecture."

"She has a good eye. I believe I spent one afternoon showing her . . ." His neck turned red again. "Well, what's important is that this seems to be a symbol in Prague. If I were to take a guess, it reminds me of something I have seen during my visit to one of the holy places in the city."

"Holy place?" Kateřina cocked her head, her voice rising. "That doesn't make sense. Why would Heydrich's driver be directing me to a holy place?"

"Who, now?" Emil raised an eyebrow, recognizing the weight of the connection.

She hesitated, realizing she might've revealed too much. "Oh, someone who provided me with some information. I suppose it's not entirely relevant now. Do you know which synagogue or church this symbol might represent?" Before she finished asking the question, Emil went to one of the bookshelves. He searched for a moment before pulling out a book titled *A History of the Old-New Synagogue*. He brought it to the table and began flipping through the pages.

"That drawing there, the Star of David as you know, is surrounded by what appears to be a structure, not just a symbol. I've seen this before, I believe . . . yes, it's right here." He pointed to a picture in the textbook of a piece of furniture that very closely resembled the drawing. "The chair of Rabbi Loew can be seen at the head of the Old-New Synagogue in Prague. I saw it myself last time I visited."

Kateřina's breath caught. *A chair? That man's dying wish was for me to have a picture of a chair?*

Emil leaned back, choosing his words carefully. "Given the current climate, everything is symbolic. Everything has a deeper meaning. This is especially true in Prague under Nazi occupation."

Kateřina's brow furrowed. "Why would something as ancient as the Old-New Synagogue be of any significance to someone like Heydrich, the Reich's Protector of Bohemia and Moravia?"

Emil sighed, pushing his glasses up the bridge of his nose. "Heydrich isn't just a brute. He is cunning and aware of the cultural significance of places. The Old-New Synagogue is not just a building. It's a symbol of the Jewish presence and endurance in Prague for centuries."

She frowned, trying to piece things together. "But why?"

"Perhaps," Emil began slowly, "because to truly dominate and erase a people, one must first understand their history, their symbols. By knowing what binds them, one can aim to sever those ties. Heydrich is intelligent enough to understand that."

Kateřina felt a lump forming in her throat. "And with the rumors . . . about the transports to the east, the concentration camps . . . ?"

Emil's gaze darkened. "Exactly. They're not just attempting to eliminate people physically but to erase them from history. Knowing about the Old-New Synagogue, understanding its significance, and potentially controlling or manipulating its narrative would serve that purpose."

Kateřina's fingers clenched. The weight of the situation, the magnitude of the stakes, suddenly became very clear to her. Heydrich and the entire Nazi machine weren't just waging a war on the battlefield; they were waging a war against memory, history, and identity.

"According to an old story, Rabbi Loew created a being out of clay to protect the Jewish community from harm. *The golem.* Some say it was a protector, some call it a monster, but its purpose was to save them. Maybe it's a coincidence, but the Jewish people need a protector now more than ever."

It's not what it seems. Kateřina remembered the driver's final words. Why would the driver of a high-ranking German officer carry an image of a chair that once belonged to a Jewish rabbi who created a creature to protect the Jews? *It can't be mere coincidence.*

"Coincidence or not, I need to investigate." She drank the last bit of her tea, placed the empty cup on the table, and then rose and turned to face Emil. "Thank you so much for your help, Emil. I don't know if I would have ever found the meaning of this drawing on my own." She headed toward the door.

"Ah, miss?" Emil stepped forward. "Pardon an old scholar's curiosity. But what sort of story leads you to old furniture? What are you writing about?"

She hesitated. She wasn't overly concerned with Emil reporting her. Still, could the truth endanger him? She felt she owed him something for his hospitality and searched for a nugget of information to share. However, Emil seemed to read her body language and stepped back again.

"I understand. I will have to wait to read it like everyone else." He reached over and opened the door for her. "Please be careful. Truth is a dangerous thing to be digging for these days."

Josef's footsteps echoed on the cobblestone streets as he approached the imposing synagogue. Its stair-stepped roof towered high above the surrounding buildings. The evening sun faded on the horizon, casting long shadows. He couldn't shake the unease gnawing at him since he had left his grandfather and Rádek earlier in the day. He had to know what they were hiding. *Is there another reason Grandfather is holding me back . . . does he have a different answer?*

The synagogue doors hung slightly ajar. He hesitated. Should he turn back and forget this nagging feeling? Curiosity got the better, and he pushed the doors open and stepped inside.

The coolness of the interior was a welcome relief. Josef made his way down the nave, his eyes scanning the space for any sign of his grandfather or Rádek.

The Old-New Synagogue was shadowy and dark, dimly lit by a few candles and the mechanical handlight in Josef's hand. Like many buildings in Prague, the synagogue was from ages past. While the intricate designs and furnishings were pleasurable to see during the day, under the dark of night, they always gave him an ominous feeling. *Ancient.* That was the best way to describe what he was looking at. His grandfather believed in the old ways but was also a creator of modern invention. There was absolutely nothing modern inside this building.

The ark holding the Torah scrolls was the very heart of the synagogue. Its doors stood ajar, showcasing the meticulously crafted wooden cases. The candlelight played upon the aged parchment, casting wavering shadows. In the dim glow, the aged stones of the synagogue seemed to murmur tales of bygone generations.

Outside, the Germans rounded up suspected enemies of the state, seeking answers, but time stood still inside the synagogue. It was a sanctuary, a place of peace and contemplation amid the chaos and turmoil. The Old-New Synagogue remained a beacon of hope and faith in a world that was all too often dark and uncertain.

Still, the history of the Loew family was deeply entwined with secrets, and his grandfather was no exception. The Old-New Synagogue, with its centuries-old architecture and dark corners, was where mysteries could be tucked away and forgotten. As he ventured inside, Josef checked the main hall, running his fingers along the ornate wooden pews and the age-old stone columns. His steps took him to the Torah ark, where he hoped to find a clue, but nothing was amiss.

With bated breath, he went to the attic, a place riddled with legends about the fabled Golem of Prague. He hoped to find another hidden treasure: his grandfather's invention. But, as he looked beneath the ancient artifacts and dusty scrolls, he was met only with disappointment.

He then ventured down to the lower chambers, their cool dampness and the faint, echoing sound of his footsteps reminding him of the gravitas of the place—still, nothing.

Each nook and cranny of the synagogue held potential, and as he meticulously checked, he began to feel the weight of despair. He replayed his grandfather's conversation with Rádek, trying to tease out any hidden message or overlooked detail. But the only solid lead he had was this very location. Time was of the essence, and Josef hoped he wasn't too late.

Just when Josef had made his way back to the main foyer and was tempted to give up, he heard the door creak. *Was I followed?* He held his breath, flipped off his mechanical handlight, and stepped behind the stone pillar at the center of the room to listen.

Footsteps echoed. Not the loud thunking of soldier boots, but soft footsteps. A custodian? He didn't want to be caught hiding. That would make him seem more suspicious. And so, he breathed, made a soft faux cough, turned his light back on, and stepped into view.

Before him was the blonde woman from earlier that day. His heart pounded. Was she going to alert the Germans? He ignored the questions. For some reason, he felt he could trust her.

Seeing him, she yelped. "I was just looking for—" She leaned in. "It's you," she said softly, then stepped closer. "I didn't mean to intrude."

"I, uh," Josef started, unsure how to react. "I won't be long. I'm just checking something out."

"Yeah." She nodded. "Me too." She stared at him for a while longer. "Could you . . . perhaps not tell anyone you saw me here?"

He cocked an eyebrow. "Shouldn't be hard. I have no idea who you are."

She hesitated as if deciding how much to tell. Then she stood taller, almost proud, and strode toward him to offer her handshake. "I am Kateřina, a reporter. I'm following a story that has led me here. Are you familiar with this place?"

"Very." Josef released a breath. "My family has been involved in this place of worship for generations. My name is Josef Loew."

"Loew." Her word came out as a whisper. She moved even closer, her face now illuminated by his handlight. She was beautiful.

"That is unbelievable." Her eyes lit up. "Then you're who I need."

Surprise and amusement bubbled up within Josef, making him grin. "Well, that's a surprise." Meeting her gaze, he was struck by the mischievous glint in her deep-blue eyes. "Have you been following me?" he asked, his voice carrying a mix of curiosity and playful suspicion.

"What? No." One hand touched her heart. "I promise you I didn't. What type of reporter would I be if I left a scene like that to follow some unknown stranger?"

"But you found me all the same?" He tried to take his eyes off hers, but it didn't work.

"I suppose I did." Her head turned down, twin creases between her eyebrows. "By way of a library and a historian, I found you. It's as if it was meant to be." Her words were no more than a whisper. "Can you help me find the chair of Rabbi Loew?"

Josef gasped. *Leave the core in the seat at the synagogue.* Grandfather had said those words. Josef didn't think to take the terms at face value. What he needed must be in the chair of Rabbi Loew! But, if that was the case . . . how had she figured this out? He refused to move and instead jutted out his chin.

He shifted the handlight. "Why are you trying to find it?"

"A story, like I said." She pursed her lips as if to keep any more words from coming out. But when Josef, too, stayed silent, she narrowed her eyes. "There *is* something special about that chair, isn't there? Where is it? I want to see for myself."

"I don't know anything special about it." The lie was so blatant that even a child would be unconvinced.

It spurred the woman into action. She pulled a mechanical handlight from her satchel and beamed the light around like a detective on a case, illuminating the room like a searchlight. She also pulled out a small piece of paper, referencing it against the furnishings—a treasure map leading her to clues.

Even though he knew he should have more questions, Josef found himself watching, waiting.

She nodded sideways toward a hallway. "Are you going to sit back and enjoy the show? Or are you going to help?" Her smile was infectious, and he found himself drawn to her.

"Of course. I can take you there."

She followed him through the labyrinthine corridors of the ancient synagogue. He'd been working on his inventions for the last few months without knowing if anyone cared. His grandfather certainly didn't. Even today, he'd been an extra lookout, but what had he accomplished? Nothing.

But now Kateřina followed him. She was right, there was something special about that chair, and for the first time since his father had left, Josef felt he had a purpose. Yes, he was helping her find a chair, but there seemed to be more. For some reason, they were in this together.

Trust in the Lord with all your heart. Josef could almost hear his father's voice, rich and steady, reciting the ancient Hebrew Scriptures. *And do not lean on your own understanding.* In his younger days, whenever Josef felt a peculiar tug or intuition about a person or event, his father would gently remind him, *Remember, my son, sometimes these feelings are Yahweh's whispers to our souls, assuring us we are on the right path.* His father's wisdom, imbibed from years of studying the Torah, was a comforting anchor.

But now, staring at this woman, a reporter of all things, in the gathering storm, Josef grappled with confusion. Could she indeed be part of Yahweh's plan for him? It seemed improbable, almost absurd. Yet the urgency of the day's unfolding events left him little room to ponder or protest. Time was of the essence, and he had to move forward.

Leading Kateřina to Rabbi Loew's chair made him feel alive. Like he had been sleepwalking for years. Josef wanted to know more about her, be near her, and protect her.

When they finally reached the chair of Rabbi Loew, Josef fixed his eyes on it, genuinely taking in its grandeur. How often had he glanced at it yet never observed its magnificence? The chair stood as a testament to its era, constructed from a deep, rich mahogany that spoke of times when artisans spent countless hours perfecting their craft. The backrest was adorned with intricate carvings, depicting scenes from the Torah, each figure meticulously etched with attention to the finest details. The arms of the chair had similar detailed patterns intertwined with Hebrew letters, perhaps prayers or blessings. To complement this craftsmanship, the seat and back were upholstered in a plush, regal fabric, probably once a deep shade of blue or purple, symbolizing knowledge and royalty. It wasn't just a chair. It was a piece of history, resonating with the wisdom and authority of the great Rabbi Loew.

Kateřina turned to Josef, eyes full of wonder. "This is it," she breathed. "This is what I've been looking for." She hurried toward it.

"Wait!" He caught up to her. "You shouldn't be here. Don't touch anything."

"Says the man hiding and trying to make up an excuse for being in this synagogue." She scoffed at him. "Neither of us saw each other here, alright? Let's leave it at that."

Then her face softened again. "Tell me about it. How is it used?"

"The rabbi's chair is an important feature in the Jewish community. It's the seat where the rabbi sits during religious services, lectures, and other important gatherings."

Kateřina inspected closer and pointed. "Now that I see it in person, I can more clearly make out the carving." She pointed. "Symbols for the Star of David and the Ten Commandments." She nodded. "The lion of Judah."

He'd seen it hundreds of times but never with such wonder.

"But what makes you so special?" She directed her question at the chair as if expecting it to respond. Her gaze then shifted to meet Josef's. At that moment, a silent understanding and mutual curiosity passed between them.

He found her presence undeniably perplexing. He was only here because he'd overheard his grandfather. How could a reporter have heard of this secret at all? Let alone the very same night? It was a coincidence beyond belief. Surely, if his grandfather had indeed concealed something within the chair, there was no way an outsider, especially a reporter, would discern its secrets.

Yet as this thought crossed his mind, and before he had a chance to again ask her intent, she knelt before the chair, her fingers delicately exploring its surface, searching.

"Ah, here you are." She popped out a small hidden compartment from the underbelly of the chair. There appeared to be a locking mechanism, but it did nothing to stop her.

Josef gasped and dropped beside her to see what she had found. Both of them fell silent as they beheld an empty compartment. No invention nor secret of any kind was inside.

"Someone got here first," Kateřina finally said. She aimed the handlight directly at Josef's face. "You unlocked it and took what was inside, didn't you? Tell me what you found."

He blinked against the brightness and gently pushed down her handlight.

"I didn't take anything." Tears pricked his eyes, and emotions rushed over him. "I didn't even know before today . . ." His thoughts swirled and spun like a whirlwind.

He swallowed back the lump in his throat, thinking of last night. Grandfather wanted to tell him something, but he'd refused to listen. His chest bore the stone of his grandfather's unspoken words.

Josef sat beside Kateřina, attempting to make sense of everything that had happened in the last few hours.

He was certain neither his grandfather nor Rádek would have been able to make it here before him since their discussion. Whatever was in there had been taken before tonight. "I can't believe it's empty."

Josef scooted down to further check the compartment. Then he searched for any additional hidden mechanism, keyhole, or anything that would show other secrets. He felt around inside, nothing at first, but then his fingers encountered thick residue. He pulled his hand back to examine it under the light.

"Clay?" he wondered aloud. "Someone stored clay in here?"

"Clay?" Kateřina echoed his confusion and reached in to feel around herself. "Why would someone put clay in the chair of an old rabbi?"

Josef's mind flashed to his dream, to the legend. *The golem*. A clay construct made by his ancestor, so said the myth. Not that he'd divulge this information to the reporter. He had no idea of her intentions. Perhaps she was even working with the Germans to uncover hidden Jewish artifacts.

He eyed her suspiciously, only to see her handlight now focused on a nearby wall. Following the direction of her attention, Josef's eyes landed on a faint reddish smear on a candle fixture. Clay. It matched the very hue that stained his own hand.

Forgetting his questions about the reporter, he went over to investigate. Upon inspection, he saw that the fixture was a very similar design mechanism to the ones he'd seen at the clock shop many times. It took him only a few seconds to understand its workings as he twisted the candle in a particular way. The section of the wall from which it was attached popped open, revealing a hidden door.

They left clay on the secret lever. That didn't seem like something Grandfather would have done. It was careless.

Yet, would he have even noticed it on his own? Likely not. Without the reporter's keen observation, that hidden passage might have stayed secret to him indefinitely. Furthermore, the unsecured mechanism within the chair only added to the enigma. How could one be so thorough in crafting concealments only to leave them so vulnerable? Two theories arose: either some interloper had meddled with these hidden treasures before he and the reporter arrived, or a sudden, pressing event had forced Grandfather and Rádek to abandon caution. Both possibilities made Josef's stomach churn with unease, and he wasn't sure which one he feared more.

"Finally, we're getting somewhere." Kateřina joined him at his side. She had her camera raised and took a picture of the hidden door.

"Hold on, who said you could come?" Josef asked incredulously.

"We're accomplices in a break-in, aren't we?" She winked. "I won't tell anyone you came here as long as you don't stop me now."

Josef frowned. He couldn't have some reporter spouting all sorts of nonsense about him. He couldn't afford to deal with his grandfather finding out. Or worse, the Germans getting on the trail of whatever his grandfather was working on. He'd need to find a way to get her off this story, but he didn't have many options. "Fine. But I'm keeping an eye on you."

"Do what you want." She shrugged and opened the door. "Should you go first, or should I?"

Intrigued, Josef opened the door fully. It creaked as it gave way. Descending the first few steps, he felt a chill in the air. The musty smell of damp earth and stone greeted his nostrils. A rush of emotion flowed over him. It was the same feeling as if he stood on a narrow ledge high above the ground, with the fear of falling ever present.

The stairs led Josef deeper underground, away from the bustle of the city above, and Kateřina followed closely, her handlight cutting through the darkness, guiding their path.

After what felt like an eternity, the stairs leveled out, and a dim light came into view. An ornate lantern hung suspended from the ceiling by a chain. Its wavering flame threw eerie shadows that danced on the walls. The very fact that it was lit suggested someone had recently been there. The unsettling thought struck Josef: perhaps the last visitor was still lingering nearby.

Rádek stood alone in a laboratory, the sounds of his work drowned out by the light buzzing of the robust electrical systems that echoed throughout the open space and tunnels leading toward it. His body ached, especially his one good arm. He had been pushing himself for weeks, working longer hours than ever.

Tools, devices, and various scraps were scattered across tables and workbenches. He was engrossed in refining a particular device, a compact transmitter. It was imperative that it functioned flawlessly. *The weapon must strike any target without fail, no matter who they are.*

He went to screw on a covering, and his right hand twitched and dropped the screwdriver. The tool clattered against the table, knocking small pieces onto the ground. Rádek cursed and gripped his twitching hand. He'd need an adjustment.

"Ah, Rádek." Samuel Loew's voice echoed through the expanse of the laboratory in a mix of surprise and conflict. The easy gait with which Samuel entered as if strolling into his office for another mundane day caused the nerves in Rádek's jaw to twitch. Seeing his old friend donned in the customary trench coat and bowtie was both a comfort and a disturbance. The warmth of their camaraderie usually brought solace to Rádek's weary soul. Yet tonight, of all nights, he had desperately hoped for solitude, yearning for the uninterrupted concentration his current dilemma demanded.

He considered hiding the device, but no. Too late. Surely Samuel would notice. "Things are escalating. There is no time for rest."

"We need time to finish it, to get it right," Samuel declared, clapping his hands together for emphasis. "Give it a few more weeks. I believe we might just see it come to life when we activate it!"

You have no idea.

"Soon," Rádek agreed as he casually finished assembling the device. "There are many more possibilities we could pursue. Like those flame launchers you added. Why are they on the rear of the machine? What will it try to burn behind it?"

"Oh, that?" Samuel chuckled. "Wait until you see it work. I'd love to take all the credit, but it was Josef who truly envisioned its capabilities."

Rádek's chest tightened. "You told him?"

"Oh no." Samuel gestured dismissively. "He was working on a tool of his own. I would explain it, but it would be easier to show you when the time comes."

"There are an endless number of modifications that could be made, but time isn't on our side."

"The sentiment of every true inventor. We might always feel our creations are incomplete." Samuel pointed past him and into the following chamber. "This device is particularly dangerous. We need to set up a test to evaluate it with as little risk as possible."

"Risk indeed," Rádek murmured under his breath, then raised his voice. "Samuel, do you ever worry it might not suffice?"

"What more would you have it do?" His old friend chuckled and motioned to the massive casing mounted on a raised platform at the back of the chamber. Its towering shadow stretched far, reaching heights akin to the building itself. Intricate details adorned the casing's surface, reflecting the meticulous workmanship behind it. "With this guardian by the side of the Jews, I am confident none would dare harm us in its presence."

Rádek took a deep breath. "I am not speaking of the construct itself. I am speaking of what we intend to do with it. Is it genuinely sufficient for the golem to guard people as they seek refuge and flee?

What becomes of them in the absence of the golem? No amount of shielding will rid them of their enemies."

Samuel's face turned dark. "I understand. My grandson shares your sentiments. He wishes to retaliate against the Germans."

"Merely the impulsive bravado of a young man," Rádek replied with a chuckle. "But with our resources, if we truly wished to fight, they wouldn't stand a chance."

"That is a dangerous path, friend," Samuel warned, his gaze piercing through to Rádek's core.

Rádek felt a tightening in his chest, the weight of the decisions they had to make bearing down on him. He could feel the heat rise in his face, and his hands clenched involuntarily. The gravity of the moment caused a swirling storm of thoughts in his mind. *With our fight, every move we make carries risks*, he internally argued.

Meeting Samuel's eyes, Rádek asserted, "It is war. There is no safe path."

"There is truth to what you are saying." Samuel paced thoughtfully. "But even if that is what we wish, there is more you don't fully understand. The machine cannot be controlled like a dog or a soldier. That is why I have yet to give it life. I cannot presume to control it completely. I do not know its nature."

But I do. Rádek gazed at the device in his grip. Should he tell him? Or would Samuel reject him, knowing what he'd been doing behind Samuel's back? *Risks.*

"That is not true. I have been working on this for some time." He offered the device to Samuel. "It works only with simple orders. But it has listened."

Samuel's gaze fixed intently on the device, disbelief evident in his eyes. "Has listened? What are you implying? You surely haven't activated it already! You shouldn't have the means to . . . Have you already procured the core?"

"Listen, Samuel."

"No!" Samuel's sudden movement caught him off guard as he snatched the device from Rádek's hand. "You dare to command it with this? When did this happen? When was I excluded? Did we not swear transparency to each other, especially when tampering with forces we barely understand?"

"I have control," Rádek insisted, his voice dropping to a hushed tone. "I even took it through the streets. It heeded my commands."

"You dared to take it out in the—" Samuel's words caught in his throat, and his mouth clicked shut, eyes aflame with rage. Rádek was taken aback by the intensity of the emotion, reminiscent of Samuel's passionate younger days. He'd never been on the receiving end of such anger from his friend and colleague. The weight of it was both startling and unnerving.

"Just examine it. It's functional," Rádek urged, trying to defuse the situation.

Samuel's searing gaze held him for a beat longer and then shifted downward, scrutinizing the device. He carefully inspected its details, even prying open a cover to get a better look at its inner workings. Spotting a specific component inside, his expression shifted from anger to reluctant acknowledgment. "I see your handiwork," he conceded, holding the device closer to his face. "It's a rudimentary design, yet it might be effective. However, its effectiveness in controlled circumstances doesn't guarantee its predictability in combat. If we weaponize it, there's no telling the chaos it might unleash."

I know that.

"It is not like our enemies can create what we have," Rádek argued. "Even if they had our plans, they couldn't—"

The door burst open. Dozens of Nazi soldiers poured into the room with weapons drawn. They shouted commands in both German and broken Czech.

They're here too soon! How did they find this place?

Rádek scanned the ranks of soldiers, searching. One face was conspicuously missing. Could she have inadvertently shared her intelligence with those less discerning? But deep down, he knew better. It had to be her handiwork. *Persephone.* He could almost picture her sly, triumphant smirk as she orchestrated his detainment.

"No!" Samuel, with a sweeping gesture of his arm, cried out, "Run! Find shelter!" He sprinted toward Rádek.

Only when Rádek saw a soldier leveling his rifle did he grasp Samuel's urgency. The sharp sound of gunfire erupted. Moments later, a chilling spray of crimson stained the floor.

In the muted glow, Kateřina snapped photograph after photograph of the underground pathways. She'd heard tales of them but hadn't realized the vast expanse they covered. These routes appeared isolated, seemingly disconnected from the main network of underground streets. She could only imagine what other hidden pathways existed beneath Prague. This story would be unlike anything that had been put to the press in years, and she was the one uncovering its secrets. After reaching the bottom of the stairs, she took the lead, her handlight lighting the way.

She stepped around a stone pillar. The heavier footsteps of Josef followed close behind. She didn't know what to make of the young man. She tolerated him for now because he seemed honest enough. He might be connected to the story, based on the name he'd given her. Besides, she had to admit he was rather attractive. A young, attractive companion was a welcome change compared to the likes of cold-blooded Hilbert.

Kateřina stole a brief look at Josef. Regardless of her father's opinions, she had unraveled this mystery on her own. A mere slip of paper had guided her to this subterranean labyrinth, leading to . . . whatever significant revelation awaited them. Her excitement swelled within her, akin to a symphony crescendoing toward its climax, painting the silent tunnels with unseen melodies.

Then she met Josef's gaze. His eyes were narrowed. The exuberance within her fell like a discordant note, disrupting the harmony. And the reality of what they were facing hit her.

The unsettling presence of the clay gnawed at her thoughts. Why clay, and why here? She recalled the familiar clay from the banks of the Vltava. But its presence in a chair? And, more specifically, *that chair?* It felt ominous. The realization hit her suddenly: the clay wasn't merely in the chair; someone had taken it out and traversed the secret passage. *Why?*

The air around her felt cooler, more foreboding. Was that person still lurking somewhere in these shadowy tunnels?

A shiver ran down her spine, her heart racing as a touch of paranoia crept in. The dim torchlight revealed long-forgotten archways and old brick walls, reminiscent of a time when the city thrived at this lower level. This was a world she'd never known to have existed under her feet. The underground had its own life, with cobbled pathways leading into darkened alcoves and the distant echoes of water dripping somewhere, giving the place an eerie resonance. The walls told tales of centuries gone by, with faded inscriptions and remnants of paintings hinting at old Prague's stories.

Is he still resentful of my presence? she mused, giving a slight shrug, pulling her coat tighter around her, seeking comfort from the creeping cold of fear. The underground was a maze, and every shadow seemed to hide a lurking danger. *He'll warm up in time.* Hopefully, before they encountered whatever—or whomever—left that clay behind.

She wasn't merely here for personal gain with this discovery, whatever it was. She wished to experience it firsthand, to put pen to paper and record this hidden piece of history. She had no intention of laying claim if there was a family heirloom. Any treasures that might emerge from this subterranean world belonged to their rightful heirs. But to prove herself, to show her worth to her ever-doubting father? That was the kind of validation no amount of gold could buy.

"How far does this go on?" she asked casually.

"How am I supposed to know?" Josef scoffed.

That didn't work. She had hoped to coax out information. But maybe he honestly didn't know what they were trying to find either.

Was it possible they just happened to be in the same place at the same time, searching for something unknown? Unlikely. Impossible, even. Unless something had drawn him to the synagogue, same as her.

Her fingers itched to write. She could practically feel them gliding across the typewriter, sharing with the world the secrets of the underground Prague and how Reinhard Heydrich had thought to unmask them before his brutal assassination attempt.

Something ahead caught her attention. Kateřina quickened her pace—a treasure hunter searching for a lost artifact, driven by the promise of discovery. She beamed her handlight like a metal detector, scanning the ground.

She saw a pile of clothes—no, wait, it was a person? She slowed her pace, unsure of what she was seeing. The crumpled man lay in a pool of water. Or . . .

Kateřina paused, her stomach lurched, and a gasp escaped her lips. Crimson liquid pooled around the body. The person was terribly injured. The blood was fresh.

Josef shouted, "Grandfather!" He raced past her toward the body and slid down to a stop at the man's side. "Why are you down here, and what happened to you?"

Josef carefully turned the older man over to his side. He was still breathing, slow and ragged. His eyes fluttered open, and with quickened breaths, he reached out. Trembling fingers grabbed Josef's arm tight.

"Josef? Is that you?" the man uttered weakly. His white-knuckled fingers quivered.

A surge of anxiety coursed through Kateřina. Unsure of the next move, she knelt beside Josef. The man's breaths mirrored the faltering ticks of a dying clock, each more labored than the last.

"How can we aid him? What must we do?" Josef's voice echoed with desperation.

The man struggled to breathe. Josef gave a cry of alarm and carefully lifted his grandfather into a sitting position. Blood drenched his white shirt from multiple gunshot wounds.

Josef supported his grandfather's weight with one arm while using the other to rub his back and soothe him. The man's eyes clouded with pain.

"Grandfather, I am here. I am so sorry. I don't know how to help." The old man's gaze flickered with a glimmer of hope as he looked up at his grandson.

Kateřina's mind raced. There had to be something they could do. *Should I go get help?* She had no idea who to turn to, who to trust. And even if she could find someone, it would be too late by the time they got back. This man was beyond help. Josef's face contorted. He seemed to know there was no chance of saving his grandfather.

With each passing moment, the man's breathing grew more labored, his grip on Josef's arm weakening.

Watching over the older man with unwavering determination, Josef recited what she believed to be prayers in Hebrew. *"Shema Yisrael."* His reassuring voice was calm. *"Shema Yisrael, Adonai Eloheinu, Adonai Echad,"* he chanted softly, his voice steady. The ancient Hebrew words seemed to bring solace to the man's troubled soul. The man's eyelids fluttered shut.

Josef's eyes widened in panic. "I'm going to get you out of here. Get you help."

The older man shook his head. "No. No. I need to tell you. It is crucial."

Kateřina found herself a useless observer. She knew nothing of medicine or even first aid. Shame rose in her, but even that could not move her frozen body.

"It can wait," Josef pleaded. Tears streamed down his cheeks. "I'll bring a doctor, Grandfather. They'll help you! They have to help you! You're Samuel Loew!"

Samuel pulled up an arm that had previously been limp and dropped something on Josef's lap. From what she could tell, it was a small device of some sort. "Speak," he said, now sounding even weaker than before.

"Who did this to you?" Josef asked, anger rising in his voice.

"Germans could still be near." Samuel took a few shallow breaths. "You cannot be seen. You must go. Now."

"Go? How can you ask me to do that?"

"Please, heed the words of a man taking his final breaths," Samuel rasped. Gripping Josef's arm, he drew him near. "Go to where he rests. Rabbi Lowe." Those words slipped from his lips as they parted for the last time. The life drained from him, and his weary body sank unmoving.

The echo of distant footsteps reached their ears—faint but growing in number.

A knot of anxiety formed in the pit of Kateřina's stomach. She rubbed Josef's shoulder sympathetically. "We should listen. They could hurt us too."

Kateřina felt the weight of Josef's shock and grief as he silently followed her lead. The rhythmic echoes of their footsteps in the shadowy tunnels only heightened the haunting silence surrounding them.

As they navigated the labyrinthine paths beneath the city, Kateřina's mind raced. She had set out to uncover hidden history and a captivating story, but the reality she confronted was far more raw and personal than expected. Each step seemed to intensify the gravity of leading Josef to his grandfather's side in his final moments. What was once a tale of intrigue had transformed into a heart-wrenching journey. The line between observer and participant had blurred.

What is going on? The thought entered her overwhelmed mind. *Did the Germans really kill that man? Why?*

For the first time since she decided to tackle the mystery of the symbol given to her at the scene of Reinhard Heydrich's attack, she did not feel excited about where this journey would lead her. This was not a mere scoop. She had become entangled with deadly forces. Despite all the death she had been reporting on, this hit her heart. Now, she found herself *again* at the side of a dying man desperately sharing what little information he could.

This is big. The biggest story I may ever be a part of.

That thought did not fill her with anticipation. Instead, it chilled her to her very core.

Josef cursed himself, his legs heavy with shame as they pulled him back into the street. He had left him—Grandfather—lying there alone. Alone. Before long, the Germans would do who knew what to his body. He had no doubt they would treat it as if they had found a dead rat lying on the street.

How did this happen?

So many questions tore through his mind, unearthing dark thoughts like a shovel digging into his brain. His view of his grandfather was shifting. What led him to work underground, beyond even the view of his community? Samuel was a simple man, a clockmaker, and an inventor. To have been working on something so dangerous that the Germans would seek him out was unfathomable.

"Go to Rabbi Loew—Rabbi Loew's grave, right?" Kateřina spoke up. "You must know where that is."

Josef's brow furrowed as he glanced her way, having momentarily forgotten her presence. To him, she appeared solely concerned with her next journalistic scoop. Was it too much to hope for a brief moment of solemn reflection amidst their harrowing ordeal?

The streets of Prague were tense. German soldiers came out in greater force as night fell. Though most paid them no mind, Josef found himself the target of distrusting glares and sneers. As far as he could tell, they didn't see him as a threat. It was hate. Hate for being born.

Josef tried to shake off his unease, but it lingered like a dark cloud. He had to stay vigilant, to keep his wits about him in this difficult time. The war had made enemies of friends and turned allies into foes.

As he turned a corner and headed down an alley, a group of soldiers stood like menacing statues ahead, their faces etched in stern determination. A bolt of fear struck him, lightning-fast and electrifying. He had to tread carefully to make it out of this alive.

Kateřina yanked him to the side as a spider-tank leg pierced the cobblestone where he'd just been. The tank didn't slow as it continued its patrol. The drivers inside had no concern for almost killing a civilian. Josef's emotions mirrored the cold metal—detached and unyielding. Without a word, he signaled Kateřina to follow him into the silent embrace of the graveyard.

"Why is this place so significant?" Kateřina mused as they navigated through the Old Jewish Cemetery in Prague, a space that felt like an ancient library of tombstones. Stacked haphazardly upon one another due to lack of space, they lent an almost chaotic appearance. Thousands of stones jutted out, marking the final resting places of many, even though many more lay buried beneath. The surrounding walls of the adjacent synagogues and buildings made it feel like a hidden sanctuary in the city's heart—the oldest graves, moss-covered and worn by time, dating back centuries.

"Why should it matter?"

He glanced at her, she looked surprised by the bitterness in his tone. "Don't you want to discover what he intended you to see here?"

"He was a misguided old man. Too cautious. Always preferring to hide instead of standing up. And where did that lead him?" Josef's fists clenched, anger apparent in his stance. He swiftly walked until he halted before a specific gravestone that seemingly held the key to his grandfather's last wishes. "So, I'm here, Grandfather! Do you have one last piece of wisdom to share? Some archaic saying that's lost its meaning?"

"Josef, you're shouting," Kateřina warned softly.

"The dead don't hear anything." He reached under his coat and pulled free his handlight. He glared at the grave of Rabbi Loew and raised the butt of his handlight.

"Whoa there," Kateřina whispered as she touched his raised arm. "*Hněv je špatný rádce.*" *Anger is a bad advisor.*

The words halted him. He'd heard them often because of his nasty tendency to get like this when he was hurt. Grandfather was always there to guide him back to where he was supposed to be. Even when the unthinkable happened, Grandfather never wavered. Josef's arms fell limply to his sides. Tears welled in the corners of his eyes.

"What am I supposed to do without him?" he asked no one in particular. His knees weakened, and he lowered himself to the ground. He closed his eyes and tried to steady himself. Yet what his fingers touched wasn't cold earth. It was soft like clay and warm. His eyes opened, and he took in the earth before him. It appeared no different from any of the dirt on either side of the grave.

He closed his eyes again and touched the ground. Soft and moist like at the river's edge. He could almost smell the Vltava. And warm, as if warmed by the sun. Yet, that was impossible.

Josef was aware Kateřina's eyes were on him. He grabbed a fistful of the earth, allowing a sob to burst forth. Then Josef gripped his handkerchief and pulled it out.

He heard quiet ticking, like one of the many clocks back in Grandfather's shop. He felt for his watch, forgetting that he had neglected to put it on that day.

"Do you hear that?" he asked. But Kateřina was already worriedly turning her head from side to side, searching for the source of the noise. He opened his mouth to inquire of her, only to be interrupted by a powerful gust of wind. He shielded his face momentarily. Then, as if a vapor hardened into a solid mass, an enormous figure appeared before him.

The towering figure loomed several feet above him, casting an ominous shadow. While unmistakably mechanical, it bore an uncanny humanoid silhouette. Its frame was sculpted from gleaming metal. Josef could see intricately designed gears in motion through gaps in its chest. Unlike a pocket watch's delicate, precise gears, these were robust and substantial, reminiscent of the grand mechanisms that powered the city's clock tower. The rhythmic ticking emanating from the behemoth added a haunting tempo to its presence.

He gasped and fell backward, his fear like a thunderbolt striking his heart. Kateřina curled up next to him, gripping his arm. Yet the machine made no aggressive action toward either of them. It merely stood and waited.

Once the initial shock faded, Josef looked at it inquisitively. The design was familiar somehow. As if he had seen something like it before.

Golem.

A name surfaced in his thoughts, echoing tales and sketches he'd encountered throughout his life. In some legends, the golem emerged as a guardian for the Jewish community, a beacon of hope and strength. Yet, in other, darker narratives, it transformed into a rampaging behemoth, mindlessly taking lives, indifferent to the cries of the innocent. Could it be? Had his grandfather aspired to reawaken this mythical entity?

Josef rose and paced in front of the creature—so different from the one he'd imagined. While Rabbi Loew smoothed clay, his descendant Samuel Loew, had connected steel with hinges, nuts, and bolts. Or that is how it appeared at first glance. But as he looked closer, the machine was covered in a different material—ceramic, crafted from clay. In Hebrew, one word stretched across the creature's forehead: *BREATHE.* In the legend, the inscription upon the forehead breathed life into the being. Was it the same for this golem?

The machine reached toward them, and Josef flinched. But long moments passed with no harm. Its hand remained stretched toward Kateřina, who cautiously touched one of its fingers.

It chose her. Golem chose her.

"Do you recognize it?" Josef uttered, a hint of desperation in his tone.

The perplexity in her eyes was clear, her eyebrows furrowing slightly as she shook her head. "I've never encountered anything like this before."

So why her? Hadn't Grandfather been the creator?

Josef cautiously approached, scrutinizing the entity from a distance. Was there someone manipulating it from the shadows? Or did it harbor an autonomous system, allowing it to move of its own accord?

Awe sparkled in Kateřina's eyes, a mix of fascination and incredulity, making her face light up. "It's astounding," she remarked with an exhilarated smile. "I've truly never seen its like."

Josef lifted his gaze to take in the towering creature. "Me neither."

Looming at an impressive two stories, the golem dominated the backdrop of the Old Jewish Cemetery. Its silhouette contrasted starkly against the ancient tombstones and the crowding buildings of the Josefov district. Not as stocky as the spider tank, it was a fascinating blend of engineering and antiquity. Steel shafts formed its arms, held together by large, rusting bolts. The assembly of gears and other components, each welded meticulously onto a central frame, hinted at its intricate design.

One arm slowly lifted its shadow, casting it over the uneven cobblestone pathways and almost touching the ochre-colored roofs of the baroque and Renaissance buildings surrounding the cemetery.

Josef watched, transfixed, from behind an age-worn tombstone. Was there a puppeteer behind this giant? Or did it possess some innate intelligence, allowing it to operate independently?

The golem's eyes, deep and observant, tracked Josef's every move. Yet, they showed no sign of aggression. "Can you communicate?" Josef ventured, his voice barely more than a whisper, but the golem remained silent, its gaze unwavering.

"What should we do with it?" Kateřina asked Josef. "What can it do?"

Josef shook his head. "I have no idea. But whatever it is, we should keep it out of German control. They killed my grandfather for a reason."

"But how do we do that?" she asked.

"I know of a place. A warehouse. If we can get it there without being seen." He beheld the giant machine before him. "Well, I don't know how we can do that."

Kateřina raised an eyebrow, her tone nonchalant. "It has the ability to become invisible, correct?"

Josef nodded hesitantly. "It seems so. But how can we command it?"

Locking her gaze with the golem, Kateřina asked assertively, "Is it within your abilities to vanish from sight once more?"

Josef scoffed but was immediately humbled as the machine faded before his very eyes, along with a powerful gust of wind. Before Josef had time to finish gasping at the sight, the machine seemed to vanish from existence.

"Incredible," Josef awed. "Is it invisible or gone?"

Kateřina reached out in front of her, like the golem had done toward her earlier. After a short moment, her arm lifted upward slightly, and she smiled. "It is here. I can feel it touching me. Also, listen carefully."

Josef closed his eyes. As the other sounds around him faded away, the faint ticking of clockwork rose once again. Muffled, but there. The same sound he had heard before the golem had revealed itself to them.

"I can hear it," he whispered.

"Will you follow us now?" Kateřina asked into the air, presumably toward the golem. She waited for a response, a light blush forming on her cheeks. "Um, where is the warehouse?"

"This way." Josef led her out the other side of the graveyard and back into the streets of Prague. His heart still felt heavy, but a glimmer of purpose was in him now. A tiny candle in a sea of inky black. He focused on that small light.

He purposefully chose roads that would have as little traffic as possible. The streets in the Jewish sector were tranquil as it was now entering nightfall. He couldn't tell for sure whether or not the golem was following them. After all, shouldn't they hear heavy metal footsteps meeting cobblestone, similar to the tanks? Or a large arm brushing against the walls of one of the narrower streets?

"You! Jew! What's your business being out after curfew?" A cluster of German soldiers approached with stern expressions.

Panic gnawed at Josef's insides. *The golem!* He desperately scanned the area, but the massive figure was still invisible. Or was it gone? Amidst the echoing footsteps of the approaching soldiers, he couldn't discern any hint of the golem's mechanical ticking.

"You think you can ignore me?" A soldier seized his shoulder, spinning him to face his accuser. "Answer the question! Why are you out past curfew?"

Before he could respond, the soldier was suddenly thrown backward, yanked as if by an invisible force. The other soldiers shouted in alarm and raised their weapons. Kateřina bolted for the alleyway. Josef rushed after her, raising an arm to protect his head as bullets began to fire.

Dashing through the serpentine alleyways, the echoes of their footsteps seemed to summon more German soldiers. Shouts in German rang out, converging from every direction. Rounding a corner, Josef met a group of agitated soldiers barking orders, their words foreign and jumbled to his ears. As he raised his hands in a hasty attempt to surrender, a volley of gunfire erupted from their rifles.

Josef barely had a moment to react. Bullets sped toward him but struck an invisible barrier with metallic clinks as if hitting solid steel. Each projectile clattered harmlessly to the cobblestones. The soldiers' faces contorted with confusion, but they fired again in desperation. The outcome remained unchanged. Neither Josef nor Kateřina bore any injuries.

He locked eyes with Kateřina. "It's shielding us! We need to move, now!"

They continued down a different alley, evading the Germans as best they could. Had it not been for the golem, they would have been killed a dozen times. Though they could neither hear nor see it, it constantly shielded them from harm.

But Josef felt their luck run out as they came face-to-face with a spider tank. The machine slowly turned its cannon toward them and halted. On the top, a hatch opened, and a soldier emerged from within.

"Halt! Are you part of the Czech resistance?" the soldier spoke fiercely in broken Czech.

"No!" Kateřina shouted. "I am a reporter! I have nothing to do with the resistance!"

"A reporter?" The soldier squinted and examined her. "Then why are you traveling with this cowardly Jew?"

"Why am I with him?" Kateřina's words faltered. Then, a ticking sound echoed, and her face brightened. "This Jew is my friend." She jutted out her chin. "He is braver than you ever dare to be."

The soldier pointed his rifle at her, and Josef sucked in a breath. Kateřina didn't waver.

With a rush, a gust of wind buffeted the area, and the golem appeared as if from thin air. It stood directly before them, arms stretched wide in a protective stance. The soldier shouted and fumbled his rifle. It clattered down the tank's side, falling to the cobblestone. The German dropped down into the tank, disappearing.

Josef stepped as far behind as possible. Could the golem even protect him? Could it stand against a spider tank like this? Would it even try? He turned toward the machine. "Golem, destroy that tank! Please!"

The golem turned back toward him, almost as if confused.

Josef turned to Kateřina, but she seemed unsure whether to try and give the order herself.

Doesn't she see this is necessary?

He remembered the device Samuel had given him and how he had told him to "speak." How had he not thought of it before? It was a crazy idea, but he would try it. He lifted the device to his mouth and spoke the command again. "Golem, destroy that tank!"

The golem lurched and turned toward the tank less naturally than it had moved before. It pulled its arms in and then launched itself forward. As the spider tank fired a round, Golem gripped the cannon and lifted it upward. The resulting shot launched into the air, crashing into the side of a nearby building.

The screech of strained metal rose as the spider tank attempted to extricate itself from the golem's grasp. A forceful tug-of-war ensued in its efforts to retreat over the tank's mounted cannon. A shot grazed the golem's shoulder, scattering shards of metal and composite material. Momentarily, the golem relinquished its hold on the metallic limb, recoiling to dodge. But soon, it grappled the spider tank's cannon again with renewed ferocity.

Side guns emerged from the spider tank, pelting the golem with small bullets. These had little effect, and the cannon started to bend. The metal twisted and cracked until the cannon became a useless hunk of metal. In response, the tank tried to move forward as if to run over the golem. In a lightning-quick motion, the golem whipped an arm down, snapping two spider-tank legs in a single sweep. The machine lurched, and the golem stepped forward, grabbed it, and then lifted the tank into the air.

The soldiers inside crawled out like insects, bailing from their positions and dropping onto the ground at the golem's feet. It watched them briefly and then threw the mangled spider tank down the street without hitting anyone.

The soldiers were too stunned to fight back and too focused on the golem to care about Josef and Kateřina.

"Josef!" Kateřina prodded him in the side. "We can escape!"

He nodded and followed her down the side road as he lifted the device to his mouth again. "Hide again, Golem! Follow us to safety!"

Josef's footsteps resonated against the ancient cobblestones. The evening's chilling wind whispered tales of distant smokestacks, burning logs, and the more immediate, acrid tang of gunpowder. The city was on edge, and the Germans' ruthlessness this night proved why. A high-ranking official was teetering between life and death. And someone, as always, would have to pay.

Gripping the intricate device Grandfather had given him, Josef could scarcely believe his absence. Grandfather was really gone.

The weight of the gadget felt immeasurable in his hand. It wasn't just the heft of the metal and gears, but the gravity of its purpose, the countless souls relying on his next moves.

The urgency of the situation pressed heavily on him, pushing him forward. Behind him, the towering silhouette of Golem and the more delicate form of Kateřina cast elongated shadows on the streets.

The frosty bite of the air nipped more viciously than he remembered from past nights, with each exhaled breath materializing in transient, ghostly mists.

As his pace momentarily faltered, Kateřina drew level with him. The fleeting touch of her fingers against his was a spark of warmth.

"How much farther?" she asked, her voice barely above a whisper.

"We're nearly there." He turned and asked Golem to turn invisible. Without hesitation, the creature obeyed.

Rounding one last bend, they were greeted by a nondescript

wooden door, seemingly identical to countless others in the Josefov district. But appearances were deceiving. With a precise sequence of knocks—two quick, one paused, and then another—the entrance groaned open. Behind it, Nikolai's eyes, first showing relief, shifted rapidly to apprehension when he saw Kateřina.

"You brought someone else here? Who is she?" Nikolai hissed.

The taste of salt from his tears lingered on Josef's lips as he licked them nervously. "She's a reporter," he began, only to be cut off by Nikolai's sharp intake of breath.

"A reporter?" Nikolai's voice was a low growl. "In these times? We don't need any reporters—we're being hunted! She could jeopardize everything we've worked for!"

Josef locked eyes with Nikolai's, the weight of recent events pressing heavily on his shoulders. "Nikolai," he began, his voice tinged with urgency, "Kateřina was there. She witnessed our attempt on Heydrich's life." He took a deep breath before continuing. "I had stepped forward, ready to confront Heydrich, and if it weren't for her urging me to leave, I wouldn't be here. I'd be . . . gone." He swallowed hard, his eyes glistening with unshed tears. "There's so much more we need to tell you, but first, you must trust me when I say I trust her."

The atmosphere grew dense, the tension palpable. Every sound seemed to magnify—the soft rustling of leaves outside, the distant hum of the city, the ticking that sounded like an old clock.

Kateřina stepped forward, her heels echoing against the wooden floor. "I know you have every reason to be wary," she said, her voice calm yet assertive. "But my intentions aren't to expose or exploit. I'm here to understand, to ally, to support."

Nikolai met her gaze, his hardened expression softening a touch. He sighed, brushing back his hair. "Alright, Kateřina, I will let you inside. But you must realize what we're involved in is bigger than any individual. The fate of our entire people hangs in the balance."

"When I saw Josef risking himself today, I had to intervene." As she spoke, the gentle lamplight in the warehouse illuminated her face, revealing sincerity. "The clues led me here to the heart of Prague's legends. To Rabbi Loew. And to the golem." A hush fell upon Nikolai, broken only by Josef's ragged breathing.

"Golem?" Nikolai took a step back and shook his head.

"You must let us in," Josef said, much to Nikolai's confusion. Josef hurried to open the tall warehouse door.

As Josef entered the dimly lit warehouse, a rush of mixed sensations enveloped him. The familiar scent of aged wood and dust was immediately present. Blackout curtains covered the tall windows on the far end, but a hint of silvery moonlight still managed to seep through the edges, casting a muted glow.

Sensing that Golem had followed them into the space, Josef shut the door behind them.

"Grandfather always believed in the tales of the golem, of its power to protect our people," Josef's voice cracked. "And now, when we need it most, it stands before us."

Josef took a deep breath, the cool, damp air of the warehouse filling his lungs as he stepped further inside. The door closed behind him with a soft thud, shutting out the sounds of the city. Almost instantly, the massive form of the golem materialized before him, its imposing presence casting a shadow that seemed to darken the space even more.

Golem's silent figure loomed large. An old memory flashed before Josef. The tale passed down through generations—of Rabbi Loew's creation and of the golem's legendary power to shield the Jews of Prague.

Beside him, Nikolai's eyes widened, clearly taken aback by Golem's imposing stature. "Is this . . . the golem of the legends?" he whispered, a hint of awe and disbelief in his voice.

From the shadows of the warehouse, the murmurs of a few other men began to rise, calling Nikolai's attention away.

"Nikolai, we need to discuss this," one of them began urgently.

"Wait," he instructed firmly. Turning back to Josef and Kateřina, he said, "Stay here. We'll be right back." He then approached the men, leaving Josef and Kateřina with Golem.

The powerful machine that had torn apart a German spider tank made only the slightest of ticking sounds as it waited before them. Its large, glowing blue orbs for eyes illuminated the otherwise dark warehouse. It all felt like a dream. The only indication of reality was Josef's legs, which still burned from sprinting through the streets of Prague.

The golem had always lived in Josef's dreams. Reddish-brown like the clay on the banks of the Vltava River and like the tiles on roofs that stretched down from Castle Hill, spreading like a king's royal robe toward the Czech countryside. He'd always pictured the creature's surface marked with divots where fingers pressed deep and spread out. Whenever he thought of Rabbi Loew, the creator of the mystical creature, Josef had pictured Grandfather Samuel. Tall, thin, with a long, serious face until he smiled. Had Rabbi Loew smiled when he'd stepped back from his towering creation? Josef guessed so. This golem was different than he had imagined. With a clean design and metallic bone structure within. There was science involved, clear principles he had seen in Grandfather's other works. But part of him wondered if there was a mystical nature he could not see.

It was a different enemy that hunted them now, but an enemy all the same. The Jews in their city had scurried into every basement and rushed to every attic to hide. Still, it hadn't stopped the predators from rounding up their prey. Yet instead of devouring them, the Nazis had shipped them off, hiding their deeds behind stone walls and barbed wire. Men, women, and children were rounded up like sheep and transported to their slaughter. How often had Josef begged Grandfather to join their efforts to hide and transport those most valuable?

Under his breath, Josef shot accusations at Grandfather, questioning why he had secretly built this massive machine instead of directly helping those around him. Even now, the image of his grandfather slumped in a pool of blood haunted him, filling his eyes with tears. Abandoned and cast off like an old coat that someone had outgrown. They needed to retrieve his grandfather's body to give him a proper burial. But first, they had so much else to do.

Care for the living before dealing with the dead. The words echoed in Josef's mind, almost as if his grandfather had whispered the advice. With the Germans intensifying their hunt, Hermina and her children—and many others—stood no chance unless he acted swiftly. It was not enough to hide them in the secret place behind the clock shop. Josef needed to find a way to get them out of Prague.

But even before that, he had to get Kateřina to safety.

Grandfather, how can I do this without you? How did Rabbi Loew do it?

The weight of memories and decisions pressed down on Josef like a millstone, grinding him to a near standstill in the warehouse. Every beam and plank of the building seemed saturated with the history of Josefov, the scent of ancient wood infused with an undertone of machine oil, serving as a backdrop to a tale of heartbreak and hope.

With each syllable he uttered, Josef felt the heaviness of responsibility bearing down on him, making his shoulders sag. "You need to leave Josefov, Kateřina," he insisted, voice thick with emotion.

In the low light, Kateřina's form seemed like a flickering shadow, but the fire in her eyes was brighter than any flame. "I need to follow this through," she whispered defiantly.

He could hear the murmur of old memories, echoing the same determination he now heard in Kateřina's voice.

"It's not just the golem or the Germans." Josef's voice trembled like a leaf caught in a tempest. "It's the treacherous terrain of our every step. Every alleyway, every turn, it's a potential trap. This isn't your battle to fight."

She moved closer, her presence like a balm to his frayed nerves. "Maybe not at first, but now it is. The pain, the stories of despair, they've imprinted on my soul. And alongside that despair, I've found hope. Hope with you."

Every word she uttered, each step she took toward him, was a tug at the strings of his heart. "Kateřina," he murmured, frustration and fear dancing in the pit of his stomach. "Every passing moment endangers Hermina and her children. I cannot—will not—endure another loss."

"Who is Hermina?"

His heart clenched, the very mention of the name triggering a flood of memories. "She's a beacon of strength, enduring more than anyone should have to. When they took her husband, when they tore him from her side, I couldn't remain idle. So, I hid her and the children away, thinking a week's sanctuary would be enough before we could find a way out."

With trembling hands, Josef pulled a photograph from his pocket and passed it to her. Its edges were worn, but the image remained clear: two angelic girls, their happiness captured in a moment, contrasting the grim world outside. The young boy beside them seemed lost in thought, as though he bore the weight of the world on his tiny shoulders.

A memory came unbidden, of Josef closing a door on them, effectively locking them in their gilded cage. The sound of the door latching shut echoed in his ears, like the final note of a dirge, condemning Hermina and her children to a prison he'd built with the best of intentions.

"It's heartbreaking," Kateřina whispered, her voice trembling. "These children and Hermina, they deserve better." She handed back the photograph, their fingers briefly touching, an unspoken commitment passing between them.

"I had hoped to give them a week's worth of food, thinking it would buy us some time," Josef admitted, a hint of frustration in his voice. "But I was only able to gather a day's worth. My hope was to get them out of the city, away from all of this. But with each passing day, the situation becomes more dire. Those children are just caught in the crossfire."

"Then let's not waste another moment. We'll do everything we can to protect them and get them out of this hell."

"You shouldn't get involved."

Kateřina's gaze met his, fierce and unyielding. "I need to follow this through," she repeated, her tone resolute.

He clenched his jaw, memories of his grandfather flooding back, each more painful than the last. The looming presence of the golem, both an inspiration and a haunting reminder of what was at stake, pushed him further into his resolve. He had to act, and quickly.

Drawing in a shaky breath, he took Kateřina's hand, gripping it tightly. "We move fast, and we move now. But remember, Kateřina, it's Hermina and the children that are our priority."

The air in the warehouse grew tense, the conversation between Josef and Kateřina becoming an almost palpable entity. She nodded, gratitude shadowing her gaze.

Guilt and memories swirled inside Josef like a tempestuous storm, making it hard to breathe. Every glance at Kateřina conjured images of others he had failed—the lifeless gaze of his grandfather, left behind in a desperate escape. The weight of past mistakes threatened to pull him under, but the immediate crisis anchored him to the present. The story of Golem, that mythical protector, felt both a beacon of hope and a distant fantasy. But the very real, very present danger to Hermina and her children demanded his attention.

From the shadows, Nikolai stepped forward, his eyes, darkened by concern, locked onto Josef. "You both speak too freely," he warned, his voice edged with a hint of panic. "This place is no fortress. Every word could be an echo that reaches unwanted ears."

A chill coursed through Josef, the fear in Nikolai's voice amplifying his own apprehensions. "And yet standing still, doing nothing, ensures our doom," Josef replied, his voice resolute despite the tremor he felt deep within.

Nikolai scanned the dimly lit space, his gaze resting momentarily on the golem. "Sometimes silence is our greatest weapon," he murmured, making Josef ponder the weight of that statement amidst the gathering storm.

Nikolai's eyes darted between Josef and the looming figure of the golem once more. His brow creased in deep thought. "And what about that . . . thing?" His voice betrayed a hint of mistrust.

Josef felt the weight of the room shift toward him, the onus of explanation squarely on his shoulders. He swallowed hard, memories of legends and tales from his grandfather swirling in his mind. "I don't want to involve the men," he began, "especially when I don't fully understand the golem or the extent of its powers."

As the conversation continued, Nikolai excused himself with quickened steps.

Kateřina moved closer to the golem, her fingers brushing its smooth surface. The two connected almost as though through a magnetic pull.

Turning to Josef, her eyes shone with determination. "But what if this golem, this protector, was brought to life for this moment? For Hermina, her children, and all the innocent souls trapped in this nightmare?"

A flood of emotions swirled within him, each one threatening to break the dam of his stoic exterior. Her eyes, filled with conviction and hope, pierced through the walls he'd built around himself. His heart rate quickened, and he felt a warmth spread from his chest, contrasting sharply with the cold, damp air of the warehouse.

Doubts gnawed at the edges of his thoughts. *Could it be? A divine intervention in these desperate times?* He swallowed hard, feeling the weight of the moment on his shoulders. His fingers twitched involuntarily, a physical manifestation of the internal battle raging within.

"You believe it's . . . a sign from above?" he asked, voice quivering ever so slightly. "That we're meant to use the golem?" The very idea was both terrifying and exhilarating, and he teetered on the edge of belief.

Kateřina nodded, her conviction seemingly unwavering. "Throughout history, there have been times when the impossible became possible, when miracles guided the course of events. Maybe this golem, this ancient guardian, has been resurrected for a time like this. We may not fully understand its purpose, but perhaps we're not meant to. We need to have faith."

Josef sighed, torn between hope and skepticism. "Using the golem could be our best chance, or it could be our downfall."

"Or it could be the miracle we've been waiting for."

Josef's gaze drifted to the oil-painted portrait hanging on the warehouse wall, portraying Rabbi Loew, the legendary protector of the Jews. What steps would he have taken in a time like this? One man had indeed achieved the impossible, defending the Jews of his era. As Josef stood, awestruck by the golem's silent majesty, he felt an added weight of responsibility. Golem was more than just a machine. It symbolized hope and protection.

"A bit terrifying, isn't it?" he asked.

"Terrifying?" She raised a genuinely confused eyebrow at him. "Of course not. He is gentle and kind. From what I recall, you were the one who told him to fight that tank."

That's it. Josef marveled at the golem's powerful arms, capable of bending metal and breaking stone. *It is a dangerous weapon if it can be told what to do.*

"He is going to help people," Kateřina's eyes gleamed as she patted a large metallic hand. "Aren't you?"

"When did we decide it was a 'he'?"

"Look at him!" She waved emphatically. "Broad shoulders, wide chest. It was shaped after a man, so it must be a he."

Shaped after a man. Josef pondered the words as he observed Golem's form. Who had Grandfather based the design on? The pain of loss stung. Based on how Josef still felt when his parents came to mind, he imagined the wound would never heal. Not really.

The reality was that Grandfather had died making this machine. He deemed it necessary enough to jeopardize his life. That alone was frustrating. Grandfather had always told him *Our lives are our greatest gifts.* He'd always dissuaded Josef from throwing his own away to fight the Germans. So why, then, had he ignored his teachings to put his own life on the line?

"What your grandfather did was amazing." Kateřina gently touched Josef's arm. "You're thinking of him, aren't you? What happened was terrible. But he still lives in you and in his creation."

A sorrowful chuckle escaped. "I think you're right. I think he would have liked you, and the golem sure does."

"You need to be friendlier, that's all." She gave a playful shove. Golem turned its glowing orbs down at her. "See? He's a gentle soul. He wants to preserve life."

Josef grimaced. He didn't want to spoil her enthusiasm, but machines could not think or feel. He needed to figure out how exactly the device interpreted commands to execute them.

Still, something that could sit there silently for hours upon end, with no stimulation, was undoubtedly incapable of independent thought. There had to be some other reason it seemed drawn to the reporter. He scrutinized her. Perhaps it was something about her appearance. Like the color of her clothes or the way she walked? How her hair shimmered in the light? Maybe something about the way her eyes glistened. Or was it the graceful way she moved about?

"What is it? Am I doing something wrong?" she asked.

Josef realized he had been staring for a while longer than was polite. He had become distracted. "Oh, no, it's nothing."

She looked skeptical, clearly doubting his words. A surge of frustration rose in Josef, causing his heart rate to spike and a flush to color his cheeks. "I need to see how the others are doing," he said briefly.

Walking a short distance, Josef soon found Nikolai just beyond the meeting-room door. The man's face was inscrutable, his emotions well-guarded.

"What's the verdict?" Nikolai inquired. "Is the creature trustworthy?"

Josef hesitated, searching for the right words. "I can't be entirely sure. But it did shield that reporter and me from the Germans, even intercepting bullets meant for us."

"Indeed, we must address the creature and your involvement with that journalist later," Nikolai declared, his voice betraying frustration and genuine concern. His eyes, which had seen more than their fair share of treachery and war, darkened even further. "We have received news. Kubiš and Gabčík are already seeking refuge in the catacombs. Even here, we're not safe. It's only a matter of time before they storm in. A journalist revealing our affairs could be our undoing."

The very mention of Kubiš and Gabčík, the would-be assassins intensified the palpable tension in the air.

"I don't know what to make of the reporter yet," Josef admitted, his voice tinged with uncertainty. He cast a lingering glance over his shoulder, catching a distant view of Kateřina. She seemed engrossed, maybe even communicating, with the golem, their shared moment from earlier hanging between them like an unsaid promise. "I believe Kateřina means no harm. At least not intentionally. I will ask her to keep our secrets."

Nikolai's eyes, hard as flint, met Josef's. "Promises are good until the torture starts," he responded, his voice cold and matter-of-fact. A pause lingered, heavy with unspoken thoughts. "Well, we may all be dead soon anyway."

In a bid to prove his trust in Kateřina and to put to rest some of Nikolai's concerns, Josef finally voiced a decision. "I'm going to take her to the clock shop," he stated firmly, determined to lay down his cards. "It's time she understands just how much I trust her."

Somewhere in the distance, Kateřina heard a church bell toll, its mournful chimes echoing through the silence of the evening. Josef, his face partly illuminated by a flickering light, stood rooted to the spot, staring intently at her.

"I'm going to show you," he began, his voice heavy, "the people I'm protecting. If you truly desire the entire story, then prepare to witness it."

Kateřina's gaze strayed to the towering form of the golem nearby. "We should bring him. The golem might offer protection."

"No. We don't know the extent of its stability. I can't risk it. If the golem was to turn. If anything happened . . ." Josef's voice broke. "I'd never forgive myself."

After a few heartbeats, with the hum of the city as their backdrop, Kateřina relented with a nod. "Alright."

"I need to know how serious you are about helping. Do you know what is happening in the city right now?" he asked.

"In our part of the city, we hear rumors." Her fingers traced the wet, cold stones of a nearby wall. "It's easy to hide from the truth. Especially when it is a truth we do not want to hear. I know now that things have gotten worse than I dared think."

Kateřina felt Josef's gaze fix on her, the dim glow of the lamp highlighting the traces of genuine concern in his eyes. What lay behind those depths? Could he discern her heart?

"There is something inside that tells me I need to trust you." Josef's voice quivered. "My grandfather often said that the Loews have an inner knowing." He swallowed hard, pain evident in his gaze. "Or that's what he used to say."

"Maybe you hear the whispers of God?" It wasn't something she thought much about, but her mind took her back to her days as a child. "I remember walking past this part of town as a little girl. Children are curious, of course. I didn't understand why the people dressed differently, especially the men in dark suits, black hats, and long side curls. I would stare, as children do, and my grandmother never stopped me. As we walked, I would grip her tighter. And once— maybe the third time after we passed—I asked why these people were different." Kateřina crossed her arms and tucked them in close.

Josef tilted his head. "And what did your grandmother say?"

"She said, 'These are the people chosen to receive the law of man and the ones who hear the whispers of God.'" Warmth and a strange longing brimmed in Kateřina's chest even as she said those words. "It's strange. I haven't thought of that in years."

With a hesitant touch, Kateřina then turned and reached out to the golem, the coolness of its ceramic surface contrasting with the warmth of her fingertips. "Go invisible," she whispered, her voice barely audible. "Stay here."

Golem remained still, like an ancient statue gazing down upon its creator. Then, slowly, it faded until it blended seamlessly with the surrounding shadows, nearly indistinguishable from the naked eye.

Satisfied, Kateřina turned back to Josef. They exchanged a nod, understanding passing silently between them. Without another word, they set off, their feet tapping lightly against the cobblestones.

The night enveloped them, its embrace cold and unwelcoming, as they moved stealthily through the mazelike streets of Josefov. Every echo, every distant conversation, felt magnified in the silence, urging them to be more cautious. They avoided the glow of streetlights, flitting from one shadow to another, like phantoms haunting the spaces forgotten by time.

After a hurried journey marked by anxious glances, Josef finally halted before a seemingly ordinary clock shop. The vintage clock at its façade ticked away softly, its gentle chimes starkly contrasting the tense atmosphere. The hands of time moved steadily, uncaring of the secrets that lay hidden behind the shop's wooden door.

Josef gestured toward the door. "Would you like to go inside?"

Kateřina nodded. He opened the door for her, letting her go inside as he followed shortly after. She was greeted by a magnificent chorus of ticking from the dozens of clocks around the humble shop. Each one appeared to be carefully carved and fitted with unique fixtures.

"Seeing it from outside is interesting, but this is amazing." She slowly spun around, taking in the sights and sounds.

"This is my family's shop, but it hasn't been open in years. It belongs—belonged—to my grandfather. My father would have inherited it were he still here, so I suppose that means it's mine now." As he talked, Josef began winding up one of the ticking clocks to keep it running.

"I'm sorry about your grandfather." She pursed her lips, unsure if she should have brought it up.

"Thank you. I cannot speak of how it was when he took it over, but this shop has become a special part of the community." Josef stopped, glancing at an antique clock for a few lingering moments. "I don't know how they will hold up without him."

"The Jewish community?"

"Yes, the remnant which remains." He nodded to her. "They often came to him for guidance. Now, I'm not sure what they will do."

They lost their leader when they needed him most. She felt an urge and followed her heart as she walked over and gently hugged him. He tensed at first, but then his body relaxed, and he returned her hug. They lingered for a few moments before separating, and Josef pulled out a chair for her to sit on while he sat down near the wall.

"Even associating yourself with me can be dangerous," Josef said. "I know what you said to me and Nikolai, but if you chose to walk away—"

"Never." The word erupted from her with an urgency she hadn't anticipated. She blinked, her chest heaving as she continued, "I realize these people you're protecting are yours, but I can't just be an observer. I won't. You must understand I have connections with many of those who are inflicting this pain upon your community. My presence here isn't just coincidental. I'm here to help in every way possible."

Josef paused, a subtle softening in his eyes. "If that's the case, I want to show you something. To make you witness the full extent of their malevolence."

Without another word, Josef led Kateřina deeper into the clock shop, every step resonating with echoes of days long gone. The familiar scent of wood and oil told of countless hours spent at workbenches and amongst ticking gears.

They reached his grandfather's workbench, a division between the past and the hidden present. "Once, clocks of all shapes and sizes chimed together," he said. "That world is gone now. Only this clock, an artifact from the sixteenth century is not kept wound, Grandfather's orders."

Kateřina eyed the iron-and-copper façade, a testament to the craftsmanship of a bygone era. It looked similar to the one in her father's office, as if they had been crafted by the same maker. "Why that clock?"

Josef simply shrugged and turned his attention to a humble wall clock. Josef's fingers deftly opened its glass face. He precisely wound the clock's hands, the minutes ticking by until they rested on 10:17.

The subtle *click* that followed sounded louder than any chime in the silent shop. To Kateřina's amazement, a grandfather clock beside them gently swung open like the pages of a book, revealing a hidden passage. With a gesture for her to follow, Josef slipped through the small doorway. After she also stepped through, it closed behind them.

They'd stepped into a secret workroom filled with the aroma of dust and machine oils. A workbench sat in the center of the room with a gaslight hanging above it. The walls were lined with shelves. One set of shelves held tools. Another set was filled with contraptions of every size and shape. There was a bookcase, too, with boxes of old documents.

Kateřina watched as Josef hurried to the center of the room. Nearing the table, he reached up to the hook holding the gaslight. For a moment, she expected him to remove the light. Instead, he grasped the hook and turned it counterclockwise.

A grinding noise caused her to jump, and the floor under her feet shook slightly, offering the vibration of a truck driving by on a bridge. A deep moan sounded from the back wall, and the section next to a built-in fireplace swung as if on a hinge. Kateřina stepped into a hidden closet, noting piles of clothes. Then the piles of clothes moved. Kateřina gasped.

They were not piles of clothes but children. As her eyes adjusted to the dimness, she spotted a hunched figure in the corner. From the smoothness of her face, she appeared to be a young woman. Still, with the way she was crouched, with a gray blanket pulled tight around her shoulders, her frame resembled the illustrated drawing of the witch in Hansel and Gretel.

Kateřina stepped forward cautiously. The woman's eyes widened as if seeing her for the first time. Her mouth opened as she pulled back, pressing herself against the wall. Kateřina paused, looking down at her own perfectly tailored coat. She touched her hair, which still felt grimy from the blast.

Does she think I am a German coming to take her children away on a transport?

"I am not going to hurt you. I want to help." The words came out, and at that moment, Kateřina knew they were true. She'd do anything to help this woman and her children.

"They would rather hide here and be together than risk being dragged away." Josef shook his head. "Trying to add sense to their senseless violence is a pointless endeavor. The Germans have no real reason for hating us."

"Josef," the woman spoke up. "My children need more food, fresh water."

"Yes, I know. I will bring more in the morning."

"But why not now? It's quiet outside. If I could just take them—"

"No!" the word shot from Josef's throat. "You have to stay here."

"But what if something happens to you? Besides, they are hungry now."

"If something happens, I showed you how to get out. But that should only be a last resort." He fixed his gaze on the woman. "Do you understand?"

The woman glanced away and nodded.

"Be safe, I will bring more food and water in the morning. I promise."

Josef led Kateřina back out and closed the hidden door. He paused and released a breath, perhaps wondering if the woman would listen and stay safely hidden.

Kateřina stepped back, glancing around the workshop once more. "I'm honored to have your trust, but why did you show me?"

Josef did not answer but held her gaze.

The throbbing pain shooting from Kateřina's heart took her by surprise. Perhaps he wanted to make sure the woman and children would be cared for if something happened to the Jews who remained. Could that be it?

She eyed Josef, seeing him for the first time. Really seeing him. Josef was a man but still part boy. Good-looking with dark, curly hair, full lips, and a pointed chin. His clothes were worn, and she lost count of how many patches covered the elbows of his jacket. Although the war had been hard on everyone, Josef seemed to carry an invisible burden she didn't fully understand.

If Josef is caught, he will be killed, she told herself. *Then again, he could also be rounded up and sent away at any time.* He was so brilliant and kind, wiped out for no other reason than the Jewish blood that pumped through his veins.

"Do you worry that something will happen to you and you couldn't return to help them?" She studied him to gauge his response, but he turned away.

Josef paced three steps to the window and back again. He had every reason to be jumpy. "Come, we must get you out of this district. You found what you were looking for, haven't you?"

"But what's going to happen next?" she dared to ask. With the golem? With us?

"Just like I told Hermina, give me until the morning. I need to think things through."

"Yes, of course."

The hushed streets of Josefov welcomed them as they stepped out of the clock shop. The tall stone buildings on either side cast long, haunting shadows in the waning light. The once-bustling district, a mosaic of life and laughter, now felt eerily quiet, as if it held its breath, waiting for the next blow to fall. The stillness was unnerving, and every footstep they took seemed to resonate, their echoes carrying whispered tales of despair and hope intertwined.

Kateřina couldn't shake off the surreal feeling enveloping her as they moved through the winding alleys, trying to avoid soldiers. The day's events played in her mind like an old reel. Images of the golem, the secret chamber in the clock shop, and the desperate faces she'd witnessed. The note—the simple piece of paper that had started this whirlwind—felt like a relic from a different life. But Josef, walking beside her, seemed like a constant, as if their paths had always been meant to intersect. There was a familiar comfort in his presence, an inexplicable bond that transcended mere hours of acquaintance.

Finally, they reached the boundary of Josefov, a threshold between two worlds. The moment lingered, suspended in time, as they stood facing each other, the weight of unspoken emotions pressing down.

Before Josef could utter his farewell, the charged stillness was shattered by the rapid patter of footsteps. Nikolai, breathless and wild-eyed, emerged from a nearby alleyway, rushing toward them. Kateřina felt the broken cobblestone beneath her feet and caught the faintest hum of a German vehicle in the distance. The soft scent of rain, a harbinger of an impending downpour, danced on the wind, tugging at the edges of her senses. She wanted it to drown out whatever dire news Nikolai was bringing.

The dim streetlight cast a soft orange hue, turning Nikolai's fear-stricken face into a mosaic of light and shadow as he darted toward them. Nikolai paused before them, voice trembling. "They're gone! Just . . . vanished!"

Kateřina's eyes narrowed. "Who's gone?"

Nikolai gasped. "It's Hermina . . . and her children. The Germans have taken them." Each word that spilled from Nikolai's lips felt like a punch, drawing all warmth from Kateřina's body, replacing it with a numbing cold.

Josef gasped. "Impossible! We were just there."

"Yes, my lookout informed me of that, too. Not minutes after you left Hermina emerged from the clock shop with the children."

"They were hungry." Kateřina's voice was no more than a whisper.

Josef looked around. "There are few patrols on the street."

Kateřina swallowed, the realization hitting her, too. "They are going to specific locations in search of rebels."

Josef turned to her, eyes wide. "The Germans must have gone to the clock shop for a reason. Are they on to us?" He raked a hand through his hair. "Where? Where would they have taken Hermina and the children?"

Nikolai let out a low moan. "How could we ever know?"

Kateřina's breath caught. "I might have a way to find out where they've been taken."

Josef started. "How can you possibly know that?"

"I know people. German officers. I can get information from them."

Nikolai scoffed. "You're going to go and tell the Germans where we are, more like! Why would we let you go to them after seeing our warehouse?"

"It's not like that! I am a reporter, and I know people. I would never tell them anything that puts you or others' lives in danger."

An angry huff came from Nikolai, and he threw his arms up as he turned to Josef. "Do you see now what I meant? Bringing a *reporter* into our midst when I told you the mere knowledge of our operation puts your life at risk? What kind of protector are you?"

Josef didn't flinch at the man's stern words. He met Nikolai's gaze defiantly. "Tonight, when the Germans had me cornered, Kateřina didn't leave my side. She could've easily left me to save herself.

Our acquaintance might be short, but I am certain she bears no ill intentions toward us. She's an honorable woman."

"Please," Kateřina said, "I know asking for your trust is difficult, but I want to help. I *can* help. If I can't use my connections to find one missing family, I have failed as a reporter."

Nikolai started to open his mouth but then closed it and slowly shook his head. "Well, it's not like things can get worse. Fine. Let's meet in three days and share any information we find. God be with you all."

Midnight's cold settled heavily on the ancient cobblestones of Prague as Josef escorted Kateřina home. She followed him out of Josefov, footsteps heavy and sorrow pressing on her heart. The occasional distant clang of a late tram and the subdued murmur of the night wind told tales of an old city steeped in fresh anguish. The dim light from the streetlamps painted ghostly halos, while the moon's pale luminescence added an eerie glow.

As they trudged through the nearly deserted streets of Prague, the haunting beauty of the city stood in stark contrast to the horrors that continued to unfold. The majestic Prague Castle, silhouetted against the moonlit sky, bore silent testimony to centuries of history, while the winding Vltava River mirrored the shimmering stars of the night. And yet, in those serene surroundings, the weight of recent events pressed down upon them.

Their footsteps, a rhythmic reminder of their journey through the cold night, seemed to accentuate the gravity of their conversation. Josef's voice, a low murmur in the stillness, shared tales of his friend Petr's miraculous escape. The stories from Terezín, however, cast a far darker shadow. Terezín, or Theresienstadt as the Germans knew it, had transformed from a fortress town into a ghetto and a transit camp. In this place, Jews from Czechoslovakia and surrounding countries were sent before being transported to camps further east.

Petr spoke of overcrowded conditions, where families were torn apart, and the elderly and infirm suffered the most. Of the façade the Nazis maintained, misleading the outside world about the true nature of the ghetto. Tales of cultural events and performances held there—music, theater, and art—but also stories of hunger, disease, and ever-present fear. Josef's words painted a vivid picture.

Kateřina softly sighed. "That's not the worst of it. At least in Terezín, souls still draw breath." Her voice faltered as she remembered the glass canisters. As the horrifying truth of their purpose took root, she watched Josef's face pale, the shock in his eyes deepening, and his features contorted with horror and disbelief as if he'd been physically struck.

"They're concocting a lethal poison, not for soldiers on the front lines, but for the defenseless—for men, women, and children." The weight of her revelation hovered between them, a chilling reminder of humanity's descent into darkness. Swallowing hard, Kateřina locked eyes with Josef, determination burning within. "And Josef, I promise you, I will do whatever it takes to find out where they've taken Hermina and the others. We cannot let this stand."

The dim glow from a gas-powered streetlamp cast a flickering light over the cobbled streets, revealing brass gears embedded into the stones. These mechanized tracks previously allowed automatic carriages to navigate the streets of Prague with remarkable precision. Yet once the Nazi trucks and tanks rolled into town, those carriages had been parked for good.

They walked until they reached the path leading to the front steps of the home she shared with Father. Kateřina offered a quick goodbye, her breath catching. Their eyes met, and she was momentarily lost in the depths of his gaze, noticing faint gold flecks in his irises. An involuntary warmth spread across her cheeks.

"Be careful, Kat," he murmured, running a hand through his dark hair. She was mesmerized by the way the faint light played upon his jawline and the curve of his lips.

She nodded, trying to calm the erratic beating of her heart. "Always," she whispered, her voice thick with emotion.

Pulling away, she left Josef by the luminescent gaslight and approached her front door. The entrance to her townhouse was flanked by two ornate brass lion statues. The lion to the right whirred, and its eyes—a pair of glowing emeralds—blinked twice in recognition, allowing her entrance. She stole one last glance back at Josef, hoping the night shadows hid the yearning in her own eyes.

The door's cog-and-gear mechanism opened smoothly. As she stepped onto the checkered marble floor, tiny steam vents in the walls released warm air, driving the chill from her bones. She aimed for the grand staircase with intricate ironwork railing shaped like intertwining serpents.

Yet, before she could ascend, a muffled conversation reached her ears—the hum of an electric gramophone mixed with deep, masculine voices from the sitting room. Heart pounding, she edged closer and pressed herself against the cool, ornate wallpaper, listening intently. The unexpected lightness in their conversation was unsettling.

"The advancements in Prague, especially in steam and aether technology, have been remarkable," Sturmbannführer Langer's voice floated, tinged with admiration.

Her father's voice followed, a mixture of pride and nostalgia. "Indeed, they have. But even as the world hurtles forward, some things remain constant." The rhythmic ticking of the gears from the room accompanied his words. "Times have evolved, Sturmbannführer Langer, but alliances built on shared ambitions are the lifeblood of our endeavors."

There was a momentary pause before Sturmbannführer Langer chuckled, a deep, resonant sound contrasting with the delicate machinery around them. "To history and innovation. And to the world, we'll shape once this war is behind us."

Kateřina's brow furrowed. The joviality in their conversation was jarring, given the day's events. What could they possibly be planning?

Taking a deep breath, Kateřina rounded the corner, noting the men amidst a backdrop of moving gears, cog-laden wallpapers, and a fireplace where green flames danced, fueled by alchemical concoctions. "Father, Sturmbannführer Langer," she greeted. "How unexpected to see you at this late hour."

"Please, as I have pleaded before, call me Hilbert."

"I was just heading to my bedroom, Herr Hilbert," Kateřina deflected. "It's been a long day. Goodnight." She turned, feeling the weight of Hilbert's gaze on her back.

"And where have you been?" Hilbert's question pierced the air. "Out late, are you not?"

Kateřina turned, a practiced smile on her lips. "Once I heard of the assassination attempt, I rushed to Josefov. Who else could've been behind it?" She added a note of theatrical intrigue, making it sound like the makings of a riveting tale. "I wasn't allowed inside, of course, but I lingered long enough to see the Jews being rounded up. Such drama, such tension—perfect for a story, don't you think?"

"And did you find your story?" Hilbert asked.

The question caught her off guard and scrambling for a response. Then inspiration struck. "The sun rises over Prague, casting shadows over cobbled streets as whispers of rebellion stir in hidden alleyways. In a city poised on the brink of change, its people are torn between loyalty and hope. The question on everyone's lips: who is our enemy?"

Her father's jaw dropped slightly; eyes widened in disbelief. Hilbert, on the other hand, raised an eyebrow, clearly impressed.

She continued, finding her rhythm. "And sometimes our true enemy is the very neighbor one shares a wall with or the familiar face from the market."

"That's quite the narrative, Miss Kateřina. You've painted a vivid picture that many can resonate with."

Feeling the balance of power subtly shift, she offered a slight smirk. "Every good journalist knows always to be prepared with a captivating lead, even during unexpected encounters."

Her father cleared his throat. "Indeed. Perhaps we should use that in tomorrow's edition, Sturmbannführer Langer?"

Hilbert nodded. "I agree. The essence of your story touches upon the underlying tensions that simmer beneath the surface. It's too compelling to ignore."

She paused, gauging Hilbert's reaction. Should she ask him about the fate of the Jews rounded up tonight? No. Hilbert's leader had been targeted, and she needed to tread carefully. To show too much interest in the Jews might make her suspicious.

She shifted her tone quickly, allowing a hint of concern to bleed. "Compelling and shocking. Is our great leader . . . is he going to be alright?" Her eyes sought his, trying to convey genuine care and concern.

"He's alive," Hilbert said, apprehension in his gaze. "Badly wounded, though. They're doing everything they can."

"Such a terrible thing to happen. Who could've been behind this?" Kateřina's gaze darted between the two men, her father and Hilbert. It struck her as strange, this camaraderie amidst the storm.

"These are not things to discuss tonight. Today was shocking, but soon we will remember who we are—conquerors." Hilbert cleared his throat, looking mildly amused. "To lighten the mood, Kateřina, there's a gathering aboard an airship in two weeks. With Prague's elite in attendance and history in the making, wouldn't it be prudent to have someone documenting the events?"

"With all due respect, Herr Hilbert," she began, treading cautiously, "that is far in the future, considering what transpired today. The city's on edge, and people are scared. It's hardly cause for celebration."

Hilbert leaned back, his smirk unwavering, his eyes a cold shade of calculation. "Ah, Kateřina," he chuckled. "You underestimate the strategy at play. The world might see it as an assassination attempt, but we view it as a godsend. What better excuse to round up ten thousand of our enemies? This act of defiance gives us the pretext we need."

"So, you're saying this whole situation . . . is favorable?"

Her father shot her a warning glance, but she didn't back down and waited for an answer.

Hilbert's laughter was chilling, devoid of warmth. "Very much so. Reports suggest that Heydrich will make a full recovery. It's as if our adversaries delivered a gift right into our laps—a reason to exert our force without drawing the world's censure."

"That's one way to look at it, I suppose." Then she smiled,

considering his veiled invitation. "And this gathering . . . I assume that was an invitation?"

"Yes, of course." Hilbert cocked an eyebrow, waiting for a response. She recognized the opportunity for what it was—a double-edged sword. One slip could spell doom, yet the potential insights she could gain from this event were invaluable. "I'm intrigued," she said, feigning nonchalance. "It's an honor to be invited."

Hilbert's eyes twinkled, a hint of genuine amusement. "Ah, the world seen from the skies offers a different vantage point. Besides, one never knows the alliances one might forge in such settings."

Hiding the fear that caused her stomach to tense, Kateřina replied with a practiced smile, "Thank you. I'll make sure it's a night to remember."

Her mind was already racing ahead, plotting and planning her next moves. The airship event would be both an opportunity and a challenge. She needed to be prepared.

Katarina's room was a symphony of whirring gears and ticking clocks. Antique airships sailed through the hazy skies in miniature, their bronze hulls glinting in the dim light, suspended from the ceiling by delicate chains. A curious collection of figurines from old Czech fairy tales lay on the wall-mounted shelves, framed by brass and worn leather. Tales that spoke of adventures and lessons, of good and evil, and of the human spirit triumphing against all odds.

Kateřina's fingers traced the contours of a rusalka, the water nymph of Czech legends, her steely blue eyes shimmering with a deep-seated wisdom that transcended her porcelain form. But as Kateřina's gaze drifted, her hand stilled over a figure that sent a sharp pang through her heart—the Golem of Prague.

A lump grew in her throat as her mind wandered to the haunting, twisting alleyways of the Jewish district. There, stories of old intermingled with the present-day horrors she was still piecing together. She reached for a tiny replica of one of the buildings from the district, its ornate architecture captured in stunning detail. The weight of it felt solid, almost grounding in her palm. Yet, its implications made her heart race, linking today's mysteries to age-old legends. It was as if their quest had always been destined, interwoven into the tapestry of Prague's past, present, and future.

A rush of memories from earlier in the day invaded her mind. Conversations overheard and questions answered. More questions building and glances exchanged. It all began to piece together. Yet, in the center of this evolving puzzle was something she hadn't genuinely reckoned with for years—faith.

Between volumes of tales and fables, a sacred book awaited her attention. Its aged leather cover, weathered by time, whispered stories and teachings from bygone eras. The Bible—a connection between the fleeting now and the timeless beyond. Memories of her grandmother and tales of faith merged, underscoring the enduring strength of stories.

Kateřina yearned to connect with the intangible in an era dominated by steam, mechanics, and palpable truths. She settled onto her bed, its blue coverlet soft beneath her, and carefully opened the pages of the Bible. Should she delve into it? Was its message still pertinent in this day and age? Or was it merely another collection of tales, not unlike the other stories on her shelf?

She pondered the golem, recalling the tales she had heard. God had often worked through people. Yet instances of God employing creatures to assist His people were few in her memory. Still, there were some. He'd directed Jonah to his destination with the aid of a great fish. He'd even enabled a donkey to speak, delivering through it a vital message. Nonetheless, she had witnessed the golem firsthand. Remarkably, she felt a profound connection with the creature's essence.

Kateřina read the thin pages of the book. It had fallen open to the book of Job. She'd read it before—or at least part of it. It was a sad story of a rich man who lost everything after God agreed to allow Satan to attack him. Yes, Job remained faithful, but at what cost?

Behold now behemoth, which I made with thee; he eateth grass as an ox.

Lo now, his strength is in his loins, and his force is in the navel of his belly.

He moveth his tail like a cedar: the sinews of his stones are wrapped together.

His bones are like strong pieces of brass; his bones are like bars of iron.

Bars of iron? In one of her writing classes in college, she'd learned that Job was poetry, and she understood the bars of iron were most likely thick bones, but she couldn't help but think of the golem.

Kateřina read the words again. Another phrase caught her attention. *Then will I also confess unto thee that thine own right hand can save thee.*

She needed to assist Josef and the resistance. They depended on her to gather information about the Jews who had been taken. She could potentially uncover vital details. But such endeavors came with peril. If discovered, she might face arrest or even execution. And yet, wasn't that the grim fate many in the city were already confronting? Like lambs led to the slaughter.

Thy own right hand can save thee. Goosebumps rose on her arms as she read the words again. Yes, there were times when God swept down and destroyed wickedness, as with the cities of Sodom and Gomorrah. But more often, God used ordinary people to do his great work.

Kateřina pushed the book to the side and leaned back against her pillow. *I promised to try. I have to do it. I am risking my life, but the people who need me will lose theirs if I do not act.*

A low hum from outside the window drew her attention. She saw some sort of contraption, a machine resembling a disk, hovering midair. Kateřina yelped, the Bible slipping from her as she almost dropped it. Cautiously she investigated, opening the window and waiting as the disk hovered in place.

"What are you?" she whispered to the flying machine, her voice a mix of awe and curiosity. She hadn't expected a response, but then she spotted a small piece of paper secured to the underside of the disk. "Have you brought something for me?" she inquired, carefully detaching the note.

Unfurling the note, Kateřina's eyes raced over the meticulous handwriting, each curve and bend of the letters evoking memories of the day's events.

The Germans have increased their presence in Josefov. We must lay low. Two weeks from today *meet me at midnight at the old synagogue. Trust no one else. We must keep safe our guardian. JL.*

Josef.

Kateřina felt a thud in her chest.

Our guardian, Golem.

The resurgence of this ancient protector was a beacon of hope in dire times. Yet why was she the one to whom the golem listened? She wanted to question, but the why didn't matter. Yet her answer did. To meet Josef would take her down a path with even greater danger. This was more than a story now.

Shifting her gaze from the open window to the open pages of the Bible, Kateřina's gaze again settled on a passage from the book of Job: *Though he slay me, yet will I trust in him.* The words, laden with perseverance and faith amidst suffering, gripped her. Kateřina felt a bridge connecting her present to these age-old truths. Like Job, her journey was one of deepening trust.

Looking back to the hovering disk, she noticed something attached to the top of it. It was the same key Josef had used to the clock shop—an unmistakable sign of trust. Attached to it was another slip of paper. Unfolding the new note, she read: "If something happens to me, tell our story." She pondered the word "our." Josef wasn't just referring to himself and the golem. She, too, was now interwoven into this narrative.

The hovering disk, sensing her contemplation, gave a gentle nod, urging her to decide. She knew that somewhere out there Josef maneuvered the small flying machine and waited.

Kateřina approached her desk and the comforting scent of pencil shavings. She wrote swiftly, her response simple:

Understood. Two weeks. Midnight.

She attached her reply to the disk's clip, watching as the mechanical messenger disappeared into the embrace of the night.

A flood of emotions swelled within her: growing concern over

Josef's cryptic message, awe of the golem's legend, and newfound courage rooted in ancient Scriptures. Kateřina was no longer merely a journalist or a friend. She had become an integral thread in a tapestry of faith and resistance that had spanned this land for centuries.

Over the last two weeks, a whirlwind of emotions had enveloped Kateřina. There was an uneasy anticipation tinged with a profound sense of dread, especially about being Hilbert's date at a prestigious gathering that would include Nazi officers and the upper crust of Prague society. The city had been on edge ever since the death of Reinhard Heydrich six days prior. Prague's citizens, already bearing the brunt of the occupation, faced even more severe repercussions.

Thankful for Josef's advice, Kateřina had kept a low profile. Yet, despite her reservations about accompanying Hilbert on the airship, part of her couldn't help but feel a flicker of excitement at the prospect of seeing Josef later that evening.

Kateřina's pace barely kept up with Sturmbannführer Langer—Hilbert—as they ascended the ornate winding staircase. Each step reminded her of the growing unease. A sharp stitch pinched her side while her breath grew ragged.

Hilbert cut an imposing figure in his impeccably starched uniform. The weight of his numerous medals, glinting in the warm candlelight, was a stark testament to his accomplishments and loyalty to the Nazi cause. His hair slicked back gave prominence to his sharp features and cold, calculating eyes. Every aspect of his appearance was meticulously crafted to command respect and fear.

"Are you really taking me to an airship?" she inquired, attempting to lace her voice with humor.

"Yes, to the sky," he replied, a hint of amusement playing at the corners of his lips.

A chuckle escaped her, but it died quickly when the stairs led them straight onto a rooftop. "I've never seen parking like this before" she remarked, glancing at the ornate statues lining the balustrade. Yet what truly captured her attention was the grandeur of the parked airship and a Nazi soldier who toyed with a cigarette case as he guarded the gangplank. His gaze then snapped to Kateřina, scrutinizing, assessing.

Walking over the gangplank and onto a lower deck, her eyes were met with the mesmerizing panorama of Prague. From this height, the city spread like a giant patchwork quilt, its iconic red rooftops shimmering under the evening glow. The Vltava River snaked its way through the city, reflecting the golden lights of the Charles Bridge and the surrounding buildings. Gothic spires and baroque domes dotted the skyline as proud sentinels of the city's rich history. The cobblestone streets she walked daily now appeared as intricate patterns weaving through the city blocks.

The grandeur of Prague Castle could not be ignored. Even from this distance it dominated the cityscape as it sat majestically atop its hill. The view from the gangplank was a beautiful contradiction: a city deeply steeped in tradition and history now under the shadow of a new and menacing regime.

The wind's chilly kiss prompted her to pull her coat closer. The breathtaking sight momentarily dulled the evening's underlying tension. But as she met Hilbert's gaze with a polite smile, she felt a firm grip on her elbow. This man beside her was the opposite of Josef. Josef was gentle yet heroic. He cared for others with a tender heart. Hilbert's goal was to oppress and control, and it was clear tonight she was viewed as his possession.

She shoved thoughts of Josef to the far recesses of her mind as she took her first step onto the airship. The passenger area of the ship was nothing short of opulent, easily rivaling the finest banquet halls in the city. Long tables, set with an array of dishes, ran the room's length and were flanked by men deep in conversation. Servers in white jackets flitted about offering drinks. The air was thick with laughter and the clinking of glasses.

Young soldiers in pristine uniforms guarded the entrance. Their gazes, however, were not on her alone but lingered appreciatively on her companion. There was an added air of authority around him, perhaps even a hint of tension. The subtle straightening of the soldiers' posture was an explicit acknowledgment of his presence and rank.

Trying to maintain her composure and act like this was just another outing, like their visit to the glass factory, she engaged in casual conversation. However, she couldn't help but notice how Hilbert's eyes frequently darted around the room as if searching for someone.

Suddenly, he nodded politely and whispered, "If you'll pardon me for a moment."

Kateřina followed his path as he went to a table occupied by a group unmistakably the Nazi elite, distinguished by their higher-ranking uniforms and an air of self-importance. She watched as he leaned in, exchanging a few words with them, all the while attempting to act nonchalant and unaffected by the unfolding dynamics before her.

Kateřina navigated through the event on the airship, the dim, amber lights casting a warm glow over the rich woods and polished brass. She was drawn toward the center of the room where a large gathering seemed to have formed, the attendees all animatedly discussing matters of importance.

The entire setting felt theatrical to her, as though she had unknowingly been cast in some elaborate stage play. But as the scenes unfurled around her, she grappled with the script, questioning her part in this intricate production.

As she continued navigating the room, she caught sight of a familiar face among the throng of German officials. Her heart skipped a beat. Father?

Why hadn't she been informed that her father planned on attending? And the more puzzling question: why had Hilbert appeared at her residence in the first place? Both men had remained enigmatically silent about their intentions.

Even as their eyes met, Kateřina hesitated. Had Hilbert been at her house because he'd been tipped off to her trip to the Jewish district? Had someone shadowed her to Josefov? Was she now under suspicion for ties with the resistance? She sucked in a slow breath and looked around. Perhaps this was all a strategic test of her loyalty. She was even more thankful now that Josef had told her to keep away, at least for a time.

She made a quick decision. Without a clear script, she'd continue to play the only role she felt she could convincingly portray: that of a committed journalist, aligned with and supportive of their German overseers. The lives of many hinged on her performance. She needed Hilbert to trust her. Only then could she find the information about the rounded-up Jews, including Hermina and her children.

She smoothed her hand down her dress and looked at her father once more. Their eyes locked, and an involuntary shiver passed through her, contrasting with the room's warmth. She approached him.

Amidst the cacophony of the room, her father's voice, dripping with playful sarcasm, pierced the air. "Have we not crossed paths before?"

She pretended to ponder, tapping a finger against her cheek. "Could be," she began with a mock-serious tone, "though I've encountered so many forgettable faces lately." She offered a teasing grin even as a weight settled on her heart. She hadn't said more than ten sentences to her father since the night she and Josef had discovered the golem. Father had often been gone when she'd awaken. And when he came home in the evenings, Father often hadn't been in the mood to talk. But maybe it was better that way. She'd never been very good about hiding the truth from him, and he'd made it easy to keep her secrets these past two weeks.

"Yes, I see what you're saying. I know I haven't been around, and I am sorry about that. Sad to hear my face is forgettable though." His smirk matched hers. "I overheard you're here to chronicle this grand occasion."

"That's unlikely," she retorted, her voice laced with bitterness. "When have my words ever been allowed to stand on their own?"

Their exchange drew curious gazes.

Choosing to disengage, Kateřina gracefully excused herself

from the gathering. Drawn to the observation deck, she needed a moment of respite. Opening the door, she was met with a cool breeze and the expansive panorama below. To her surprise, they were no longer anchored to the building. The airship had silently taken off, disconnecting from the terrestrial world below.

Staring out, she couldn't help but draw a parallel to her life. It had lately lifted off, seemingly without her noticing or granting permission. Everything felt untethered and out of her grasp. She leaned against the railing, contemplating the unsettling thought: perhaps she'd never honestly had control over her life.

Below, Nazism's dark shadow was evident. Marching soldiers and tanks ready to pounce painted a grim picture. Outside was just as stark as within.

Returning to the grand hall, the ostentation of the Nazi regime surrounded her. Everywhere banners emblazoned with swastikas, tapestries showcasing their might, and the unmistakable order of hierarchy of men seating themselves at the tables spoke of power and control.

An orchestra tried to lend some normalcy with their soft tunes, but the notes were lost amidst hushed conversations. Kateřina moved through the room as poised waiters presented trays bearing exotic fruits, cheeses, and meats. She picked up snippets of conversation from various groups of officers. Their voices carrying easily in the grand space, making it impossible not to overhear their discussions.

"You should've seen it," one officer said, a glass of brandy in his hand, his voice laced with perverse excitement. "The village of Lidice. Completely leveled. Nothing left but ash and rubble."

Another officer chimed in, the glint of his medals reflecting the soft light of the chandeliers. "A necessary action to send a clear message to those who would dare oppose the Reich."

Her hands clenched involuntarily, knuckles whitening. The pride in their voices was palpable, and it sickened Kateřina. She forced herself to keep walking and to maintain her neutral expression, although every fiber of her being wanted to shout at them, to demand answers, to make them see the atrocity of their actions.

She overheard another conversation between a group of younger officers, their faces flushed with drink.

"Did you hear about the children from Lidice?" one said, slurring slightly. "Shipped off to German families, the lucky ones. The others . . . well, they won't be causing any problems anymore."

Kateřina's heart felt as though it had been gripped in a vise. The horrors the village had faced were beyond comprehension, and the casual way these men discussed them was enraging.

She took a deep breath, attempting to calm her storm of emotions. The information she had gathered was invaluable, but she needed to remain incognito to avoid drawing attention to herself. Every revelation made her mission more vital. She had to bring the truth to light.

The chime of a fork against a glass silenced all chatter, demanding immediate attention. Kateřina and everyone else turned their focus to the evening's host, who stood tall amidst the opulence.

"Most of us are still in shock of the Obergruppenführer's death," he began with an air of authority. "Even though the brave Reinhard Heydrich succumbed to his injuries, our ranks remain strong. And our prisons, ever more so, are filling with the enemies of our great Reich." Cheers erupted, and glasses were raised in salute, many vocalizing their admiration for the Führer and just as loudly grieving the loss of the Obergruppenführer. The atmosphere was electric—a mix of triumph and vindication.

Feeling suffocated by the boisterous adulation, Kateřina stood to return to the observation deck. The room behind her echoed with hollow laughter and praise, a jarring reminder of the regime's machinations. A waiter near the door handed her a delicate pastry, and she allowed herself a fleeting moment of diversion, the sweetness providing a brief respite from the oppressive ambiance.

She stepped onto the deck and gazed at the expanse of Prague below, with its cobbled streets glowing softly under the streetlights. The peaceful scenery contrasted sharply with the tempestuous events she had recently entangled with. The distant melodies of the orchestra wafted out. For a split second, she entertained the thought of letting go, allowing the dance, wine, and flirtation to numb her senses. However, the stark reminders of the Jewish community's fate, the mysterious tales of the golem, and her growing worries for Josef loomed large in her mind. Her once-beloved haven in journalism now seemed overshadowed by the weight of reality she had to confront.

Her thoughts were interrupted by a presence. She turned to find Sturmbannführer Langer, aura unmistakably commanding. His almost invisible pale eyebrows accentuated piercing blue eyes that seemed to dissect her soul. An unsettling shiver coursed through her as he offered a disarming smile.

"Such a serene night, isn't it?" His voice was velvety, but the undertone hinted at a concealed sharpness.

"It is," she replied cautiously, "but it's hard to enjoy fully when unsettling rumors are circulating the city."

His eyebrows twitched ever so slightly. "Rumors? Do elaborate."

Hesitantly, she ventured, "I've heard whispers about the village of Lidice . . . that it was razed today."

For a fleeting moment, she detected a glint of surprise in his eyes before his façade returned. "Ah, Lidice," he mused, a trace of coldness creeping into his voice. "A necessary action, a reminder of what befalls those who defy us."

Kateřina's heart raced as the implications of her new knowledge washed over her. The fate of those recently rounded up loomed large in her mind. Would they face the same outcome? Thoughts of Hermina and her children surfaced, making her stomach knot with anxiety. The thought that the children of Lidice, being Czech, might potentially find a more favorable outcome—perhaps even being assimilated into German families if they lacked distinctly Jewish features—was a bitter pill to swallow. But the realization gnawed at her. Hermina's children, with their distinct Jewish appearance, wouldn't even be granted that slim hope for life.

She had to gain this officer's trust. It was the only chance to unveil the fate of those whose lives hung in the balance.

"People are scared and confused," she began, choosing her words carefully, her voice betraying a hint of desperation. "Perhaps understanding the reasons behind such actions might help calm the masses."

He eyed her warily. "It's not a story for the faint-hearted. But if you think it will serve your cause, maybe you should see it firsthand. Witness the consequences of betrayal."

She swallowed, the gravity of the invitation weighing heavily on her. "I think it's essential to know the truth."

Their exchange was brief, but the revelations were profound. The tranquil cityscape now seemed to carry a somber undertone. Kateřina felt an even stronger resolve to uncover the truth and stand against the looming darkness.

Laughter erupted nearby, pulling her attention to a group of soldiers, visibly in high spirits, reveling in the ambiance. But their joviality was abruptly overshadowed when another set of doors flung open, releasing a rowdy group of drunken soldiers onto the deck. Their merriment was a stark contradiction to the atrocities they committed. It was haunting to juxtapose these vibrant faces with the mental image of them violently pulling innocent individuals from their homes, displaying no hint of remorse as they enforced their brutal regime.

After arriving home, Kateřina had changed out of her evening dress into a simple pair of dark pants and a dark gray sweater and made her way by foot to Josefov. Even though he asked that they meet at the Old-New Synagoguee, she didn't want to wait. Instead, she'd hurried to the clock shop, using her key to enter. Once inside, she closed the door behind her, finally releasing the breath she'd seemed to be holding for the past two weeks. Kateřina didn't understand why she felt so drawn to someone she'd just met, but she had to know for certain all was well—that he was safe and Golem had remained hidden.

Inside the dim room, every nook and cranny vibrated with

ticking, whispering the passage of time through the rhythmic chorus of countless clocks. Their hands moved in synchrony, but each had its unique tale—much like the people of Prague. The dim light from a solitary candle made the room seem almost ethereal, casting elongated shadows and highlighting the exquisite details of hand-carved cuckoo clocks. She found Josef deeply engrossed in an ancient map of Prague, which sprawled across his workbench.

He looked up abruptly, his eyes widening a fraction. "You're early," he observed, his voice taut with concern.

She took a quick, nervous glance over her shoulder. "I felt eyes on me as I moved through the streets. I had to come when it seemed least suspicious."

Josef's expression darkened. "We can't delay any longer. We must devise a plan, Kateřina. We must save the Jews."

Her fingers played with the hem of her sweater, her voice wavering. "I've yet to pinpoint the exact location, Josef. It seemed unsafe to attempt to pursue information. However, I'll be in Lidice tomorrow." They exchanged a laden look. Worry reflected in his eyes. He had heard the whispers about Lidice, too.

Josef leaned back, rubbing his temples. The weight of their mission was evident, yet amidst the shadows of uncertainty, their unbreakable bond shone brightly, offering a glimmer of hope.

"Josef, how is he?"

"Hidden." Josef's answer was simple.

Kateřina nodded once. It was all she needed to know.

Wind washed through Kateřina's hair as she gazed out the auto window. She took in the sweet smells of a small bakery as they soared past. The sun caressed her face gently, coaxing her toward a tranquil surrender. Her guide, Hilbert, had been extraordinarily gentlemanly today. He treated her with the utmost care and kindness. They conversed casually, and she would consider this a wonderful date if not for the nagging dread that had sunk deep into her gut. Hilbert had been involved in a slaughter. She dare not enjoy such a peaceful afternoon when she thought of families being locked away in some cellar, awaiting a terrible fate at the hand of the man she accompanied, among others.

"They built the synagogue in the thirteenth century," Hilbert continued the conversation, unaware of her hidden discomfort. "When digging under the hill, the workers discovered intact walls of white stone, then a Torah scroll made of deerskin and a few prayer books written in Hebrew."

Kateřina met his eyes directly. "The Jews have been here for that long?"

Hilbert smiled back at her. "They believe from the time of the Second Temple. They built this synagogue on the old and used the white stones as a foundation."

He continued to speak for some time, but she couldn't focus on his words. As the road stretched, she noticed fewer and fewer people about their business. It was quiet and still. For a beautiful day like today, that shouldn't be the case. Her dread grew as she pieced together what they would be visiting. And as they neared the destination, she swallowed the threat of vomit.

She hadn't wanted to believe it was true. As Hilbert parked the car, her body tensed in the seat. *I can't do this. I can't pretend this doesn't matter.*

She stepped out of the car, and the air was too still. The road led to a pile of stones that extended as far as the eye could see. The fields stretched out green. Too green.

In the distance, a cluster of jeeps parked on the road leading to the shell of a building that she guessed once was a church.

Acting like Hilbert wasn't watching her, Kateřina pulled her portable dictation machine from its satchel and placed it on the car's hood. She leaned close and spoke into the voice box. The gentle tapping of the recording key assured her the words were being captured.

"A haunting hush fills the air around the town of Lidice. If traitors believed they could hide in the beauty of the Czech countryside, they were mistaken. Green fields spread in every direction around the rubble, proving that life goes on. No more boastful proclamations will rise from this square. No stone is left unturned when it comes to rooting out enemies of our protectors."

She continued her story, trying not to spit the word *protectors*. Hilbert shuffled at her side, and for the briefest moment, she hoped he'd see the truth. *How could destroying a whole town be protecting anyone? And even if a traitor is hidden in one of these houses, could that justify killing every man, young and old, and shipping off the women and children?*

Yet when she dared to glance at Hilbert, Kateřina recoiled. Where she witnessed pain and despair, his chest puffed out with pride and power.

"The rubble, lifeless and cold, should make each of us consider our alliances," she continued. "We choose to join the cause or be cut down like the trees that line the village. Just stumps, they remind us to choose wisely."

We should weigh our fight and consider what is right. If our walls still stand, a decision must be made to keep them standing. Lidice is no doubt a graveyard of regret.

"You are a gifted reporter, if I do say so myself." Hilbert beamed. "I had wondered how you might act upon seeing a sight like this. But now I see my worries were unfounded. You can see the bigger picture and how this destruction is merely the price paid for treason."

These people had nothing to do with the assassination. You slaughtered a town for pride alone.

Kateřina tried not to think of children's laughter as they played, the glow of brides on wedding days, or stolen kisses behind backyard sheds that no longer stood. Hilbert touched her back, and she tried not to flinch.

"Have you seen all you need?" His chin jutted out.

"I would like to take photos, of course." She retrieved her camera from her satchel, carefully removing the lens cap as she prepared it for some shots.

"If I had known you were interested, I would have brought you here during it all. It was quite the sight. You would have gotten some excellent photographs for your story."

Words could not express how much she didn't want to see that. But she tried to remain curious as she tilted her head toward the man. "You were here?"

"Of course."

"So, can you tell me what it was like?" She feigned approval and lifted her dictation machine close to his lips.

"My soldiers gathered up the men and boys. Others took care of the children." His gaze narrowed. "They begged for their lives and questioned their crime. As if all of Bohemia didn't know. Didn't understand why they had to die." Hilbert opened his mouth to speak more, and Kateřina raised a palm, halting his words. Her stomach lurched, and she thought she'd lose her breakfast all over Hilbert's shoes. And why did she believe eating this morning was a good idea?

"My father is the editor, you know." She batted her lashes at Hilbert. "He still tries to protect me. I'm sure you understand."

"Of course. An editor won't understand the ways of war and what is necessary to preserve the best future for all." He gently directed her back toward the auto. "Shall we head back to the city for lunch?"

"I would be delighted." She couldn't manage a smile, so she bowed her head instead and stepped back into her seat. She silently prayed that once they returned to the restaurant, her stomach would be still, and she would not arouse suspicion.

"Do you think you caught the traitors who attacked Reinhard Heydrich yet?" she asked as the vehicle began to pull away from the horrific scene.

"Oh, we must have gotten a few traitors here." He shrugged dismissively. "If any are left in Prague, we will find them. Rest well. You will be safe as long as I am here. I will make sure no scum brings you harm."

"I am sure you will. I hear you are cleaning the city in more ways than one." Her mind formulated the words as she chose them with utmost care. His guard was down, and she needed to strike.

"I think I know what you mean." He chuckled. "Yes, I am sure you have dealt with the annoyance of animals infesting your city. We clean more out every day, I promise you."

Hearing good people like Josef being referred to as "animals" caused her fist to clasp tightly. But she kept her tone neutral as she turned and took in the countryside again. "The coordination it must require is impressive. How do you go about managing so many people?"

His cheeks flushed a little red as her flattery took hold. "It takes no small effort. But German technology and infrastructure are the finest in the world. A few of our newest trains can transport hundreds in only a few hours."

"New trains?" As she looked back at Hilbert, Kateřina did not have to feign interest this time.

"The finest in the world, as I said." Hilbert grinned. "That is why the cowards surely attacked Reinhard—Obergruppenführer

Heydrich—because they could never hope to stop our powerful machinery."

Or they did not know its purpose.

"Fascinating. Perhaps not as much as your work here at Lidice, but I feel safer knowing my city is under your leadership."

Rádek sat alone in a small hotel room. It was quiet except for the rapid thumping of his heart. One of his palms sweated profusely, the only palm that still could. How had it all gone so wrong? It was just like all those years ago. When bullets flew and fire blazed, all around him perished, but he always remained. He always lived. And now, he'd lost the one closest to him for the second time. He could still hear Samuel's scream in his ear. His best friend had given his life so that *he* could live. Taken a bullet that was made for him.

If he had known . . . if he had only known what I've been doing, he would have never taken a bullet for me. That was the thought that had come into his mind. What he had done, what he had been doing. It all felt so necessary. He was making sacrifices to achieve his goal. He needed his revenge. They needed to pay. He felt prepared to make such sacrifices before. But now that the price came due, he could not bear it.

A knock came to the door, followed by a series of knocks in a specific code. *Persephone.* It could be no one else. He cursed quietly enough so she would not be able to hear. He didn't want to deal with that woman or whatever vile lies she had to twist this time. Still, she surely knew he was in here. If he tried to run, they would find him. The fact that they'd found his and Samuel's hideout meant their intelligence network was far more comprehensive than he had anticipated. He grudgingly went to the door, knocked his return sequence, and twisted the knob. The viper disguised as a kitten stood before him, trademark smirk across her lips.

"Quite the evening, isn't it?" she chirped as she showed herself in.

He didn't respond save for a glare.

"Don't be like that." She waved playfully. "It would have all gone fine if the golem wasn't active."

"They tried to *shoot* me," he growled. "I would be dead if not for . . ."

"Your friend, right? So sorry about that. These things happen sometimes. Soldiers can be rather jumpy, you know?" She walked over to a nearby table and threw down a map of Prague, unrolling it to show the intricate details of every street and building. It showed his and Samuel's hidden laboratory and other points of interest he was unaware of. "But that was weeks ago. Time to move on. Tell me where the golem has gone. I imagine you'll need our assistance in recovering it, yes?"

"You think I'm going to work with you now? I am surprised you didn't shoot me when I opened the door. Tie up your loose ends and be done with it."

"Nonsense! Besides, we have the same goal, do we not? There are vermin to be exterminated." Her voice was grating. Her ungenuine enthusiasm made his stomach turn. "This was your project. I am not so dumb as to get rid of the man behind it all. What if you made a mistake in the design? It's much more convenient to keep you around to fix it rather than try to have our own engineers dig through your research."

That's her play. She wanted to keep him around so he could modify the golem however they wished. He had suspected this day would come. He had proven his capabilities. Sourcing weapon parts from the Germans was always a risky ploy. However, it was not only risky for him. The Germans now knew what he was capable of creating. If they let him get away, they would have a significant problem if he decided to work with their enemies instead. And they were right. They were absolutely right. He would show her how right she was.

Rádek stepped back swiftly and ungloved his metal hand, pointing it at the woman. He had kept this much a secret from her. Her arrogant façade dropped, and genuine horror crossed her face. For all her bluster, she was still a human.

With a single flex of his muscle, he could trigger a mechanism that would douse her in flames. "The deal is over. I will use my weapons of war however I see fit from here on out. If you play your cards right, you may leave with your life. Anything beyond that I cannot guarantee."

"You think killing me will save you?" Her voice quivered. "I am not some messenger. I prefer to work in the field, but I *never* move alone. Half a dozen men are waiting in the hall as I speak. Kill me, and you will be ravaged to no end."

Rádek did not flinch. "Prove it or die."

Persephone tapped on her watch, causing a small light to turn on. After only a few seconds passed, six men rushed into the room with weapons drawn. They all wore plain clothes, same as Persephone, but their features were clearly German.

Rádek cursed under his breath and noted the custom-built grenade in his coat. If he acted now, it was very possible he could kill them all. But he could just as likely take a fatal wound in the process. As his gut boiled with anger toward this miserable woman before him, it felt like a good enough trade. But no, he could not die. He would be willing to make that sacrifice, but he knew now more than ever that his goal *must* be met. Still, swiftly, he tore the grenade from his belt and held it toward the men as they trained their guns on him.

It was a standstill. None of the Germans knew what Rádek's weapons were capable of. But after the golem had torn apart a spider tank, they no longer underestimated him.

"We could all try and kill each other," Rádek started. "I may die, but I can guarantee that none of you will survive this encounter. However, you were right, Persephone. I may not be able to recover the golem alone. *You* can help *me* recover him, and we can keep working together. I do not care for you, but I have big plans for Germany. But I will be no prisoner. I am the only one alive who knows how to control the golem. It is *mine.*" He glared at her. "I return your threat. If you kill me, that golem will ravage your entire army to no end."

There was a long, terrible silence as everyone waited for Persephone's response. She let out a long breath, her façade seemed to rebuild, and she smirked at him. "Well, that's one way to negotiate. I underestimated you, Kelley."

"That makes one of us." He kept his weapons raised. Persephone sighed and then waved for her soldiers to leave. They did so without any pause, and the two were left alone in the room. "Good. Now, let's discuss new terms for our partnership. There are a few things I still want to make, and I need your help acquiring the parts."

The warehouse pulsed with nervous energy as Josef listened to Kateřina recount her entire trip to Lidice, including everything Hilbert had told her. Nikolai cursed several times as she described the ruined buildings and charred houses.

Josef remained quiet.

"Which train are they loaded onto?" he finally asked, eyes forward.

"There is a new train. She's right." Nikolai shook his head. "I saw it only once. It was massive. I believe it was made to withstand an attack with no trouble."

"Explain."

"It is large, with thick metal plating. I do not know all the details, but I saw guns mounted on the top."

That didn't sound good. They wouldn't have the numbers to assault even a regular train, let alone one built for war. Any rescue attempt would be easily thwarted, and their names would simply be added to the names of the lost.

Josef pounded a frustrated fist against his leg. He felt powerless, useless. All his efforts, every action he had taken didn't prevent his people being taken away, imprisoned, and killed. Because of what, the circumstances of their births? He needed something, a weapon that he could bring to bear against the Germans. But what?

He turned toward Golem, which was still preoccupied with Kateřina a few dozen yards away. While it was docile now, the sight of the living construct tearing apart a tank was still fresh in his mind. It was powerful—powerful beyond anything else he had ever seen. He could use it. Use it to save Hermina, the children . . . and others from their community.

"I can tell what you're thinking, and I think it is unwise," Nikolai interrupted his thoughts. "We must learn more about this before sending it against a train. Besides, our people will be on that train. If it is destroyed, we will lose them for sure. There is still a chance they could be rescued from wherever the Germans are taking them, but not if they are killed in a desperate attempt using something we do not understand."

"He listens," Kateřina argued. "And he protects even when he is not told to."

"And he's powerful," Josef added. "My grandfather built a weapon unlike anything I've ever seen."

"That doesn't sound like Samuel," Nikolai mumbled.

"I would have never thought he'd make something like this in the first place," Josef agreed, gesturing toward the machine. His tone deepened. "But now we have it—us. Those who have already fought despite the terrible odds. This is our chance to even those odds. Do we want to think of this day and curse ourselves for refusing to act?"

Nikolai seemed stunned at his passion. "You remind me of Samuel, but you are also very different. Fine, we should try and use the golem. But my point about the train still stands. How can we attack a transport full of our people? How do we prevent the golem from hurting them?"

That wasn't an easy question. Josef didn't know the specifics of what orders Golem would and wouldn't follow yet. It had protected him and Kateřina from the Germans, but there was no telling who it would deem a threat. That wasn't all. If German soldiers were stationed near the prisoners on the train, the rescue could soon turn into a hostage situation.

He considered his options. The longer he thought, the more the only viable solution came to his mind. It was a dangerous but inevitable part of any rescue plan they would have to attempt.

"I will need to infiltrate the train, find the exact railcar our people are in, and secure it." The plan was still formulating in his mind as he said the words aloud. "I don't know if I can do it alone."

At those words, a smirk cracked Nikolai's face for the first time that evening. "That I can help with. Do you remember Petr?"

Kateřina leaned forward. "You said he escaped from Terezín, yes? Is he well?"

"That camp took a lot out of him. He saw many terrible things and was given nothing to survive on. He's gotten better since. He's healed and grown strong once more. He's been talking of ways to help hide people. But he wants to do *more*. If I asked him, he would join your mission without hesitation."

"I will take him." Josef nodded. "Anyone who can escape the Germans without being seen is exactly the type of person I need on that train with me."

"I will let him know right away. Get ready." Nikolai headed out the door.

"This has to work," Josef said. "Once I am on the train, you must direct the golem from outside."

"Josef, how do you plan to get on the train?" Kateřina asked.

He hadn't considered that. There was no way they would ever let a Jew on board one of their trains.

"I ask because I can help with that," Kateřina spoke up. "Or rather, my father can. He's the head editor of my newspaper. He can get boarding passes for the train easily."

His mind flashed to the countless headlines spouting nothing but lies, German propaganda. "You can't tell me your father isn't on the side of the Germans." Josef's words were terse.

"If you wish, I won't say that, but I will say I know my father well. Instead of fighting, he has given up." She paused for a moment before continuing. "But he was once a fighter. I know I can get through to him."

"What do you mean by that? He was a fighter?" Josef asked.

"The man my mother married wasn't the father I knew growing up. I saw photos of them when they were young and in love—the only place I'd seen my father smile. The Great War took so much from him. But even still, he wants me to be safe. I can't believe he agrees with the Germans. I won't."

Josef sighed and shook his head. "How can you be so sure? So many Czech people have sided with Germany."

"He slapped me once." Kateřina couldn't help but touch her fingertips to her face, remembering the pain—the shock. "I told him I didn't want to be Czech. I said I loved Germany more. Germany, to me, was visiting my mother's parents' beautiful home. It was dressing for dinner and tasting fine foods. It was boarding school with private tutors, riding horses, and finely tailored clothes for a time."

"I don't understand. How did a Czech patriot fall in love with a German woman?"

"They had known each other since childhood. My grandfather worked in the German Embassy in Prague. I don't believe my grandparents ever approved of my father, but they adored me."

"And so you wanted to be German?"

Kateřina shrugged. "I wanted the easy life until I saw it was not easy on my father when I returned with all my fine things."

"And your mother and grandparents now?"

"My mother died when I was nine. After that, I went to see my grandparents only once. I knew how much it made my father unhappy. One night, not long after my return, I heard this horrible wailing. I left my room and saw my father in the living room. He was kneeling, and a broken picture frame lay before him. Glass shards spread over the floor, and my father scrambled to pick them up as if not realizing they were cutting him. Blood dripped from his fingers, pooling in dark puddles on the floor." She pressed her eyes closed.

"What happened?"

"I went to him. I touched his shoulder and told him I missed her too. In my desperation to ease his pain, I told him I wouldn't go to Germany anymore. I believed I needed to stay to make him happy, to make up for my mother's death."

Josef's eyes reflected compassion, and she quickly turned away.

"What did he say when you told him that?"

"At first, nothing." Kateřina's voice wavered. "But as I wondered if I had even spoken, my father looked my way. His eyes held a vacant expression. There was a deadness in his gaze. It felt as though I had become invisible to him."

"Do you still feel invisible to him?"

"I'd be lying to say I didn't."

"Is that why you became a reporter?"

"Maybe so." Kateřina pressed her fingertips to her forehead and then rubbed her eyes as if that would stop the tears from coming. "Maybe I believed that since he seemed to look right through me, my words in print would make a difference."

"Have they?"

She paused. "No, not at all," she admitted. "But maybe things aren't as complete as they seem. I think he is fighting the war the only way he knows how."

"That's not fighting. That's hiding," Josef said, but then felt a pang of guilt. He had once accused Grandfather of the same thing. And Grandfather had been fighting in his own way, which had now given them a chance at doing good. "Maybe you are right. You never know what a person is thinking. You can try to guess based on their actions, but it is easy to get wrong."

"I think he's protecting the Czech people. Think of the lives lost by these reprisals. Maybe instead of stirring the pot, he's attempting to lull the Czech citizens into a drowsy state. The less they know, the less they'll fight, the less they'll die."

"I understand, but what good is that? Is it better to live under German rule than to die knowing you're fighting for your country's freedom?" He winced. The words were easy to say until lives were lost.

"I know that," she said quietly. "I believe he does too. You've already risked so much in trusting me. I shouldn't be asking any more of you. But let me do this. Please."

Josef slowly nodded. "Okay. I trust you."

The usual sounds of typewriters and excited mutterings were noticeably absent as Kateřina stepped into the newsroom. The place was dark except for a singular lamp at the back, from Father's office. Her legs trembled as she walked the path lit by the open door. Her footsteps were almost as loud as her beating heart in her ears as she knocked.

"Who is it?" he demanded with unexpected intensity. "Evka? What do you want now?"

Evka? "No, it's me, Father." Her voice cracked at first, but she strengthened it partway through her words. "I need to talk to you."

"Oh, Kateřina." His voice softened. "Come in."

She pushed the door open the rest of the way and stepped inside. Her father was groomed and alert, odd for this time of night.

"Why are you back?" he said coldly.

"A lot has happened," she said. "I have been following a story on my own, and—"

"You *what*?" He stood up out of his chair.

"It does not matter. I am not bringing it to print. Not yet." She moved to a chair in front of the desk and sat down. Her father narrowed his eyes and sank back into his seat. After a moment of quiet, she saw his eyes grow larger.

"Are you in trouble?" A slight quiver weakened his voice.

"No. But I need your help." She reached into her satchel and pulled out two pieces of documentation. Forgeries that the rebels had been making for their members. "These men need boarding passes onto a German train. It leaves in eight days, in the early afternoon."

Father's eyebrows pinched as he read over the documents. "Who are these men?"

"They are not real," she said softly. "These papers are forgeries. But the men who intend to use these *must* be aboard that train. Lives are at stake."

She waited for the outburst of screaming and shouting as he demanded to know what she had gotten mixed up in. She even readied herself for a slap or for him to forcibly move her and lock her away somewhere where she could not cause trouble.

But Father sat in silence, reading the documents. "You came to me. Why?"

"I know you can help. And I believe you will."

"I would be committing a great offense to the Germans," he said slowly. "If they find out, it will all be over. They would not take just me; they would take you, too. You understand that, right? You know the cost you are asking me to pay?"

"Yes."

It was another few minutes of silence. She wanted to beg or plead. But she wouldn't. Josef had given her many opportunities to back away from all of this. Her father had to choose for himself whether or not he would risk his life to try and save others.

"As your father, I cannot allow it," he said. "The price is too high."

She nodded and took the documents back. "Good night, Father." She rose from her seat and started toward the door.

"Kateřina."

She froze and closed her eyes.

"This is real, isn't it?"

She nodded.

"I see." He let out a sigh. "I have been here before. Far too many times. Over and over the question is posed to me. Will I do the right thing, or will I keep those near me safe?"

Kateřina turned. His head hung. She had seen him like this before.

The day her mother died. Years of being a cold, uncaring man had passed since then, but it was clear this pain was still inside of him. He must have been carrying it with him every single day.

"Why must it be me?" he asked slowly. "Couldn't you have asked someone, anyone else? At least then I could work to save you from your choices. Why must I always be the one to have to choose?"

She stared, mouth agape.

"I cannot approve of this." He choked on the words. "I disapprove of what you are doing." He paused and then continued. "But I will help you. Where do they need to go?"

She held out the documents to her father. "It doesn't matter as long as they are aboard that train. Whichever way that draws the least suspicion."

Her father took them once more. "Just the two of them?"

"That is all we have." She hesitated, unsure how much she should tell. "Others and I will be outside of the train. There are not many of us. Two will be enough, or it won't."

He nodded.

Finally he said, "I can get those passes. But there is still a chance they will be arrested. Security has grown tight these past few weeks since the attack."

"That will be up to them. I trust them."

Her father wrote down various details from the forged identities and then returned them to her. "I will place the passes on your pillow tomorrow at noon. Do *not* bring them here."

Those words struck her like a knife. "Father, is there something I should know?"

He shook his head. "Focus on your task. Leave this place to me. Now go, and don't be seen."

Kateřina resumed her exit but paused. "Thank you, Father."

He didn't respond. She didn't need him to. As she walked back into the dark of the night, she prayed for his safety. For the safety of all involved.

Saturday, 20 June 1942
Prague, Protectorate of Bohemia and Moravia

A train unlike anything Josef had ever seen stretched before him. Tall, thick, and covered with giant metal pipes releasing puffs of pressurized steam through valves. He had heard of this monstrosity, but this was the first time he had witnessed it. Rumors claimed it would transport anything the Germans needed to move during wartime. It could withstand attack from a modern military and give back as good as it took. As though to prove that point, mounted gun stations rotated on the top of every few carriages.

The train stretched beyond what he could see down the tracks. It was a lot of carriages, a lot of distance to search and secure before the train got to where the rebels were waiting. Where, hopefully, a fleet of automobiles would be waiting to take the prisoners to freedom. An unlikely prospect, as they'd had little time to prepare. But that was their job, Nikolai's job. Josef had to trust them to do what they could, and it was up to him to ensure there were prisoners alive to save.

Despite the death hovering around its metal shell, passengers waited to board the vessel, gossiping or exchanging idle talk about what meal they would choose aboard the train or their evening plans once they arrived at their destinations. Josef's stomach churned. Did they know what other purposes the train had? He couldn't imagine a sane person caring so little for human lives. They must be ignorant, right?

He tried to push recent news out of his mind. Just days ago, most of the other men who'd plotted and executed the assassination attempt against Heydrich were dead. The Germans also executed Alois Eliáš, the former prime minister of Protectorate of Bohemia and Moravia, for resistance work. There were few men left to stand against the Nazi horror—and even the head of state had been eliminated—which made today's efforts even more critical.

Josef took stock of himself, noting his self-crafted tools and a concealed singular pistol. Hopelessly outgunned wouldn't begin to describe how he felt. He had to focus on Hermina and the others to find the courage to step into the line to board.

Think of all who fought to get you here.

Just as she promised, Kateřina had managed to get him boarding passes. A German propagandist had aided in their effort to save Jewish lives. That alone invigorated him. There were more out there willing to risk themselves for their community than he expected. He could not let them down.

Soldiers inspected everyone who tried to board, German or otherwise. While it was not immediately apparent that Josef was a Jew, he still worried whether or not his false identification would pass scrutiny.

Stay composed, he reminded himself. *If you carry yourself as if you belong, others will believe you do.* Summoning all his acting prowess, he tried to project impatience with the tedious boarding process rather than his underlying anxiety. He tapped his foot, a gesture that eased some of his nervousness, and checked his pocket watch.

His actions were not unnoticed by the Germans, who were slightly insulted at his impatience. A little offended was a much better reaction than suspicious. With any luck, they had already profiled him as a nuisance rather than someone to be worried about. They were reluctant to deal with him as his turn to be searched came up, and he let out a small scoff. "Efficient as always, I see."

He'd chosen a risky approach. Still, he couldn't deny the satisfaction that came from a chance to insult a German soldier to his face. The soldier before him scowled and snatched Josef's satchel to search through it. Another soldier flatly received his identification and boarding pass, which Josef provided without hesitation or second glance.

"Careful with that!" Josef barked as the first soldier retrieved a device from his bag. It resembled a hand-cranked handlight. He found himself fully taking character as he unleashed an unasked-for explanation into the finer apparatuses of this mechanical handlight, aside from his personal modifications and how easily the soldier could break the "expensive" device. The result was as he hoped as the soldier tossed it back into his bag before roughly shoving the whole satchel into his arms.

"Just get on and keep quiet." They returned his boarding pass and identification.

Josef let out another small huff and climbed onboard. Only after he stepped up onto the train and out of view of the German guards did the reality of the situation come crashing back onto him. A bead of sweat dripped down his brow, and he sent a quick prayer of thanks for his body's delayed reaction to the stress. His infiltration was a complete success. He didn't receive a single glance as he chose a seat at the furthest end of the carriage.

Once seated, he glanced at the satchel he had brought himself. The weapons he had been working on for the past few years were all intended to seem ordinary to the uninformed viewer. They were pretty impressive, mostly simple tricks to buy time when needed. He didn't have anything strong enough to stop a train this size. In that, his grandfather's creation had far outclassed anything he had the ability to create.

That's if Kateřina can get Golem to actually stop this train.

That was his primary worry. He had given Kateřina the commanding device to force the creature to stop the train in its tracks. But would she instead try to *convince* it to protect the prisoners inside? Talk to it? Was it even capable of that level of abstract instruction?

He shook himself. He couldn't waste any of his energy worrying about something far beyond his control. It was up to him to secure the prisoners on the back of the train. As long as soldiers controlled those carriages, everything else would be pointless. Josef steeled himself and took stock of his situation to decide the best course of action from his current position.

As far as he could tell, the soldiers were not actively monitoring the passenger coach. They had little reason to suspect anyone would try to do something as crazy as Josef planned, so moving past a few soldiers was not too dangerous. But once he approached the rear end of the train, he would be prepared to defend himself at a moment's notice.

And as for Petr. He had yet to see him board. Perhaps he'd gotten onto a different carriage? Or maybe he was prevented from boarding altogether. Even worse: arrested at the security checkpoint. He silently prayed for the man's well-being.

The train horn boomed throughout the chamber. It was not the shrill whistle he was used to hearing from the old trains that usually came through Prague. This was a deep droning that was more like the higher-pitched horn one might hear from a large carrier ship. At least, as best he could remember. He had little experience with boats while living in the landlocked country of Czechoslovakia. Still, he found the noise this horn made far more haunting.

Shortly after came a few loud *thunks* of interlocking metal, and the train accelerated ever so slowly. He scooted over in the seat and glanced out the window. They would be close to the center of town for a little while. If he didn't want any outside interference, he might need to wait before he made his move. He feigned boredom as he watched the city outside the window. The soldiers outside all had their backs to the train as it left. They had no reason to be concerned. They likely felt safer right now than they usually did. After all, who would ever think of challenging their powerful war train?

This fact spurred him to move sooner rather than later. He casually rose from his seat, walked toward his coach's back door, and peered through the small glass window separating his coach from the next. No one stood guard, so he cautiously entered the open air. The otherwise muffled sounds of the thundering train came into full force as he opened the door and stepped through, closing the door behind him.

He quietly stepped toward the next carriage. Thankfully, it was a freight unit, and no visible soldiers would bar his path. Valuing swiftness in this situation, he entered this carriage as well and made his way between the tall wooden containers. As he stepped around a giant crate, he faced a German soldier reclining on a small chair. The

German seemed to have heard the door open, but his eyebrows shot up when he spotted Josef.

Heart racing, Josef retrieved his hammer from the inside of his coat. This reaction was a mistake. The soldier rushed for his own weapon at the side of his chair. Josef lashed out with his hammer, instinctively twisting the hilt and activating the mechanism built inside. Flames spewed from the *back* of his hammer and past his side in a short burst, propelling the hammer through the air. It struck the German soldier on the side of his head. A sickening *crack* sounded, louder even than the clack of the train. The soldier slumped to the ground.

Josef stumbled as he fought against the momentum from his weapon. His heart raced, and he stared at the body, shocked. He had killed a man. He had never done it before, but he didn't regret it. Not when carriages *full* of his people were pulled a few coaches away. However, it did mean he had a complication now. It would only be a matter of time before this soldier was found or reported missing. He'd need to move faster.

There was blood on the floor. Even if Josef hid the body, the alarm would be raised. There needed to be another way. His eyes drifted to the boxes around the compartment. They were secured but seemingly in haste. He loosened a nearby set of straps then dropped a medium-sized box on the floor next to the fallen soldier's head. With any luck, the staged "accident" might cause a diversion believable enough to buy him time to get to the back of the train.

I need to be more careful now. He hurried past the scene of his blunder. *I can't afford another mistake like that.*

A glance through the door window showed a clear path. He exited that carriage and moved to the next, peering inside. Another freight unit. That meant there would likely be another guard posted up in there. Opening the door would alert the guard to his presence.

Just how do I get through?

A nudge in his back made him spin around. It was Petr, crouching behind him. Josef clutched his chest, drawing in deep breaths to ease the surge of adrenaline. Petr should have known not to startle him, but his silent approach was admittedly skillful.

"You move so quietly, Petr. It's good to see you." His words struggled to compete with the roaring train on the tracks.

"I didn't escape from Terezín being loud." Petr grinned. "I saw what you did back there. Brutal. Do you think there is a guard in this carriage as well?"

Josef nodded and scanned again for any sight of the soldier. After moments, he saw a large man mulling about inside, inspecting the cargo. He headed in their direction slowly.

"I will deal with this." Petr nodded to him. "Open the door once he gets near."

Josef nodded and gripped the doorknob. It took about half a minute for the soldier to be in position. Josef swung the door open. Petr rushed inside and flung an arm around the soldier's neck from behind. He wrestled him to the ground. Josef, unwilling to be a bystander, rushed in and stole the soldier's firearm. After a few agonizingly long moments, the soldier slumped to the ground.

"Where did you learn that maneuver?" Josef asked, shocked at the precision of the older man.

"You want to sit down and have a chat?" Petr said in an amused huff as he dragged the soldier off.

Josef shook his head. "Fair. Let's get moving."

A singular carriage separated them from the one holding his people, but this one worried him the most. It was an armory with gun stations mounted on top of it to shoot at anyone who would attack the train from the outside. He didn't necessarily fear the guns themselves, but rather the half dozen or more soldiers manning the station.

"Do we try to climb over?" Petr asked worriedly. "There is not much to hold on to. It will be dangerous."

"No, I have something for this." Josef reached into his satchel and pulled out the device resembling a torch. While it seemed only slightly odd to the naked eye, it was perhaps the most effective tool he and his grandfather had ever made together. The Torch of Gideon.

The biblical name was his grandfather's idea. He took the tale of Gideon's assault against the Midianites seriously, and they had planned how to replicate the effects. They'd never fully tested it, but Grandfather said he preferred it that way. After all, he said God was the reason for Gideon's victory. *Toss it and pray*, Grandfather had told him. Though Josef had been silently praying his entire time on the train, he would surely kick it up a notch.

The two crept across the coupler to the armored carriage, Josef in the lead. It was too risky to try and look inside as they had before. But from a quick glance while they crossed, Josef was sure there were at least five men in the lower section, and there could be a few more in the gun station above. He steeled himself, readied the Torch, then grabbed the doorknob. It didn't budge. Not even slightly.

Locked.

He hadn't even considered this. The device relied on the element of surprise. How could he pull it off now? His mind searched furiously for an answer. Except for the small gap in the gun station where the soldiers inside could maneuver the guns, there were no openings beyond the locked door. There was, however, a *possibility* that something thrown in that small gap could make it down into the carriage, and the device could do its work. There was no way he could toss it in from a distance, though. He'd have to shove it in up close.

His chest tightened at the answer to his problem. And the terrifying implication of what he needed to do to use the Torch of Gideon effectively. He examined the walls of the armored carriage and began planning his way up.

"Are you insane?" Petr asked, having deduced Josef's intentions. "You'll slip off before you make it up, and even if you do, a soldier will shoot you long before you could reach the gun station."

"We're two barely armed men taking on a German train alone. We are already insane."

Josef hoisted himself up the side of the train carriage. The buffeting of the wind intensified once he moved from between the carriages to the outer-facing side. The metal was smooth, and the footholds were sparse. Every tiny sway or shift of the train felt deadly without a steady platform to stand on.

His foot slipped. He gripped the shallow handholds. Only by a miracle did he manage to stay on the side of the train. He would require plenty more to make it to the roof.

He focused only on each step. Not worrying about what would happen once he saw the gun station. He came into what he knew would be full view as he pulled himself onto the roof. From here, he could see that the opening for the gun station was only slightly larger than a head. It would be too narrow for a grown man to crawl through but plenty large enough to drop the Torch inside. From his current viewpoint, he didn't see anyone actively manning the gun.

Josef fought against the air current as he crawled across the smooth metal roof toward the gun station. There seemed to be a sealed hatch separating the gun station from the train carriage below.

No! He cursed under his breath. He had no way of opening the hatch from the outside.

Just as he thought to turn back and try to climb back down, the hatch door creaked open. Before he had time to think, Josef surged forward. His arm arced as he tossed the Torch of Gideon straight at the soldier emerging from the carriage, whacking the soldier cleanly on his head. He ducked back down, and the Torch tumbled after him into the carriage below.

A terribly haunting sound echoed from the interior, incredibly loud despite the already deafening sounds of the roaring train. It reminded Josef of a chorus of shouting men with different pitches and tones. The sound alone filled him with dread even as he knew that it emanated from a device. In addition, flashing lights shone up from the open hatch in sporadic intervals. The combination of the two was incredibly disorienting, and he shielded his eyes and moved away from the open hatch. A mistake, as he slipped backward and fell.

The world spun around. He couldn't tell which way was up. He expected to feel his body crash onto the stony ground, tumbling like a rag doll as his life was cut short. Instead, a harsh jerk slammed his back against a metal floor. He gasped, eyes wide to see Petr crouched over him.

He was back on small platform above the carriage's coupler.

Petr's mouth moved, but Josef couldn't hear his words over the ruckus inside the train carriage. Then he realized it wasn't only the haunting calls from the Torch anymore. The German soldiers were shouting and panicking, and gunfire came from inside. The noise doubled as the metal door swung open. A soldier rushed out wildly, only to trip over Josef and tumble straight off the train with a cry of terror.

"Watch out!" Petr said as he pulled Josef to the side, bullets pummeling the grated platform where he was lying a moment before. "It's chaos in there! They're . . . they're killing each other!"

Josef painfully pulled himself to his feet. Though the Torch was waning in volume and brightness, the soldiers still fought amongst themselves. Those who remained, at least. He saw three bodies, and with the soldier who fell off the train, that meant four had been killed. The remaining three struggled against each other. One seemed to be coming out of the panic and realizing what had happened.

Josef turned to Petr and shot him a severe expression. They each pulled out their concealed pistols and rushed into the train carriage. A shot rang out. A bullet tore through the collar of Josef's coat. He aimed his pistol at the culprit and fired. The recoil shocked his arm, but his years of hard metalwork made him sturdy, so he kept his form true.

His first shot struck the soldier in the shoulder, causing a flinch from the impact. A small spray of blood and torn fabric marked the point of entry, just below the soldier's collarbone. Despite his initial aim for the man's chest, the bullet had veered off course, finding an unintended target. As a result, he quickly fired a second shot.

This time the soldier gripped his chest and fell backward. Dead.

Two soldiers remained. They, too, had recovered from the effects of the Torch of Gideon and now turned their aggression toward Josef and Petr. Petr was already firing madly, piercing a German multiple times without mercy. His death was not left unavenged, as the last remaining soldier shot a few rounds back, catching Petr several times. Josef pushed in front of his friend and returned fire. He hit the soldier, but it was not a fatal wound. He ducked behind a nearby chair.

With the number of shots fired, he'll have to reload or find another weapon. Josef gritted his teeth and charged around the wall, knowing he had at least one or two bullets left. The soldier had finished reloading his weapon and raised it straight at Josef. Josef didn't give him a chance and shot the German point-blank twice. The soldier crumpled.

Josef frantically looked around at all the fallen soldiers, waiting to see if any of them were still alive and trying to fight back. It was a long, tense wait, but soon he realized none of them were getting back up. In fact, he was the only one still standing.

Petr!

He rushed to his friend's side. There were multiple bullet wounds across his chest. Josef tore off his shirt to create bandages, but Petr stopped him. "There is no time. Please, get everyone off this train."

"You want me to leave you to die?" Josef asked.

"I died in Terezín. All I want is for no one else to experience that horrible place."

At the mention of Terezín, an image of his father's face filled Josef's mind. Another person he cared for that he could not save. Could not reach. He had failed again and again to protect those close to him.

"Go," Petr coughed. "I will guard your back for as long as I can."

Josef gritted his teeth. For the second time, he was asked to leave behind a fallen man and live. But he knew he had to do it. If he were the one who'd gotten shot, he would be telling Petr the same thing. There were too many lives at stake. Innocents who weren't even given the option to make their choices. With a heavy heart, Josef took a gun from a nearby fallen German soldier and placed it in Petr's lap, then made his way to the far side of the carriage.

The next carriage did not have any doors for him to get into. From what he could deduce, the only way to open it was from the broad side. He leaned out to confirm his deduction, noting that it was closed with a heavy lock. *This has to be it,* he thought. If there was any place where hidden prisoners would be stored, it would be in a carriage like this.

Kateřina tried to quell her shaking as she followed Nikolai through the streets of Prague. She had never felt this way before. Like she was being hunted. In truth, there wasn't much difference between now and any other time she had walked the streets since the Germans occupied the city. The soldiers would have no reason to suspect an upstanding citizen like herself. Only a few specific soldiers had actually gotten a good look at her when the golem protected her. And when questioned, her reporter credentials could quickly get her out of most situations.

But it wasn't the Germans who had turned against her. It was she who turned against them. Even if they didn't know it, she was now directly aiding an effort against them. The thought terrified her. She imagined what it would be like to be taken to a place like Terezín.

"Are you alright?" Nikolai asked. "Your face is pale."

Her eyes darted around frantically to see if there were any soldiers in sight. They were alone in an alley. She hadn't even noticed that they had left the streets. "I have never done something like this before. I . . ." She struggled to say the words. "I am terrified."

"We all are." Nikolai shook his head. "Do you want to know what I did before this? I was an optometrist. I never asked to be targeted by the Germans. I made glasses for anyone who came through my doors. Why my birth was such an inexcusable offense, I will never know. I'm not doing this because I want to or because I'm the man best suited for the job. I am doing this because I am needed."

Someone needs to be the one to do it. Her mind went to her stories. She always wanted to write the ones no one else would.

"Kateřina," Nikolai prodded. "To keep the terror at bay, you must focus on what is important. Why are you doing this? Why help our resistance?"

She didn't want to admit the truth to him. That she was just a reporter who had been following a story, going places she didn't belong. Or at least that's how she started. "I saw Samuel die, though I didn't even know his name at the time. Seeing Samuel die . . . made it all real. I don't want anyone else to be hurt. Not if I can do something to help them."

"Think about that. Nothing else. Think about how your actions today can save lives."

She closed her eyes and took deep breaths. She couldn't shake the fear. Couldn't stop the dark thoughts of her likely fate from rolling in. But the more she thought about people who might or were *already* suffering those fates, she knew she had to do something to help them. That focus caused the trembling to lessen. Her heart rate slowed. She opened her eyes to Nikolai, who nodded his approval before leading her on.

They made their way toward the outskirts of the city. It was a slow process, a fact that clearly frustrated Nikolai as they had to wait for extended periods at necessary checkpoints. But they eventually reached the location and saw the promised auto waiting for them. Two other men already waited inside, both of whom were extraordinarily relieved to see Nikolai and her arrive safely.

"You think it will be able to keep up with the auto?" Nikolai asked her.

She paused and listened. Now without moving, she could hear the faint *tick tick* of the golem. *Good, he made it, too.* He had followed her here without fail. "He has to."

To be sure, she turned to face what her eyes deceived her into believing was empty air in front of her. "Golem, follow behind this auto. You will need to move quickly."

She couldn't see whether he even understood what she had asked him to do, let alone whether he would follow her instruction. She had to believe he would. She nodded to Nikolai and followed him to the backseat of the auto in front of them.

The calm winds of the evening seemed to wash through her coat with ease as they drove down the countryside. It sent chills through her as she watched the empty train tracks on the quiet fields to their side. The buildings became sparse as they drove until there were not any buildings in sight at all. Despite them being so exposed and out in the open, she felt much calmer out here than in the city.

She let her mind relax, even for a few precious seconds. It didn't last. Far too soon, the auto stopped, and she would need to get out and walk to their final destination.

How had she managed to get mixed up in something so serious? Each step seemed correct, yet now she ended up on both sides of this conflict. What would her father think if they were to find her body at the scene of a rebel attack? What would the other Czech people believe? For many, it would be seen as aiding their enemy. Traitorous.

But I'm not here to attack the train, she thought solemnly. She didn't care about hurting the Germans. But she could think only of the people they had captured and were taking to terrible places. She thought of Hermina and her children. Could helping innocent people escape really be bad, even if it wasn't what her people wanted to happen? She pulled her coat tighter and stretched out to her side. She brushed something—something she couldn't see. Kateřina closed her eyes. Golem waited patiently at her side. Despite the metal feeling even cooler than the air around her, its presence was comforting.

"Is it still there?" Nikolai asked with a touch of worry in his voice. The middle-aged man was poised to pull his gun. Not a threat, but an unintentional reaction, she guessed. He eyed how she was pushing against the golem—invisible to them both.

Kateřina nodded. She could faintly hear tapping metal, but it was muffled somehow. She smacked it even harder but didn't hear a significant increase in noise.

How odd.

Nikolai's fingers tightened around his gun's grip.

She offered him an apologetic smile. "He is tame. He won't hurt us."

"How can you be so sure?"

She turned in the direction of the invisible machine, pondering the question. "I can't explain it, but I feel it. He's here to protect. Not harm."

It wasn't a lie. She truly felt that way. It had destroyed that spider tank, but only after Josef commanded it using that device. She reached into her pocket and retrieved the strange transmitter. A twinge of disgust poked her as she examined it. Golem was so gentle. It protected her without being asked. If it did that, why was a device like this even made? Josef had given it to her in case the golem didn't listen, but his true meaning was clear. If it came to it, she was supposed to command the golem to attack the train or kill German soldiers. Commands it might not do of its own accord.

Own accord. Was she now considering a machine sentient? A foolish thought that would probably invite mockery. Machines, even complex ones, followed the commands they were given. The way they were designed. Once she spent more time seeing the golem operate, she would understand exactly what it meant to do. Until then, she would be careful not to rely on the assumption of any function or action it had not explicitly done before.

"The train should be here soon," Nikolai warned. "Stay low, and stay as far back as you can. If the Germans believe you are part of the attack, they will not hesitate to harm you."

"I never expected them to hold back," she said plainly. "They are taking women and children to horrible camps. I know they won't show me mercy. That's why I am here."

A loud, ominous noise, barely resembling a train whistle, sounded in the distance. The terrible noise spawned goosebumps across her neck and arms. That feeling intensified when the massive train rounded the corner and came barreling down the tracks. It was not moving as fast as she had expected, but it was far larger than she had imagined.

"Are you with me, Golem? When that train comes, I need you to stop it. Please. There are people aboard who need us."

She heard nothing for what felt like ages. "Golem?" A gust of wind passed by. Moments later, the golem became visible to all and was on the tracks, directly in front of the oncoming train.

A shrill screeching split the air as the brakes on the train clamped tightly. The train began a slow deceleration.

Golem was a giant and had proven to be powerful already. But seeing that train flying toward him worried Kateřina. Some sort of projectile launched from the front of the train, exploding upon contact with Golem's body. The shockwave knocked her to the ground, and she covered her head with her arms to protect it from possible shrapnel. A new noise caused her to give up her cover. Golem flew toward the train, covering hundreds of feet in a few seconds. It grappled with the engine, adding more stopping power to the already enabled brakes. But even with the giant's might, the train was still set to roll far beyond them.

"It is not enough!" Nikolai shouted. "We need to move further down!"

The darkening skies flared as if a second sun had dawned before them as flames came to life and then roared from the back of the golem's feet and arms. Kateřina shielded her eyes, but soon peeked out to watch the phenomenon in wonder. Golem placed tremendous pressure on the head of the train, yet he did not cause the train to derail. He controlled his flames and movements perfectly, never using too much force in a single direction.

What are *you, Golem?*

As the flaming mass of steel and metal rolled toward them, Kateřina and the others rushed away to avoid being caught in the blaze. She dove to the ground as rocks flew their way. One landed with a heavy thud a few feet past her.

Finally, the train slowed to a stop.

An eerie silence followed. Those inside the train were likely taking stock of themselves and trying to recover from the shock of the event. Though Kateřina felt dizzy from all the commotion and deafening noise, her conscious mind managed to focus on the task. This was precious time they needed to get the passengers off the train to safety. She surveyed the side of the train, jogging as she traveled down its length.

There.

Josef stepped out of a carriage alone. He looked ragged and weary. But he'd survived. Before she realized what she was doing, she ran up and wrapped her arms around his neck. He tensed at the sudden show of affection but relaxed in her embrace momentarily before separating.

"We have to move quickly. There are a lot of people on this train." He hurried to the next carriage and smashed his hammer at the lock. It snapped off, and he pulled open the container to reveal hordes of people who had been pushed inside like cattle. They looked hungry, tired, and terrified. Though once they saw it was not soldiers who had opened their confinement, hope brightened their faces.

"Come with us!" Josef extended himself to help the first one out.

Bile rose in Kateřina's throat. She had expected prisoners in less-than-ideal conditions. But the Germans were not even treating these people as *humans*. She watched in horror as each man, woman, child, and elder stepped down from the cart onto the grass. They were ordinary people of no threat whatsoever. Not captured enemy soldiers or influential persons whom the Germans would want to usurp. These were people. And they were being led to their deaths or a fate that could be considered even worse.

"Help, please!" Josef broke into her thoughts as he directed her toward an older woman struggling with the step down. As Kateřina moved over, a loud *thud* sounded from the front of the train. The older woman startled, and Kateřina had to use all her strength to keep the woman from tumbling down through the grass and stones.

"The golem stopped it after all," Josef noted. "It's drawn

their attention. It is giving us a little more time than I expected. It is amazing."

"You have no idea!" She shook her head as she recalled the flames. Though now she couldn't help but worry. The golem was mighty, but what would he do on his own? Neither she nor Josef was near him. Up ahead at the front of the damaged German train, the golem was surrounded by enemies.

Josef watched the warm glow from the front of the train subside. The golem cast a silhouette as it was left in the dark of late evening. The engine of the train was twisted, crumpled, and lay in a heap on the ground at its feet. The amount of effort and resources required to repair it would be better spent buying an entirely new locomotive. But the train had stopped. Their plan, for now, was working.

The golem's great head turned this way and that, looking for something. Was it Kateřina? It moved around the scrap pile it had created and toward the field surrounding the train. Soldiers scrambled from the wreckage and surrounded it, weapons drawn. It paid them no mind.

Josef gritted his teeth and glanced back to the slow-moving crowd of Jewish captives. It was extremely fortunate that the golem was drawing all the attention. No one had even noticed the resistance fighters had started emptying their carriages. However, what would become of the golem? He shuddered to think of what would ensue should they take command of the creature. *If* they even could.

The golem shifted, catching the soldier shooting at it off guard. A bullet sped toward the golem, striking its ceramic exterior. Normally, such an impact might crack or damage ceramic, but the bullet fell to the ground, deflected by some unseen force. As more bullets were fired, each proved ineffective, like mere blanks. Josef knew he should be assisting the crowd but was compelled to watch the machine's reaction.

It turned as if scanning the area and taking note of everyone it saw. As quickly as a bird taking flight, the golem vanished. Its body was now completely invisible to their eyes. The men waved their guns about as they searched desperately for their unknown enemy.

Where is it going?

He shook himself. Now that the golem had chosen to go invisible, he could not know what it was doing. But for now, he could not worry about it. He came to the side of a younger girl struggling to keep up with the crowd and hoisted her onto his back.

"Josef! You came!" He recognized the small voice in his ear. It was Hermina's youngest, Amalie. He felt incredibly relieved to have her in his grasp. He was equally horrified that the young, innocent girl had been subjected to such savage circumstances in the first place.

"Of course. I would never let anyone hurt you." He forced a smile at her. "Where is your mother?"

"I don't know. She got taken somewhere."

His eyes darted around, aiming to find her. In the darkness, it was hard to recognize anyone. All he could do was hope everyone had made it off the train.

Shouts in German came from the direction of the engine. He didn't know many words, but he understood they had said something like "being opened," which he could only assume referred to the carriages. He and the other Jews had a decent head start, but with elders and children, they would need help to stay in front of the soldiers. They needed distractions and protection. His mind rushed like a whirlwind as he tried to think of possibilities. Where were Nikolai and the other rebels?

More shouts sounded from behind. This time they sounded like commands. The soldiers were indeed on their tracks now. Someone touched him from behind, and his heart dropped. He spun only to see Hermina. Her face was flushed, and she was breathing deeply.

"Thank God for you, Josef," she whispered as she followed close behind. "And you have Amalia. I was so scared!"

"I have her. Are your other children safe?" he asked.

"Yes. All of them are being taken care of. But how will we get away?"

Josef shook his head. "We did not have time to come up with a full plan. Every step has been a choice made at the moment. Even Petr died to get us this far. Our only hope is to hide these people in Petrin Hill."

"Back toward Prague?" Hermina gasped.

"They will look for us in the countryside. It is the only option until we find somewhere better. But it will mean nothing if they chase us down now. I'm sorry it's come to this. I did all I could."

Hermina's pace slowed until she was barely moving. He stopped and looked at her, calling quietly for her to come along. But she shook her head.

"Please, Josef, watch her. Watch all my children. Take them to safety." Before he could protest, she darted to the side and started being noisy. She shouted and yelped as she ran.

No! She can't!

"Mama!" Amalia cried out, and Josef immediately covered her mouth. He wanted to run after Hermina, but with all the noise she was making, the soldiers would be on her location swiftly. He couldn't bring Amalia into that, no matter how much he wanted to stop Hermina from doing this. His eyes blurred, but he fought back the tears as he ran again.

The Germans shouted upon seeing her, and they altered their course. They'd capture her in minutes. Josef cursed Hermina and then blessed her. He hated how she was the one to sacrifice her freedom to save them. He would have done it. He *should* have done it. He could have done the same thing if he had passed Amalia to her.

I will find her again. I will save her.

The distance between him and the German soldiers grew, but the shouting took a turn. Hermina's hollers turned to pleading. Gunfire sounded out. Josef's blood turned cold. Hermina's cries for mercy were cut off. The reality of the situation came crashing down on him.

They were not taking prisoners, not anymore. Anyone who was

caught would be executed on the spot. Man, woman, or child. The soldiers robbed three children of their mother without hesitation. They were monsters. Complete monsters.

I was wrong.

Josef caught up to an able-bodied young man. He passed Amalia over to him, despite her protests. He searched the crowd for someone in particular. Someone with something he needed. It wasn't long until he found Kateřina. He rushed over to her and grasped her shoulders firmly. "The transmitter, do you have it?"

"Who did they shoot?" Kateřina all but shouted in a panic.

"The *transmitter,*" Josef commanded. "I need it now."

Kateřina fumbled in her pocket. "I didn't need to use it. Golem did as I asked. It must be nearby. It has to—"

When the device emerged, Josef snatched it and made his way to an open spot. He activated the transmitter and held it to his mouth. "Golem! Reveal yourself and come to me!"

Golem appeared between bowed trees it had been pushing aside. It was only a dozen yards or so behind them. It took only a few long strides for the machine to stand before him.

If you were so close, why didn't you save her? He shook his head. That didn't matter now. He put the transmitter close to his mouth. "Golem. Chasing us are soldiers. Kill them."

"Josef!" Kateřina cried out in shock. "What are you doing? We need it here to protect us!"

"They killed Hermina!" he shouted back. "She ran off to save her children, save *us.* And they killed her! A kind woman, a mother!"

The golem had yet to obey his command. It stood there, looking at them. Its arms twitched, and it almost turned a few times. It was like its body was trying to follow Josef's order, but its eyes were trained on Kateřina. Watching her. It was like . . .

It doesn't want to leave. It wants to stay with us.

Kateřina scowled deeply.

Who cared what a machine wanted? It wasn't human. It was a tool, a weapon his grandfather had made to help them. This was the way it needed to be used. "Golem!" he screamed into the transmitter. "Kill the Germans chasing us!"

It was as if a switch flipped on Golem. Its eyes dimmed and then changed from blue to orange. Its strange, fluid movements turned robotic as it faced its pursuers. Its arms opened up in shifting mechanisms to reveal hidden guns and cannons. It looked around, fixing on a soldier in the distance. Without warning, it raised an arm and released a barrage of bullets. The projectiles tore through brush, trees, and soldiers alike.

Josef watched it move at incredible speed, bearing down on its targets. It crushed, blasted, and even spewed flames that washed over an entire squad of soldiers. They were more than outmatched. Golem massacred them as if they were helpless and not the manpower of a powerful country. They often didn't have time to mount any resistance against the overwhelming force. When they did, their meager weapons were ineffective and did nothing but alert the monstrosity to their locations.

Few Germans survived, but those who did called for retreat. They scattered like roaches, scurrying away from the golem and the escaping Jews.

No one would be following them any longer. But Josef kept watching. Hatred burned in his heart. He felt nothing but satisfaction as his enemies were crushed underfoot by a machine built by his people.

Never thought we could fight back like this, did you?

Rádek sat alone in his workshop. The hidden lab hadn't changed since the previous weeks, but it felt different. The room had always been large. It was necessary for the construction of something as mammoth as the golem. So, of course, there was always plenty of open space. Before, that space was filled with his and Samuel's lofty aspirations. Now it felt empty and hollow. But his own feelings didn't matter.

He moved his metal limb to grab a small part, but the mechanical appendage twitched and shuddered. He groaned and used his other hand to pick up the part instead.

His work was quick, even with the malfunctioning limb. He needed to make a new transmitter and fast. What had become of his last device? Samuel had it when the Germans had rushed in before. He didn't find it on his body, nor did the Germans mention it. If they knew what it was and that it could control the golem, he would probably be dead right now. He needed to assume someone else had it, as strange as that sounded. Upon hearing the golem had attacked a spider tank, that was the only possible explanation. Samuel was a gentleman. The golem had taken after him, somehow. It would not attack. It would only ever move to protect. Whoever controlled it had tested that functionality for him.

Josef.

That was the name that came to his mind. Samuel's grandson was willing to fight. That was where the two differed most. He must have the transmitter. Rádek didn't mind that the lad was running around with his machine as long as he didn't kill himself. It kept the golem out of German control, and if a few of those backstabbers got crushed in the process, good riddance.

"What are you working on now?" a gruff voice asked from behind.

Rádek groaned, annoyed. Persephone had insisted on keeping one of her men in there with him. A "show of unity" that he had to tolerate for now. The fool was too chatty for Rádek's tastes but overall harmless. And with the explosives Rádek had hidden near the man's chair, he had nothing to fear from him.

"It's part of the tool we need to track down the golem," he lied. "It's very intricate, so I would *appreciate* some quiet."

"How does it work?"

Rádek wanted to snap at him but barely managed to hold his tongue. He took a deep breath, which only slightly calmed him. "In the time it would take for me to explain it to you, I could finish it instead. Which would *you* rather I do?"

The man shrugged. "Suit yourself."

Rádek sighed and returned to his work. It was almost complete. All he needed was to install a final component. He reached into his pocket and pulled out a small glass vial. Inside was one of the few remaining clay pieces of Rabbi Lowe's original Golem. With it, his transmitter could speak directly to the spirit within, or at least that's how he assumed it worked. Even after all these years and technological advances, he still did not understand everything that went into bringing the golem to life. Samuel knew, but the knowledge might have died with him. Rádek needed to regain control of the golem. He could not make another one.

The sounds of multiple heavy footsteps alerted Rádek. He leaped to his feet and grabbed a few nearby weapons to aim at the door. Persephone entered the room, as he suspected, and waved dismissively to Rádek's show of force.

"No need for that. I'm here with news. The golem has been found, so you no longer need to make the locator." She crossed her arms, her face unusually serious.

"Where is it, and how did you find it?" he croaked.

"We didn't. *It* found *us*." She spat the words as she spoke. "It attacked one of our trains. That train was supposed to be able to withstand cannon fire, but if the report has been told correctly, a 'giant ceramic man' has ripped it from its tracks like it was a toy. Sound familiar?"

Rádek nodded. "Let's go. We can retake control of it, but I need to get close. Can you accomplish that?"

Persephone merely turned and waved for him to follow, which Rádek cautiously obliged. He hadn't finished his second transmitter yet, but maybe he didn't need to. Not if Josef was there.

This was it. His chance. Everything was finally in place. Persephone might not trust him, but he didn't need her to. Her justified fear of the golem was enough to keep her in check until it was too late to stop him. He could initiate the precise command he needed. His goal could be met.

Time to end this. End it all for you, Tomas. They will finally pay for what they did to you.

The night sky was constantly lit by the flashes of guns, cannons, and flames. Each of the loud *booms* and explosions had startled Kateřina at first. Now all she could do was stand motionless, covering her mouth as the gentle golem tore apart soldier after soldier. It was a terrible sight, even for people who intended to inflict vicious harm on others. How long would it continue? Would Josef ever stop the golem or call it back to guard their retreat?

Kateřina looked for the escaping Jewish people. She couldn't see them anymore. She wasn't sure how long she had been watching the golem inflict its destruction. She needed to find them and help guide them to safety. Where that safety was, she wasn't quite sure.

Yet, the people were likely terrified right now. Even with the soldiers abandoning their chase, they would not know the golem was on their side. They had not seen the gentle giant that was so careful around her or took bullets for her. All they knew was this monster wreaking havoc.

She spotted Josef nearby still. He, too, was enamored with the scene before them. But he was not watching in horror. She couldn't tell *what* his expression meant. But it scared her. She reached over and pulled on his sleeve. "Please. Stop him. We need to go. It's enough, Josef. More than enough."

"It isn't close to enough," Josef spat. But as he met her eyes, his face softened, and shame crossed his expression instead. "No, you're right. We need to get them all to safety." He held the transmitter close to his face. "Golem, stop your attack and come here."

They watched for a few moments, but nothing changed. Golem finished with the soldiers in the area and then headed toward the train's wreckage.

"Golem!" Josef called again. "Come back!"

It slowly turned, its eyes flickering between blue and orange. For a moment, it struggled with the commands. It raised a gun toward them as it started to approach.

Kateřina gasped and grabbed Josef to pull the transmitter toward her instead. "Please, Golem! Don't hurt us! There has been enough death today!"

It stopped; its gun still trained on them as its eyes transitioned colors. After a few agonizingly long seconds, its eyes turned blue and stayed that way. Its arms shifted until the guns became hidden once more. It slowly approached them and stood motionless, staring at Kateřina expectantly.

She motioned for Josef to put the transmitter away and approached the golem. She swallowed her fear and reached toward him. It loomed over her hand and reached out its own to meet hers. Kateřina let out a sigh of relief. Despite all the death and destruction it had wrought, it was still gentle. "Follow us now. Protect us, Golem."

As if to respond, the golem became invisible once more. She

turned to Josef, nodding, before heading in the direction she had last seen the crowd go.

It did not take them long to catch up, and she spotted Nikolai ushering the crowd along.

"You are alive! Thank God!" She stopped near the man as she helped watch over the crowd.

"It was a close call." He nodded to her. "Our group was spotted, and we had to circle around to ensure that we were not followed. This all would have failed if not for you and the golem. For now, they are hiding in Petrin Hill."

"We won't be able to hide them in the forest for long."

"No village will accept us, not after Lidice," Nikolai said in a low voice. "We need to take them back into the city. Find them places to hide."

"We have to scout the city, find somewhere to take them. Kateřina and I have already found old tunnels underground. Surely we can find some way to get them there," Josef insisted.

"I will watch over them. Keep them quiet and in place as long as I can," Nikolai said. "Will you be okay alone?"

"I'm going with him," Kateřina said. "After all, I was the one to find the underground tunnels, unless you forgot."

It was a long and slow trek through the night as they made their way back to Prague. There was no sign of any soldiers in the countryside, but each time they needed to stop and rest they feared they would see a swarm of tanks rushing toward them. By the time they reached the outskirts of the city, it was well into Sunday afternoon.

Kateřina scanned the nearby buildings and streets. It was strange not to see any sort of German activity, even out here. Were all their resources going to manage the crash site for the train?

Or is something else going on?

"Something isn't right. There should be soldiers everywhere," she said. "Where are they?"

Josef looked around and nodded. "You're right. After last night there should be tanks surrounding the city. They must know something."

Things were even quieter as they entered Prague. The streets were empty, and all the buildings were tightly closed.

"The golem is still with us, right?" Josef whispered to her.

She paused, hearing the soft ticking, and nodded.

Just then, a small group of German soldiers appeared before them. They had guns drawn and trained on her and Josef.

A trap. I knew it. But these soldiers had no idea the power they were trying to stand against.

"Golem, reveal yourself," she said. Then she addressed the soldiers. "I recommend you stay back." Collective gasps followed from the soldiers as the massive figure of the golem barred their path.

"Oh, there's no need for that!" Kateřina heard an oddly, *impossibly* familiar voice as Evka stepped out before the soldiers. It was her. There was no doubt in Kateřina's mind, but she wore the attire and decorations of a German officer.

"Evka?" she asked in disbelief.

"Wow, if it isn't the boss's daughter! I knew you were following this story, but to think you had gone all in with the Jews!" She smirked and cocked her head coyly, like when letting Kateřina in on juicy gossip. "Rather lucky you're still out here, really. Saved you from getting rounded up like your pops and the rest of the crew down in the office!"

Kateřina couldn't fathom the situation. Evka had been working at the paper for *years*. Longer than even Kateřina. Was she a spy the entire time? How was that possible? How had Kateřina, a supposed reporter, never noticed anything suspicious about her? She had been played for a fool. "Why, Evka? My father is a good man. Why would you betray him like that?"

"My name isn't Evka, of course. Call me Persephone. I've grown to like that name as of late." She giggled to herself. "And *betrayed* is a harsh word. I never *really* worked for your dear old dad. He knew that, and yet he *still* went behind my back to buy a few boarding passes! And for the same train that was attacked. Life sure is strange, isn't it?"

The way this "Persephone" callously talked about her father's life caused Kateřina's eyes to narrow into a glare. "Where is he?"

"Oh, you'll see him soon enough." She waved. "Rádek, come get your machine so we can leave."

Josef was disgusted when Rádek—his grandfather's dearest friend—stepped out beside a German officer. He sympathized with Kateřina when her friend turned out to be a German spy, but *Rádek*? While he wasn't Jewish, he was as close as someone could become. Josef couldn't count the times Rádek had joined his family for dinner. How he had spent countless nights working with both him and Samuel in the clock shop.

Rádek was family.

No, it can't *be right.* He observed the man. He did not seem comfortable around the Germans. Rádek shifted and glanced at the woman, "Persephone," beside him. It was subtle, but Josef noticed the undertones in his eyes. Hatred.

Something more was at play here. At least, he really wanted to believe that.

"Kelley, take control of your weapon, please." Persephone motioned for him to move forward.

Rádek advanced with both arms raised, his expression earnest. "We can struggle for control of the golem and all die here, Josef, or we can talk this out." Sensing the tension, the German soldiers exchanged uncertain glances but made no move to interfere.

"Let's talk. I need answers." Josef narrowed his eyes. "Alone."

The two stepped to the side and out of earshot of the others, their conversation shielded from the prying ears of the German soldiers. Josef struggled to contain his anger. His fist clenched, but he restrained himself from punching his family friend in the face. He needed answers.

"What are you doing with Germans, Rádek? You'd better give the best explanation I've ever heard."

"You may not know this, but I built the golem alongside Samuel. We've been working on it for years now."

Questions raced through Josef's mind. Why did they never tell him? He had proven himself countless times and made great inventions alongside Grandfather. Why had they left him in the dark? And how did they make a machine that could think for itself? He wanted to know those answers, but a single, glaring issue rose to the forefront of his mind.

"You put the weapons in, didn't you, Rádek? Those guns and cannons. That was all you."

Rádek's mouth parted, and he swallowed hard. "So you saw them."

Josef nodded. "That golem is a weapon beyond anything the world has seen. It killed dozens of Germans like they were cattle to be slaughtered. They couldn't raise a single effort against it."

Josef noticed that Rádek was trying—and failing—to hide a grin. "Yes, I added those on without Samuel's knowledge. Samuel was the mastermind behind animating the golem, but I have always been . . . secretive. I made all the hidden passageways necessary to hide our work, even at the clock shop. Hiding weapons from your grandfather was a great challenge but necessary."

"Necessary for what?"

Rádek looked behind him in the direction of the Germans. "We don't have time to talk about this. Once bullets start flying, I don't know what will happen. You have the controller. Please give it to me."

Josef shook his head firmly. "I can't give this up. Not if it will go to the Germans."

"It will not." Rádek glanced back again and then leaned in close to Josef. "I put the weapons in because we need a weapon. We do not need a protector. I know you think the same as me. I heard Samuel talk about how you want to fight. I wanted to fight too."

"That's what I intend to do with it. I will use it against the Germans *and* to protect others. So leave it with me, and we can work together. As you and Samuel did."

"Better hurry up!" Persephone called. "Tanks are on their way. Try to cross me and you're signing your own death certificate, Kelley!"

"Now, Josef." Rádek reached out toward him. "I know how to use it. Let me save us all."

Josef stared down at Rádek. His gut told him not to do it. That Golem belonged with him. But what if Rádek knew some vital information he didn't? What if the golem turned on him like it almost had before?

Despite his best judgment, Josef pulled out the transmitter and gave it to Rádek, who nodded and turned back toward the Germans.

"Good work." Persephone clapped slowly. "Let's get out of this dump and start the real work. Your weapon can finally exterminate vermin as intended."

"Indeed." Rádek lifted the transmitter to his mouth. "Golem, kill the Germans, that loud woman there first."

Golem crushed Persephone. Just like that. Josef hardly had a chance to process Rádek's command. The rest of the soldiers followed after in the span of a breath. The ground rumbled as the soldiers were stomped flat, like ants. Josef almost tumbled from the fierce shaking. The sudden and intense violence overwhelmed him, even though the targets were German soldiers.

Rádek chuckled and shook his head. "I waited way too long for that. Insufferable woman. You had best leave town, Josef. It's going to be dangerous from here on out."

"What?" Josef tried to regain his footing.

The question was ignored as Rádek raised the transmitter to his mouth again. "Now, Golem, kill every German you see. Kill every last one in the city, then head west. Stop for nothing and no one." Then he looked at the transmitter, took a small piece out of it, and tossed the rest to the side.

Josef and Kateřina gapped in horror as the golem's eyes shifted again—first from blue to orange and then finally deep crimson. Its weapons emerged, and it began moving slowly down the street, scanning its surroundings for any targets. Based on a gunshot only seconds later, it had located one.

Now murdering in cold blood, the sight of the golem on its warpath was horrifying. Using it to stop pursuers was one thing, but what Rádek had commanded it to do . . . who knew how long it would fight? No, it would only stop if it destroyed every German it could find or the German military managed to destroy it after a long and bloody battle. That level of destruction would be talked about for generations.

But why? He searched for Rádek, but the man was already gone. He was a dear friend, but what would have driven him to such extremes? It couldn't have been Samuel's death. He had been working on this outcome for *years*, even stooping to work with the German military. So, why?

A nearby explosion rained cobblestones. Josef grabbed Kateřina and pulled her behind a car. Stones pummeled the vehicle, metal crunching and glass shattering into pieces. One heavy rock landed right next to his foot with such force it cracked the street.

"We need to stop him, Josef!" Kateřina gripped his arm. She trembled violently. He wanted to comfort her but found his body shuddering just as badly.

He took a deep breath and ran over to the transmitter. It appeared operable overall, but a piece was missing, leaving an obvious gap in its otherwise intact structure. He raised it to his mouth, hoping it worked even with the missing component. "Golem, stop! Stop this!" His command did nothing. It wasn't like before. It was as if the golem couldn't even hear him. "Stop, stop!" He shouted in vain. Rádek had taken an essential part.

"Please, can't you do anything, Josef?" Kateřina asked him again.

He shook his head. "Rádek did something to it. He's the only one who can stop the golem now."

"Where has he gone?"

Josef tried to think. But he couldn't manage coherent thought under the massive booms that sounded repeatedly. "I don't know. Follow me. Stay close."

He reached out to her, grabbed her hand, and ran. Amidst the screams and sounds of battle, his mind blurred. His legs moved without any conscious thought. He realized where he was going when the familiar entrance of the clock shop appeared in front of him.

Home.

He took Kateřina inside and closed the door behind him. While the sounds were still intense, the door alleviated the chaos, and for the first time since Rádek had grabbed the transmitter, Josef felt like he could breathe again. He sucked in each calming breath greedily. Neither he nor Kateřina said anything for a few minutes while they tried to slow their racing hearts.

"What are we going to do?" Kateřina finally asked. "We can't let this keep going. It's a terrible fate for anyone. And a terrible end for the golem."

Now that he could think, Josef considered all he knew. Rádek and Samuel had made the golem, but it wasn't made in the clock shop. They had nowhere to store it; he would have noticed *something* off with the building. That meant they had to have built it somewhere else.

"Remember those tunnels under the Old-New Synagogue?" Josef asked.

"Of course. That's where we met."

"My grandfather was down there. I wasn't sure why, but that must be where they built the golem." He shuddered as the image of his dying grandfather crept back into his mind.

"Is there something down there that can help us?" Kateřina asked. "Some sort of device that can turn him off?"

Josef shook his head. "I can only speak for my grandfather's character. He must have made some failsafe, but I have no idea what. Without Rádek, I can't think of any other way to stop him."

"Me," Kateřina said simply.

"What?"

"Golem and I have always had a connection. I can't explain it, but

I understand him. He is a protector. He's being forced to destroy right now. I can stop him, or at least try."

"That's insane!" The words left his mouth before he could think to stop them. He closed his eyes and then spoke slowly. "You have no idea if that will work. It doesn't seem like anything will stop it now. If you got hurt . . ."

"So what if I get hurt? People are dying, Josef."

His eyes traveled along her face, her beauty giving him pause. Throughout all that had happened, one person always stayed by his side, working with him to help others. She risked her career—no, her *life*—constantly. She was the kindest person he had ever met. And a steady voice in his ear to keep him on track. "I don't want to lose you. Kateřina, I—"

She held up a finger, her eyes filling with tears. "Not here. Not now."

He pushed the rising feelings down and nodded. "I'll find a way to stop it."

"So will I."

Josef felt nothing as he gazed upon the Old-New Synagogue. The black angles of the roof jutting into the sky had felt ominous before but now were nothing but the architecture of men long passed. Not long ago he'd come here seeking answers and met Kateřina doing the same thing. Little time had passed, but he felt like a completely different person. He hurried toward the candle fixture on the wall, twisting it. As expected, the hidden door popped open.

He peered down the dark stairway. The thought of going down there again churned his stomach, and he shook himself. He didn't know what had become of Grandfather. What if his body was still down there? What kind of person was he not to be brave enough to come back to get it? He instinctively held a shield in front of him. A simple one he had retrieved from the clock shop along with a few other inventions of his.

Do it for Kateřina. She's facing worse.

He swallowed hard and forced each leg to step before the other as he descended into Prague's old, buried streets. The air felt damp and stale. He thought he smelled blood. But it was either a trace amount or his mind playing cruel tricks on him. He traversed the passageways he had once searched with excitement. Before long, he saw a dark stain on the ground. He knew what it was but didn't allow his mind to register it as he continued past.

After several more minutes of walking, he came across a

peculiar-looking door. There was some locking mechanism, but it was left open. He carefully moved forward and peeked in to discover a wide-open facility hidden behind.

This is it.

Josef stepped inside and scanned the room, a nerve twitching in the hinge of his jaw. Yellow light radiated from a cluster of bulbs hanging from the ceiling and set within a wire cage as if to protect them from an explosion that could happen at any moment.

This lab was different from the one in the clock shop. Every invention seemed to be a weapon. Guns, bombs, and what appeared to be attempts at robotic weapons of war.

What is this? Grandfather wouldn't have been a part of this.

Then he noticed a section in the far end of the room. One mostly packed away in boxes and crates. There he saw a simple workbench with well-designed tools. It was almost identical to the workbench on which Grandfather had first taught him to make a clock. He moved past all the weapons to that spot and started searching.

This was no doubt his grandfather's workbench. When had Grandfather given up the gentle work of a clockmaker to create tools of destruction? His grandfather had been far too skilled at crafting intricate timepieces to be dabbling in these dark creations. It didn't seem possible, but here was the proof. Or perhaps his grandfather had gotten caught up in the schemes of another.

Rádek appeared to have been putting all of Grandfather's clockmaking paraphernalia aside to make room for his weapon creation. The contrast was stark and unsettling.

Then, as Josef continued to sift through the clutter, he stumbled upon a journal that had been carelessly tossed under a pile of papers. Its leather cover was worn, and its pages appeared well-used, hinting at a hidden world of secrets and revelations waiting to be discovered.

Josef spent little time flipping through the pages for clues. Much of what he saw was what he expected. Pieces of Scripture were written in between thoughts and observations. In one section, he saw talk of some sort of "haven" to be found in the shadow of Rabbi Loew. Those words may have hidden meanings, but he didn't have time to try to decipher it all. He needed something concrete.

Just as the endeavor began to feel hopeless, he saw a familiar story written toward the back of the pages. It was a section of the original story of the golem and Rabbi Loew. The part where the words of life had been placed in Golem's mouth, the act that brought it to life.

Does that mean removing the words could make it rest?

That was a long shot. He had never seen the golem open its mouth. Could it even do such a thing, or was the design merely cosmetic? But Grandfather had written this in here. It had to mean *something*. Even if it was that simple, it would be complex in practice. He'd need to get close enough to the golem to make this work. Only one person even had a chance of getting that close. He needed to let Kateřina know somehow.

"I thought you might be here."

Josef spun around.

Rádek casually walked over to a raised platform and the workbench atop it. The madman stood before what appeared to be an empty holding chamber for Golem.

"Rádek! We need to stop Golem. It's going to destroy the city!" Josef set aside the journal and carefully approached the man.

"Some of it, yes. But then it will move on."

"It's killing people!"

"Mostly Germans—the same people who would kill your own with little hesitation. What is so bad about their deaths?"

Josef balled his hands into fists. He had no love for the Germans, but what he saw was destruction incarnate. "How can you be so sure?"

"I was training the golem for weeks before I was no longer able to control it. I would take it through the city and show who was a German and who was an innocent. It has learned and understood. At least as well as it could." Rádek sat in a chair and assembled a device before him. "Even now, the non-German casualties are probably only in the dozens. Once it leaves Prague, that number will drop even more."

"Dozens of innocent lives? And you're fine with that?" Josef spat.

Rádek slammed a fist on the table. *"Fine* with it? I have not been *fine* in many years, boy. Every day of my life is agony. Every day. I do not want anyone to die. But the Germans are like roaches, ingraining themselves anywhere they go. I do not relish in the deaths of innocents, but I will do whatever it takes until every last German is gone, scorched from this world. I'm doing your people a favor."

"I don't have any sympathy for the soldiers waging this war," Josef started. "But I can't go along with innocents being killed. We're going to stop the golem. Stop you."

"We?" Though his expression was unreadable, his voice hinted of mockery. "Did you send that girl to stop the monster alone? A brutal death at the fury of the golem is a cruel fate, I must say."

Josef gripped his hammer and cautiously stepped forward. "I trust her."

"Trust her? To do what?" Rádek casually moved toward a nearby worktable and retrieved an altered pistol. "My design was flawless. Upon my command, the golem became a machine. It will stop at nothing to do what I instructed."

Josef raised his shield in preparation for any attack but kept his eyes on Rádek. "It's not that simple. She can convince it to stop. I know she can. It's gentle."

"Yes, your grandfather's workmanship. A flaw I couldn't remove completely. However, that's only when it's not following a direct order, is it not? I commanded the golem to never stop fighting. It will kill anyone who tries to stop it. *Anyone.* Feel lucky it is heading toward Germany."

Don't listen to him. Trust her. Trust God.

"You thought you could come here, right? Find out what I did to the controller to keep it from working? Cancel the order I made?" Rádek chuckled and shook his head. He reached down and retrieved a metal mask, which he placed over his face. "Foolish. I only designed this to give commands. Once given, it will follow them no matter what. From here on out, all it will do is destroy." Rádek's voice rose, and he grasped what appeared to be some sort of weapon.

He's not going to back down. No matter what I say.

Josef reached into his pouch as stealthily as possible and grasped a Torch of Gideon. Rádek turned his weapon on Josef.

In a swift motion, Josef flung the Torch, simultaneously rushing forward. Rádek fired rounds. Bullets crashed against the shield and ground around him.

The Torch of Gideon started to go off, but a second device landed right next to it, exploding in green fire that completely destroyed it.

"Don't insult me with your *toys!*" Rádek pulled another bomb and threw it at Josef. "I make weapons of war!"

Josef unlatched his shield and hurled it at the bomb, knocking it away before it exploded. The blast threw his battered shield far across the room.

Rádek fired another shot, piercing Josef's shoulder. Pain surged through his body, and his vision blurred. Rádek tried firing again, but his weapon clicked against an empty chamber. Out of ammo.

Josef lumbered toward him, unwilling to back down. Rádek grabbed a long staff from his table. A simple twist of the shaft caused long blades to extend from either side.

Rádek and Josef became locked in battle, Josef with his hammer and Rádek using the bladed cane. Though younger and stronger, Josef's wounded left shoulder kept him from fighting at full strength. Each time he gained the advantage, Rádek would retreat or separate them using a shelf or table.

"Why, Rádek?" Josef asked between breaths. "What have the Germans done to you that you would sacrifice so much to kill them?"

Rádek threw his arm in the air. "You think your people are the only ones those animals hurt? They didn't start with the Jews, boy. They've been cleansing 'undesirables' for *years*. Anyone they deemed to be worthless."

Josef was caught off guard by the comment and almost sliced by a swing of Rádek's cane.

"You didn't even know, did you, Josef? So ignorant of the truth of the world." Rádek paused, his voice cracking as he spoke. "My own son. He was called 'simple' and put down like a stray dog. The last part I had left of my wife was my *life*. They say they want a perfect world, but that isn't true. All they want is to kill anything they dislike."

Josef's will to fight wavered, and he stumbled back a few steps. His entire life he'd thought Rádek had chosen to stay alone. He never knew he'd had a wife and child. Such a loss didn't go away with time, not when an enemy was responsible. Josef understood the hate; he couldn't imagine living quietly while it boiled under the surface for so long.

"This is pointless," Rádek mocked him, regaining his composure with a laugh. "You're fighting me for nothing. Even I couldn't stop the golem if I wanted to. How could you?"

Rádek again went on the offensive. He snapped forward and swung a blade at Josef's chest. A well-timed deflection was the only thing that kept the edge from piercing him.

"We need to fight, yes. Everyone does." Josef didn't feel sure of the words even as he spoke them. "But you're murdering."

"I'm murdering *animals*," Rádek spat. "The Germans are not human. You should know that better than anyone! You fought against them, too. You killed them, too! Are you going to pretend you didn't command the golem like I did? I saw the marks on its cannons. I know what you did."

Rádek was lost in his rage, and finally, Josef saw an opening. A time when Rádek swung too wide out of anger.

Now!

Josef's hammer cracked across Rádek's face with a loud *clang* as it hit the metal mask. Rádek reeled back. The mask flew off, revealing a face twisted with pure fury. As Rádek fell, he held out his metal hand. A stream of flame shot out. Josef ducked, barely in time.

"You should be *helping me*!" Rádek's eyes went wild. "You wanted this! Wanted a chance to fight back! Do you think the Germans will hesitate to kill you? If they had the golem, would they refuse to use it to its fullest potential? They wanted me to make it for them as a weapon to exterminate any who opposed them! That's who you're protecting!"

Rádek took the offensive once more. The sweeps of his bladed staff pushed Josef back as he tried to get out of range.

He's not wrong. A blade nicked Josef's shoulder, spewing a few drops of blood across his sleeve. *They wouldn't hesitate to kill me. But . . .*

As Josef tried to hold his own, he stared into the eyes of a murderous man. He caught a glimpse behind those eyes. A reflection, perhaps. As much as he didn't want to admit it, he *did* feel the same way as Rádek. He wanted to let the golem loose, let it tear everything down. Make every German suffer the same suffering they had inflicted on his people. It wasn't a desire. He had the *right* to do this. He had the right to take revenge in the fullest way imaginable.

But now, as he looked at how twisted Rádek had become, he saw the truth his grandfather had warned him about. If it were not for his guidance, Josef would have turned out *exactly* like Rádek. A wild animal who would stop at nothing until everything he hated was gone. Destroyed. Not caring who was hurt or what lives could have been saved instead. A man who would spend his entire life inventing new ways to kill.

"They murdered Samuel!" Rádek screamed. "One of the greatest minds in this world. A true friend! I will make them die for that! Every single German will die for that!"

"Don't you dare say his name!" Josef activated the jet on his hammer and crashed it sideways into Rádek's weapon. As intended, both weapons flew out of reach. Using Rádek's shock as an opening, Josef charged. "Not when you are betraying *everything* he ever wanted!"

Josef closed in and punched Rádek across the face. They crashed to the ground with Josef on top. "He wanted to protect everyone! He gave his life making something that could save us!" Josef punched again with his right arm and then again. "He made the golem into the ultimate shield. And it worked! It would have worked. But you— no . . . *we*—"

Flames spewed from Rádek's metal hand. It set Josef's sleeve ablaze. Josef pushed through the flames, grabbing and twisting the mechanical limb. He had seen how it worked, how it was built. It only took a breath to unlatch it and toss it aside. Then, raising his still-burning arm, he prepared a final punch. *"We turned his shield into a monster!"*

His fist collided with Rádek's head, slamming it into the ground. Rádek went limp.

The city was in chaos as civilians ran to hide within the confines of the surrounding buildings and businesses. The once-overwhelming power of the German military was in complete disarray, with soldiers moving either toward the golem in a vain attempt to stop it or fortifying sections of the city to protect key locations or important individuals.

Kateřina, a mere reporter, found herself fighting against the crowds to move toward the source of the trouble. She hadn't even begun to think of what she would do once she got close to the golem. Based on the sounds of destruction far ahead, she doubted she would even make it close enough to try anything before being hit by a stray bullet or flying chunk of debris.

She ignored the shouts of soldiers as she passed one of their blockades. They made no attempt to stop her—putting their own lives at risk—from continuing toward the golem. Her courage faltered at the sight of flashes up ahead. She rounded a corner, and there stood the massive figure, battling against multiple tanks. Her legs froze beneath her.

"Kateřina! What are you doing?"

She barely registered that someone was speaking to her until a familiar face stepped in front of her. Father's. She blinked a few times as he shook her. Was this real?

"Kateřina!" his voice called again. "We must run!"

This is real.

"Father?" she finally spoke. "How are you here? I thought they had taken you."

He dragged her back around the corner. "They did, but many Germans are fleeing the city. They no longer cared about a few presses when that *thing* was on the loose. Are you alright?"

This still felt like a dream, but she threw her arms around her father and pressed her cheek to his chest, as she used to do as a child. Then she felt how much thinner he had become over the years. "I'm so sorry," she sobbed. "I had no idea Evka was a spy. I was harsh on you, but you were under so much pressure."

"It's alright. It's alright." He put his arm around her. "I was scared. I did not want you or anyone else to get hurt. But you wanted to fight for the truth while I stood by and let them use me to spread their lies. In the end, they still threw me aside. I was powerless when they came for us." His voice sounded so different. It was how she remembered his voice, back when he was still the kind, caring father she had adored. "But it is over now. We need to leave the city. Find somewhere safe from all this."

She didn't want to let go of him, but she forced her arms to drop to her sides as she stood up straight. "No, I can't." She shook her head. "I need to stop the golem."

"What are you saying, Kateřina? You cannot go near that thing!"

"I may be the only one who can." She took a long breath to calm herself. "There is so much I need to tell you. I found the story of a lifetime. I saw everything leading up to this. But that does not matter now. I have been close to that golem. It was gentle with me. It protected me. It is being forced to do this but doesn't want to. I can save us."

"No!" He grabbed her shoulder firmly. "I do not want you to save us. I need to save *you*. That thing is fighting the Germans. Let them deal with this."

"It is hurting everyone right now." She gently pulled away. "Father, I have only ever wanted your approval. I wanted you to see I was strong like you have always been. But right now, I am telling you I will do this, whether or not you approve. I have to."

She ignored his protests as she sprinted around the corner and down the street. In that short conversation, the golem had already dispatched one of the tanks. He whaled on another with its mighty fists. Around her, soldiers shot at him until their ammo ran out. They were either staring in horror or abandoning their positions.

Kateřina was alone in her charge against the golem.

Golem hurled the tank overhead. It crashed with a heavy force behind her. The impact caused her feet to give out beneath her, and she tumbled to the ground with a scream. That action drew the attention of the golem, and his deep-red eyes bore down at her.

"Golem." The words were barely a breath. She climbed to her feet and inhaled deeply. "Golem! Stop this! Stop the killing!" She reached toward him, trying to mimic the gentle reach they'd shared before, but she quivered, and it took all her strength to keep her legs underneath her.

Golem looked away from her and revealed his guns to fire at some soldiers trying to escape, then took aim at an older man, who had climbed out of a crumbled building. Emil! Her stomach flipped as she recognized the man. The professor who had been nothing but kind to her.

"No, Golem!" Her cry went unheard over the cannon fire. She winced at the horrific sound of the explosion behind. *He's going to kill anything that moves.*

Against all her survival instincts, she waved her arms frantically and shouted. Once again, her actions drew the attention of the golem. This time, he aimed his cannon toward her. She squeezed her eyes shut.

"Golem, stop!" Tears fell down her face. "You are a protector! You were not made to kill like this!"

A few long moments passed in which she neither felt nor heard anything. She slowly opened her eyes to see someone standing before her, holding his single arm as a barrier between her and the massive machine. Her father.

"No! You should not have come!" she cried.

He shook his head. "We were one day away from finding the

Romanovs, *one day*. This is happening here and now. I will not be too late to save someone who needs me again."

Kateřina looked past her father to the golem. The guns were still trained on her, but Golem had not fired. Red eyes focused on her father, and then her, then Father.

"Please," she said. "I know you were forced to do this. Forced to do terrible things. But you are a guardian. You have saved my life. You must stop this."

His eyes flickered blue and red in a strobing effect. He managed to point his gun away from her, but did not put the weapon away. The giant's gaze darted around, scanning for more targets, and then back to her for a while.

"He's trying to stop," Kateřina whispered to her father. "But I do not know if he can. Pray."

"I have been praying since I followed you, dear," Father whispered.

A German soldier shouted something about retreat. Golem immediately launched a blast toward the man. But Golem's other limb reached out and grabbed the weaponized arm, trying to pull it downward. Metal groaned from within as he struggled against his own body.

There has to be more I can do!

"Kateřina!" a voice yelled weakly.

Josef limped down the street toward her. He was severely beaten, and one of his arms was hardly recognizable from burns. "Josef! Stay back!"

He halted and almost dropped to his knees. "His mouth! Take it out! He'll go back to sleep!"

His mouth? A strange sensation washed over her. She moved forward, stepping past her father and reaching out. "Golem, come now. It's time to rest. Open your mouth for me." She couldn't explain it, but those words felt like the right ones to say.

Golem shuddered, his eyes still flickering between blue and red. After several failed attempts, he slowly dropped into a sitting position and opened his mouth. Though it was high up, Kateřina could see something in there.

She carefully climbed up Golem's leg and onto his chest. From there, she could see inside a simple paper bearing the word *Emet*. *Truth*. She removed the paper, the effect immediate as the golem leaned forward, falling limp.

It worked.

She started to climb back down, but the world around her faded to gray. Her body became weightless, and everything darkened. She slipped and fell backward, landing with a heavy *oof* atop her father, who was waiting below.

After a few moments of catching her breath, her vision cleared. She saw the blazing sun setting perfectly behind Prague Castle. She marveled at it, a hint of nostalgia hitting her as she lay in the ruined street.

"We saw this once, didn't we?" she asked her father.

"Yes." He chuckled. "I brought you here when you were young. It happens during the solstice. It was your mother's favorite view in the world."

Looking at that, she knew. The golem was finally resting. And the biggest story of her life was coming to an end.

The world felt deathly quiet as Josef stood beside Kateřina and the now-lifeless Golem. The streets of Prague were ravaged, with tanks and cars torn into shreds. There wasn't a single soul in sight. Not a civilian or soldier. Josef knew that would not last long. Once they realized the golem was no longer a threat, the streets would swarm with German soldiers once more.

"Josef, are you alright?" After all that had happened, Kateřina's voice was the most soothing sound he had ever heard. She inspected his arm, which was severely burned from Rádek's flames, and the bullet hole just below his shoulder.

"Those wounds are bad." A man he didn't recognize stood next to her.

"I will live." Even to Josef, his voice sounded hollow. "I cannot say the same for Rádek. It was not my intention, but we fought. He would not back down, no matter what I said or did." His eyes flicked past her. "He died."

"Then the golem truly will rest forever," Kateřina said quietly.

"No, there might be a way someone could revive it." Josef moved like a machine. He walked toward the golem and climbed onto its leg. He examined its chest cavity. Golem was more than mere machine. Technology couldn't explain all the things it had done. There had to be a secret within.

Josef raised his hammer and struck down. A burst of flames

enhanced the blow. The casing cracked as he suspected it would. Without the mystical protection, each swing of his hammer broke off a piece of the ceramic covering.

He kept dismantling his grandfather's construction until he reached the core. A final compartment sat in the middle of the golem's chest. Without time to think, he pulled it open to reveal a lump of clay. It was not even that large, only about the size of his fist. He pulled it out and presented it to Kateřina. "This is the key. Clay from Rabbi Loew's Golem. I suspect it was hidden in his chair in the Old-New Synagogue."

Kateřina gasped. "We nearly found it first."

He nodded. "Rádek must have taken it out and started the golem alone. Without this, no one can make a golem again. No matter how hard they try."

"What are you going to do with it?" Kateřina asked.

He stared down at the clay heart. His family's legacy. His grandfather believed it could be used for something greater. That dream had died. And with the world knowing the truth, it wouldn't be long before those seeking power would try to replicate the work.

"If someone has this, they might be able to bring it back to life or create something even worse." Tears built up in his eyes, and he tried to hold them back as best he could. "I need to get rid of it. Destroy it."

"Do what you need to do."

He looked down the street. As he suspected, German soldiers were already emerging from their hiding places and fortifications. They would resume their destructive path through Prague with nothing holding them back. His people would be rounded up at an unprecedented pace. "We have to find a haven. . ." His words trailed off.

"But where can we go? Where can we be safe?"

"Please tell Nikolai I will be in hiding. The Germans will come searching for me. They will also be searching for *this*."

Josef reached into his coat, pulled out his grandfather's journal, and tossed it to her. "Look in there. I think Samuel had a plan for how to use the golem. Even without it, he might have known where to take everyone he saved. Find a haven of protection for our people, Kateřina. I know you can find it."

Josef then put the clay in his coat and started to jog away. "I know you can find the truth," he called back over his shoulder. "Be quick. Once they find me, they'll retake control of the city!"

"You're trying to draw them away from us, aren't you?" The worry in her voice was evident. "They'll find you and kill you."

He paused and held his fist to his chest "I need to protect them. It's my job. I'm a Loew, after all."

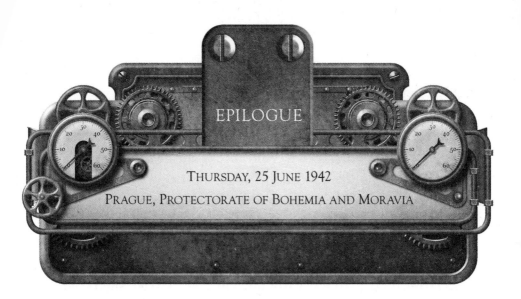

Kateřina lifted rubble, garbage, and shattered pieces of clocks from Josef's family clock shop, setting them into piles of what could be saved and what couldn't. The Germans had torn the shop apart in their search, leaving only a few things undisturbed. Even in Josef's absence, she wanted to clean this place up. It did not deserve to be left in such a state. Even more, she kept thinking about Josef's final directive: *Find a haven of protection for our people, Kateřina. I know you can find it.*

She had read Samuel's journal cover-to-cover twice and had not found anything. Her mind drifted to all the people quietly funneling into Nikolai's warehouse, waiting for salvation born from their old leader's plans. Her forehead glistened with sweat and dirt, and she wiped it away with her wrist. What if she couldn't decipher the clues before the warehouse was found? What if nothing was to be discovered, and she had provided nothing but false hope? It wasn't only Jewish people anymore, either. She had pulled in others, including her father.

Her heart felt as if boulders were being stacked on it. She wished Josef were here. She needed someone she could confide in. She could still remember the image of his burned, bruised body jogging away, deliberately drawing the attention of the German forces. They would pin the massacre on him. Make him out to be the worst war criminal ever known to man.

Worried thoughts overwhelmed her, and Kateřina leaned heavily on the counter. "I can't do this alone."

Just then, the front door of the clock shop opened. A woman with bright-red hair peeked inside and waved. "Hello? Are you open?"

Kateřina jumped, startled. Her cheeks flushed at the foolish mistake of leaving the door unlocked. Kateřina's mouth dropped open in surprise as she stood to face the woman and recognized her. The woman from the tram stop the day of the assassination. Despite such a fleeting interaction, the woman's face had fixed in her mind.

Kateřina recovered her voice quickly. "No, sorry." She looked around at the wreckage. How could anyone think they were in business right now? "The owner is away."

"Are they now?" The woman furrowed her brow. "Well, that's a shame. I find ticking clocks very relaxing, so I hoped for one for my home during these dark times."

Kateřina looked around the walls. Of the few that remained untouched, a couple still had a price tag listed on them. "The shop is currently not open for business."

"I understand, but I hoped to purchase that one." The woman pointed to the silent clock on the wall. It was the one that looked similar to her father's office clock—the one Josef said his grandfather had never wound. It was an important clock, she knew. Something deep inside told Kateřina she shouldn't allow this clock to remain in the shop. She couldn't let the clock to fall into German hands. Yet could this woman be trusted?

The redheaded woman had been at the tram stop, and here she was now. Kateřina wasn't sure, but she had a feeling this woman was on their side.

Kateřina hurried to the clock. *Well, a little business won't upset Josef, right?* "I don't think I should let you come all the way in with the shop in this condition, but I will bring it to you."

The woman beamed and accepted the clock. "Why, it's beautiful! I can tell it was made with great care." She pulled out an envelope and pressed it into Kateřina's hands. "This should cover the payment."

Kateřina felt no need to count the money. Instead, her smile expanded, pulling against her cheeks. It was a welcome feeling. "I can assure you the owners never miss a detail."

"I've heard the Loews love leaving their marks in the most interesting ways. I had been meaning to visit this shop for a while, you see. I find the passage of time fascinating. So, a shop owned by a family with a rich history and is also a clock shop? Paradise."

The woman's gaze moved toward a painting on the wall. Kateřina didn't know how it was possible, but the painting, too, was untouched.

"That's him, isn't it? Rabbi Loew?" the woman asked. "He was an important man. It would be difficult to live in his shadow."

Rabbi Loew's shadow? Kateřina's eyes moved over to the painting and then back to the woman. Kateřina had a strange sense. Like she had met this woman long ago or had seen her in her dreams. As Kateřina started to open her mouth to question the woman, the redhead waved goodbye.

"I apologize for intruding like this, and now I am prattling on. Have a good day, Miss Kateřina." The woman exited through the front door as swiftly as she had appeared.

"I never told you my name!" Kateřina stepped outside to talk to the woman but didn't see a trace of her. The street was empty in both directions.

Who was that?

She couldn't shake the oddity of the interaction. But it had given her an idea.

Kateřina returned inside and locked the door. Then she looked over to the painting of Rabbi Loew, approaching it. She lifted the painting off the wall as carefully as she could. As she did, papers fluttered onto the floor. She glanced down, her breath leaving her. Then she returned the painting to its place and snatched up the papers.

The map detailed a complex network of ancient tunnels

reminiscent of those she and Josef had discovered beneath the Old-New Synagogue. This network, however, was located under a designated area marked by a triangle bisected horizontally—the alchemical symbol for earth or land. *Could it be?*

The gardens of Wallenstein Palace were right beneath Prague's German stronghold! There were multiple entry points, but the closest and most accessible were nearby. If the map was to be trusted, an entrance to these tunnels was just one and a half kilometers away, on the other side of the river. She delicately rolled up the map and concealed it within her coat.

With quickened steps, Kateřina exited the shop and hurried to a nearby bridge that crossed the Vltava River. The patrols of Germans were sparse, and she only encountered a few casual passersby as she hurried to the other side of the river.

Is it really so near?

They would have little trouble moving people between the warehouse and these tunnels without suspicion. She hoped and *prayed* these tunnels weren't merely future plans. But as she reached the marked location of the entrance, her heart began to drop. There was no entrance. All she could see was a wall.

There has to be a button or lever. Find it, Kateřina.

For a half hour, she meticulously searched the wall. Bit by bit, she noticed oddities. Scuffs and marks that seemed natural at first or even second glance.

But soon she began to see a pattern. These could be viewed as alchemic symbols if viewed from the right perspective. Two, in particular, stood out the most to her. Earth, the same symbol the gardens were shaped as, and its counterpart, the oppositely shaped air. She touched both at once.

A section of stone slid into itself, revealing a passageway. Kateřina gasped, then gave a quiet cheer. She rushed in, only to find someone already standing in the doorway. The woman with fiery red hair.

"You again?" Kateřina's heartbeat quickened.

The woman furrowed her brow. She spoke in a whisper. "Tell

your allies about this place. They'll be safe here." The woman leaned in close. "Be quick about it. Because afterward, you and I have a *lot* to talk about."

THE END

ACKNOWLEDGMENTS

First and foremost, a heartfelt thanks to Nathan, my coauthor and easiest kid I raised. (All my other children will agree this is true.) This novel would not be here without you taking my nugget of an idea and growing a world and plot around it. Thank you writing the first draft when I was sinking under other deadlines. Thank you for not just going along with my ideas but coming up with something far better. Thank you for joining me in all-night writing sprints. This was a fun book to write because of your ability to take my average plot and up the games at every turn.

I want to extend my deepest gratitude to Janet Grant, a remarkable agent whose belief in my writing career never wavered and who stood steadfastly by my side. To the incredibly talented team at Enclave. Your meticulous attention to detail, insights, and unwavering dedication transformed this manuscript into the masterpiece it is today. To Steve Laube: Look, it only took thirty years for you to publish one of my books. I did it! We did it!

Lastly, to amazing husband John Goyer. Your belief in my dreams of becoming an author all those years ago has made this possible—all of it. I love you.

ABOUT THE AUTHOR:
TRICIA GOYER

TRICIA GOYER is a well-known speaker and author who writes compelling historical fiction with a faith-based twist. She is the author of over ninety books, covering a wide variety of topics and styles, although many of her works center on World War II.

Biblical themes, profound emotion, and meticulous historical research are the hallmarks of Goyer's work. Set against the background of pivotal moments in history, her stories frequently revolve around characters who, through faith, discover hope and redemption. Her distinctive combination of styles has won her both readers' and critics' devotion.

Tricia Goyer is devoted to her family and homeschooling in addition to her literary career. Speaking publicly about these experiences is a common way she encourages and inspires her listeners. Readers and listeners alike are moved by Goyer's unwavering dedication to her family and faith, which runs throughout her works.

Goyer isn't just a writer. She's also very involved in mentoring and community service. At church and community events, she is a regular voice for young writers and young mothers. Her considerable volunteer work, which includes mentoring adolescent moms and conducting writing workshops, is a reflection of her love of storytelling and her desire to help others.

Tricia Goyer has received many nominations and awards in the Christian publishing industry. She also hosts two podcasts: The Tricia Goyer Show and The Daily Bible Podcast. Please connect with Tricia at TriciaGoyer.com

About the Author:
Nathan Goyer

NATHAN GOYER is an upstart designer and science fiction author who has been writing since he was young. He has written the novel *Bask: City of Shadows* and solo-developed the mobile RPG game *Heedless*, which has surpassed 30,000 downloads. After graduating with a Bachelor of Science from the University of Arkansas Little Rock, he is now pushing forward with new endeavors, starting with his newest novel, *Breath of Bones*, which he wrote alongside his fellow author and mother, Tricia Goyer.